ACCLAIM F...

Innocent Cit...

"Readers who enjoy Hodgins' free play with reality, his ability to see the magical in the everyday, to take the surreal easily in his stride, will find much to beguile them. . . . [*Innocent Cities* is] an elaborate and entirely welcome monument to the genius of its creator."   – Montreal *Gazette*

"[*Innocent Cities*] has the masterful touch of a writer who knows his setting intimately. . . . Hodgins's greatest talent lies in his ability to create memorable portrayals of vivid, sometimes disturbing, individuals. . . . His examination of the crippling effects of hatred and hypocrisy is at times stunning. . . . *Innocent Cities* digs deep into the human character, seeking out the hidden, often nasty, baggage that people carry with them."
                                                        – *Maclean's*

"It's a luxuriously written book, full of Hodgins's wit, quiet wisdom and graceful turns of phrase."   – Halifax *Daily News*

"Jack Hodgins tells a rattling good tale. . . . One cannot but be delighted by the romping of such a fertile imagination, and cannot help but participate in the evident delight of this storyteller in the miracle of words as they shape . . . a most entertaining narrative."   – *Globe and Mail*

"*Innocent Cities* is both humorous and enchanting, with its cast of oddball characters."   – Saskatoon *StarPhoenix*

"[Hodgins's characters] are as remarkably distinct and memorable as one's own friends and relatives. . . . Jack Hodgins has sung into existence a world that is at once as real as the Inner Harbour and as magical as the antipodean wilderness."   – *Monday Magazine* (Victoria)

"*Innocent Cities* is just the kind of enjoyable, funny and endearing novel one has come to expect from Jack Hodgins. . . . A rollicking read."
                                                        – *Nanaimo Weekend*

BOOKS BY JACK HODGINS

FICTION

Spit Delaney's Island
The Invention of the World
The Resurrection of Joseph Bourne
The Barclay Family Theatre
The Honorary Patron
Left Behind in Squabble Bay
Innocent Cities
The Macken Charm
Broken Ground

NON-FICTION

Over Forty in Broken Hill
A Passion for Narrative

Innocent Cities

Jack Hodgins

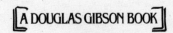
A DOUGLAS GIBSON BOOK

M&S

Cloth edition published 1990
Mass market edition 1991
Trade paperback edition 2000

Canadian Cataloguing in Publication Data

Hodgins, Jack, 1938-
Innocent cities

ISBN 0-7710-4197-7

I. Title.

PS8565.03I49 2000   C813'.54   C00-931996-4
PR9199.3.H63I49 2000

We acknowledge the financial support of the Government of Canada
through the Book Publishing Industry Development Program for our
publishing activities. We further acknowledge the support of the Canada
Council for the Arts and the Ontario Arts Council for our publishing program.

This is a work of fiction. Though a few of the events in the Horncastle story
were suggested by the lives of actual people, I have not attempted to write
either a biography or a history. The people, the events, and to a certain extent
even the places, should be taken as imaginary.

Cover design: Ingrid Paulson
Cover image: Marco Prozzo/Graphistock

Set in Goudy by M&S, Toronto
Printed and bound in Canada

A Douglas Gibson Book
McClelland & Stewart Ltd.
The Canadian Publishers
481 University Avenue
Toronto, Ontario
M5G 2E9
www.mcclelland.com

1 2 3 4 5   04 03 02 01 00

for Bill New

1881

THE world was farther away then, in Logan Sumner's time, and we were only an infant city out on this edge of the continent by ourselves. Mountains, forests, sea. For the most part this was no enormous hardship. The regular arrival of ships bearing travellers from India, Chile, England, San Francisco – from every corner of the Empire and the vast new world – gave us the sense, occasionally, of living at the centre of things. New arrivals came spilling down the gangplanks every week, demanding to be shown the wonders of this little city which had been named for the monarch but set down on the southern tip of an island Her Majesty had possibly never heard of – an island where little had previously happened since the beginning of time, they believed, except for the eternal falling of leaves, the constant murmur of dark-skinned natives in pursuit of berries and fish, and the occasional arrival of raiding-parties from northern tribes intent on acquiring new slaves.

Within moments of arriving, these newcomers demanded to be shown the famous mud puddles which were reported to be so deep that no bottom had ever been found. They begged for a glimpse of the legendary Broadwood square piano which had been transported through dense forest on the shoulders of Indians who set it down in Sheepshanks' hayfield and watched in astonishment while Mrs. Sheepshank ran out of her house and joyously fought her way through a great crashing storm of Mozart. They sought out the homes of famous sealing captains, and the hideouts of notorious smugglers of illegal Chinese immigrants into the United States, villains of legends involving sea battles, chilling murders, and bodies dumped overboard in the strait. And only later would they ask someone to point out the way to the Driard House, or the Windsor, or James Horncastle's Great Blue Heron Hotel.

Amidst this constant hubbub of debarkations it was hardly possible to detect the arrival of someone who would later prove to be unwelcome. Certainly Logan Sumner had no reason to think he should have sensed the approach of the Australian widow, or the danger she represented. He was not a seer, after all, despite his reputation for being rather distracted and fanciful. "At any rate," he would later say of that crucial morning in June, "there was no room in my head for anything but the resolution I'd made – after a long night spent tossing on damp sheets – to swallow my terror at last, face Miss Adelina Horncastle before the day was out, and speak the words which would alter the course of my life."

So far, it had been mostly a life of too many losses. No wonder he possessed the melancholy eyes of a deserted orphan peering through those small round spectacles which were forever sliding down his nose. What was surprising was that his mouth appeared to be always ready to burst into shouts of surprise or joy. A tall man, taller than most, he possessed long, angular limbs, and hair the pale colour of ripening hay. He was a builder; his pockets bulged with plumb bobs and pencils and bits of paper covered with calculations. Fine sawdust could be seen in the hairs at his wrist – in the midst of a conversation he would lift a forearm to his nose and inhale the scent: western red cedar, maple, hemlock, Douglas fir. Then, quite suddenly, he would sneeze.

"Still a child" was the opinion of some – an affectionate view. Even in his thirty-first year he was still uncertain what sort of man he was to become. Everyone knew that his house servant bullied him without any fear of reprimand. When he rode through town – from home to office, from office to building site – his red mare assumed a resigned and patronizing manner, making allowances for a man so distracted by his heavy weight of sorrow, his constant internal calculating, and his persistent uncertainties about the future that he tended to forget that even the most sympathetic horse expected occasional instructions.

Often his progress was followed by amused stares and jocular commentary from members of the chain gang repairing the ruts and mud holes in the road, and by modest smiles from young ladies who knew that even the most sorrowful of grieving widowers would not be content to mourn forever. Because he had grown up here when the island was still a colony and the city not much more than a palisaded fortress of exaggerated dreams, he moved through the landscape as though it did not even register itself upon his sight. In this way he was unlike most of the population of newcomers who still regarded the crashing waves and the giant coniferous trees and the wild green forest undergrowth with expressions of alarm, amazed that the monstrous elements of their adopted home had not yet been reorganized into tidy European gardens or reduced to familiar stretches of horizontal California desert.

He was quite a gifted singer in those days – a soloist with the St. John's choir, even a performer in the occasional concert. Peculiar as the practice seemed to his fellow townsmen, it was not altogether out of character that he should rise early every morning in order to cross the wooded park to the grassy slope above the headland cliffs, climb the Garry oak above the Pest House ashes, and lend the modest assistance of his voice to the sun's daily efforts to raise the world up out of its nightly dark.

To raise, that is, a pale membrane of yellow light up the eastern sky. To sing up the great blue wall of snow-capped mountains across the strait in Washington Territory, sometimes distant and misty, sometimes crowding in to wrap themselves around us, unbearably close. To bring an endless invasion of swollen grey waves rolling in off Juan de Fuca Strait, to crash repeatedly against the cliffs and fall back on themselves and sink into their own swirling foam. To plant the grey twisted oaks and the colossal firs and the fragrant cedars amongst the rocks and willows along the coastline cliffs, to raise up the masts and funnels of the sailing vessels and steamships in the inner harbour, to erect the brick shops and tall Italianate houses and the Chinatown opium factories and the conspicuous church spires in their proper places, and to set out the small collection of red legislative buildings which people had taken to calling The Birdcages, perhaps for their resemblance to peculiar Oriental bamboo prisons made for exotic fowl. He sang up the cows that roamed through town, the wild roses that bloomed over picket fences, the hacks that waited for business in front of the Post Office, even the tombstones that clustered in little villages throughout the giant wooded cemetery to the east of town.

"Each morning I hoped to see more than just the same old world reappear, of course. I imagined more than I ever received. The mountains would be more than mountains, the streets far more than streets. The endless succession of waves would bring me messages from God. Who did I think I was – St. John? I hoped for the perfect world this world obscured, so to speak. A glimpse of a larger truth." But he was daily disappointed on this account, as he was on others. He did not even succeed in his all-too-fanciful, foolish hope of raising up the Pest House from the ashes at the foot of the tree, or his poor lost mother who died within it.

He had been born on this windy headland in an abandoned cottage his mother had claimed immediately upon arriving here, her husband having died on board the ship that was bringing them to the place of their promised new life. Within a few days of the child's birth she fell ill and took to her bed, where she was discovered too late by a retired whaling captain out for a walk along the cliffs. After several more years of sitting empty, the cottage was used as Pest House during a brief outbreak of smallpox, and then one night caught fire and burned to the ground. Perhaps it was the cabin's absence that drew Logan Sumner to the spot again and again, to dream of singing up the building and his lost family into renewed life, perhaps so that he could hear his mother's silenced voice, and feel her gentle heart beating within her breast as it had done in the months when they had shared a body and known each other without ever looking into one another's face.

If he did not succeed in raising up a better world that morning in June of 1881, or in resurrecting the past, neither did he suspect that when the *Steamship Sardonyx* sailed into sight from the direction of the Pacific – beyond the pale-blue sequence of western hills – it was bringing into their midst an enigmatic widow from the Antipodes whose presence would soon bring drastic change to any number of lives. Regrettably, he felt no sense of foreboding whatsoever of the sort one finds in certain English novels, no skull-tingling hint of danger, not even an uneasy sense in his kidneys that something was about to go wrong.

Instead, his attention was distracted by a colony of male sea lions – unheard-of at this time of year, when they should all be far to the south with their abandoned mates – great grunting creatures who heaved their quivering tobacco-coloured bodies onto the larger rocks around the foaming shoreline at the foot of the cliffs, grumbling angrily all the while about an invasion of flotsam which followed them shoreward out of the strait. A wide flotilla of shattered debris rode the heaving surface of the waves – crates and barrels and broken lumber, nodding and sliding into the shallower ripples and troughs and bobbing up again. Pieces of boards leapt out of the waves, rolled and drifted and then went under, disappeared, and shot up to slap on the surface of water and race shoreward. Churned under again, beneath the breaking waves, they almost immediately reappeared, and slid or sailed or leapt ahead onto the gravel slope of the beach where the sea lions growled indignantly down from their rocks. Debris from the sidewheeler *Nebraska*, he supposed, which had yesterday foundered on rocks and lost much of its cargo to the sea.

Sumner followed the narrow trail down the cliff-face for a closer look: empty crates and barrel staves and broken boxes had been flung up onto rocks and wedged between driftwood logs and tangled in the high-tide rows of twisted seaweed. *Antwerp. Made in England. California Oleomargarine.* Intrigued by this spectacle of broken lumber and painted words being flung up onto the rocky beach, he began to walk, keeping his distance from the cranky sea lions and stepping cautiously out of the way of newly tossed pieces of wood. *Barnett's Cocaine Hairdressing. Calf Shooting Boots. Dr. Treat's Celebrated Toothpaste and Corn Extractor.* Because the boards had been so brutally smashed, many of the words existed without any context, almost without any meaning. *Napkins. Leder. El Dorado. Chlorodyne. Sauterne.* The sea continued to toss them up as he passed on down the beach. *Cider. Kid. Sapone da barba. Waggon. Asphalt Roofing.* This same thing was happening, he imagined, all up the southwest coastline of the island, printed debris washing in like spawning smelt to leave, where smelt left eggs, a perplexing and untidy deposit of words from every corner of the world.

But even the grumbling of misdirected sea lions and this continuing spectacle of wooden syllables throwing themselves upon the beach were not enough to distract a man like Logan Sumner for very long from his morning's preoccupation. As he would later quite often explain, he could hardly forget that this was the day he'd decided to renounce the sad life of a mourning widower and seize certain opportunities for happiness which had presented themselves. "I was determined that before the sun went down again I would swallow my terror and ask Miss Horncastle of The Great Blue Heron Hotel to consider marriage. Enough of this mooning around, I could bear it no longer! Life was too impossible as it was, I had to do something about the way just thinking about her would turn my lungs into tight, reluctant bellows choked with steaming soup. It would take far more than an invasion of wooden words to keep me from my battle for a better life."

MR. SUMNER'S TROUBLESOME
GRAVESTONE, AND THE ARRIVAL
OF A MYSTERIOUS WIDOW IN OUR
REMOTE CORNER OF THE EMPIRE

I

He might have met with the young lady immediately and got the business over with if he had gone directly to the Police Barracks courtroom where James Horncastle would soon be locking horns once again with Her Persistent Majesty the Queen. But before attending today's trial he rode out to the cemetery, to put fresh flowers on his wife's grave and at the same time make sure that the reluctant Peter Schlegg had made the latest amendments to his headstone exactly as he'd ordered. The stubborn stonecutter had resisted at first, complaining that most of the space had been already filled. "I'm used to engraving the names of those who lie quiet and satisfied, Mr. Sumner – which is exactly the way I like it."

Sumner left Cleo to graze by the gate and crossed the first clearing in what was still largely uncut forest, passing the white marble of Mary Pearse's gabled stone, the granite mausoleum of the MacKenzie family – tidy, fenced-in histories. He passed the marble obelisk above Mr. Simon Clearwater's grave: *lovingly remembered by all his admiring children* – erected by the only son who had not long ago repudiated his father. He skirted the cluster of evergreens which only partially obscured the gilt-edged hearse that Mary One-eye had salvaged from the bottom of the cliff where the four terrified horses of Smith's Burial Parlour had plunged with the small white coffins of the Harrigan twins. Often seen about town or passing through the cemetery in her ill-fitting, mismatched second-hand clothing, she sometimes wore a tiny round crown and veil in the manner of the monarch, and referred to the mended hearse whose stained sea-smelling silk interior provided her with a place to sleep as her Summer Palace.

No sign of her today. Slanting down through a stand of Douglas firs, sunlight spread broken moving patterns over this vast region of quiet sorrows and across the characters carved into the glittering face of his own two adjacent stones beneath the holly tree. His wife's stone had of course remained unaltered in the five years since it had been erected: a simple record of her name, Julia Morrison Sumner, the dates of her birth and death (1853–1875), and the words LOVED FOREVER. Beside it, his own stone had originally been as simple as hers: HUSBAND OF JULIA, INCONSOLABLE. Though his purchase of the second stone was considered by some to be an eccentric and even morbid act, acquaintances were willing to understand this as the gesture of a young husband grief-stricken by the tragic ending of a happy marriage after less than a month, the pair of matching headstones an admission that he had not himself entirely survived that overturned rowboat.

Within six months of the funeral he had discovered that the original words were inadequate. Still wild with grief, he ordered Schlegg to inscribe a small comma after the INCONSOLABLE and to add, after it: CURSING GOD, AND UNABLE TO FIND ANY MEANING IN LIFE. He was a very young man then, willing to risk the anger of the churches which had divided this enormous new cemetery into little sectarian villages of the dead. Also, he could not have guessed that very shortly, when the town had entered a brief period of encouraging growth and his business had begun to prosper, his heart would occasionally find itself singing songs that were not entirely sad. Peter Schlegg's task the next time was to add in slightly smaller letters below the original inscription: BUT PREPARED, ALWAYS, TO GIVE THANKS FOR NEW HOPE. But hope, like building-booms, can come and go. A year later, he filled in the letters of ALWAYS with mortar and replaced the word with

OFTEN, reflecting the less intemperate attitude Sumner had achieved as he approached his thirtieth year. Business had slowed, his life was still empty of anything beyond his work – no successes had been large enough to encourage a resurrection of his early dreams of designing splendid buildings that would last forever, no real adventures had caught him up in their grasp and tossed him around, no new love had come along to grab hold of his heart and make him stop mourning that poor girl who lay beneath the holly.

But this was before he'd been captured by the challenging eyes of Adelina Horncastle, at this moment preparing to walk the distance from the family hotel to the courtroom where she would observe her father's trial and think at least a little, he dared to hope, of him.

To Sumner's relief, old Peter Schlegg had swallowed his objections and recorded this latest change in attitude. After GOD, which was already an insertion, he had inscribed a small wedge, as requested, and had found just enough room above to add the further interjection: BUT ALSO PRAISING HIM FOR HIS TENDER MERCIES. Surely his lost Julia would not be unhappy about this renewed interest in life. Surely the Almighty, too, could be counted on to approve.

He knelt and laid the roses against the base of the stone, but just as he was about to empty last week's flowers from the vase, a slight movement caught his eye. Not far away, something that might have been a long, thick snake hung down from the higher branches of a fir. Of course there were no large tree snakes on this island, and his eye quickly travelled upward to find that this was an uncoiled whip of the sort used by horsemen to round up cattle, and that it was attached to the waist of someone who sat high in the shadowy boughs, close against the thick trunk. This was a long, extremely thin figure, a man with a dark complexion. Sumner could see a large black hat with a wide brim, a pair of huge boots, a long hide-coloured drape of gleaming oilskin coat.

The stranger appeared to be interested in something at a distance, across the cleared portion of the cemetery.

The heavy boughs of cedar and Douglas fir gently rose and fell in a breeze from the strait; oak leaves shuddered; wheels of arbutus leaves fluttered, bobbed, and turned themselves inside out like weak parasols; bushes of ocean spray seemed to swell up from inside, to fill with air, to shift, nod, deflate, and to swell up again, their creamy flower panicles floating and drifting like foam upon the heaving surfaces. The entire cemetery was in gentle turmoil. And here was someone who had appeared from nowhere, a woman in a black dress who stood in an expanse of grass beyond the cluster of high white Church of England monuments, looking steadily at him while she removed one finger after the other of a glove.

Suddenly the air was split by a long, horrendous wail, and a child, two children, ran out from behind a tree to throw themselves at the woman, who greeted them with a shout of hearty laughter. Holding on to either outstretched hand, the children began to run, forcing her to turn like the pivot-post of a carousel. Faster and faster the children ran, until it seemed that she had taken command – their feet left the ground, they dipped and rose in a great wide circle, all three of them uttering a sound that seemed to combine both terror and hilarity. Then the woman stopped, staggered, tried to steady herself, and fell back onto the grass with her arms laid out wide while she continued to laugh at the sky. Most peculiar behaviour in a widow, he thought – since there could be little doubt that this was a widow who'd come to visit a husband's grave. When both children threw themselves in a heap upon her to make a wrestling-match of this, one couldn't help wondering at the manner in which some poor husband and father was mourned.

Perhaps his disapproval could be sensed at even that distance. The laughter stopped, the children having discovered that they did not have the cemetery to themselves. The little boy and girl stood up and awkwardly brushed themselves off. The woman lay silently gazing up at the sky for a few moments, then stirred and allowed the children to assist her to her feet. All three of them slapped at her skirts and brushed grass from her sleeves before she stooped to pick up a carpet-bag from the ground and began to make her way in Sumner's direction. The children followed, still beating the back of her dress, then ran off and disappeared behind a stand of wind-stirred cedars near the fence.

"We've shocked you!" she cried. She sounded quite pleased to think so.

As she approached, past trees as uneasy as sea, he saw that she was at least a decade older than he – a tall, erect woman, dressed in a black walking-dress, with a tiny black hat of a rather masculine style riding high on a complicated mound of coppery hair. A powerful uneasiness arose within him, as though she were someone he ought to recognize, yet this was no one he had ever seen before.

"I came in search of my brother's grave – he died while I was still crossing the ocean. What you've just witnessed, what you've just *seen*, is the joy of three people set free after too many weeks on a ship."

Now that she had stepped up quite close, Sumner could see that her eyes were the red-brown colour of fox fur, and that the long, pale hand which held her gloves was freckled, as if she'd been sprinkled with the dust from crumbling brick. There was something foreign in the sound to her words, but nothing he could identify.

"A long journey from . . .?" As was always the case whenever he found himself in an uncomfortable situation, Sumner fished around amongst the pencil stubs and bits of papers and finishing-nails in the pockets of his coat until his hand closed around a small wooden ruler and brought it out into the light. This piece of varnished wood, no longer than his hand, divided and swung open upon a hinge to become twice its original length. Then it unfolded to double itself once again. And again – until Logan Sumner was holding a length of connected wooden segments with numbers reaching to thirty-six. A yard.

She did not answer his question. She lowered the dark-blue carpet-bag to the grass at her feet, and gazed a moment at its pattern of leafy vines and exotic long-tailed birds. "Perhaps you knew my brother, who owned, who was the proprietor of, the Bottomless Saloon on Johnson Street."

Sumner admitted to having only a nodding acquaintance with this gentleman, though he knew the location of his business – a source of ear-splitting roars and vociferous argument whenever you passed by its door.

"Some of his friends may be known to you then, whose names have appeared in his letters." She regarded Sumner with the steady, unprotected gaze of one who considers herself entirely safe in the world. "A certain Mr. Hatch. A Mr. Hatch was mentioned often."

"A quarrelsome man, I'm sorry to tell you. Before the morning is out, he will be before a magistrate, suing for slander and assault."

Whenever he found himself with an unfolded yardstick in his hands, Sumner could not help measuring the first thing that came to his attention – doorways, carriage wheels, a standing horse. In this way, he was constantly discovering how the world could deceive his eyes. In the present circumstances, however, there was nothing immediately available. He could hardly lay the numbers out along the nearest grave. So he allowed the yardstick to swing down and measure his own left leg, not for the first time. From the outer edge of his foot to hip-bone: thirty-six inches was not enough; he guessed an additional six.

"And a Mr. Horncastle too, a Mr. Horncastle was a friend," she said.

Adelina's father! Perhaps this woman could read his thoughts. Did the blood rush to his face? He folded up the yardstick and returned it to the obscurity of his pocket. "I think not. Not a friend. There has always been great rivalry amongst the saloon-keepers in town, and your brother was amongst those who chose to treat Mr. Horncastle as an enemy."

"An enemy!"

"They're envious of his success, madam, and often circulate slander. It is unlikely the two men ever exchanged more than a few words, except for insults."

This was too vehement a denial by far! He was left stumbling for words while this woman marvelled that her innocent questions had generated such passion. Already she appeared amused enough to have guessed the presence of an Addie Horncastle somewhere in the picture.

"Then perhaps I'm mistaken, perhaps I'm *wrong*, perhaps my brother wrote letters filled with lies." This possibility did not appear to concern her. In fact, she seemed to find it amusing. "Maybe he was not William McConnell at all in this country, he may have passed himself off as someone else."

"Bill McConnell is the name he used, but he wouldn't be alone if he'd changed it. Mr. Hatch was Mr. Zeltstange in Germany, we only recently learned, before he shot his brother-in-law in the neck and decided to leave."

She appeared delighted with this. "And this is the man who takes others to court for assault?"

"In England, Mr. Smith was known as Mr. Price before his employers discovered his habit of altering their account books to his own advantage and suggested he find another country to live in. He has laughed about this himself, since a traveller from his village gave his secret away."

She laughed at Mr. Smith's unmasking but shifted attention to Sumner himself, who seemed scarcely less amusing to her. "Perhaps you have plans, perhaps you have something you intended to *do* with those flowers?"

He had forgotten the bouquet of Chinese roses lying on the granite slab. Now he knelt before his wife's grave and lifted the vase containing the blackened remains of old flowers. A small envelope lay beneath it. Inside, above his elaborate Germanic signature on a folded piece of paper, Peter Schlegg had recorded the cost of his labour – hardly his usual practice. He had also printed the words: "And I also PRAISE HIM, that I've run out of space at last!" At the bottom of the paper, this peculiar man had then appended a hastily scribbled postscript. "Don't come to me when you decide to start adding your nonsense to the backside of this poor-man's little stone."

Sumner laughed. Then, remembering himself, he quickly folded up the piece of paper and closed his hand around it. Had his habit of making changes seemed so obviously the actions of a madman? People, even strangers, had probably joked with one another about the survivor who could not decide once and for all how he felt about things. He saw them inventing possible new adjustments: "Erase everything and replace it with *On the other hand*. That would say it all!" Now that the terrible seeds of doubt had been sown, he even imagined his wife to be laughing: "If I'd lived, he would have driven me crazy with his indecision. Why doesn't he give that poor block of granite a rest?"

He looked about him: a multitude of silent stones, all speaking precisely the same message that had been put on them in the beginning. Permanent histories. He should throw the tombstone into the sea where no one could see it, where the persistent waves could begin the slow task of wearing the inscriptions away. But what if he were seen doing this and arrested? What if a swimmer should find it? It would be raised and put on public display, with all its legible words reproduced in the newspaper for families to chuckle over at dinner.

A smile began to play around the edges of the woman's mouth as she read the confusion of words on Sumner's headstone.

"A passionate man, I should think, though wondrously erratic."

There was nothing to do but join in the world's derision. "A lunatic, I think I have decided." He decided to laugh as well.

"At any rate, I hope this will not become the fashion." Her smile also became laughter – she displayed a wide mouthful of teeth. "Suppose we were all required, suppose we were all *forced*, to run to the graveyard with a chisel every time we changed our opinion of life? I would have worn these legs off long ago!"

"And emptied several quarries!" Having thrown himself into the pleasure of laughing at his own foolishness, he was in danger of overdoing it. He abruptly snatched back sober dignity. "Of course, I intended nothing like this at the beginning. How was I to know that everything would prove to be inadequate?"

"There you have it – the very problem. I hate to see *anything* set in stone! Even paper is too permanent for my tastes. I'd rather flow like a river through life, leaving nothing behind."

As if to live up to her own ideal, she snatched up her bag and moved on across the grass without even taking her leave. A black parasol sprang open, and at the same moment the two small children hurled themselves at her from behind the trees, to accompany her out through the gate and into the street.

Sumner had altogether forgotten about the man in the tree, who dropped to the earth now without a sound and moved off in the direction of the gate. Were the woman and her children aware of his presence? He was so long and thin as to seem fashioned from wire – or perhaps (he was of a darkened complexion) from fire-scorched roots and vines, sinuous things of the earth. With the large fingers of his nearer hand clasped to the coiled whip against his thigh – the long hide-coloured coat pushed back to snap at the heels of his boots – he strode across the grass with unnaturally long steps, and looked at Sumner briefly from beneath a level bar of dark continuous brow, apparently without the smallest flicker of interest.

Sumner resolved to forget them both. And to leave as soon as possible this region of peaceful sorrows which had decided to mock him. Should he seek out the caretakers and arrange for the stone to be removed and somehow destroyed? Smashed into gravel, perhaps, by prisoners brought out from the jail? (What did he care if drunkards and petty thieves should have a good laugh at his expense? He had laughed often enough at theirs.) Perhaps he should try to persuade Peter Schlegg to erect a new stone where the old one had been, blank and pure as a fresh piece of vellum paper, to be left in that state until the day that someone else would be required to write his story on it. He would never add another word himself.

2

THROUGHOUT that long, warm spring, fragrant with honeysuckle and wild roses, Horncastle's rivalry with the one-armed saloon-keeper Samuel Hatch had escalated to the point where Horncastle would seize any opportunity to test his long-nosed terrier against the reigning champion, Lillie, a newcomer who had killed ten rats for every one of Vicky's in all their recent contests. When the May 22 match in Horace Sheepshank's barn terminated in bloody fisticuffs, Horncastle was once again charged with common assault and slander, and required to face a magistrate who had heard this all so many times that even before the business of the courtroom had properly started he had already begun to yawn. "They'll have to find a murder in it somewhere if they want to keep me awake."

Of course, the tirelessly optimistic Mrs. Horncastle sat in the front row as usual, flanked by their several children, to make certain the Crown did not lose sight of Horncastle's reputation as a faithful husband as well as loving father to half a dozen adopted orphans. Amongst these was the lovely Adelina, with her eyes downcast upon a book in her lap and a long hand pressed to a blushing cheek. Logan Sumner pushed in to claim an empty chair behind them, and sat with his long legs angled out in the cramped space and his hands on his pointed knees, interested mostly in observing the oldest daughter's graceful neck while he hoped for just a glance. Turning to look over the crowd, he could see that Sam Hatch's unpleasant wife had arrived too late to secure a prominent location for herself and had chosen to sit against the back wall, where she rustled her taffeta skirts and muttered a variety of complaints about the manner in which the universe was being governed.

"Well, Horncastle!" The magistrate leaned forward over his desk and arranged his long, thin mouth into the shape of a smile which he directed at the accused – perhaps the smallest man in the room. "You must feel right at home in my little court, having spent nearly as much time in it as I have." He had the habit of seizing his own mutton-chops with both hands when he was pleased with himself, as another might grasp his lapels. "If we move quickly you'll be back behind your own bar soon enough, pouring a whiskey and planning to get yourself hauled up before me again."

Sitting in the relaxed, turned-sideways manner of someone entirely familiar with the wooden chair of the accused, one leg thrown over the other and a polished black boot bouncing impatiently, Horncastle lowered his great antlered eyebrows while he listened to these opening remarks, the fingers of one hand slowly stroking the ends of his white moustache. He wore a scarlet rose in his lapel, picked at dawn from the garden of his hotel, and briefly sniffed at it now with his small, sharp falcon's beak of a nose. "Save your breath for your porridge, Will Cleland." He looked up at the roomful of chuckling spectators and smiled. "Just do the job you're overpaid to do and let's go home!"

No one was surprised by this example of Horncastle's disrespect. Those who had come in from neighbouring shops and from nearby homes, and even from out in the country, had expected nothing less. They had little interest in the entirely predictable outcome of the case but a large appetite for the defendant's habit of responding in a perilously entertaining manner to almost everything that was said about him. Those like Logan Sumner who had joined the family out of loyalty to long-standing friendships had seen it all before. So had Mary One-eye, whose unmistakable smell of woodsmoke and dead fish drifted out to tickle every nose in the room despite her care in choosing a seat in a back corner and in pulling her blanket tight around herself. In order to be admitted, she had had to promise not to wear her crown, and especially not to repeat her performance of a month before when she'd put a spell on the magistrate which made him ill for several days.

In her customary position high up the front wall, Her Majesty allowed the unfaltering gaze from her heavy-lidded eyes to express unshakeable confidence in the ability of appointed officials to deal appropriately, on her behalf, with incidents of misbehaviour amongst her subjects.

The matter before the court was something the Crown counsel could summarize quickly enough in his eagerness to keep the magistrate awake. The usual crowd had gathered shortly after dawn in Horace Sheepshank's barn; the usual boasts were made; the usual bets were laid in Sheepshank's hand. A bottle was passed around. Sheepshank held his watch in his open palm and studied the moving hand. "Last chance to make your fortune the easy way, men, before y's has to go to work and earn it."

The incredible Lillie Langtry once again proved herself to be the superior killer, depositing rat after rat on the dusty chaff in front of Hatch's toes, each with its neck broken and its whiskers glistening with tiny dots of blood. When the ageing Vicky had brought back only three dead rats in the same period of time, Sam Hatch regarded her with pity. "You should put her out of her missery, Chames. Zat beast vill your life-savings lose for you – she's nearly blind!"

Precisely as he had done in similar circumstances which had led to similar appearances in this same courtroom, the red-faced Horncastle threw his hat down onto the barn-floor straw, rolled up his sleeves, stuck out his quivering chin, and accused his opponent of cheating: "You've been killing the rats yourself – and telling that flea-bitten hound where you hid them!" Several men laughed, but Horace Sheepshank took offence at Horncastle's attitude and asked him to vacate his barn. A few supported this suggestion, while others did not. Soon the entire crowd had erupted into a loud exchange of insults which led to the occasional blow. Horncastle's fist connected with Sheepshank's indignant bottom lip, then withdrew and delivered a felling wallop to Samuel Hatch's nose.

"A coward's nose!" Leaping to his feet, Horncastle shouted as though he intended the town outside the Barracks to hear. "That humpbacked lump of purple flesh bleeds out of craven fear – like a dog shedding hair." Assuming a pugilist's stance, he jabbed at the air. "I have only to curl my fist and he commences to gush."

Ignoring the repeated pounding of the gavel, Hatch roared up out of his chair with his one great fisted hand well above his head – the stump of the other raised as well, as though he wished to lift up Horncastle and toss him, like a log, on some fire. "You see how Herr Hornshvoggle giffs me abuse! Behind bars you should put him for ever! And shoot his shtupid Wicky!"

"Silence! Silence!" The magistrate also rose to his feet, screaming. "Or I will throw you both behind bars. And throw both your dogs behind bars. And leave all of you there until you have finished one another off – saving this court from the unpleasant prospect of having to deal with you again." His furious eyes raked through the entire roomful of spectators, to stop the outbreak of giggles and snickers from developing into full-fledged hilarity. "As usual, Horncastle, this trouble comes from your inability to resist a bet. Is there nothing in life you don't see as an opportunity to make a wager?"

"I hope not!" An extravagantly indignant Horncastle faced his audience with a smile that clearly said: I cannot resist! In planting his fists on his hips, he pushed back the sides of his dark-blue double-breasted reefer to display a brocaded satin waistcoat of the same scarlet hue as the rose in his lapel. "Your Honour, I stand to win ten dollars from Horace Sheepshank Jr. if this case is adjourned before noon."

This combining of exaggerated insolence with a large dose of self-mockery had been noted by Lady Roxanna Honeydew in the journal of her travels throughout the Empire, which she published soon after her return to England. She referred to her host at The Great Blue Heron Hotel as the ideal prototype of the race that would constitute the new country's future: raised to the civilized standards of Victoria's Britain, tempered by a period spent amongst the lawless uncertainties of the American west, and set down on the far edge of the world where he had taken advantage of both heritages to succeed with whatever rough resources came to hand, he was a perfect specimen of the breed one expected to see dominating his country's future. This passage was quoted in the local newspaper with the accompanying suggestion that Lady Honeydew return and encounter our Mr. Horncastle when he has just seen his horse lose a race, taken one too many whiskeys in his own bar, or had to endure the indignity of being asked to pay his debts. "If this extravagant overacting and mocking disrespect is a glimpse of our new race's future, we had best take a good hard look at how we educate our children."

During the loud burst of hilarity which drowned out the gavel, Sumner's own laughter was suddenly chopped, his breathing interrupted, when Adelina Horncastle turned her pretty head just a little and directed a smile in his direction. Only a brief smile before she turned again to her book – but it was meant just for him. Enough to set his heart racing. Racing? He would have stood up and burst into song if he were not afraid he would look the fool – not to the others, nobody else's opinion mattered at the moment, but to her. Being a young and beautiful woman, she was the most dangerous person in the room. And yet – he had not forgotten – he was determined to ask her, before this day was through, if she would consider becoming his wife. Her parents, who already knew of his intentions, would only wonder what had taken him so long.

All laughter was brought to a ragged end by a high, thin sort of chant coming from the back of the room. Eyes turned to discover that Mary One-eye had risen to her feet, straining against those who would push her into her seat. Her words were incomprehensible to spectators and officials alike, but their intent became clear enough when one long arm stretched out from beneath her blanket to point at the magistrate. This august official with the distinguished record in jurisprudence must have decided that his shouted "Take her out of here!" would be more effective if it came from the floor behind his desk, believing, perhaps, that Pacific Coast magic was not designed to penetrate solid walnut imported from another continent. On the wall, Her Majesty's expression of sublime confidence was not at all affected by this confusion, but the magistrate remained in his haven until Mary One-eye and the danger she represented had been removed entirely from the building and windows opened even wider to eliminate the overwhelming smell of woodsmoke she'd left behind.

"Now!" cried the magistrate, into the wild disorder of laughter and excited conversations amongst people congratulating themselves on having the good sense to give up a morning of housekeeping or cattle-butchering for this. The gavel had been lost somewhere beneath the desk but he was experienced enough at pounding his fist. "Now! We will dispense with this business quietly. And we will deal with it as speedily as possible!"

But of course Logan Sumner knew that this battle between Her Persistent Majesty and the hot-headed James Theodore Horncastle would not be settled speedily at all. Horncastle would challenge every one of Hatch's statements, and pass up no opportunity to entertain his expectant supporters. There would be applause before long, despite the magistrate's efforts. Horncastle would once again be told to apologize to Mr. Samuel Hatch for punching him in the nose. He would also be placed under his own recognizance and ordered to keep the peace for three months – an impossible demand he would not even try to observe. You did not remain in the courtroom in expectation of a surprising outcome; you stayed to the end in order to be entertained by James Horncastle's flair for the dramatic, and – if you were Logan Sumner – to hope for further smiles from his beautiful daughter.

3

OF course Logan Sumner ought to have been at work – in his office at least, or out on one of the work sites supervising his carpenters – but he had no intention of treating this morning like any other. If he was only one of many who considered themselves to be close to the Horncastle family, he was one who never failed to attend all of Horncastle's court appearances. As an orphan from soon after birth, and abandoned repeatedly in the years since, he valued every moment spent in the company of this exemplary family, and could not neglect an opportunity to demonstrate his loyalty, even when it meant ignoring his business for a part of the day.

Like the bachelor uncle who'd raised him and made him his apprentice and then abandoned him by unexpectedly dying, Sumner was a designer and constructor of buildings. In the earliest years of his adult life, he'd dreamed of erecting magnificent structures which would be admired and photographed and later imitated by strangers who had come from all parts of the globe to see them. "More beautiful than Versailles!" they would tell the gangly, short-sighted young man with the forlorn eyes while they gazed on his latest mansion, or his most recent cathedral, or his newly completed hotel. "Bavarian palaces will crumble in shame, when they see that they've been eclipsed." Nothing was impossible in those early years. Why should it be? If he had not come into this world in order to bring about a few miracles, then why was he born at all?

At any time, Sumner could slip a hand into his coat pocket and find, amongst the papers and pencil stubs and folded wooden yardstick, the small piece of stone which his uncle had pried from a corner of the Ca' d'Oro in Venice. The uncle had spoken of university in England, of architectural studies, of a partnership between them that would see fabulous buildings rise, attracting widespread admiration. But his uncle had died when Sumner was barely a man, leaving him to take over the business. For a few years he erected new structures according to the designs of others, however uninspired. When the town had entered this present period in which many buildings stood vacant and they could only hope for something like another gold rush to bring it new life, he earned a modest reputation for a particular skill in handling small additions, out-buildings, interior renovations, and various minor constructions. Eventually, Sumner Construction became known for an expertise in a particular *spécialité* – giving to the buildings they renovated an appearance of having been just newly erected, by applying new and inexpensive façades over the old. Houses, shops, warehouses, even factories – when they were undergoing needed alterations – could put on the style of any foreign architecture desired, in the manner of ladies' fashions, depending upon what books had been recently read, what photographs admired, what foreign travel just completed. When a small addition was commissioned by an owner who'd grown tired of having a residence or business that looked as though it were situated in Rome, say, or London, Logan Sumner could make it look as though the building had just been brought in on a barge from Madrid, or Dublin, or San Francisco. In the privacy of the workshop he and his carpenters spoke of "putting on m'lady's newest face."

It was in this capacity that he had become acquainted with Mr. James Horncastle, who had quite possibly put more new faces over old than any other property-owner in town. When he sat at his desk in the office of The Great Blue Heron Hotel, he was surrounded by the successive layers of his own expanded business – by the walls of the small log cabin he'd purchased for his saloon in 1860 upon arriving in the Colony, by the rooms of the boarding-house he'd constructed around the saloon, by the additional rooms and storeys added for his first hotel, and finally by the brick exterior of the grand Blue Heron, which had been inspired by some provincial hotel in England but which he was now in the process of altering once again, despite the current lull in business. It is difficult to imagine two men more unlike one another – the cocky but popular little hotelier, always in a scrap, and the lanky, sad-eyed engineer of false faces who seldom offended anyone – yet they got along remarkably well, and hardly ever raised their voices to one another in genuine anger.

As a child, Sumner had been well aware that Horncastle was a notorious figure about town. He and a few of his friends incited minor riots with their squabbling, offended public morality with their loud language, and provided exuberant entertainment with the inventions of their robust imaginations. They found in any occasion an opportunity for betting heavily, and for cheating as well. Though Sumner's Uncle Charles did not entirely approve of these gentlemen, he never failed to keep the boy informed of their scandalous behaviour: playing practical jokes on the undertaker, dressing as women and attending dances where they were always found out, racing on horseback across farmers' fields and through croquet parties and even up the steps and down the hallways of Sir Joseph and Lady Riven-Blythe's stately water-side home.

Most of this behaviour was fairly harmless, his uncle would suggest. Invariably he would be holding one of his golden pheasants in his arm while he commented upon these exploits, stroking the beautiful feathers as he sat in the branches of an apple tree behind their home. Raised with Sumner's father in a Sussex rectory, he had learned how to put this sort of behaviour into perspective for a growing boy. "It would be acceptable, one must suppose, if only it did not interfere with the performance of duty." Sumner had been instructed thoroughly in the performance of duty. Horncastle, the uncle solemnly regretted, behaved as though *he* had not. "He fancies himself some sort of rebel – perhaps because he lived for some time in Yankeeland. He accepts all of Mr. Darwin whole, for instance, without ever having read a word of the fellow's books, because it nicely suits his own dislike of being preached at from a Sunday pulpit. He will stay home, impersonating the man of science, while merely trying to bring order to the hotel accounts. There is no sincerity in it. I like the man myself, but see his faults all the same."

After the uncle's death when Sumner was twenty-one, Horncastle stopped the young man whenever they met in the street, to inquire about the state of his business, to bring him up to date on the latest horseflesh he'd acquired, to give him tips on the week's races in case he should decide to renounce his promise to his uncle and place a small bet, or to pass on some of the taller

tales he'd heard from the sailors of the Royal Navy who patron-
ized his bar. "Seventy-eight bodies in one room! Can you fathom
such a thing?" Occasionally he invited Sumner to join him and
his friends for a three-day deer-hunting expedition into the woods
north of the Malahat, or to substitute for an absent team-mate on
the cricket field. But it wasn't until Horncastle made the suggestion that Sumner design him yet another new face for The Great
Blue Heron Hotel that they began to spend longer periods of time
together, and a friendship was able to grow up between them
despite the difference in age. Eventually Sumner became a frequent guest at family gatherings – the larger dinner parties,
occasional Sunday dinners, musical evenings at the Theatre
Royal, boating picnics up the Gorge, and riding parties put
together by the older children for day-long horseback excursions
out into the country – opportunities to fall under the spell of the
oldest, Adelina, whose beauty seemed to become more astonishing at every encounter.

Naturally, as soon as Horncastle's trial had come to its predictable conclusion he stood up to wait for Miss Horncastle, his
heart hammering in his throat and his lungs drowning in the
familiar lava of steaming soup. But even as the young lady was
putting a marker in her book, apparently annoyed that the
adjournment had interrupted her reading, Constable Edgar Bragg
approached and placed a hand on Logan Sumner's arm. "If you're
wondering where your head carpenter is this morning, we've got
him down the hall."

"Again?"

The policeman nodded. "Overnight. And he's angry as blazes
that we wouldn't come in and drag you out while the court was in
session. He's waiting for you now."

"You're making him pay a fine?"

"No. He just says he won't leave the calaboose until his boss
comes and gets him."

"And the crime?"

"The same as usual."

Sumner followed Bragg down the hallway and under the GAOL sign and into a little whitewashed office, where Zachary Jack sat waiting on a chair. He did not look impatient, he looked as though he was prepared to sit for ever if necessary, with his wide, soft face impassive and his legs apart and his hands laced together across his hard enormous belly, just below the hole in his cotton shirt. When Sumner entered the room, Zak pursed his lips and looked at the policeman as if to say, "Is this the best you could do?" Then he shrugged his soft round shoulders. "H *wah*. Another night in the damn skookum-house just for opening my mouth."

"Perfectly innocent, of course." Sumner knew that he was expected to join in Zak's little bit of play-acting for the benefit of Constable Bragg. "You didn't even suspect that you might give offence."

"Hnnnnf." Zak grinned the grin of a man who was pleased with himself.

"What was the criminal word this time?"

Even the policeman smiled while Zak explained. He had stopped to chat with Mr. Gristle on the street while Mr. Gristle's new bride stood gazing in through the window of Mansell's Shoes. When Zak complimented Mr. Gristle on his handsome klootch-man, Mr. Gristle objected. His wife, he said, was a lady, and would be described in no other terms. "Maybe he wasn't so sure himself about this, his face went all hot and red." As anyone who knew him might have predicted, Zak adjusted his vocabulary only so far as "squaw," but this was not good enough for Mr. Gristle. An exchange of insults followed, with raised voices, and with passersby stopping to see how far the Indian carpenter had stepped out of line this time. Eventually Constable Bragg intervened and decided that it was Zachary Jack, rather than Mr. Gristle or Mr. Gristle's new wife, who had been disturbing the peace.

"I guess you just wanted an excuse to find out if the cell was still as comfortable as it was last time," Sumner said.

"Blame your uncle. He brought us both up wrong. He forgot to tell me this tongue in my mouth don't belong to me. Now, tell me, *tyee*-boss – before I leave this place – why is Mr. Gristle's wife a lady but not a squaw?"

"I don't know," Sumner said. "Let's go." That Zak already knew the answer did not mean you could deprive him of the pleasure of seeing you try. "The Queen says Mrs. Gristle is a lady but not a squaw. It's simple."

Zak heaved himself upright off the chair and laid an arm on Sumner's shoulder and looked close into the side of his face. "Does the Great Mother say Mary One-eye is a lady too?"

"Her Majesty hasn't noticed Mary One-eye yet. When she does, no doubt she'll tell us what to call her."

Zak's laugh was a deep-throated gurgle. "I guess that means if *you* called Mary One-eye a lady they would throw you in the skookum-house too."

"You know they wouldn't."

Zak flung his arms out in a sort of mock fit of frustration and propelled himself through the door. He was all shoulders and chest and belly, with legs so short they seemed to have little use for their knees. "H *wah!* Me no understand white man nohow!" His favourite expression, whenever he wanted to make Sumner cringe.

"Don't try. The rest of us aren't any better at it than you are." Sumner went after him, into the hallway. "And you can act normal now, Bragg isn't watching any more." For a moment they stood together in the Barracks doorway, squinting into the light. "Isn't it about time you got to work?"

Zak rolled his shoulders in a sort of shrug and scowled at the collection of people standing in the sunlight. Then he laughed. "The Horncastle party. They don't want to be too far away when he decides to buy them a drink."

"Just reluctant to return to normal life. I guess you understand that."

"I'm going," Zak said. Then he laughed again. "I see Miss Horncastle, wearing out her eyes on another book." He thrust his shoulder against Sumner's, and leapt away, still laughing. "Don't worry. I'm going. One thing I don't want to see is any more of this courtship business. I hope I never get to see England, I would bring up my breakfast if I saw a whole damn country full of men and women pretending they'd never even thought of what it is they can hardly wait to get."

Out in the street he turned, flashed a broad white smile at Sumner, and shook his head. One of his hands had found its way in through the hole in his shirt to slap against the flesh of his belly. "I'll tell the men you're too busy to show up at work today. I'll tell them we can hammer that thing together any way we want and you won't care, you're too busy acting like you were born in London with a silver spoon in your mouth and a poker up your —"

"Tell them I'll be there a little later."

"Sure. I'll tell them something you've been sneaking up on for years is suddenly taken care of in an hour." He swung around the corner of the Barracks and disappeared, but not before he'd looked back, grinning, to shake his head in the manner of one who would prefer not to believe what he knows to be true.

The crowd of Horncastle supporters showed no sign of breaking up, so long as the guilty one was still inside offering his mandatory apology to Samuel Hatch. Apparently the red-faced Captain Trumble (ret'd) was prepared to let the Royal Navy survive without his free advice while he took part in a post-mortem of the case. Mr. Harris, the former mayor and racing champion — still as tremendously stout in his early sixties as on the day he first took office and fell through the mayoralty chair to the floor — agreed with the captain's opinion that Horncastle had yet to disappoint his friends when it came to putting on a good show before a magistrate. Mr. Drysdale (or Mr. Stackpole, if you preferred the name he used in Missouri before his activities during the American Civil War compromised his future in that state) agreed with Mr. Harris, but wished the magistrate would put more imagination into his sentences. "Same old thing every time." Clyde Munro, a veteran of the infamous Pig War which settled the international border question for the islands without the loss of a single life except for that of a farmer's hog, could find in every situation an opportunity to criticize Ottawa's continued delay in locating the western terminus of the cross-country railway in the city as promised. If having John A. Macdonald, the Prime Minister himself, as our Member of Parliament wasn't enough to get things done, then perhaps we should reconsider joining with our neighbours to the south. "If we'd had the brains to join with the States, a man like Horncastle would be elected to the Senate by now, instead of having to listen to tongue-lashings from a foreign queen."

Sumner joined the Horncastle family, who were just around the corner in the narrow noontime strip of shade thrown by the Barracks. Here, the topic of conversation was neither politics nor the trial they had witnessed but the identity of the woman in black who had entered the courtroom a few minutes before the end and then had disappeared. "She and her great flowery bag have been seen everywhere," Miss Horncastle said without looking up from her book, "but she seems to have no name. Or purpose."

The children rushed in to report that they had decided the mysterious woman was almost certainly a Russian. Russians had been much in the papers recently.

"A wandering Jewess," said young Jerome, the oldest of the boys – a stout lad of thirteen. "In search of a husband who was taken from her during the St. Petersburg purge."

Adelina was still sometimes drawn to be one of the children. "If she's a Russian, I say she is one of those nihilists who murdered the Czar, fleeing the hangman's noose that punished her friends." Her pale-blue eyes danced merrily, but did not quite meet Logan

Sumner's admiring ones. She moved out into the sunlight and swung up a white parasol, throwing new shadow across her curls and much of her pretty face. For a moment, only her mouth was in sunlight – her perfect glistening teeth pressed momentarily against her bottom lip – and of course her dress, which was a white muslin embroidered with tiny blue flowers.

"Perhaps she's the widowed Czarina herself" was Sumner's contribution to this game.

Abandoning his wandering-Jewess theory, Jerome immediately agreed, as he tended to do with almost everything Logan Sumner said. "Chasing the old bugger's mistress around the globe after revenge!"

Several cried his name at once, his sisters slapping their hands across their mouths, delighted and shocked. His exasperated mother took hold of an ear and twisted. "We'll wash out your foul mouth later."

Red-faced Jerome moved away from the group but did not altogether abandon them. It was unlikely that a forgiving woman like Mrs. Horncastle would still consider his misdemeanour to be important by the time they got home.

Though he would have preferred to forget all about the woman in black, Sumner could not neglect an opportunity to bring some truth to the situation. Miss Horncastle, Adelina, seemed to expect something more from him, and he was in a position to oblige. "I met her earlier this morning and she says she is William McConnell's sister. Hardly a Russian name."

This news delighted Miss Horncastle. "She'll take over the Bottomless Saloon and become one of those notorious woman saloon-keepers." She moved back into the building's shade and lowered her parasol, clearly expecting more.

"Not without a legal battle first," declared her mother with confident authority. "Isn't it common knowledge – he left the business to that Negro who worked for him."

They were joined by Mrs. Horncastle's friend, the tiny Lady

Riven-Blythe, who trembled beneath her enormous hat of yellow ostrich feathers with the need to bring new light to this conversation. "I happen to know that the woman is resident at the Driard House," she said. "A chambermaid is a friend of my kitchen-maid, Bess, who reports that she has come from Australia!" Her little dark eyes twinkled with the pleasure of imparting information, especially in full view of those who considered her friendship with the wife of a mere hotel owner to be highly irregular.

"Timothy Robbins is from Australia and he steals!" cried Jerome, bravely rejoining the party. He lowered his voice just for Logan Sumner. "His ma says he was sired by a bush-ranger during a stage robbery."

Lady Alice would not be distracted from her topic. "According to the chambermaid, she is a Mrs. Jordan – recently widowed! If she is McConnell's sister, as you say, he may have sent for her and the children with the intention of taking care of them. What a shock it must be to find him gone – and the saloon in the hands of a darky!"

Although her late husband had employed Sandwich Islanders and escaped slaves in his furniture factory, she'd persuaded him to discontinue the practice as unseemly for someone whose distant relative the Queen had rewarded with a title for his important contributions to the laws of the new Dominion. Lady Alice, who had never shared Sir Joseph's fascination with the laws, or indeed the humanity, of the new Dominion, had twice sailed Home to escape for ever this rough world she saw creating itself out of too many mediocre races – only to return each time equally discontented with all she had found in the soggy town of her birth.

When it became clear that the head of the family was not finding it easy to bring his apology to an end, the Horncastles started downhill towards the harbour – the youngest children running ahead, Mrs. Horncastle moving, as always, in the warm, clean smell and cheerful rustle of freshly ironed clothing. Sumner accompanied them, determined to stay with them long enough to discover whether an invitation to lunch might be forced upon him, though Adelina had opened her book and begun reading again, even as they walked. It was far too fine a day to worry about responsibilities – the sky was a pale cloudless blue, the sunlight made even the darkest buildings look cheerful, the sweet breeze off the sea was almost warm. He walked with a light step, leapt over an obstructing wagon's tongue, and greeted the pair of Indian women who stood talking at the corner while their baskets of onions and fish sat ignored against the wall. He accompanied the others right past the doors of his own offices and did not consider stopping.

Beyond the Customs House they began to follow the shoreline curve of the inner harbour, where steamships unloaded goods onto the docks.

In the constant shifting of positions amongst this progressing throng of noisy pedestrians, Sumner moved closer to Addie, who did not look up from her reading. "Your father says he regrets giving you Dancer, since you only neglect her. A good horse must be ridden every day, or will quickly decline. I think he will not deny us permission to ride together more often."

"And Jerome, of course."

"I shall speak to him about this, then?"

"For the good of the horse, I suppose it is a necessity."

They stepped onto the planks of the long bridge that spanned the shallow bay between the town and the legislative buildings. To their left, the soap factory released its steady flow of white fat juices into the shallow water, where it divided into wandering rainbow streams on the rippling surface, curled around the tall, narrow poles that held up the Sandwich Islanders' cabins, and joined with the food scraps from the cabin windows and bits of wood from the furniture factory to leak over the small waves towards the bridge and the harbour beyond it.

Amongst the younger Horncastle children a decision had been made. If she was not the Russian they had formerly made her, the woman in black was undoubtedly someone famous who had a reason for wishing to go unrecognized. "Lillie Langtry in disguise!" cried Moira. "Not Hatch's dog, of course – the real one! Somebody told her she might find the Prince of Wales here, far from his mother's eyes. If only it were true!"

But Lady Alice's little hands erased this talk from the air. "All this idle conjecture!" She almost sang this. "When you might only have asked me what more did I know! We must assume the woman is a criminal, of course, fleeing from justice!"

It was difficult to tell whether the chorus of protests was for the information or for the smugness with which it was delivered. Nevertheless, Lady Alice ploughed on. "It is impossible to tell the seriousness of a crime to which she has not yet confessed, but according to my Bess's friend a thousand clues point to something dreadful. Murder or treason at least. One has no trouble imagining those eyes squinting down the barrel of a gun."

"Surely not!" exclaimed Mrs. Horncastle, stopping dead in her tracks and widening her own green innocent eyes – she could not bear to hear evil spoken of anyone.

Adelina protested. "But she may be someone quite heroic. Perhaps she merely protected her honour from villains." The eldest of the lovely Horncastle daughters had for more than a year been addicted to novels sent by a relative from England, including the stories of the late Mr. Dickens, whose son, while he resided here, had been a guest at the family dinner table more than once with other sailors when she was a little girl. In particular, she was fond of the three-volume novels of Mrs. Oliphant, whose *A Rose in Spring* she was reading even now.

Lady Alice raised a hand to ward off both their protests. "Have you not seen a certain strange gentleman on our streets? An unusually tall man, and thin, with – you would notice this – one missing ear? He has followed her here. He has sworn vengeance on behalf of the victim. Bess's friend says he booked passage on the same ship from Melbourne without her knowledge, and is staying at the very same hotel. He keeps an eye on her while he awaits an opportunity to act!"

Keep an eye indeed. Sumner shuddered, recalling his glimpse of the man spying from the branches of a cemetery tree! Did he intend to administer vengeance with that enormous whip? "Then why did he not 'act' while he had her trapped on the ship?"

"Perhaps she was protecting her children from a villain," suggested Addie, without looking up from her story. "She may have had to kill him, to save her babies' lives." Addie had once confessed, to her parents' horror, that she had considered following in the footsteps of Mrs. Oliphant, Miss Thackeray, and Miss Broughton. Using a false name, of course.

Lady Alice grabbed at her own necklace and presented a determined jaw. "And a second gentleman? Also registered at the same hotel! A balding bespectacled man." This nameless chambermaid was proving to be a truly wondrous detective. "A lawman of some sort, who boarded the ship in San Francisco. Bess's friend discovered him sneaking around the hotel. He too is awaiting his moment."

"Then she is doomed?" a distressed Mrs. Horncastle asked, all of the starch deserting her clothes. "Poor soul! It is only a question of who will get her first."

"Oh, we shall see her hang yet," promised Lady Alice. "And once her neck has been stretched, beware! – those two children will be looking for a new home and *your* soft heart is well enough known, Norah! You'll find them on your doorstep, you'll have two little criminals stealing the very silver they eat with at your table."

"Innocent children!" cried Mrs. Horncastle. "How could you blame them for the mother's sins?"

"Let us not forget that she is Australian!" Lady Alice cried in the direction of the harbour. "Her mother rode with a gang of cattle thieves, undoubtedly. Her grandmother was transported for stabbing a neighbour in an English public house. It is all in her face. Take a good look at her next time she is near enough – but don't let her get *too* near! She'll take your money, slit your throat, and run off with your husband as well!"

For a moment they proceeded in silence. The children looked to Mrs. Horncastle, waiting for her to find the usual silver lining. It seemed for a while that she might not this time succeed – an astonishing possibility. What a struggle was going on behind that wide, pleasant face! "Didn't I like her better when she was the poor distracted Czarina!" Their footsteps, thumping hollowly on the wooden planks, seemed to insist that the world be set right again. "But surely we mustn't forget that the poor woman cannot help where she was raised. Doesn't she hope to atone for her crimes by living a sinless life amongst strangers!"

She blushed with the pleasure derived from her own conclusions, then reached out with mock anger to swat at Jerome, who led the applause.

They had left the bridge and were now on their way up Bird Cage Walk past the red-brick legislature buildings, where the clock on the cupola of the Executive Building clearly showed that the time was now twelve forty-six. The warm air was sweetened by the wild roses blooming in the bushes along the picket fences. Addie had once again happened to fall into step beside Logan Sumner, who once again found himself with a ruler in his hand – without purpose. He let it unfold downward to lay its final section alongside his own foot. Almost the full twelve inches.

"Perhaps your mother can be persuaded to invite me to dinner this evening. For the sake of Dancer."

The yardstick measured the pale-pink face of a rose – an inch and a half. A bee protested its accidental imprisonment behind the varnished wood, then flew off crookedly in search of safer pollen. Sumner picked the rose, careful not to jar the fragile petals free, then leaned in to wrench another off between his fingers, and stepped in farther still towards the buried pickets to break off a twisted stem that branched out into several flowers – a bouquet in itself. Turning to present the prize to the waiting one, he discovered his jacket was caught on thorns – his pocket, now his sleeve, now somewhere his back as well. The rest of the pedestrians had gone on, unnoticing, leaving only Adelina to laugh as he twisted and shook himself into the even tighter grasp of the thorny bushes.

When he bent, cautiously, to retrieve the fallen yardstick from the leafy ground at the base of the thorny stems, he found himself hooked at the shoulders as well, and even by the hair. He could stand up again only by enduring a long scratch on his scalp and snags torn from the tweed – yet he remained a prisoner.

Down along the inside of the fence came a Jersey cow to investigate, mooing softly. Encouragement or muted threat, he couldn't tell.

"Shoo! Shoo!" Addie Horncastle waved her arms, but only whispered the warning. "She would only be able to drool on you, but we cannot have her interfering. Unless, of course, the flowers were intended for her."

"For you, of course. Please take them."

"Go into the bushes after them? Mother would have my head. You must bring them out to me."

"I have tried," protested Logan Sumner, "but I seem not to be very good at it."

"Or at much else?" she ventured, tentatively. "Like speaking your mind while you have the chance? *We are alone!*"

"You want me to speak now? Like this? You would never let me forget it. 'He revealed his heart while hiding inside a bush.' No – I shall sacrifice my clothes and tear myself free to speak, if necessary, in tatters."

"Oh, very well," she said, coming closer. "Give me the flowers to hold. Now, carefully, slip out of the jacket – careful! Now take my hand and step . . . out. . . . *There!* Now, you are free to rescue the jacket or not, as you please. And you may decide whether these flowers were intended for me, or you may ask me to attend to that scratch on your hand."

"Now hurry, Addie," complained her mother, leaving her flock of younger children to come back towards them. "Will you keep Mr. Sumner to yourself? Wouldn't the rest of us enjoy his company as well – since he has been good enough to escort the ladies and children this far."

Only now did it occur to him that he had no idea why they were walking in this direction when the Horncastles lived in the centre of town and Lady Alice's home was in quite the opposite direction. His confusion must show all over his face. Even dear Mrs. Horncastle laughed. "But we're invited for luncheon with Lady Alice's sister-in-law, Mr. Sumner! With Mrs. Limpet. Didn't you know? Ladies and children!" She lunged at Jerome: "And wicked family outcasts, of course!" She gave his ear an affectionate twist and laughed at his yelp. "Perhaps you didn't intend to accompany us at all, but meant to stay behind for Father." Her broad red cheeks were made even broader by her smile. "Once he has growled at the help for letting the hotel fall apart in our absence, he will expect to argue business with you. He enjoys nothing so much as talking hammer and nails with Logan Sumner, and would be most alarmed to discover you'd chosen to lunch with the ladies before him!"

4

Although it was not yet the largest hotel in town, or the most impressive either, The Great Blue Heron was perhaps the most popular amongst those who wanted to drink at a friendly

bar, or eat in a comfortable dining-room, or stay in a clean and
tidy room within easy walking distance of all the downtown businesses. Guests in the upstairs rooms tended to be travelling salesmen and businessmen from San Francisco, and occasionally
families of immigrants whose husbands and fathers had not yet
found or built them a home. A few had become more or less permanent, like poor little Miss Thurlow, who arrived from Kent to
join a fiancé no one here had ever heard of. And old Colonel
Willoughby Stokes, who every afternoon went out in his carriage
and allowed his horses to pull him up and down a regular pattern
of familiar streets for two or three hours while he slept, his great
yellowed moustaches fluttering under his snoring nostrils.

The hotel was located close to the centre of town and the
harbour, within a few minutes' walk of the Police Barracks, the Post
Office, and the Theatre Royal, with the mysteries of Chinatown
just a short distance to the north. Situated between a stationer's
and a tobacconist, the building was a plain two-storey red-brick box
set back a few steps from the sidewalk, the entrance to its main
foyer in the exact centre of the front wall and the doors to its billiard parlour and bowling alley down the narrow lane that separated
the building from the tobacconist. Inside the foyer of oak walls
and royal-blue rugs and potted ferns, where one or another of
the smiling Horncastle children could always be found behind the
reception counter, the bird after which the hotel was named stood
guard at the foot of the staircase – waist-high, its beak upraised on
the end of its long, snaky neck – a heron waiting for food. Mrs.
Horncastle had spotted the dead bird and ordered it brought home
as though she expected her husband to give it back its life. He gave
it all he could, the attentions of a taxidermist and a sort of immor-
tality as central feature in his beloved hotel.

At one time, Horncastle had decided to make himself an expert
on the enormous bird which had given its name to his hotel and
its silhouette to the rectangular sign by the door. After reading all
the information he could find on the *ardea herodias*, he set out on

bird-watching expeditions. At first this meant spending the occasional afternoon boating on the saltwater arm of the Gorge, observing the long-legged, long-necked birds that waited near the shoreline for whatever fish or crustaceans or reptiles or amphibians should come by in the shallow water. He admired their regal crests and ornamental plumage, he watched for one of them to comb the oil and grease and mud from its feathers so that he could explain to others – as boastful as he might have been if he had invented this wondrous detail himself – about the claw on the middle toe with the teeth along its inner surface.

But eventually this proved to be a much too sedentary sort of entertainment for a man like Horncastle. Soon he was climbing up the pitchy branches of a Douglas fir in search of the nest that was responsible for the great riot of squawking that could be heard from a mile away, and for the droppings that had spread like a spilled bucket of whitewash down the boughs and trunk to the needle-carpeted ground. Neither the furious parents nor the panicked fledgelings were happy to share their great wide floating nest of twigs with the human who poked himself up over the edge, but Horncastle had a way of disregarding protest. There proved to be room enough for them all, at least for the time it took Horncastle to examine the situation from every angle, drink a little from his flask of whiskey, sing a few verses from HMS *Pinafore*, and congratulate the birds on training their offspring to hang their rear ends out over the side of the nest, fouling the world below instead of their home.

Like all enthusiasms that did not involve some form of gambling, this one quickly faded, but at least it gave him the sort of information he might turn to his advantage in the bar. Why was the hotel named for this great awkward bird? Simple. "You've seen him. Stands at the side of the water. Waits for his dinner to come to him." What else were any of them doing here, he challenged his listeners to tell him. Waiting for the next boom. "Waiting for gold to be discovered again somewhere so we can all become rich.

Haven't you noticed? This city's how those foreigners get into the country." Many like himself had got their start during the Cariboo gold rush, and now they waited for the opportunity to take advantage of the next lot to come chasing after wealth. "Will have to buy their licences here. And their supplies. Will have to stay in hotels here until they're ready to move on. Will have to stay in hotels again later, too, while they wait for the boat to take them and their fortunes home. Every damn business in town could be named the Great Blue Heron. Waiting for our dinner to come swimming by!"

When Horncastle did his accounts at his office desk, he sat at the very centre of his hotel's history. The office was the same log cabin he'd purchased for a saloon soon after moving to the Colony from San Francisco with his wife in 1860, one of the squared-log fish warehouses built by French-Canadian carpenters in the Hudson's Bay fortress that had been dismantled just before the Horncastles arrived. Although he'd come here expecting to find a familiar British flavour and had found the little city swarming with Yankee businessmen agitating for annexation, he was capable of adjusting quickly to any circumstance and put a false board front on his saloon in the manner of the California buildings he'd become accustomed to during the gold-rush days. Almost immediately Horncastle became the most popular saloon-keeper in town. Enterprising American businessmen applauded what they called his Yankee energy, especially in his enthusiastic and dramatic defences against accusations arising out of disputes at the race-track. At the same time, British sailors found their welcome at Horncastle's superior to that at other establishments, and could not resist a proprietor whose tall tales about his travels equalled their own – "Down in the Grand Canyon country I spent a week with this eight-foot Indian woman who'd set up her teepee amongst the rattlesnakes!" British sailors and American businessmen were as pleased as local farmers with Horncastle's willingness to lay bets on anything – his horse, his dog, his fists, his cricket bat, or the length of time a spider might take to drop from the ceiling to the floor at their feet. Occasionally someone succeeded in tripling a month's wages in the course of an evening.

When the combination of his own success and Mrs. Horncastle's ambitions suggested that it was time to expand (this was shortly after his second appearance in police court for assaulting Dr. John Meredith in an argument after a horse race), he'd decided neither to tear the building down nor to move from his location in the centre of town. Why risk losing what he had worked so hard to establish? Rather, he'd hired Charles Sumner to build a large home and lodging-house in the style then being widely copied all over town from the better class of villas in San Francisco, but he kept the cabin within it as his saloon. He continued to spend most of his working hours inside those four log walls, even after he and his wife had begun to adopt orphans and other abandoned children whose care would prevent Mrs. Horncastle from devoting her time entirely to the business.

A few years later, shortly after the success of his libel suit against the saloon-keeper William McConnell (who'd posted a large notice in his own premises suggesting that anyone using Horncastle's bar was unknowingly being robbed), he converted the lodging-house to a hotel and added an entire brick exterior in the simple, dignified style of some sober hotel he remembered seeing in England. A brand-new bar was added, along with a billiard parlour, a bowling alley, and a livery stable, and the log-cabin saloon became the owner's office at the heart of the building – its floor the original oiled planks, its walls the same rough squared-off logs that had protected fish from thieves and extremes of weather.

Glass doors opened onto a small garden situated at the rear of the building, where guests might enjoy the solitude or soak up the warmth of the sun – an iron bench, a marble fountain, several flowering shrubs, and a large old cedar whose heavy boughs laid green moving shadows down across the floor of the office. In spite of the limited space, Mrs. Horncastle had followed the local pattern of including plants from various corners of the earth: a monkey-puzzle tree from Chile, fuchsia bushes from Ireland, a redwood from California, Canterbury bells from England, even a little maple from Quebec. This was soon after her husband's courtroom victory over the saloon-keeper Samuel Hatch, who'd been heard suggesting in public that the history of Horncastle's youth included a period as a transported felon.

Sumner thought of the establishment as growing rather in the manner of a tree, adding continuously to its sequence of interior rings. Miss Adelina Horncastle took quite another view: "Imagine a home that is constantly changing! Nothing is ever considered completed, or even capable of being completed. It has taught me to see the world in constant need of being remade – an exhausting, hopeless task." Now Horncastle was anxious to proceed with plans for yet another new face to be applied over all the others, once he and Logan Sumner had agreed on the design – which was likely to include a balcony above a long verandah, sturdy pillars, and much fancy fretwork around the edges.

When Sumner entered the office late in the afternoon following the courtroom appearance – just in time for dinner – Horncastle stood at the glass doors looking out on the beds of hollyhocks and irises and lily of the valley. A mock-orange bush was in bloom. "Aha! The jay escaped! Would have won if you'd been here to place money on the cat." He did not turn from the window. "Well, my friend, I disappointed you this morning?"

"Far from it! It was all I could do to keep from applauding when you announced the wager with Sheepshank Junior."

"Stupid move on my part, to confess it. Damned magistrate deliberately slowed things down to spoil my chances of winning." When he turned his head to glance at Sumner, the green light of the cedar boughs moved across the window side of his face. "Saw

your attention wandering, you traitor. What do you expect of me –
gunshots? Confessions of infidelity? Should I accuse His Honour of
selling his wife? He considered it once. Told me himself. Regrets he
didn't follow through." He turned and advanced on his desk where
Sumner's drawings were laid out, his fingers stroking his moustache.
"Now, we have a disagreement I think, about the pillars. Would
prefer the round, solid hearts of sturdy trees myself, but you have
something square and flimsy and fabricated in mind. Let us have it
out now." He narrowed his dark eyes down to glinting slits and
grinned, prepared for battle, the network of tiny veins on his cheeks
reddening as they did whenever he anticipated a brisk encounter.

"I'd intended to arrive earlier, but when I stopped by the house,
Chu Lee was in a panic – that black and white cow that's running
loose had found a weak spot in my fence and pushed in to feast on
his young lettuces. I spent the afternoon replacing old pickets
with new."

Horncastle rested a hand on the black telephone that hung on
the wall. Naturally, he'd been one of the first in town to install a
telephone, but it was very seldom used, since none of the other
telephones were owned by people he cared to speak to. "Edgar
Greer saw you taking orders from your own cook, who stood on
the step and criticized while you mended the fence. Has there
been a reversal of roles in your household? Or has Chu Lee saved
up wages enough to hire you to repair your own property?"

This was a familiar sort of teasing, which Sumner did not mind
at all. "Chu Lee claims to have been an aristocrat in China, where
his nod caused heads to roll." He placed his hand against the
rough log surface of a wall: dark knots, adze-nicked crescents, and
wide slanted cracks from the years of drying. "I'm expected to
humour him occasionally, when he's overcome with nostalgia."

Horncastle consulted first one and then another of the watercolour racehorses on his walls. Eclipse about to be mounted. The
astonishing Iroquois in full canter. "Will you humour him still, I

wonder, when it's your own head that rolls? While he converts your house into an opium den for his homesick countrymen?"

"Very well, then," Sumner said, "the pillars will be round, the solid hearts out of giant firs, if that's what you want."

Horncastle's face showed disappointment. "That's what I want but, dammit, not so much as I wanted a battle over them. You give in too easily, boy. If all your clients have this effect upon you, you will end up with no mind at all of your own, and everyone thinking he has the same privileges as your cook! Speak up for yourself!"

"If you wish! Fabricated pillars would be less expensive, and every bit as solid to the passing eye. And they would adequately serve their only purpose, which is to keep the upper verandah from collapsing under the weight of ladies taking the sun."

"By the lord Harry, I'll have round, solid pillars or none!" He began to roll up the drawings. "And I am the one who will pay for them. Argue with *that* if you will!"

"And I am the one whose uncle was an expert on these matters. Who taught me what he knew. Round pillars will look ridiculous, if you'll forgive me. You aren't building a monument after the fashion of Mr. Jefferson. I am assured that slim rectangular pillars are far more admired amongst the leading contemporary designers of hotels in England."

Sumner knew nothing about the contemporary designers of hotels in England, of course, but Horncastle expected his opponents to stop short of nothing, as he would himself. The drawings were abruptly stuffed inside a cupboard. "Not a word more. The matter is settled."

"Your way or mine?"

"Come, we'll join the others. Mrs. Horncastle will scald my ears off for keeping you to myself. Your way of course. Do you think I want my hotel to look like a damn university in Virginia?" He held the glass door open and stood back for Sumner to go through to the garden. "You're not our only guest today – which explains why I've hidden in here for as long as I have. The newspaperwoman again! My brash Yankee cousin with her opinions. Let us discover how much, between us, we are able to endure."

Sumner's enormous affection for the family had no difficulty expanding to include those who showed up at the Horncastle table from all parts of the globe claiming to be relatives – a trader in Oriental art works from Hong Kong, a colonel's widow on her way home from India. But he found little pleasure in the company of the long-jawed newspaperwoman from San Francisco who never failed to attend at least one family dinner while she was in town, though she slept a few blocks away at the more luxurious Driard House at her employer's expense. Excessively and defiantly emancipated, this woman went everywhere in a fringed leather jacket she claimed to have won off a notorious gunman in a California poker game. Her face was as dark and roughly creased as her jacket, though presumably it had taken more than a single poker game to acquire. Some believed she was really a man. Sumner found her too loud and confident for his liking, and always reacted to her presence with a disappointment which he knew would eventually become, in her continued company, an extreme case of irritation.

"Well, it's the melancholy bachelor again – lookin' more pale and wan than ever!" She met them in the garden, where she'd evidently been wandering with a glass of their host's whiskey, a white petal from a mock-orange riding her buckskin shoulder. "Every time I come up here I wonder how many of the buildings are wearin' new faces because of you. I can tell the people down the street have visited Rome."

A second guest rose from the bench to greet them – this one a young man with an unusually pointed nose and a strange twitch in both eyelids. Sumner's disappointment sank to bad-tempered impatience. This young gentleman – a long, thin fish-hook of a fellow, with tiny white hands – was introduced by James Horncastle as a "son of a friend in Ottawa," living for the time being in the Blue Heron. Employed by the federal government, he'd been sent out to earn enough experience in the Customs House here to justify a transfer home. "Want him to make all his mistakes where it doesn't matter," said Horncastle, grasping the young man's sleeve and giving it a friendly shake, "before they send him to somewhere important." The young man blushed, and stuttered, and tried to find something in the flowers to distract attention from himself – then gave up and drained his glass. He put Sumner in mind of a timid traveller set down in an alien court where he was terrified of violating customs he'd never been told about, possibly bringing upon himself a punishment that ended in a painful death. He was not the first visitor from Ottawa to exhibit this look.

"Must write your father that I'm still waiting for that railway!" Horncastle shouted, as though the young man were deaf. "Still expecting them to put the terminal just down the street. Deliver visitors right to my doorstep!"

In a thin voice that seemed determined to give him difficulties, the young man explained that, according to his father's letters, every effort was being made to fulfil expectations. "But it is impossible for people here to realize what obstacles insist on arising." He sat down upon the bench again, as though this explanation had required an exhausting effort, and took a bough of the cedar into his lap for companionship.

"Eight years of obstacles," Horncastle said. "Tell him we're waiting to see if we made a mistake."

The newspaperwoman from San Francisco laughed. "Of course you made a mistake! You've had enough time to see that. Instead of joining with a country you can practically touch across that strip of water, you've joined up with a lot of stuffy Loyalists and shrill Frenchmen three thousand miles of impassable mountains and empty prairies away. As ridiculous as if Georgia decided to join up with Belgium."

"The railway, madam," declared her annoyed cousin, "will change that."

"So would a steamship between Brussels and Atlanta. A railway, by the way, that I bet you'll never see."

"Let's see your money," Horncastle snapped. "Come on. How much are you willing to lose?"

The young man from Ottawa stopped blinking and twitching long enough to reveal that he was more in control of the issues than the others might have thought. "Of course, you have been influenced by your friends in town." He added, for anyone who might not already know, "Who were amongst the businessmen petitioning President Grant in '69, on behalf of annexation."

"Oh dear," said a voice in one of the windows above them. The sash was pulled closed. But Horncastle greeted the young man's rejoinder with cheers and hoots, as though he had scored four runs in a cricket match. "Tell us what you think will happen," he said to his cousin, when he had regained his composure. "Will the Republic of Dollardom invade us?"

"We won't have to do anything. We'll forget you're even here. Sooner or later you'll grow ashamed of being invisible."

"Bah!" Horncastle turned away, as though he would retreat to his office. "Where's Captain Trumble? Thinks we threw it all away. Exchanged the attentions of London for government by a lot of rascals in a frozen city that doesn't know we exist – but he wouldn't go with you! Still mourns for the lost colony. Important thing is what we make of ourselves."

"You think those easterners will lead you with any courage or imagination? They're the men who intended to call this country the Kingdom of Canada – remember? – but changed it to Dominion in order to avoid offending us. Not an inspiring start. And anyway," said the Yankee woman, one of her boots holding down a fallen iris by the stem, "there's bound to be someone amongst you eventually – an Irishman, probably – who'll be glad to take you away from *them* and give you to *us*. You'll let him do it when our successes have made you ashamed of everything about yourselves that's different from us."

Perhaps this was too far-fetched to be considered. Horncastle said, "Let's go in, then, and see what there is to eat. Norah will think we've finished one another off behind the bushes."

The newspaperwoman's prediction of vengeful Irishmen had set the direction – the latest news from Ireland was spoken of during the meal. Several riots had broken out during recent evictions in Counties Clare and Cork. Many had been injured, some killed. Horncastle expressed the opinion that, despite his considerable sympathy for the Fenian cause on their own soil, he hoped the two who'd been convicted of plotting to blow up the Liverpool town hall were quickly hanged. "Too close to Manchester – my childhood home. Let them blow up their own town halls if they must blow up anything." The Irish-born Mrs. Horncastle was not here to respond to this, having rushed off at the beginning of the meal to take care of some hotel emergency – kept vague and mysterious in front of dinner guests – but Mrs. Stark, the newspaperwoman, rebuked her host for his British hypocrisy. Raising her voice in a manner that Sumner found to be almost a donkey's bray, she made certain everyone understood that her own country would have handled the Irish business in a far more intelligent, far more compassionate, far more effective manner. "Of course, you haven't realized yet what tyrants you chose to take your orders from."

The watercolour swans on one wall, Queen Victoria on another, and several ancestors on every side received this proclamation in silence. So did the young man from Ottawa, whose nervous gaze kept returning to Adelina's pale wrist. Conversation shifted, during dessert, to a variety of matters – a phantom ship that had been haunting people along the banks of the Fraser River, Disraeli's funeral and the old woman who'd left him her fortune on the condition that he be buried beside her, the one hundred lashes received by the St. Petersburg executioner for his mismanagement of a recent hanging where the rope broke twice.

Whenever the young man from Ottawa stole glances at Adelina, he was overtaken by fits of feverish blinking. Perhaps he had begun to feel irrelevant at this table, Logan Sumner hoped, having found little to say about any of the topics raised. But when he made an effort to revive the earlier debate by mentioning the promised railway again, Mrs. Horncastle returned from her mysterious mission and informed him that she forbade political talk at her table. "I dislike the colour it brings to Mr. Horncastle's face." She tightened her mouth and glanced in the direction of the woman who must know, surely, that she would never have been very welcome here if she had not been a relative of their host, and if Mrs. Horncastle had not been incapable of withholding hospitality from anyone.

The young civil servant leaned close to Addie and remarked, in his thin voice, that he had admired the horse he had seen her riding earlier in the week. "A match for my Horatio, I think. Perhaps we could discover whether they make good riding companions?" Adelina looked squarely into Logan Sumner's eyes and said, "A fine idea, Mr. Callow. Papa thinks I ride him too little." All previous failures vanished from the civil servant's suddenly beaming face.

Since ladies were not in the habit of withdrawing from the Horncastle table after a meal, they found themselves speaking again of the mysterious woman in black. Horncastle had not seen this person for himself, being too involved in his own affairs even to hear of her, so Mrs. Horncastle took up the task of telling him what others had seen and heard. But it was quickly discovered that again the newspaperwoman from San Francisco knew more than the rest. Perhaps she considered it her birthright to be always better informed than those who lived north of the border, even about matters that took place in their own community.

"She's already received two proposals of marriage since she got here. What d' you think o' that?" Lighting up a cigarette, she looked as though she expected someone to replace Mrs. Horncastle's dishes with a deck of cards. Exclamations of disbelief were waved aside by the hand that shook out the match's flame. "One from a fellow who was on the ship from the start. Another from a medical man who came aboard in San Francisco, on his way to the Cariboo."

Raising his cigar to just beside his ear, Horncastle leaned back and suggested that they send someone out this minute to bring the woman here. "Should have a good look before those others snatch her up. May want to put in a bid myself."

Scooping up pink rose petals which had fallen from the bouquet in the middle of the table, perhaps from shock, Addie asked what he planned to do with Mother.

"You've probably seen one o' them on the streets," the news-paperwoman said. "Carries a whip. He knew her in Australia – made his proposal there. When she turned him down, he booked passage on the same ship and renewed his offer. I reckon his hopes are as slim as he is himself."

Mrs. Horncastle flushed. "Heavens! But this is not at all what Lady Alice told us!"

"Lady Riven-Blythe said nothing about proposals," Sumner protested. "She spoke of punishment."

Horncastle laughed. "Question is: when a proposal is accepted, who is the punished one?" He winked at Mrs. Horncastle, who picked up the sugar bowl and made as though to hurl it at him.

Fringes on the newspaperwoman's leather sleeve trembled with scorn. "Has your *Lady Alice* seen all this for herself? I've talked to everyone concerned." Her jaw seemed to grow even longer as she spoke. "I'm at the same hotel, remember."

Addie said, "He must be very much in love, that he could not bear to stay behind without her." This was said to the hand that held her cup, and not to any young man in the room. But wait, a smiling glance was directed at Sumner after all, though more briefly than blinking.

"No more so than the second fellow," said Mrs. Stark. "The physician who got on the ship when I did has postponed his journey up the Fraser River into the depleted gold-field. People are dying in the Cariboo this minute while she refuses to give him an answer! At least four times he's offered to cancel his plans and open a practice here, or take her to live in California, or take her back to Australia. The man is desperate for an answer – tossin' back more alcohol than he should. He hammers on her door and begs her t' put him out of his misery. Says he'll blow his brains all over the ceiling if she turns him down. Presses his face against her door and weeps like a child – then later, when he's sober, he comes back to apologize for his behaviour."

"Mercy!" cried Mrs. Horncastle. "Haven't they only had time to get their land-legs and already they're engaged in such melo-drama!" Lest this comment appear to be unfairly critical, she added: "Spirited people will live by their own codes, I suppose, and would find the rest of us a lot of old bores." She moved a bowl of happy irises off the shining walnut cupboard and onto a white table-cloth which could be considered boring, she imagined, without platters of food. Even the falling leaves on the wallpaper, or the dark-green velvet drapes, were not as colourful as some might have wished them to be.

"The thin man offered to put him out of his misery if he'll step into the park. But the woman insists on patience."

"Let us discover the physician's name," said Mrs. Horncastle. "If he sets up a practice here, we'll not make the mistake of calling for his services." She paused, before adding what the rest expected from her: "Though he's a fine enough physician I'm sure, when he is not in his cups."

"The story seems the more remarkable," Sumner suggested in Horncastle's direction, "when you consider that the favoured gentleman can expect to inherit two small children in the package. Not every widowed mother is pursued so avidly."

"Good lord!" Horncastle said. "This woman becomes more and more impossible to believe in. I'll marry her myself."

"Papa!" Addie warned.

"Isn't there only the one explanation for it, then?" said Mrs. Horncastle, giving her husband a warning frown. "And an obvious one at that. She is not the destitute widow we took her for at all, she's as wealthy as a duchess."

"She doesn't wear jewellery!" The American cousin was brashly vehement. "She hasn't many possessions with her – mostly clothing for the children."

Horncastle exploded. "You've been through her things?"

The newspaperwoman spoke with her cigarette still in the corner of her lips. "I'm good at my job, if that's what you mean. She told both suitors there's somethin' here she has to do before she answers them. She won't tell them what. She wouldn't tell me either. Maybe she'll tell Mr. Sumner – she seemed uncommonly taken with him. She told me you'd met."

"But did not even exchange names."

"Well – she knows yours anyway. She's even better than I am at finding out what she wants to know."

"She wishes to invest some of her fortune in a business!" This inspiration put the young man from Ottawa back in the picture. His face displayed his confidence in having achieved a triumph.

Addie was expected to respond to this demonstration of superior intelligence, but Mrs. Horncastle recognized his brilliance first. "By the time we have made the Blue Heron the finest hotel in town, with Mr. Sumner's help, she will have built an even finer one across the street and made paupers out of us." She clasped her hands together as though to control them. "May the medical man drag her off to the North where her money will do her little good. The two of them can drink it away." Because she was incapable of wishing ill on anyone for long, she quickly added, "Sure, they could build a lovely hotel up, there with her money and be as happy as children together."

Though the younger children were no longer present to laugh at this typical expression of their mother's determined good will, Addie and Logan Sumner exchanged amused glances. They would have been disappointed if she had suddenly become no better than the rest and left her uncharitable thought uncancelled. She knew this herself, and smiled in a manner that said, There, I have made the world right again for you, as I do a thousand times every day.

The planned after-dinner ride – which threatened for a while to become a trio – was postponed when Adelina declared the air to have become a little chilly. When Sumner took his leave of the Horncastles, it was still without a private word with the young lady. Out on the street, he found himself walking with the newspaperwoman towards her hotel, and began to sing the praises of the entire Horncastle family for her benefit. "They should be written up in your paper, Mrs. Stark, as a model that families all over the continent might do well to imitate."

The newspaperwoman did not commit herself to the project. Instead, she seemed to feel that her companion would be interested to learn that she had been out to the cemetery that afternoon. "To visit the grave of a friend."

"Yes." Sumner resigned himself to the inevitable. "And could not help noticing –"

"I don't pay any attention to the sentimental nonsense you see on those poor slabs of stone, but I couldn't help but notice how temporary all your final words have turned out to be."

"To be truthful, I find it difficult to understand how others can be more definite."

"Maybe that's why most epitaphs are composed when it's too late for the subject to have second thoughts."

She found him amusing! Here was proof that Sumner had been right to imagine people laughing at him, when even a casual acquaintance should so quickly notice! He was glad the subject had not been raised indoors.

And the worst of it was, he had already thought of something else he wished to add. The thought of smashing up the old stone was unbearable to him after all, however foolish it made him look. Somehow, it mustn't be destroyed but enlarged rather, for just this one final addition. Positively the last. *Bereft of parents, relatives, even wife, he was blest nevertheless with extraordinary friends.* He would use his tombstone to celebrate the one true blessing of his life: the Horncastle family. Peter Schlegg could not be approached to do it, of course. But Sumner was himself a builder after all, with skilled employees. He would secure more granite himself, a much larger piece, and would direct one of his employees to find a way of fitting the old stone onto the top of a newer larger one, and to add these words as a final statement on the unblemished surface below.

So involved was he in his own thoughts that he was not aware of what his companion was talking about until it became clear that she was onto the woman in black again, whose presence in town had expanded to preoccupy the entire day, pushing his own hopes quite aside. "Of course, I couldn't mention this at the table," she said, "with his wife in the room. I reckon he'll learn for himself soon enough."

"I'm sorry," he said. "Who will learn what?"

"My cousin. That he's the one she's come here to find."

"If she had come here to find James Horncastle, she would have found him by now. No one is more easily located."

"She's been scouting. Findin' out all there is to know about him. It's not just to find him that she's come, but to *have* him."

Sumner was appalled. "How could you know such a thing?"

"I'm a newspaperwoman, Mr. Sumner. It comes natural for me to discover what no one else knows. I need to be even better than the lawyer at putting clue beside clue."

"Then you are only guessing."

"I'm tellin' you what I know."

"And you have facts?"

"I've spoken to the woman herself, something nobody else seems to have thought of doin'."

"But why? Why? What does it mean?"

"What does it mean to her? She wouldn't tell me. We'll have to wait to see what it means to him. He won't be able to treat this as a joke. She claims to know him. To have known him all her life. Or did you mean to say what does it mean to *you*?"

"To us all. To us all." She might have told him that this city where he had spent his entire life was about to disappear into a chasm. She might have been saying that this lovely June night was actually all theatrical props, camouflaging a bitter December noon. "God help me, Mrs. Stark, but I've gone as cold as that graveyard stone you saw this afternoon. What can it possibly mean?"

"Ask her yourself. She talked as though she felt some affection for you, after your little conversation. Somebody like you – a young fellow with sad eyes – can sometimes win the confidence of a certain kind of woman where others can't. Just go to the hotel and *ask*."

MRS. KATE JORDAN'S ACCOUNT OF
WHY SHE LEFT AUSTRALIA, SOME OF
WHICH SHE TOLD TO MR. SUMNER
IN THE LUXURIOUS FOYER OF
SOSTHENES DRIARD'S HOTEL

5

ALTHOUGH Mrs. Jordan could hardly confess this to Logan Sumner immediately, she had not forgotten that back home in Ballarat she had begun to fear that the pressures of widowhood were beginning to have an unfortunate effect upon her mind. Because her hatred of the cockatoos had grown so large that she sometimes had trouble breathing, she began to go out onto her narrow verandah at dawn when the great white birds had gathered in the upper branches of the blue gum across the street and, with her eyes closed, to discharge her husband's ancient musket at the vacant sky. Though the blow to her shoulder continued to send her staggering back against the weatherboard every day, fewer and fewer of the ten, eighteen, thirty-nine birds exploded off their shivering branches to go screeching down the street and resume their squabbling in the sturdy old bloodwoods at a safer distance. Stepping inside to lean the firearm into the corner behind the door, she knew of course that she had changed nothing, that others would come, and others, or the same ones again, that there was no end to the great white hated parrots, or to their persistence – there was a whole continent of them out there prepared to hang their weight on the limbs of the blue gums and bloodwoods of Ripon Street in order to drive her mad. "Nobody should be expected to live in a world where birds are the size of pigs that laugh in your face."

For some reason which she never learned, neighbours did not complain about the widow's new habit of catapulting them out of their dreams every morning with a blast from a flintlock musket that dated back to the Eureka Stockade. Perhaps this was out of respect for her husband, dead now for less than a year, who had not permitted the loss of an arm in the rebellion to prevent him from performing his job in the drapery shop, or from starting a family, or from expressing admirable sentiments amongst the crowd at the Loafers Tree on Saturday afternoons. Perhaps their silence was motivated by a self-protective caution as well, a horror of the sort of unpleasantness that might be unleashed by mentioning something even mildly critical to a woman of Kate Jordan's temperament.

Even more surprising was the fact that no delegation approached her on behalf of the town council to discuss this violation of certain city statutes. No mayor, no councillors, no councillors' wives. No irate-but-careful leading citizens. Not even a deputation from Christ Church Cathedral, which might have added gentle remonstrances concerning other matters – that she had not been seen in her pew since the funeral, for instance, or that she had not approached any of the ladies of the congregation for the sympathy and comfort they felt they deserved to be asked to give.

There was no immediate response from her sisters, either, who must surely have heard the gunshots in the family boarding-house three blocks to the east. Susannah, the eldest of the McConnell sisters, seldom passed up an opportunity to speak plainly to the most spirited member of her family. But she had not been speaking to Kate at all since the day they'd quarrelled publicly during the preparations for Tom Jordan's funeral, when Susannah had insisted that for a new widow who owned a cottage but had no money the only solution was to take in boarders as she and young Annie did – as Kate had done herself, along with them, before her marriage – and Kate had responded that she would rather

throw herself and her children on the charity of the parish than
make herself the servant of every demanding butcher and brick-
works labourer who pounded on her door.

Annie still visited occasionally to take tea in Kate's kitchen,
but she did not make direct reference to the explosions that had
become a regular introduction to her day. She spoke, rather, of
local concerns given space in the *Courier*. "You remember that
boy at the Theatre Royal who accidentally discharged a gun into
his thumb while putting it away after a performance – he has
developed lockjaw!" She also repeated rumours that had travelled
up the track with Cobb and Co. from Geelong: "A shooting at the
Melbourne opera! A man shot both his wife and her lover. Some
Frenchman sent here to help set up the Exhibition. And then he
shot himself. He was the only one who died." And she reported
on letters received from their brother in Canada. "He seems to be
accumulating a fortune in his saloon, having no wife to spend his
profits. He says he had to fight off two would-be thieves wielding
revolvers." Cheerful, energetic young Annie behaved as though
she were not aware of any common element in the stories she
related, almost as though the world had undergone no very
significant change.

On the morning of Her Majesty's sixty-first birthday, Kate went
out onto the verandah as usual and, bracing herself against the
post where scarlet roses continued to climb and bloom without
regard to season, pointed the musket at the sky, and closed her
eyes. This time, when she'd recovered from the shock of being
slammed against the wall, she saw that not a single cockatoo had
left the branches of the blue gum across the street. As indifferent
as the citizens of the town, they continued to screech and tear at
the leaves as though she and her husband's musket did not exist.
Kate Jordan went back inside the house, slammed the door, and
tossed the gun into the corner, where it slid down and lay along
the skirting-board. She strode through to the kitchen, where she

stopped and pressed her palms together beneath her chin for a moment of silence; she threw open a door to look in on her children, both undisturbed in their beds; she marched back to the front of the house and snatched up the musket from the floor and found the small half-filled carton of bullets in the corner cabinet. This time, when she steadied the barrel against the post of fragrant roses, she took careful aim at one particularly confident sulphur-crested male. Though the intended victim did not plummet when she pulled the trigger, a nearby cluster of leaves detached itself from the upper limbs and wheeled earthward from the tree. Uncertainty rippled amongst the great white tenants of the upper branches. A third shot tore off still more leaves and caused a general confusion of wings. One, two, three birds deserted the no-longer-to-be-trusted blue gum in favour of safer branches farther down the street, but did not give up their first choice without indignant protests. A fourth shot also failed to find a victim, but a fifth succeeded finally in persuading the rest of the stubborn inhabitants to evacuate the tree. At the same time, cottage doors squeaked open, eyes appeared at windows, someone's voice shouted something from down the street. But a sixth and seventh and eighth discharge were necessary – aimed at upper branches all over the neighbourhood, in random order – before Annie McConnell came into sight, running from the direction of the boarding-house and crying "Katie! Katie! Katie!" as if all this had somehow caught her by surprise.

"You frighten me half to death!" she cried, catching up her sister's hand in her own. An earnest, sombre look had tightened all the curves in her freckled face. Poor Annie – her immense tangle of red curls seemed never to cease moving about her head! She yanked on the great thick plait she'd brought round from the back, as though it were a rope for summoning aid from some invisible servant. How could you take her seriously? "If you'd come live with us, we'd keep you far too busy to care about silly birds."

"I hear Susannah's voice in that."

"Susannah says that if you're planning to become a bush-ranger with that gun, you should do your target practice up on Misery Mountain, out of our hearing." Annie was not reluctant to laugh at their common cross, but sobered quickly. "It isn't because of Susannah that I've come. I can't bear it myself. If you refuse to put this house to good use, then sell it and help us as you did before, when we were sisters together in a new country. I don't see that you have any choice."

"Dear Annie! If I truly thought I had no choice I would use that gun on myself, I would *turn* it against myself! Surely by now you must know I would rather starve, I would rather *die*, than start again with *her*. I would rather bum this cottage down around us. I would rather see us throw ourselves down a mineshaft."

Laughing at her sister's habitual tendency to see things in extremes, Annie knelt to comfort the little girl who had appeared in the doorway. Beside her, James began to whimper. Kate told him to hush, but this only sent the child sobbing to Annie, to throw his arms around her neck. Now Laura also began to cry. "Hush! Hush!" – it was Annie who comforted them. Kate glared. Two sobbing enemies glared back, from the safety of Aunt Annie's trustworthy embrace.

Kate leaned the musket against the wall. Choking back what might have become a sob, she grabbed up her parasol and went down the steps and out through the gate to the sunlit street. Then she opened the parasol and laid it across her shoulder and set off down the footpath in the direction of Sturt Street past the row of plain-faced little miners' cottages with their rust-stained iron roofs, her eyes ahead, scarcely aware of her children's voices calling her back, conscious only of the heavy silence that reigned at last, at least for the time being, in the branches of all the fragrant eucalypts of her neighbourhood.

6

SUMNER'S first opportunity to speak with the Australian widow occurred while he was returning to his office after a visit to the cemetery, where a brand-new stone had been erected according to his orders. A little more than twice as tall as before, it cradled the original stone in its embrace and displayed his new final words in tall, sharply inscribed letters, the tribute to his friendship with the family at The Great Blue Heron Hotel.

Already he had begun to wonder about the wisdom of this. Had he presumed too much? Perhaps the Horncastles only pitied him, or laughed behind his back at his obvious devotion to Adelina. What right did he have to make any assumptions about people he could know, after all, only as they wished to present themselves to him?

He was in a state of confusion as he passed by the Driard and recognized the figure of the widow stepping out through the doors with her familiar carpet-bag in hand, preparing to descend to the street. Her children were not with her. She and Sumner spoke for a few moments about minor affairs – the weather, the knifing last night in her late brother's saloon – as though they intended to take their separate ways within moments. But, recalling the newspaperwoman's suggestion, he resolved not to leave without finding out how much of what the Yankee had said was the truth. "You have been asking questions of everyone."

Laughing at his bluntness, she suggested that he might wish to join her inside, amongst the travellers who sat on the red plush couches in the window that overlooked View Street. "I have thought of you more than once, to be honest, since we met."

Inside, she said, "You did not make me feel invisible, or merely *tolerated* – something your fellow townspeople communicate even before they open their mouths. When I saw you just now, I thought,

Ah, how pleasant if we could only have tea together and talk. About anything."

She encouraged him to speak of his work, "since I have always had a keen interest in architecture." Naturally Sumner could have spoken of his own work for an indefinite length of time, sharing his vision of the splendid city he hoped one day to build. But however enthusiastic he might be, a gentleman must eventually allow his fellow conversationalist an equal opportunity. In Mrs. Jordan's case, Sumner admitted to being interested in learning why she would choose the inconveniences and miseries of a long sea voyage when it meant exchanging an exotic southern colony for this more conventional corner of a fledgeling dominion of the north – if indeed it was her intention to stay.

Why she so quickly agreed to explain her choice was unclear at the time. It did not occur to Sumner to wonder. Perhaps a young man is more easily flattered than he would like to admit – he assumed that she'd found some quality in him that inspired her confidence. Perhaps she believed his friendship with James Horncastle to be more intimate than it was, and hoped that he would pass on some of what she told him, or in return would confide what he knew of Horncastle's story to her. More likely, it was simply a matter of curiosity not wishing to raise the question of "why" so long as it was being satisfied with an interesting story. And of course he hoped that eventually she would explain how it was, as the Yankee newspaperwoman had suggested, that her story connected somehow with Horncastle's life.

"I am a *widow*, Mr. Sumner, as you see. With little but my own resources to rely upon. What use I make of them will determine my future. When I lost my husband – when I was given the *blow* of my dear Tom's death after a long illness, leaving me with the two small children – life seemed altogether too miserable if I were to remain where I was, it was *impossible*. His business had failed. I had very little income. All I possessed was the small cottage. It seemed that if I were to survive at all I would have to take boarders into my home, or take my sisters' advice and work together with them – to rent out my cottage and help them in *their* boarding-house, as I did before I was married.

"Did they think, did they seriously believe, I would consider going back to where I'd begun? In my younger sister Annie, the impulse was a generous one – a friendly one at least. She cared! In Susannah there was only, there was only *spite*; she would love to see me down on my knees, she would love to see me scrubbing those floors again, knowing I would hate it now even more than I had hated it the first time. To witness my daily humiliation would give her a little of the satisfaction she'd hoped to achieve through far worse punishments than this.

"Of course, I cannot deny that it seemed an exciting prospect when we first arrived in Ballarat in '63. This is in the colony of Victoria. The four McConnell sisters running a boarding-house. We would take in only the best people, only the *best*! We would work hard, we would quickly become respected members of that community, we would find our way into society and marriages and even, possibly, wealth. We hadn't been in Ballarat a week when the cousin who'd persuaded us to emigrate removed to Kalgoorlie in pursuit of another man's wife, but we decided, we determined, not to follow him – we'd already found a perfect little house. Larger than the other cottages on the street, with a nice bay window at the front. I wrote the advertisement myself, after studying others in the *Courier*. I'm sure I remember it still, just let me *think*. 'WANTED KNOWN that the McConnell sisters, recently of Manchester, have taken a residence in this fair city, and respectfully intimate to all residents, travellers, and families that they are prepared to accommodate them with BOARD and LODGING.' Yes, and then: 'Every attention, so far as domestic arrangements are concerned, can be relied on. Shower and plunge baths in connection with the bedrooms. Good stabling free.' I must have read it aloud to the others twenty times before we were satisfied!

"But typically – and of course I was hardly surprised by this – Susannah ruined, Susannah *poisoned*, the entire adventure from the beginning. With her resentment, with her spite. She needed only to put all that distance between us and home in order to begin her campaign against me in earnest. Away from the restraining conventions of our Manchester home, my merely bossy eldest sister turned out to have been concealing the cankered heart of a shrew. No, no, no – I would not, under any circumstances, after living a life of my own, return to where I had begun, to endure that life again. I remembered all too well that the McConnell sisters' boarding-house hadn't been open for business a week when I began to look for opportunities to escape, began to *pray* for escape. How could I consider going back?"

What she saw, from the little front yard of their house, and from the streets while she performed errands in town, and from the family pew during the Sunday service, was a population mostly of men who seemed to be drawn from every corner of the earth – Germans and Chinese and Irish and Americans – busily hauling fortunes in gold up out of the ground. Golden Point, Canadian Gully, Bakery Hill. She saw no harbour, no lake – only a reedy swamp, a narrow river, some low, rolling, arid brown hills, some sparse ragged trees, and smokestacks spewing black clouds into the air above the mines – yet the sort of brick and bluestone structures that were being erected clearly showed they thought they were building a major city.

It was almost impossible not to share some of this excitement. Only a decade before, a handful of brave and stubborn diggers had risked and lost their lives to defy an unfair licensing fee and the bullying police who tried to enforce it. And everyone was still talking about Lola Montez! Just a year earlier, they'd witnessed her infamous performance of the spider dance on the stage of the Victoria Theatre, then learned the next day that she'd taken her whip to the editor of the *Times* for what he had written about her, and that he had responded by punching her in the nose. The notorious courtesan had moved on to scandalize other audiences by the time the McConnell sisters arrived, and "One town is the same as the next" was Susannah's opinion. "Boarders expect the same cleanliness, the same good cooking promptly served, and the same respectable atmosphere wherever you are in the world." But Lilian and Kate and young Annie thought otherwise. This strange bustling place was *different* – as exciting as it was frightening. For Kate, almost any other life in that bustle was preferable to a lifetime spent in drudgery under the watchful eye of rancorous Susannah.

That Lilian was the first to escape did not surprise anyone. She was not so slow as Kate to realize that certain things were done in much the same manner there as they had been done at home. Besides, she was prettiest. She could do no wrong in the eyes of Susannah, who assisted her at every step in her campaign to shake off family and enter the world of the squatocracy. To undertake such a spectacular metamorphosis seemed a risky business to Kate, but Lilian had always been a convincing actress and Susannah stood by to assist in all the deceptions, pretences, manipulations, flirtations, and gambles that were needed for Lilian to become, first, a close friend of the daughter of a squatter family down for the season from the northwest corner of Victoria, then a regular visitor to their terrace house on Lydiard Street, and finally the most popular figure at the round of parties thrown by their circle of acquaintances. "Our parents would be so proud of her," Susannah said. "A well-turned-out lady." She really meant that their parents would be proud of *Susannah* for fulfilling their roles more successfully than they could have done themselves had they been alive.

When a handsome and well-to-do cousin of this family arrived from Queensland for a visit, just as though he had read all the appropriate books and knew what role he was meant to play, Lilian arranged for him to fall in love with her while dancing on the great verandah of the squatter family's country home, and then propose to her, and even marry her, without once thinking to ask if she had a family of her own. He took her off to reign in his Queensland mansion and the sisters did not receive even a word of news from her until years afterwards, when she had produced children about whom she wished to complain.

Although it was clear that the only road leading away from Susannah's boarding-house was the popular thoroughfare of marriage, for Kate to try imitating Lilian's example would have led to nothing but failure and ridicule. She could count on no co-operation from Susannah, who clearly had plans to make a lifelong Ella-of-the-cinders out of her. "To spend more time on your knees would do you some good." In addition, she had none of Lilian's ability to act as though she'd been born into another class. Nor was she willing to act the empty-headed light-hearted coquette. She was a blunt, efficient, stubborn young woman in her twenties, with little patience for expected rituals. Though she had been pretty enough to win a few hearts in her earliest years, and had kept a figure fine enough for any man to admire, she possessed a face that seemed to have gone on ahead of her to take on the sort of appearance that is most attractive in a woman of middle age. She could be pretty yet, she could be a *beauty* yet, she thought, if she ever caught up with herself. But in the meantime, proposals of marriage came only from men who were old enough to want a middle-aged beauty who just happened to be in her twenties, and only from amongst their boarders – men who wished to rescue her from Susannah's kitchen in order to set her up in their own. She concluded, eventually, that the miracle of escaping The Four Sisters Boarding-House would have to come about through some other route than marriage.

Dozens of unattached women demonstrated nightly that marriage was not the only way to gain independence, but their example held little temptation for her. It seemed they had given up the few advantages of marriage in exchange for all the disadvantages several times over – every man with enough coins in his pocket could buy the privileges of a bullying spouse. She waited for a third option to appear.

In time, it did. Four years after their arrival, the town went crazy one day and remained in a continuous state of insanity for four months. From September through December everyone behaved as if all the laws governing the universe had been suspended. Perhaps they had. Word was received that the Duke of Edinburgh – the Queen's son, Prince Alfred – was to pay them a visit. Here was an opportunity for everyone to demonstrate loyalty to the Empire even while they at the same time displayed ample justification for having left the Old Country. Meanwhile, they could also reap huge financial rewards from the preparations. There would be parades and balls and banquets and sporting events. Once it was seen that the orphanage was hardly large enough for the celebrations, it was decided that a hall of enormous proportions would be built as a permanent memorial – the largest hall in the southern hemisphere! Consider the employment possibilities. Consider the clothing that would have to be purchased, the decorations, the food, the entertainments that would have to be prepared! The entire population saw this as an opportunity to gather in still more profits to add to the wealth that was already surfacing daily from deep in the earth.

Kate's own hopes were less extravagant – she saw a way the Prince could help this Cinderella escape at last from the ashes. If she was not to get out of the family business through conventional means, perhaps she could make enough money to buy her independence without any need of a man. In Manchester she had taken it upon herself to become an apprentice to a certain dressmaker named Miss Collins – a move that had caused the sisters such pain that it hastened their decision to emigrate. So now she purchased a sewing-machine and set up business in her bedroom. How many flags would be needed, how many pieces of bunting and bows and decorative backdrops, how many new *gowns*! Advertisements in the *Courier* and the *Star* brought in enough work to keep her busy right up until – even after – His Royal Highness arrived.

Susannah was displeased, to say the least. But Kate was far too busy to care. She was too busy to notice the rest of the preparations either, or the sort of civic wrangling that inevitably accompanied this type of enterprise. She leaned over her sewing-machine while the Alfred Hall went up, while the arch was built, while ladies and gentlemen shopped for new clothing. Because she left the house only rarely, and then only to purchase more material from a little shop that had been recently opened by a gentleman on Main Road, she heard only snatches of the arguments currently raging – who would get the contract to make the royal carriage, and who would make the socks and boots and flannel suit for the Prince to wear when he descended into the mines, and who would choose the sixteen girls from all the girls in town to wear sailor suits and throw flowers at His Highness's feet when he entered the Hall for the children's special reception. Her arms ached, her eyes burned, her back threatened to develop a permanent hunch. Yet profits daily mounted in the hatbox on the top shelf of her wardrobe.

On the day of the royal visitor's arrival, she still had more work to complete but granted herself a recess to go out into town amongst the thousands who'd gathered to greet him. Bodies crammed themselves too close against one another in the December heat. People who'd got there early enough to take up positions on the first-floor galleries of the hotels behaved as though they had come to a party. Conversations leapt from balcony to balcony. On the street, people around her complained of the heat, or the lack of room, or the smell. The mixture of perfumes could choke you if the dust and the pipe-tobacco smoke did not. Fathers bounced whingeing infants on their shoulders. Mothers pushed daughters to the front: "Maybe the Prince will fall in love while he's here and it might as well be with you!"

A stout woman in an enormous hat said, "I should imagine his mam warned him not even to look at any female south of the equator."

"Mothers have been ignored before now," said the first. "Have you heard what a fortune the Kennedys have spent on gowns for their thick-necked daughters?"

Their reward for waiting in that overheated crowd was not to see the Duke of Edinburgh snatching a local beauty up off the street, but to witness the confusing spectacle of councillors and MPs chasing all over town in open carriages. Because they couldn't now agree on where they'd previously decided His Highness would arrive, they seemed to be trying to be in all places at once – first the anxious governor would dash by in one direction, the royal carriage with its scarlet postillions throwing dust up into the faces of spectators; then minor dignitaries in their own carriages went rushing past in the opposite direction, worried and short-tempered, mopping their sweaty brows. "Lord!" cried an astounded countryman. "The fools have gone and lost 'im!" And there went the governor again, rushing back to wherever he'd been before, with the carriages of several impatient mayors behind him.

Then carriages full of grim-faced politicians clattered past in some other direction altogether, as though they had just been given privileged information. The first of the frantic carriages had been greeted with silent bemusement, but the crowd had begun to cheer each of them now as it passed, as though to offer encouragement. Someone on the gallery of the Union Hotel threw a bouquet of hibiscus down onto a passing carriage, but the flowers fell to the street, where the next team of horses trampled them into the dirt. The whole thing soon took on the appearance of a game of hide-and-seek where everyone was so stirred up by the blind panic of the others that no rational searching would ever get done.

Apparently this went on for three hours, but Kate McConnell grew tired of the noise and the dust, and returned home to put the

finishing touches to a number of last-minute flags for Alfred Hall.
So she didn't hear until later that when the Prince finally arrived
at the cattle-yards as he'd been instructed to do, he found no one
there at all to greet him. Officials were all still madly chasing
one another back and forth across town. His mother would not
have been pleased!

Children were everywhere – school was out for a week. Nearly a
hundred thousand people had come in from the surrounding countryside and from all the corners of Ballarat, East and West, to
perform dances, or devour food, or make speeches, or watch
fireworks, or attend the theatre, or simply stand on the streets to
cheer while the Queen's son rode by. Hundreds of Chinese dressed
themselves in brilliant costumes to make speeches and perform a
sort of music you seldom heard on these streets. Four hundred
Germans serenaded His Highness on his journey from the Theatre
Royal back to his rooms in Craig's Hotel. Twenty Scottish clans
rallied in Highland costume to fill the air with the wail of bagpipes.
Midsummer hailstones ruined a regatta planned by the Learmonth
farmers but did not save one thousand rabbits from being killed in
a royal shooting-party or keep seven thousand schoolchildren from
consuming two tons of cherries at a single meal.

While she was out delivering completed flags, Kate stopped to
watch the Prince lay the cornerstone of the Temperance Hall – a
duty performed with such dignity and solemnity that you might
not have guessed, if you hadn't been told, that he'd asked to be
assured that this symbolic gesture did not in any way commit him
to the cause. Silently she thanked him for providing her with this
opportunity for earning her independence. She had stored away
enough in that hatbox to take her home to England if she chose,
or to finance a move to Melbourne, where she could open up her
own shop as a seamstress – not that she was especially good at it,
having concentrated on a fairly imprecise sort of work that
required more haste than skill.

But she was never faced with having to make a choice. When she got home, the money had disappeared. Nothing could persuade Susannah to admit that she'd taken it, though Kate had no doubt that that was precisely what had happened. She had probably burned it, so that she wouldn't be tempted to give it back or spend it herself.

Of course, her tragedy was small compared with the shocking news that soon arrived from Sydney. The Duke had been shot in the back while eating a pie and drinking lemonade at a harbourside picnic. This act had been committed by someone from Ballarat, a familiar red-faced figure Kate had often seen haranguing crowds at The Corner, an excitable produce-dealer named O'Farrell who'd wasted most of a fortune on drink and lost the rest to falling gold-mine shares. Now the same town that had thrown itself with such lunatic vigour into its preparations for his visit leapt with equal crazy abandon into an orgy of remorse, outrage, hatred, horror, and sympathy. Flags came down. Thousands of citizens assembled in the new Hall to shout out their rage and sorrow and loathing of Fenians. Town officials and clergymen gathered for a frenzy of speech-making intended to purge themselves and everyone from any guilt by association with the assassin. Business came to a standstill. Families couldn't pull themselves away from the telegraph office even to eat, for fear of missing the next bulletin from Sydney. Prayers were sent up from pulpits, and tirades were delivered from the stages of theatres. When word arrived that the Duke had recovered, two charity concerts were performed in the Hall and a decision was made to purchase a special set of bells in honour of the narrow escape from death of Her Majesty's popular son.

The new bells had not yet begun to peal out their sorrowful penance and fearsome loyalty the afternoon she walked up the slope from Bridge Street and saw a man weeping on a bench not far from the Union Hotel. This sight aroused some pity in her despite the disappointment and anger that still sat like a stone in her chest.

"The Prince didn't die," she informed him. "The braces that hold up his trousers deflected the bullet."

"Nevertheless, the world is about to end," he said. He reached out blindly and took her hand in his. "Will you marry me quick before there's no more marrying?"

Though he hadn't looked up, she realized that this was the gentleman from behind the counter of the drapery shop on Main Road. "This is very kind of you, Mr. Jordan, but rather surprising. I know nothing at all about you. Beyond, of course, your consistently gentlemanlike behaviour in your shop."

"But I have admired you in my way, Miss McConnell," he said. "Only the calamitous atmosphere of the times and my conviction that things will soon get even worse have shaken the shyness off me. For me, Miss McConnell, success is merely a pinnacle from which to look down, trembling, at what must certainly follow." He had a history to support this view of things and recited it for her. He'd been a successful digger over in Golden Point, until the soldiers put a stop to that at Eureka. He indicated his empty sleeve, which of course she had been aware of since she'd first met him. Earlier, he'd been a shearer up in western New South Wales until his back gave out. He'd worked for a baker down in Melbourne until his employer decided to move to South Africa. "Now I have my drapery shop, and have made good profit from the Duke's visit, but I'm holding my breath – something is bound to come along and spoil things: silkworms will die, or the cotton weevil will multiply unnaturally, or ladies will decide to make their gowns out of fur."

"Not in this climate," she said. "Are you already married, by any chance?" He was fifteen or twenty years older than she. He wore an expensive suit, and a cabbage-tree hat with blue streamers down his back. And he seemed to have most of his teeth, though they were slightly crooked and stained. Susannah would loathe him.

"Not exactly," he said. "Except for a few days to a lady in New South Wales who was attacked by a tiger snake and died in my arms."

"Any children?" she asked. "Any children you're expected to pay for?"

His eyes were strong and clear, once he had wiped the tears away. And he spoke with a soft, gentle voice. "No children that I know of," he said. "Though I would dearly love to have a family to raise."

"Let's walk back to your shop," Kate McConnell said. "I've often been tempted to suggest how you might improve the display of your goods. I have a small talent for such matters. Have you ever considered selling ready-made curtains? This town throws up a new hotel every week, it seems, and every one of them has a need for dozens of window curtains of a certain size. The man who has a large supply in stock will find himself to be never short of business."

7

"AFTER thirteen years of marriage, to be a new widow in Ballarat in the year of our Lord eighteen hundred and eighty was not without its difficulties, Mr. Sumner – especially since my sisters chose to believe, chose to *insist*, that my grief was not entirely genuine. My marriage may not have been a storybook romance, but it was a contented one. My husband was never again as prosperous as he was the day he proposed to me – in fact, he eventually lost the business to the banks, for all the effort I put into helping him, especially while he was ill – but he was always a faithful husband and an affectionate father to the children until the day the consumption took him. I felt his loss with considerable sorrow, I feel it *still*. Yet my sisters began their tactless and shocking campaign to marry me off again almost immediately after the funeral. Any old bachelor in need of an unpaid housekeeper was given a shove in my direction. When I declined to co-operate, when I *refused*, they concentrated their energies upon trying to get me back into their own employment – an extra pair of hands to make beds and wash floors and scrub out the dunny. Since I was famous for my stubbornness, they were not entirely surprised by my resistance, however bleak my future promised to be.

"Eventually I resolved to escape their campaigns and to take up Lilian's written invitation to join her in Queensland, where she was bravely raising her houseful of brats amongst the cabbage-tree palms. Susannah did not object. She spoke of it as a rest for me, but she hoped the difficult journey might kill me off, I think. Or the impossible heat. It is more likely, however, that she hoped I would become so attached to Lilian's brood that I would stay on, that I would *want* to stay on, in her household as a sort of house-keeper nanny. Heaven knows she needed someone to help her. Her letters had made this clear. One after another of her hired women had given up trying to tame her tribe of savages, escaping back into the same bush from which they'd emerged only weeks before with expectations of employment in a household of polite, civilized, wealthy folk.

"For a short time I thought there might be some hope for me in this move – a change at least, a temporary escape from Susannah's venom, perhaps even an opportunity to find myself a place in Lilian's society. But of course it came to nothing, as I suppose I should have known it would. I found I did not belong there, I did not belong there at all, I was *desperately* unhappy there – I had little to say to the stranger my sister had become. And I was temperamentally unsuited to remaining under the same roof as her husband, who did little to make me want to stop in his home for long."

Rumours of Lilian's wealth had not been much exaggerated, even by the three imaginative and envious sisters she'd left behind. The husband owned large cattle- and sheep-raising properties near Longreach, west of the Great Dividing Range, but they lived on an inherited block of land near Brisbane, in a great sprawling house that looked, with all its verandahs and lattice-work and its abundance of poles holding it up off the earth, like a giant seaside carnival building spread out along a wharf – in the midst of a heaving forest of local and exotic trees that the husband's father had planted thirty years before.

"I was on my way to visit an ailing frangipani," the husband said when he was introduced to his house-guest. "You must come along. I understood Lilian to be without family, you see. To be confronted with a breathing sister-in-law comes as something of a surprise. Nevertheless, I am prepared to hear an explanation."

Her sister's husband was a tall grey-haired man with a military stiffness in his shoulders and a manner of tilting his head to watch you with a slightly sidelong look from under the wide brim of his hat, as though he were both amused and suspicious at once. He dressed in white, of course, as she had heard the northern men of property did, and took long, deliberate steps in his high leather boots.

"My father made it clear how I was to handle my own avaricious cousins, who would appear from nowhere with their hands out, but he left no instructions on what to do with unheard-of sisters, particularly when they are both attractive and bold enough to arouse one's curiosity. Place your hand against the flesh of this lovely jarrah."

Once a lover of trees himself but robbed by his father of the opportunity to be the creator of this private botanical garden,

Mr. Longspur explained that he had become, instead, a lover of the *names* of trees; for him, his property was a jungle of exotic words. Leading Kate through the complicated pathways, he sang out introductions: banyans, jacarandas. "*Ficus bengalensis* was how my father would speak of them. *Jacaranda bignoniaceae.* But I prefer the greater intimacy of their common names. Vulgar, perhaps, but somehow I wish to speak to them in a living language." The cabbage-tree palms were introduced, the windmill palms, the frangipani. *Eucalyptus grandis*, the flooded gum; *Eucalyptus maculata*, the spotted gum. One hundred and seventy-five varieties of eucalyptus were represented here, he said, as he led her down a long slope, addressing them all by their common names. Swamp mahogany, red mahogany, tallowwood, brush box. Down in the deep green gully they followed a creek through a dense growth of tree-ferns, flame trees, coral trees, Moreton Bay figs, bottle trees, lantanas, and banksias. The naked passion she saw in his eyes when he uttered the names of these trees did not diminish when his glance crossed hers.

Perhaps he was interested in nothing else. At the dinner table, he managed to weave the sounds of his trees through every conversation: "Tomorrow evening, Lilian, when we introduce my sister-in-law to our friends, you must wear my favourite gown – the colour of the jacaranda flower." And: "There is a koala visits the manna gum just off the western verandah." And: "I'm worried about the paperbark." Within days, she began to think she could almost smell the earthy green scents emanating from the sounds themselves, could very nearly feel the sounds reaching out with limbs and vines and fronds to touch her flesh – her exposed neck. "Consider how straight those bloodwoods grow." She could easily imagine the sounds of the tree-names sending down extra sets of aerial roots like the banyan into the carpet. "Have you noticed how beautiful are the twin rows of casuarinas up the driveway? We must walk the length of them just before dusk, you and I, when the horizontal light adds something to their mystery."

She'd arrived, foolishly, before summer had begun to weaken into a more tolerable season. The heat was unlike anything she had experienced, though she had survived Ballarat summers so hot that birds dropped out of trees like overripe fruit and people collapsed into their own sudden deaths on the streets. In the afternoons here, even in Lilian's luxurious home, you could do nothing but lie inside the mosquito netting on your bed, sometimes even on the floor, fanning yourself while rainbow lorikeets squabbled in the windmill palms outside the louvres and you tried to think of something else to get you through to sunset. The news of the world. It did no good to think of the poor boys dying for the Empire at this very moment in Afghanistan. (Where could English boys find the strength to resist the ambushes of the tribal rebels, having been raised on watery sunlight?) You scoured the newspaper for accounts of arctic expeditions, and cared nothing for Chile's advances against its neighbours.

It was during some of those long, horrid afternoons in her room that she made herself a bag from a piece of old Chinese carpet that Lilian was about to throw away. She was not sure why she took such satisfaction from knowing the bird was supposed to be the emblem of the Empress – she certainly did not feel like anyone royal. *Feng-huang* it was called – part stork, part peacock, part pheasant. An Oriental phoenix. Perhaps, amidst so much discomfort, she simply found great pleasure in spending some time with such beauty.

Meanwhile, beneath the floorboards, she heard the children conducting battles of their own around the thicket of stumps that held this enormous house up off the heated earth in hopes of encouraging imagined breezes to circulate. Presumably they would not kill one another with their improvised weapons. Lilian undoubtedly wished that Kate would show some gratitude for her husband's hospitality, by joining the children beneath the house and exercising some control over them (over her own as well). Some sense of guilt disturbed whatever rest she might have taken, but resentment steeled her determination to do nothing about it. What benefits did widowhood offer, if not the right to take advantage of whatever little sympathy might be found? She would, for as long as she could get away with it, feign innocence of the expectations of others.

Certainly she hadn't the heart to pursue the children when they disappeared into Paul Longspur's jungle, which she could look out upon in any direction from the house. Wattles. Cabbage palms. Bottle trees. Silky oaks. Her own children became indistinguishable from Lilian's at a distance. Within a few weeks she had to remind herself that two of them were her own. Her fear of snakes, on their behalf, was ignored, as was her terror of the poisonous spider whose bite would bring instant death. The snakes, the spiders, were only more sounds; they were part of the jungle of names, and no more frightening to the children than were the other names. Tuart. White mallee. Desert kurrajong. In the morning the children flew out of the house and disappeared into the forest; at noon they returned to speak excitedly and mysteriously of having "climbed up to heaven in our secret beanstalk." Kate did not know what they meant; occasionally she tried to follow them, but soon lost her nerve and returned to the house.

She was little real help to Lilian. Did she want to be? She felt she must try, for the sake of the letters that were undoubtedly being sent to Ballarat West. Perpetually exhausted, Lilian had barely enough energy for light conversation while they prepared meals together – deserting servants had not been replaced. But how did one take charge of a household of children who seemed determined to behave like a tribe of Aboriginals? It seemed that she stood by helplessly and watched her own two children run with the pack. There were black children amongst them. Hadn't anyone noticed? She read to them on the verandah, for as long as they would tolerate her. She paid visits to the world beneath the house, but discovered herself in alien territory. She contented herself with helping prepare the meals, and hoped for no disasters.

At mealtimes, Lilian's husband continued to plant his forest of names around her. He taught them all how the tree-fern grows, building a trunk out of its own dead fronds. He spoke as though to the children, but his eyes would not leave hers, or permit hers to glance away. "Have you noticed the large staghorn growing on the coconut palm? A parasite, living off the host tree, yet so beautiful, don't you think." He raised his fork to his smiling lips without lowering his steady gaze. "At certain times of the year I swear the beefwood smells of the marriage bed." Lilian neither confirmed nor denied this. Kate doubted such information could be found in the library. "The grass-tree we call 'black boy' thrusts a spear up higher than this ceiling." He demonstrated the force of the black boy's thrust with his fork, and smiled into her eyes, so that she felt the thrust somewhere inside. Lilian stood up to bring in another course.

"Jarrah," he said. "Say it. Jarrah."

"Karri," he said. He held his mouth a certain way, so that you could almost taste the word with him. You could almost taste him tasting the word. His lips, beneath the heavy grey moustache, were always moist.

Though she continued to resist the children's attempts to lure her out into their forest world, Paul Longspur was determined that she not get away with this for long. They would make a picnic of it, he said; they would take the field-glasses with them, to make a game of watching for unusual birds. Prizes were thought of, for the most unique sighting. "Perhaps you could take advantage of the opportunity to rest," he suggested to Lilian. "We know you despise picnics."

Kate liked picnics even less than Lilian, and had little interest in trying to find birds amongst the movements in the branches above them. But she occasionally took the glasses from her brother-in-law as a courtesy, and pretended to admire what others claimed to see. Somewhere the cry of a whip-bird was slung out, snapped back. But only a blur of limbs and leaves swam by. A second whip-bird

answered. *E-e-e-e-e-e-*WHOOP! Nothing focused, nothing made
sense. Then, when they had penetrated the dense forest along the
creek gully, it seemed that despite her determined indifference she
had spotted a rather enormous bird of a peculiar colour. "You have
mustard-coloured birds in these woods?"

He laughed, and leaned close to point where Kate should look
again, his hot breath passing her ear. The rough sleeve of his
tweed jacket smelled of the honey scent of wattles; creases ran out
from the outside corners of his eyes, she saw, in a permanent
network of laugh-lines pressed into his sunburned skin. With her
unassisted eyes she could see that what she'd spotted well up in
the branches was not a bird at all, but the frock belonging to one
of Lilian's daughters. At the moment, it was being worn by her
own daughter. Freckled, red-headed Laura was up there, high in
the trees, laughing down at the adults.

So were the others, the other children – faces laughing down
from high in the tangled confusion amongst the leaves and
branches, faces blooming out of various gaps and irregular holes in
the trunk of the most peculiar tree she had ever seen, even in this
continent of eccentric vegetation.

Though it was perhaps six feet across at its base, it seemed not
to have what was normally thought of as a trunk, but to have been
woven and knotted out of a variety of twisting smaller trunks. A
great soaring braided tube, a long, long tower that sprouted both
leaves and children from all its orifices. The children had climbed
up inside where it was hollow, Paul showed her – a round venti-
lated spire, a soaring turret. "There was a tree here once. But what
we are looking at is really just a giant vine that strangled the life
out of the tree long ago." What he called a vine was sometimes as
thick as her arm, she saw, or even thicker, and sometimes a snarl
of little snakes. "The tree itself has long since rotted away in the
steamy heat."

Paul's hand at the small of her back urged her closer, to enter
through a large opening in the base. This meant approaching the

tree between two of the flying buttresses it had thrown out – a foundation of narrow upright grey blades that swept out from as high as her waist to go knifing down into the soil amongst the less spectacular trees. She shrank from brushing against these, which might have been made from the hip-bones of giants, the shoulder-blades of mammoths, upholstered with tough stretched hides peeled from a herd of strangled elephants who had somehow wandered onto the wrong continent and been ingested into this monster's twisted internal ducts.

But when she looked up – a dark, round, soaring tunnel populated by the headless bodies of all their children, her own children and her sister's children, all those children to whom she was expected to devote her life – her knees weakened, and she found it necessary to throw out a hand and hold onto some part of that twisting vine. Paul's hand moved along her waist, so that his arm could support her.

Somewhere a whip-bird's cry again lashed at the air. A second, far off, did the same.

"Come down out of there!" she called. "Come down immediately. We must leave!"

Laura pulled her head inside, and looked down. "No!" Her bottom lip was out, her brow lowered. "This is our magic tower! You go away!"

"James! James – bring your sister down. Think – if you should fall!"

James was no more pleased with her than Laura was. From below, his expression might have been one of contempt. "We shan't fall. Why do you want to spoil things for us? Uncle Paul, do take her away!"

Paul Longspur seemed to find her behaviour amusing. "Why should the children not enjoy themselves? This tree might have been put here especially for them."

His arm had remained around her waist, though she was quite capable now of standing on her own. A gentle pressure might have been meant to draw her closer. Not, she thought, the way one might handle someone he thought of as a potential governess. Had he found that one wife was not enough for him? Having worn Lilian out with the care of his seven children, did he hope to make an auxiliary wife of his sister-in-law? She pulled away, and insisted sharply that he bring the children down out of the tree immediately. He laughed, while squinting at her in his sidelong way. But he called the complaining children down out of their tower and into the small amount of sunlight that penetrated the ceiling of leaves. "We shall move on, to see what other wonders await us."

"But we shall return tomorrow!" said James. "Without you."

Again the pair of unseen birds lashed with their snapped-off whip sounds at the air around the upper branches; you almost expected snatched-off leaves to fall.

That night a wind came up and from her bed she could hear the trees thrashing in the dark. Limbs clattered, like swords in combat. Leaves whipped and tore. This might have been happening outside the house; it might have been happening inside her head. Everything was trying to pull itself out of the earth and go flying off in the roaring storm. She dreamt that she had become lost in the dark, roaring storm of Paul's laughter, a thrashing jungle where tubular vines all leaned into the blackened sky with their snakish arms around her children, carrying them up and away from her into the thrashing turbulence of the upper limbs. Their sharp cries for her help could be heard even above their uncle's laughter, but she had become rooted herself in the soil and could not pull free to assist them, even when the first small tendrils of vines began to wrap themselves around her legs, weaving and braiding a strangling tube up her struggling body, shackling her to the earth. Gravity had never been so insistent. When she awoke, he was sitting on a chair against the far wall of her room.

"You cried out," he said.

"Only a dream," she said. "Please go."

"I shall stay, until I am content that you are safely asleep again."

At breakfast, her brother-in-law reported on the damage done by the storm. "A cabbage-tree palm has been uprooted," he said. His smile unfolded around the words, which grew, soared up to the ceiling, filling the air, choking the room with great clusters of broad green leaves. "Cycads," he said, sending fernlike leaves spraying out in all directions. His eyes were the colour of rusted chains. "I must show you a lovely pair of boronia plants, if they have not been harmed."

After breakfast, she threw herself into Lilian's arms and wept. What else could she do? She couldn't stay, she couldn't bear to stay. Life was hopeless; she wept against her sister, though she shuddered to feel even *Lilian's* arms offering comfort in the only way they knew, by wrapping themselves around her.

"Ah, Kate, Kate," she said. "You might at least have tried."

"By the time I left Lilian's plantation I realized that something disturbing had happened to me since I had first arrived on that continent. You must understand, Mr. Sumner, that when I left my childhood home in England I left behind a comfortable world of *things*, of real places and real trees and birds and buildings. But now I saw that I had exchanged it for a world made up of nothing but beautiful *words*. The lovely, lovely sounds of the place had deceived me. When we'd first arrived on that continent I was charmed, I fell in *love* with the strangeness and beauty of their words, but in return they pushed and jostled me aside in their greedy rush to germinate, it seemed to me, to sprout and burgeon and multiply, and throw out feelers and send up shoots. They intended to crowd me out! Do you think this is a kind of madness? Listen! It is the fault of that old lunatic Adam who started it all, I think, and all his lunatic offspring males who became explorers and geographers and dictionary-makers – all of them wanting, I'm sure of it, to nail everything down into some sort of rigid identity in order to perpetrate some awful fiction upon us. That whole ancient worn-down flattened-out continent wished to strangle the breath out of me with the arms of its endless forest of *names*! The tree at the centre of their braided tower had not had the choice of escaping, and neither had I an effective way of holding off the jungle; instead, in my frustration I went home and grabbed up my husband's musket one morning and declared war on the great white cockatoos in the neighbourhood trees – giving my sisters all the proof they needed that I had taken leave of my senses."

8

INSTEAD of turning right to plunge down Sturt Street into the very centre of town – where crowds would soon be gathering outside the Union Hotel and around the Loafer's Tree and along the grassy boulevard in front of the Town Hall to help the Queen celebrate her birthday – she turned left for a block, then crossed the street and proceeded in the direction of the lake. She had no desire to be where she must eventually listen to speeches. At this early hour, even today, the shoreline of the little swamp which had been tidied up and called a lake would surely offer more peace. Annie would feed the children; Annie had always been a better mother to them than she had been herself.

Yet it soon became obvious that she would not be alone, even so early in the day. A few small sailing boats were already out on the glimmering water, flying the Union Jack. Silent fishermen stood in their rowboats amongst the weeds near the shore. People could be glimpsed in small clusters out on the balconies of the hotels on the far side – the Regatta Club and the Lake View seemed busiest. From here, with their low roofs and long galleries, they might have been river boats about to steam out onto the water.

Others strolling along Wendouree Parade nodded greetings. Some paused to chat. "We're expecting our grandchildren to join us later, for a picnic."

She continued to think of their lake as Yuille's Swamp, though everyone insisted on calling it Lake Wendouree now, and had been calling it Lake Wendouree for a decade, since the improvements had been made. Having eliminated the Aborigines who once lived in the area, they would make romance of their memory now, by stealing the magic of their names. She did not hesitate to refer to Yuille's Swamp in conversation either – took some pleasure in doing so, in fact. The town was all too willing to believe in the miraculous power of its money to erase the past.

And to influence the future. She had been as bad as the rest of them once – had gathered here at the lakeshore on more than one occasion to witness the sort of miracle you could achieve with the powerful combination of money and nostalgia. As far back as '65, crates of sparrows were brought from England and released to the air here. And as recently as last year she and Mr. Jordan had come down again, like the others, to witness the introduction of blackbirds and thrushes. Where were they now? Small, dainty, subtly coloured birds – the melodious voices of Home – they'd become pitifully unremarkable here, treasured but rarely noticed, amongst the brilliant colours and riotous squawking of the local breeds. They'd been absorbed into the darker undercolours of *Terra Australis* itself.

As she had been, she feared, as well.

She was not unaware of how attractive a figure the widow Jordan made. She had indeed caught up to her own handsome face which had for many years been that of a mature woman. She could carry black as well as any other colour, and make it seem the only possible choice – even in this autumn warmth. Occasionally she shifted the parasol so that the sunlight might find her thick weight of copper hair. Yet she knew that in her years here, her appearance had undergone a subtle change not accounted for merely by the passage of time. The continent itself had had its influence – her pretty red hair had become this burnished copper; her white skin had taken on the palest of brick-dust freckles; even her eyes had darkened to that rich red-brown colour of iron-filled soil. Had she taken the country in through the food she had eaten, the minerals that had deposited themselves within her? She was becoming a part of this continent herself, had been given no choice in the matter. Her limbs had the heaviness of living wood, or mineral-laden earth. Sometimes she hated being part of something so old, and flat, and so indifferent to her. She remembered English sunlight in a garden of forget-me-nots.

A family of black swans had begun to travel alongside her, a very short distance out from the shore. Others glided in to join them, and still others – perhaps they were determined to become a parade. To mock her? Every one of them in widow's black for life. She despised them, of course, but despised them less than the cockatoos and the galahs and the other raucous birds that inhabited this world. Perhaps she forgave the black swans for being black swans in Ballarat because they had relatives in the parks of the northern hemisphere.

The botanical gardens had been laid out on the site of the old Police Paddock as though for an array of English flowers and trees, with walkways and carefully separated sections, but the trees themselves were mostly the same species she had seen on Paul Longspur's estate. Though they were young yet, and still politely contained within their orderly borders, she foresaw the day when they would explode into a jungle as dense and uncontrolled and frightening as his.

"Without the young 'uns this mornin', Missus Jordan?"

You noticed his long, thin, angular legs first, in their dark trousers, and then the enormous size of his dark, rough hands. Beneath one hand along the bench lay a coiled stockman's whip which hung from his belt – souvenir of an earlier life in the bush. The other hand held his black hat by the brim.

"My sister has the children at the moment, Mr. Hawks. I wished for some solitude."

Long and narrow and hard, Mr. Hawks's face was eroded by weather out of sandstone, his complexion stained and coarsened from the years of working on a station in the Gulf Country. The McConnell sisters referred to him as Old Stonybrow, and mim-icked his uncommonly long stride. The missing ear, according to local knowledge, was the result of a dispute with a drunken sailor in his youth, while he was working aboard the ship that brought him to Sydney from his native America, where he had been a cowboy on the King Ranch in Texas. Now he lived in Craig's Hotel, and made no secret of the money he was in a position to spend – though saw no need to reveal its sources. "Here, sit a while beside me. A word or two? The sunshine's sort of pretty on the lake when y'r sittin' here."

She acknowledged his invitation with a smile, but did not join him. "I'm sure the sunlight would hurt my eyes. I prefer to con-tinue my walk."

"If I invited m'self to walk beside you, would I be unwelcome?" He did not, ever, allow the steady, uncomfortable gaze from his unblinking eyes to stray from hers.

"No more unwelcome than anyone else, Mr. Hawks. Stay on your bench, just *stay* – this morning I am not fit company for anyone."

"Then I reckon this ain't the time for a bloke to ask if you're ready to give him an answer yet. To my overture of the other day, I mean."

"Not if you hope to be happy with the answer when you hear it."

The long, heavy dark brow lowered. He had told her often enough that he was a man who'd become accustomed to getting his way in all matters. "I hope it's understood that I'll go on makin' the offer so long as you haven't accepted nobody else. If I have to, I'll follow you to the Arctic."

"If I were foolish enough to go to the Arctic, if I were *crazy* enough, I should be grateful to have someone more sensible than myself to get me out. But please do not follow me while I stroll around Yuille's Swamp, where polar bears are not too much of a threat."

She had not progressed far when it became clear, from the shouts that pursued her, that Annie and the children had decided to join her. So had a congregation of swans, which had come up out of the lake to gather on the grass where they might observe her – perhaps hoping that she had brought them food. Solitude had been cruelly short. She turned, and gave herself up to the inevitable by sitting on the first unoccupied bench and waiting for her sister to overtake her. The black swans waddled closer, unable to understand why she was taking so long to fulfil their expectations. They tilted their red-eyed red-beaked heads as though to study this person who had not thought to bring even a few dry breadcrumbs. The children were less disappointing; taking for granted that the swans had gathered for their benefit, they began to distribute crumbs from small bags they were in the habit of bringing.

"You ran off before I could tell you – I've received another letter. Yesterday. From our brother, of course."

"Oh William! Crowing about his profits – crowing! – and complaining about his bachelorhood. I have no interest in his letters, you know that. And you know, you *know* how he feels about *me*." She lowered her voice. "Dear Annie, this must not be repeated at home, but I have been proposed to again! Who can understand men? Far from making a woman dull as it should, the widow's black only arouses their interest."

Annie responded with enthusiasm. "Oh, Kate! There can't be anyone in town who has received more proposals!"

In fact, Annie herself had had more. Though she was generally considered to be a young woman of beauty, Annie had reached the age of twenty-nine without marrying, chiefly because she was reluctant to give up what little independence she had. She claimed to have other plans for herself, but her sisters believed that she regretted turning down a proposal from the youngest son of a merchant family from up around Bendigo when she was barely eighteen. She would not discuss whether she'd expected him to pursue her. At any rate, he had not, and had married a friend of hers within the year.

"Mr. Hawks again."

Annie was unable to hide her disappointment. "And did you give him your answer?" She started pulling for help again at the thick rope of her hair.

"I did, I suppose. And tried to make it as oblique as his proposal."

"But what does it mean? Will you be his wife? When it is proper, of course."

Kate Jordan looked into her sister's freckled face. The topic of marriage never failed to bring the blood rushing to her complexion. "Old Stonybrow? I shall make a proposal to you, Annie. Listen. I shall agree to marry him if you will agree to be the one who sleeps with him."

For a moment, Annie looked too shocked to respond. Her colour deepened. She looked towards the children, who were deep into the crush of swans. She looked off in the direction of the lake, where sailing boats went racing in the breeze. She began to tremble a little, and put a hand over her mouth. Then, laughter exploded through her fingers, and she threw herself into her sister's arms. Between them, they set up such a racket that the children abandoned the swans for the moment in order to see what was the matter. "Why are you laughing? Why are there tears on your faces? Aunt Annie, Aunt Annie, are you crying?"

"Your mother," Annie said, "has been behaving shockingly again."

It took some time for them to regain their composure. Even then, it was necessary only to catch one another's eyes for them to go off into peals again. Eventually they drooped, exhausted, groaning, too weak to break into new hilarity even when couples went walking by so stiffly that they might have inspired some satirical commentary.

"But now let me return to my excuse for following you here," Annie eventually said, straightening up her skirts. "I've brought William's letter, as you can see. And I am determined to share it with you, for all your pretence of indifference." Annie shook the folds from the thin paper, which she had concealed beneath the wristband of her sleeve. "He says he has seen James Horncastle." She paused – a silence filled with intended meaning. "Perhaps you are less indifferent now?"

"Annie!" She meant this as a warning.

Annie held up a hand, as though to hold off protest. "Listen. I shall read just this one paragraph. 'Although I have not spoken to him myself lately, I have seen JTH often in the streets and at the races. I have no doubt that you and our sisters will remember him, perhaps with mixed feelings. He is a prosperous and popular man, and has appeared before a magistrate several times in order to protect his reputation from the slanders of jealous men.' Imagine! The slanders of jealous men!"

"Annie, I will listen to no more of this."

"If he is the object of envy, he must be enormously successful!"

Kate stood up from the bench. "And I wish no more of anyone's company today. If you'll excuse me." She might have been asking permission of the assembly of swans, who had gathered in close around the bench, apparently more interested in the conversation than in the children's crumbs. For a moment it was impossible to move; they surrounded her. Black feathered bodies pressed against her skirts. Their silence made them seem all the more coldly determined to trip her up. Silence! Who could imagine a silent crowd? It was necessary to push her way through, almost with violence, in order to escape. And to hurry home.

When she reached Ripon Street, the eucalyptus trees were once again decorated with the heavy white bodies of cockatoos. Dozens, perhaps hundreds, of them quarrelled, squawked, flapped from branch to branch. Were they laughing at her? She grabbed up the flintlock, tamped down the bullet, and without even steadying herself against the verandah post of roses discharged it in the direction of the blue gum across the street. The backward kick of the firearm threw her against the wall so forcefully that she dropped it clattering to the boards. The responding chorus from across the street might have been either protests or laughter. A second discharge, from the sitting position, ripped off leaves and persuaded one bird to leap into flight – but he chose to alight once again on the same limb. A poor decision; a third shot blew off his head. The body crashed down through limbs to thud on the ground. A fourth shot was equally successful – this one a bird that had opened his wings to consider flight. Blood flew, but his wings were no use in the downward plunge to earth. It appeared that the birds had been stunned into silence at last; or was this only a roaring in her ears that obliterated sound? At any rate, it seemed for the moment that the birds were more interested in what would happen next than in saving their own necks. A third body crashed down through the tree before a general consensus was reached. White birds rose in a noisy body, and continued to rise, altering shape, a shifting cloud of white movement. It seemed that they had chosen immediate ascension into some other sphere rather than risk the alternatives.

When they had receded to a small puff of cotton wool, slanting off a little to the west, she became aware that neighbours had come out to stand before their houses, and that her sister Susannah stood between the gateposts, directly in front of her.

"She has shown you the letter."

"My aim has improved, as you can see. Maybe sitting makes the difference."

"I told her not to. I know precisely what you're thinking now, you selfish creature."

"Go home, Susannah."

Though she came no closer, tall Susannah placed a hand firmly on one gatepost and steadied a malevolent gaze at Kate, who held the muzzle of the gun against her chest. "I know what you will do. I know your mind."

"You know nothing, you know *nothing*! Go back to your boarders."

"I shall write and give him warning."

"You hate him as much as you hate me, you vindictive long-memoried old hag! You will write to no one."

For a moment, it seemed that the sister at the gate might lose her resolve. The hand left the post and struck uncertain fingers at her throat. Even the eyes wavered, the small hard grey eyes in that wide-boned face. But she seemed to become aware of the silent watchers on the verandahs and boardwalks – perhaps remembered the slaughtered white bodies behind her. She set her feet apart, and once more held onto the post.

"She might better have read you the letter from Lilian, which suggests you caused trouble there. Between husband and wife. I should have expected nothing better. I'm not surprised by anything you do. From the beginning you were determined to demonstrate just how cruel you could be. And selfish. And grasping. And hard."

"If you are surprised at nothing I do, then you'll have no trouble believing I'll pull this trigger if you don't go home immediately."

To look into the barrel of a loaded musket might have been something for which Susannah McConnell had spent a lifetime preparing. There might have been a camera inside it, to record her courage. She called up resources equal to bullets and sent them, out of furious eyes, to meet gunmetal and lead. "Of course you are mad. Perhaps you have always been mad. Only a madwoman would take up arms against birds! Shooting your sister would mean no more to you than shooting those poor birds down out of their own natural world."

"Any jury would understand. You know this. Any jury would *understand*. When they have been told what I've had to endure from you, any jury would wonder why I hadn't done it before."

"Of course, there is another matter to be considered here, Mr. Sumner, as you have undoubtedly guessed. If we are speaking of my reasons for leaving Australia, if we are speaking of my *reasons*. It was not only that I needed to escape a malicious sister before I was provoked to some horrid act of violence. A bitter woman, eaten up by jealousy and resentment and loneliness and fear. Nor was it simply that I wished to flee from a crowded, strangling jungle of words, of beautiful *names*, to live in a world of ordinary *things* again, a world of regulations and laws that created some human order. No. It was at this point, it was only *then* – after everything else had failed – that I considered taking advantage of the piece of paper I still possessed containing two signatures, mine and another's, representing the old familiar world of principles and law as nothing else can. Annie's letter had reminded me of this. I suspect that this will not come entirely as a surprise. Your friend James Horncastle is my husband. He has been my husband for twenty-three years. In spite of all that has happened since I saw him last. I have come here to set things right."

FROM MR. JAMES HORNCASTLE,

AN EXPLANATION OF HIS

EXTRAORDINARY BEHAVIOUR IN

ENGLAND AND CALIFORNIA

9

I**F** Logan Sumner had joined the Royal Navy as he'd briefly considered doing after his wife's death, he would almost certainly have traversed the world's oceans in the lofty isolation of the crow's-nest. Every crisis seemed to send him climbing. Through most of the starry night that followed his conversation with Mrs. Jordan, he sat up in the branches of the Garry oak above the Pest House ashes, his heels braced in a crook of a limb and his pale hair lifting in the breeze, his mind a boiling stew of impossible thoughts. What was he to do? How was he to behave? His hands rubbed up and down his chilly shins; he peered through bushes and over rooftops in the direction of the dark blurred muddle of vanished buildings at the head of the little harbour. Somewhere was the space defining the bulk of the Driard House, somewhere the slightly smaller volume of The Great Blue Heron. What was he to do with what he had learned? He wished again that his Uncle Charles were here to give advice.

Quite often on summer evenings his uncle would take the young Logan Sumner up into the branches of a backyard tree for special talks "between two gentlemen" on matters he considered most important in the proper conduct of a life. One of the things he considered important was duty. As he leaned back against the trunk and stroked the soft feathers of the lovely ring-necked pheasant he held in his arm, he explained that whatever it was your duty to do you must do with all your heart. Recalling his visits to the Great Exposition where he claimed to have personally drunk at least four of the one million bottles of minerals sold by the Schweppes company, he recited from memory the words of the Prince Consort as they appeared in the programme. It was the duty of every educated person, he said, to add his humble mite of exertion "to further the accomplishment of what he believed Providence to have ordained." According to Prince Albert and Uncle Charles, man was to make of himself a divine instrument, contributing somehow to the eventual unity of all mankind.

Uncle Charles had suffered no doubts that he was doing his part towards this marvellous goal, even all these thousands of miles from the centre of things, whether he was building a butcher's shop or collecting old clothing for the poor. Occupational and social obligations were much the same. Success as a builder did not come about from idle dreaming; success as a citizen did not come about in timid isolation.

But where could duty be found in *this* conundrum? All hell was about to break loose, and he had not the faintest idea of what he should do. He didn't especially want to look Horncastle in the face. He certainly didn't want to speak to his wife. And he hated to think what the news would do to Adelina.

Assuming, of course, that the woman had told him the truth.

In the end it was this that brought him down out of the tree. Here was his duty: to discover if anything he had heard was based on fact. Give Horncastle the chance to deny it. At the very least, give Horncastle an opportunity to explain how he intended to protect his family and his own reputation from this shocking development.

At dawn he went home to face the bacon and eggs Chu Lee put before him, but could not eat them. He dressed, and rode in to the Blue Heron wearing perhaps the longest and saddest face ever seen in the city, his pale hair in turmoil, his waistcoat misbuttoned, his boots in need of a shine. When he arrived, he did not take the time to tie the reins to the hitching-post, leaving Cleo on her honour while he went inside to the dim light of the great foyer. Hotel guests came and went – families of recent immigrants from Sweden, from Germany, farmers and merchants from up-island in town for business. Chinese servants hurried past in their loose white shirts and cloth shoes. An agitated Mr. Callow could be heard claiming to have news from Mr. de Cosmos, now with the Prime Minister in London, where together they hoped to convince the Privy Council that the railway must be extended to Vancouver Island. At the reception desk, Horncastle's second daughter, Moira, gazed with admiration upon the excited civil servant, though he seemed totally unaware of her existence. Brushing past everyone without so much as a greeting, Sumner stopped outside the door to the former saloon and took a long, deep breath before going in to confront Horncastle with all the Australian woman had said. Or try to.

"Stop!" Horncastle stood up from behind the desk, a hand raised against Sumner's words, his face taking on the same rosy hue as his satin brocaded waistcoat. He found something in the portrait of Eclipse to dominate his attention for several moments before he spoke. "Encountered her myself, last evening. In the street. Thought I would drop from the shock. So this was your Mrs. Jordan! Of course I know everything you were about to say."

"And it is true? That she is your wife, I mean."

"I am not denying it."

"And Mrs. Horncastle –"

"Told her last night." It was still the racehorse Eclipse who held his attention. "Must find some way of getting shut of the unexpected lady. The children will suffer too, when they hear."

"You put the request to her – that she leave?"

"Refused."

"I'm not surprised. She did not appear to be someone who gave up easily."

"Looks bad. Looks terrible. The gossips will be chewing on this till their graves." Horncastle turned his eyes from the lithograph and contemplated Logan Sumner. "You might help me with the children."

"Help?" It was hardly his own voice he heard. He would rather swim the strait than face the Horncastle children with this. Especially Addie.

"They'll be shocked. Upset. Won't speak to me, I suppose, for a while. You could help them see the world hasn't ended."

"Are you so certain that it has not?"

Horncastle slapped his palms against his thighs. "Ah, Sumner, Sumner! Dammit, you're too serious by far. Can you see none of the humour in it, lad?"

"Humour? I would describe it as calamitous. I should imagine that Mrs. Horncastle considers it a calamity as well. As Addie will. And Jerome."

Horncastle frowned, and raised a finger to stroke the grey moustache beneath his little falcon's-beak nose. "Come come! Of course it could prove to be calamitous, but that only adds to the humour if you're capable of seeing it." He showed his teeth in a brief unconvincing grin, and tugged at the front of his waistcoat. Even in shirt-sleeves he made Sumner feel drab in his familiar brown tweed. "Think! The very model of a husband and family man is confronted by a legal wife from the past. Even I can laugh at that, and I'm the one who must somehow survive the mess! Ha ha! A bigamist exposed! Ha ha! Shall be laughed at everywhere I go. May as well enjoy the damn thing myself." He took a cup and saucer from the side cupboard and poured coffee from the tall pot on his desk, then added a dash from a bottle before handing it to Sumner. He splashed more from the bottle into his own cup and put it back in the cupboard. "Can't deny that she is a handsome woman. You've seen her. If a lady must rear up out of the past bearing a marriage certificate, one might as well be grateful to discover she is not a hag. What man would not be flattered, even, to be pursued by such a woman? Expect I'm as envied about town as I'm laughed at." He held his own cup aloft, as though to toast the lady in question, then tipped back and drained it in a single draught.

"Excuse me," Sumner said, placing the cup and saucer on Horncastle's desk. It wasn't possible to stay. "I've just remembered – There's something –"

Out through the foyer and onto the street he went, trying to look like someone who had just remembered a still-untended emergency. But where, when the hotel was safely behind him, was he to go? His carpenters were building a new wing along the south wall of the Barton house, but they were unaccustomed to visits from the boss on Saturday mornings. Chu Lee would sigh and complain and clash things around if Sumner arrived home before the morning housework was done. Into the Company building he went and up the curving staircase to his silent office, where he tried to find something that demanded his urgent attention amongst the various papers on his desk. Outside, a wagon-load of Saanich fruit was being transferred to the *Cariboo-Fly* by labourers careful not to put unnecessary strain upon themselves. Morning shoppers hurried towards the Queen's market. Eventually, forgotten Cleo moved into view, with reins dangling, and stopped to rip up grass where her neglectful owner would be sure to see, a rebuke for his insulting oversight.

Down the staircase went the remorseful one to apologize, and to lead Cleo up the block to the Livery. When he returned, James Horncastle was waiting outside his door.

"By the lord Harry, you will allow me to explain myself!"

Inside, Sumner did not lead his guest up to his office but behaved as though the half-finished oak cabinets being built for Noah Shakespeare needed the immediate attention of someone with the proper tools. He took off his coat, turned back his sleeves, set one cabinet door in the vice, and took up the nearest plane.

"Damn!" Horncastle kicked his way through fragrant curls of yellow cedar which had been swept into a heap on the floor but not yet carted away. "I did not intend to suggest I find this business merely comical. Find it abominable, in fact. Find it damned *impossible*! But can you see how a man must *try* to laugh?"

Cursing himself for playing the prude when he was really only unable to rise to the occasion, Sumner nevertheless planed on, shaving up long unbroken curls of paper-thin oak. The pencil mark was still an eighth of an inch into the wood. No knots or sudden shifts in the grain had complicated the easy, confident strokes.

Horncastle picked up a handsaw and fingered the teeth before putting it down, then picked up a claw hammer and carried it with him to the street window, where he stood looking out across to the loading-docks. "Kate McConnell," he said. There was some wonder in it, Sumner thought. "Katie McConnell she was then – a pretty lass, one of the four McConnell daughters. Well, I did not *intend* to marry her!"

"Sir?" Sumner halted the stroke of his plane but did not straighten up from his task.

"She just *surprised* me into it, I think." The hammer's head struck three times into the cupped palm of his hand. "That's right. She surprised me into it. Didn't see it coming."

"You mean it was an accident? Somehow you found yourself married to someone, a stranger, you did not mean to –?"

"You could say that. No. She was hardly a stranger. Look – first you have to understand this: the McConnell family was related to our own. Lived, like us, in Manchester. The old man's textile mill was just beginning to make his fortune. Mattress ticking. They often came by to visit their poorer relatives. As a youth, I was never disappointed to see that crowd of pretty lasses turn in at the gate, though their brother was an ill-tempered sort of lout I was glad to see the back of when he left for the colonies. The father liked me. By the time I was ready to leave myself, expecting to make my fortune in New Zealand, an engagement had been arranged between me and one of the daughters. We were to be married upon my return."

"But an engagement is not a marriage! Can she claim you after all this time on the basis of a promise?"

"This was not our lady with the carpet-bag! You're not half listening to me! This was her eldest sister. Susannah."

Horncastle dragged a saw-horse into the window light and perched upon it. Then he stepped down, dragged it a few more inches, and sat up on it again, tapping the head of the hammer repeatedly into his palm. "So I was engaged to be married, you understand. To Susannah. When I returned, more years had gone by than any of us had expected. The mother had died of cholera in one of those epidemics that swept through the country. The old man was killed by rioting workers – he'd gone in to town when he heard of the uprising, to protect his property, but they burned his mill, dragged him down off his horse, and threw his body off the Ducie Bridge. Into the foul mess of textile dyes and piggery muck and tannery-bloodied waters of the Irk. The son refused to come home. They'd tried to get in touch with me but I was always on the move. Suppose they hoped one of us would take over the business." He stopped while Sumner released the cabinet door from the vice, examined its perfect corners, stacked it against the nearest wall, and took up another to replace it. Then he went on, still tapping that hammer into the palm of his cupped hand. "But the mill had been lost. What was left of the family money was being eaten away by the living expenses of the daughters, still in that big house out in Broughton without the means to keep it up. Governess dismissed. Servants let go. Susannah had taken over the raising of her sisters. Knew she wouldn't be free for a few years yet. Youngest was less than six years old. When I came home a year after the death of the old man, I wasn't in a financial position to marry, anyway, and certainly not prepared to take responsibility for her three sisters as well. So there you are. Everything had changed. Continued to keep company, however. And spoke of our future marriage. But she'd grown older. No longer the pretty young woman I remembered. Time had coarsened her. At the same time, her younger sisters had grown older too, of course, and two of them were young ladies already, prettier than Susannah. To my own astonishment, I must confess there was a period in which I courted Susannah by day and her younger sister by night!"

"And were not found out?" How tame and uneventful Sumner's own relationship with Adelina was made to seem by this. Deception. Risk. The flaunting of convention. His friend had lived a role in a comic opera. Of course, Sumner was not entirely surprised to hear this from a man who even now was constantly getting into scraps over racing debts, appearing in court cases because of insults, and engaging in public shouting-matches about political matters. Yet he could not erase the picture of poor wounded Mrs. Horncastle from his mind. And now, it seemed, the equally innocent Susannah McConnell was to join her there – the company of the betrayed!

"Of course, I knew soon enough that I wouldn't stay long in that city of smoke and grit. The colonies had spoiled me. Hated the filth. Hated the poverty. Families dying in the streets. Children dying in the factories. Needed to get out of there to breathe! Saw myself joining the great armies of the dying poor if I didn't. Didn't let on to the sisters, naturally. In the daytime, I called to assist Susannah with her responsibilities, discussed the problems of running the household. Of raising children. Laughed. Might have been already married. But once they'd retired to their beds at night, I made secretly for the orchard where the next sister was waiting for me. We did not discuss the problems of running a house or raising children, we walked the endless roads by moonlight, we huddled in carriage sheds out of the rain, we rowed a little wooden boat on the river.

"Of course, this could not go on forever. I was not a landed gentleman of leisure. Had no trade. Nothing but a small inheritance which was dwindling fast. Time eventually came when I saw I must do something about this – leave for America, where I could try again to accumulate a fortune so that I could finally make

Susannah my wife. She was a patient woman, as she'd already proved, but she was not pleased to be asked again to wait. She pressed for a quick marriage. Even said she would abandon the others if I would only ask her to – they were old enough now, except for young Annie, and Annie could look to the others for help. She would accompany me and never complain, even if we should live in poverty. Somehow I persuaded her this second wait would not be for long. Would send for her, this time, as soon as I had accumulated enough for her passage. Her sister, having over-heard these plans, jumped down out of the apple tree that night when I arrived, and demanded that Susannah be told of our feel-ings for one another immediately. Wanted me to announce my betrothal to *her*. An uncomfortable spot to be in, let me assure you. Would not recommend it at all."

Sumner had altogether given up on the second cabinet door and now leaned back against the work-bench with his arms folded. "So you married the sister – and left Susannah howling with rage behind you."

"Not at all." Horncastle grinned – happy perhaps to have Sumner's full attention at last. "The sister consented, reluctantly, to a secret understanding. Agreed that Susannah should not be told about our feelings towards one another. At least not yet. As the eldest, and the one who had taken over the role of mother, she had every right to present herself in public as a woman engaged to be married, while the sister only needed to have the private assurance of a future wedding."

For a few minutes it seemed that the narrative might have come to a sort of end. Horncastle narrowed his eyes and examined his own fingers, one nail at a time. He heaved a peculiar great sigh. "Then the most astonishing thing happened."

"The sister changed her mind," Sumner guessed, "and insisted on an immediate marriage after all."

"Wrong again, my dear, sober, earnest young Logan. She was content." He had become quite agitated now. "Said my farewells to the entire McConnell family, and to all their relatives, and mine. Set out for Liverpool, where I was to board the ship for New York the following morning. Yet, had hardly established myself in the little dockside hotel for the night when there came a knock on my door. Was told a young woman waited below! Of course I thought that Susannah had decided not to be patient after all. What if she had packed her trunk and was ready to go? Would I let her bully me into a marriage? If I were truthful, would she take the news bravely, or insist that I save her honour by marrying her anyway? Perhaps it would not be her at all, but her sister, as you suggested – demanding that I honour the secret engagement. All this went through my head even before I had left my room. Believe me, was all in a sweat!"

"One way or the other, serious trouble."

"Except that I had not anticipated all the possibilities!" Horncastle raised an antlered eyebrow. "The lass who waited for me below was neither of the two women I had expected but the *third* McConnell sister! I almost tumbled down the stairs. Have been found out, I thought, and she has been dispatched to convey warnings, and a demand for satisfaction! Thank God the brother was not around, or I could be faced with a duel! But pretty Kate stood up with such a radiant smile on her face that I knew at once that she had come with no ill intent. 'Oh, James, they shall kill me when they discover what I have done.' You can imagine this, can you not? 'What have you done, my dear?' I said, taking her hands in mine. 'Why, followed you, of course, without their permission. They will be frantically searching for me this minute! But I had not the opportunity to wish you a proper farewell, with the others fussing over you!' By heavens, I thought, I have fallen amongst the Brontës! Yet, 'This is most touching, my dear. To think that you care so much for a future brother.' She pulled a face. 'Oh, fah,' says she, and launches into a speech that she's rehearsed no doubt during the coach ride from Manchester. She was aware of what had been going on, she said. She knew I had no intention of marrying Susannah, that I had continued my engagement to Susannah out of a sense of duty – and cowardice. 'And you have courted Lilian simply because she threw herself at you in a shameful manner.' (This lass had followed us on more than one dark evening! She admitted it.) 'But all the time it was obvious where your interest lay,' she says. 'Don't think I didn't see the way you looked at me, the way your face grew red and burst into great broad smiles at my approach. I am far more interesting company than either of them. Also, I am in love with you myself.' This she says as bold as you please! 'I did not realize it entirely until I saw you preparing to leave,' says she. 'We shall be married tonight, here in Liverpool, and sail for America tomorrow.' Now what do you think of that?"

"A third arrangement!" Sumner exclaimed. "Will the six-year-old be next? Perhaps she is already hiding in your trunk with plans to leap out when the ship has left sight of land! Men dream of having to deal with this sort of abundance – but you have outdone us all!"

Horncastle fell silent – awe-stricken perhaps by the extravagance of his own life. "By Jove, Sumner, but she was right! She was by far the most engaging of the sisters. The most intelligent, the most energetic, the most imaginative, the most courageous, obviously the most resourceful – as well as being very attractive in appearance. I did not leap into this, mind you. We did a great deal of walking along the waterfront, engaged in conversation. Stopped at a respectable public house for something to warm us up and talked some more. Strolled some more. Finally, tracked down a parson who was a distant cousin, roused him from his bed, insisted he marry us. Fortunately he was a timid man, easily bullied. Married us before grumbling witnesses also dragged from their beds, then sent us back to the hotel. 'You are old enough to be responsible for your hasty actions, I hope,' he said. 'I trust you both know what you are doing.' How he would laugh today, if he could see what it all has led to in the end!"

"I can imagine how you laughed together that night," Sumner said. "Thinking of the two other sisters at home in their beds, dreaming of their wedding nights, while you –"

Having begun to see the humour in it, as Horncastle had wanted him to, Sumner felt he might have forgotten himself and overstepped. Horncastle did not seem to know where to look. "Yes. Well. Ahem." Even after all he had confided to Sumner, here was something he could hardly joke about with someone who'd confessed an interest in his daughter.

"Yet she did not accompany you to California?" Sumner said, hoping to steer himself out of the perilous waters as quickly as possible.

Horncastle shook his head. "Went home! By morning she had been persuaded to wait, with her sisters, until I sent for her. And to keep our marriage a secret from them for as long as she could. They would have made her life intolerable otherwise, you see. Impossible to predict how much time I would need in the gold-fields before I could afford to send for her."

How he must have smiled as he sailed off into the Atlantic, to think of the household he was leaving behind! Sumner smiled himself to think of it. Of the four McConnell sisters, three waited with expectations of becoming his wife. One of them wore the ring that told the world he had promised to marry her, the second held in her heart the secret knowledge of his promise to make her his wife, while the third had possession of a piece of paper that proved she had already usurped the position anticipated by both of the others. "This is amazing!" Sumner said. Unable to think of an appropriate way to express his astonishment and even admiration without abandoning his serious concerns for the present situation, he was left gasping out inanities. "A regular Don Juan in your youth and a model of staunch fidelity ever since. Who will ever know what women see in one man rather than another!"

Again, laughing, Horncastle threw out his arms and stepped down from the saw-horse. "God knows – not I! Had nothing to set me above the next man, that I know of. Thought every healthy male to be as sought after as I was. Took it for granted we *all* got into this sort of mess!" He kicked his way through the yellow cedar curls on the workshop floor and put the hammer back in its place on the bench. "Though I hope we are not all subject to this boomerang ambush in later life. Had more to do with a competition amongst those sisters, I think, than with any charms I might have been born with, since the situation did not repeat itself very often in my life. You can stop playing at carpentry now that you've probably ruined those doors. Come on with me. Need to get over to the racetrack – see what my new Kentucky filly can do. She's about to pay for her journey."

Logan Sumner rolled down his sleeves but did not put on his coat. Did he wish to spend the rest of this day at the races?

"She's boarded out at Sheepshanks' with the others. Horace is bringing her down." Horncastle opened the door to leave but closed it again. "And about that other. There's more to tell, but later. Come along. Can't have you thinking that I married the lass and then forgot her. Life is much more complicated than that, as you must have begun to find out for yourself by now."

10

THE rest of the story would have to wait until after they'd put the races behind them, since Horncastle was far too excited about what lay ahead to keep his mind on the past, or even on his present predicament. "Son, you're about to see the finest horseflesh that ever stepped onto this island. Straight from blue-grass pastures – a champion for sure." Though he did not have Sumner's long legs, his pace was quicker – he could not get them across the bridge and into the park fast enough. "Almost bought a chestnut gelding before this filly caught my eye. Called her Nugget at first, to remind me of a great hunk of gold I won in California – a fortune, until it was stolen by a shifty assayer. Decided to rename her after Mrs. Horncastle, who stayed with me longer than the gold!"

Sumner made a point of displaying interest in the sleek grey horse, throwing his leg over the saddle and walking her around in a circle so that he could see for himself what a treasure Horncastle owned, a lively beauty with intelligent eyes. He stroked her silky neck, and spoke appropriate words of admiration into her ear. He even placed a small bet on Norah in the first race – breaking his vow to his uncle just this once in order to demonstrate his absolute faith in Horncastle's new purchase. Then, while officials and owners discussed the business ahead of them, he strolled off through the scattered groups of picnickers on the grassy slope below the Beacon Hill summit where they could see a good portion of the track and at the same time enjoy the view of sunlight dancing on the strait. Screaming children chased one another, occasionally rolling over and over down the slope. More carriages pulled in, and families stepped down to set themselves up for the day.

Here individual pines and scrub oaks, isolated from other trees, created strange paradoxical shapes out of their tensions: trunks thrust south towards the source of light, while limbs strained north away from the winds off the strait – each tree struggling as though to pull itself apart. Oaks and pines which stood in the thick timber stands farther along the slope, on the other hand, grew untroubled – straight towards sky. Up in the branches of one of the nearer oaks, Queen Victoria's local understudy trailed skirts and veils, and swung her boots like someone pedalling through air.

Sumner nodded to the O'Hara family, to the MacKenzies, to Albert Pinch and his son Jeremiah, but did not intend to accept any of the invitations to stop, to view the races from a crowded blanket, even to taste Millie Crenshaw's new pickles. The Hogans would demand to know his opinion of their beloved uncle's suggestion, from the floor of the legislature, that every citizen be given a musket for fighting the traitorous federal government. Horace and Lizzie Sheepshank would insist that he eat fresh bread and sliced beef and boiled eggs out of their picnic basket while Lizzie tried to encourage a report out of him on whatever progress he might have made in his courting of some imaginary young lady who may or may not be their friend's oldest daughter.

Seated alone with his back against the scabby trunk of a scrub oak, Zachary Jack attracted Sumner's attention by waving both arms over his head and whistling, though he did not lift his heavy body from its sitting position on the ground. "*Nah sikhs!*" He clearly assumed that Sumner would want to join him. And, indeed, once his attention had been caught, Logan Sumner laughed and turned to work his way across in that direction. "You're spending a Saturday at the *races?*"

Zak shrugged his soft round shoulders and pulled his face into an expression of extreme innocent confusion. "Me trying to figure out why white man get-em all excited, go chase around in circles like him *pel-ton.*" In Sumner's presence he often improvised an inexact form of pidgin English – but only when they were certain to be overheard, and always in a manner that was clearly intended to mock himself and the language and even his listener all at the same time.

"Maybe because he *is* crazy, Zak."

"Sit down," Zak said. "I didn't bring no blanket like them others there but you can have one of these." He lifted his broad posterior off the stack of splintered boards upon which he was sitting and drew one out. *Damask* for Logan Sumner; the word on top of the remaining pile was *Proof.* "I've been picking them up down along the beach there. Using them to cover up the cracks in my walls – they keep out the wind."

When Sumner had folded himself down to sit on the piece of broken crate amongst the grass and pine cones and twigs and tiny stones, Zak leaned close and drew in a deep noisy breath through his quivering nostrils. "Oh, that Hysolime Soap! The cleanest-smelling man on the Pacific coast."

"Or under *this* tree, at least."

"Never mind. It means we're the only carpenters in the world that can tell when the *tyee*-boss is sneaking up on us. The air starts to smell too clean."

"Uncle Charles would be pleased to hear you say that."

Sanitation and personal hygiene were amongst Uncle Charles's many obsessions. "We must all be Mr. Scrubwell, Logan." On Saturday night he was not satisfied until he and his nephew and the Indian boy he'd taken into his home had all, in words he quoted from some newspaper writer of the time, been "scrubbed and rubbed and small-tooth-combed till the tears run into our eyes." Cleaning up themselves was cleaning up the world, he said, and cleaning up the world was defeating disease!

"At least I had the sense to go out and roll around in some dirt afterwards," Zak said, "just to feel human again. But you – I guess you *like* to smell like someone on his way to the whorehouse." He slid both hands down over his enormous stomach, then ran a finger in through a hole in his shirt to scratch at his flesh. "Poor old chap – he's probably red in the face with shame up there in heaven, to see how you and him failed so bad to get me civilized."

Sumner raised his forearm to his nostrils and smelled, not Hysolime Soap but the fine sawdust in the tangle of fair hairs: oak, and cedar. "It's more likely he's apologizing all over the place, for not leaving you to fend for yourself when he had the chance." He sneezed.

Zak was still a small boy when his mother, a Nootka woman employed at Craigflower farm, walked into the woods one morning and never returned. Since his father was generally believed to be one of Uncle Charles's carpenters – an Alexander Cameron, who had been killed by a runaway horse a year or so earlier – Sumner's uncle took the boy in, and later made him an apprentice carpenter, and treated him not too differently from the slightly younger nephew who would one day be his employer. Zak had never taken his father's name, or ever mentioned him, and though he lived much like any white man, as he had been raised to do, he would drive his fists into anyone who called him a Smoked Scotchman or otherwise suggested there was any blood in his veins but that which had come from the woman who had disappeared into the woods.

"What I meant was," Sumner said, "you're here instead of working on –" The sentence could not be finished where it might be overheard by those who would take it as all the proof they needed that these two friends were a pair of lunatics.

"So are you. That's why I came. Thought I'd track you down and drag you away from this place."

"Not today, Zak. I came with Horncastle. He wants me to watch the race."

Zak grunted. "One more thing I didn't know about them courtship rituals your people brought from that other place. You have to jump up and down and holler and yell for the old man making an ass of himself on a horse before he'll let you slip your fingers inside his daughter's dress. To me, the blue grouse makes more sense. Stand on a stump, puff up, and *drummmmmm*, and watch the ladies come running from every direction." He did not mind that heads turned to investigate his impersonation of a male blue grouse on a stump.

Most Saturday afternoons and Sundays Zak set aside his role as the most reliable and skilled employee in Sumner Construction and met with Logan Sumner for activities unconnected to their work – occasionally in the popular bar of The Great Blue Heron, and sometimes at the Rock Bay bridge, from which they rode out together past Craigflower farm to where a distant relative of Zak's lived in a shack in the woods, and even more often at Sumner's house, where they sat over a game of chess on Uncle Charles's chess-board before taking dinner together beneath Uncle Charles's enormous etchings of scenes from Sir Walter Scott. Wherever they were – at the bar, in the relative's shack, or in Sumner's parlour – they would eventually find themselves plotting the next stage in their plans to build a flying machine.

When Sumner first agreed to co-operate in this preposterous scheme, it was only to the extent of contributing Company lumber scraps. But almost immediately he had found himself becoming more involved than he'd intended, sending to England for books containing drawings of machines that had already failed to fly, poring over the pictures and descriptions in order to figure out where the designers had gone wrong. He allowed Zak to make use of a neglected barn on a piece of property Uncle Charles had bought shortly before his death, hidden behind trees not far from this park, so that he could work on his project in secrecy. And then he found himself spending far more time than he'd expected in the barn himself, helping to build the machine.

Of course, their latest creation had not been the great imagined Aerial Steam Carriage one saw in magazines, fashioned out of nothing but wishes, nor would it remind anyone of Sir George Cayley's triple-winged Old Flyer which was supposed to have lifted a ten-year-old boy off the ground. Instead, it made Sumner think of a giant horsefly. Gauze wings drooped. Slender legs seemed to be clinging to earth. When they had brought it out onto these grassy slopes for a trial run last Sunday midnight, a moonlit night, their faith in the invention had not been so great that they'd risked riding in it themselves. Cayley had written somewhere that "a hundred necks will have to be broken" before man would successfully fly, and they had agreed that two of those necks need not be their own. Instead, they'd lifted two boulders inside, to act as passengers for the hazardous experiment.

Perhaps their timing had been bad; perhaps there was no helpful breeze at the moment; perhaps the stones were too heavy or the wings too short. When Zak urged his horse into a gallop and towed his invention across the grass, the machine eventually consented to behave like a clumsy kite and to lift just a few inches above the earth, and then eventually higher; but while Sumner and Zak watched from the edge of the cliff, the combination of carriage wheels and scrapwood body and cheesecloth wings plummeted to the rocks below, where it exploded into pieces and disappeared beneath a wave, surfacing almost immediately in a hundred fragments floating outward from the beach. Zak had been brooding about this failure ever since.

Now he leaned back against the trunk of the oak and put his hands behind his neck. "This time I think I've solved the problems, eh, *tyee*-boss. I didn't spend my childhood watching the sky for nothing – I was keeping my eye on those birds. I think I've figured out how they do it. Next time she'll sail right over them Yankee mountains there."

The "Yankee mountains" had moved their great blue bulk up so close in today's light that they might be thought of as keeping an eye on this Indian with the absurd plan for challenging nature's laws.

"First it will learn to glide, like an eagle, off these cliffs. When I've got that right, I'll figure out a way to keep it up. You seen any bicycles lying around?"

"You intend to *pedal* across the strait?" Sumner had early fallen into the role of sceptic in this enterprise, though possibly he was even more stirred by the business than Zak was himself. Whenever they spoke of this, everything within him strained to see that machine leave the ground. He strained to leave the ground himself. To lift above the pines, to soar above the rolling Juan de Fuca waves, to sail over the mountain peaks, and enter the sky. He hardly dared hope that between them they might make it possible one day, and shored himself up against disappointment by regularly voicing sensible doses of doubt.

This had been the case even when they were boys. While Uncle Charles attempted to teach them the construction business, enchanting Logan Sumner with his excited talk of quarrels, quirks, and quoins, bored Zak would dream of making pieces of construction lumber fly through the air. It was left to Sumner to fill him in on what he had failed to learn. Whenever the two boys were invited to accompany Uncle Charles and James Horncastle and their friends on hunting trips into the mountains north of town, with responsibility for collecting and carrying the bagged wildfowl, Zak would disappear for hours on end in the woods and be eventually found by Sumner sitting on a log in some small clearing, closely examining the feathers, the bones, the joints of a dead willow grouse's wing, looking for its secret. Drawing Zak back into the practical world was, even then, more of an expected role he was fulfilling for his uncle than an act of real conviction. He would rather have been party to the preposterous secret quest.

"I've been studying them pictures by your Mr. da Vinci," Zak said now. "I think I've figured out where that fellow went wrong. I'd steal an engine out of one of them steamboats if they weren't so damn heavy! You think they could be taught how to make wings flap up and down?"

At that moment, horses came thundering along the track, boiling up dust. Sumner had forgotten about the race. Picnickers rose to their feet all over the slope to shout encouragement. Sumner counted horses – two hired jockeys were vying for first – until Horncastle and his Norah passed by. They were fourth, though a Bluejacket riding on a spotted gelding was coming up fast from behind. Even the drunken naval captain Joshua Trumble (ret'd) was ahead of him, shouting and laughing and all but falling off his mount. This was not at all what anyone had expected.

Perhaps Horncastle was deliberately holding back so that he could win all at once with a last-minute burst of speed, a risky display of bravado that would not be uncharacteristic.

"He's going to lose," Sumner said. "At least he knows how to lose, being a thorough sportsman."

"A seasoned gambler knows how to take a loss with grace."

"So long as nobody says something he doesn't like."

"That's right," Zak said. "It's the *not* losing he's not so good at. It means he has to bloody the nose of everyone he catches even *thinking* he might have cheated."

When Horncastle and his grey filly came in fifth, behind even the sailor, Sumner decided to stay where he was for the time being rather than join the crowd rushing in to congratulate the winners and compare their winnings. He could think of nothing he might say to Horncastle. He had no winnings to collect, or any intention of placing another bet. There were other heats to be run, and other opportunities for Norah to justify her expense, but he would prefer to watch things happen from this distance.

"Too bad, Horncastle!" Someone had seized the megaphone. "I guess that long trip from Kentucky just wore her out."

Laughter and cheers. Sumner could not see how Horncastle was handling this. So long as he was willing to laugh at himself, matters would not become too uncomfortable.

Now someone else had the megaphone. "That filly just don't like the colour of our grass is all. Hornswoggle ought to get Horace to spread a little blue paint around his pasture, that ought to speed her up enough to come in fourth at least."

"I'm leaving," Zak said. "Nobody told me I had to jump up and down and holler for a fool on a horse. If I want to put my hand in somebody's daughter's dress I just do it. Today I've got plans for that big perambulator Mrs. Carey brought over from England. The wheels. She finally threw it out."

"Mrs. Carey doesn't throw anything out. She would keep it for her grandchildren."

For some time two young Indian men had been moving in this direction across the grass. Heads down, apparently speaking to one another without looking up from their feet, they did not seem to Sumner to have any particular direction in mind, nor were they paying any attention to the commotion surrounding the race, or to the little clusters of spectators they passed. Yet they came to a stop not far from Sumner and Zak and continued to speak, in subdued tones, to one another.

"All right, Mrs. Carey she gave it to me then. I told her: me got-em cousin up in Ahouset, she got-em six papoose but no got nothing to push them in." Zak had raised his voice for this, as though he hoped to be overheard by the two men. "I told her if my cousin up in Ahouset could use that perambulator she would be the first one in the tribe to push her babies like an English lady. That Mrs. Carey she starts to cry every time you mention hard-up Indians, she wants to write her sister in London how she's helping out."

If this were indeed intended for the two men, they gave no sign of having heard. They did not even glance this way.

Nor did they look up from their own conversation when Horncastle, still in the saddle, took hold of the megaphone. "That's all right, folks. You don't need to worry about placing your hard-earned money on my pretty Norah. It's still safe. We thought we'd take it easy the first time around so you could have a chance to admire her properly. Anybody with an eye in his head can see she'll take the money in the next two heats."

"So, you coming with me?" Zak said. "To work on Mrs. Carey's wheels?"

"I came with Horncastle, Zak. He'll expect me to stay."

Zak grinned. "Tell him it's not his horse you want to marry, you want his daughter for your pretty klootchman, no? He taking you home for supper?"

"I don't know. To tell you the truth I don't know if I want to face any of them right now – Mrs. Horncastle or her daughter or any of them."

"Yes, Jimmy," Zak suddenly said. "What d'you want me for this time?"

The two men slowly raised their heads. With fingers tugging at the front of his hat's brim as though he wished to yank it right down over his eyes, one of them cleared his throat. "Hey there – Zak?" Then he said, to the grass not far from Zak's feet, "He told us to come over here and find you – my brother Jubal."

Zak heaved himself up and brushed the grass and needles off the back of his sagging trousers. Whatever their business, the two men would not speak in front of Sumner – Zak was taken aside for a few moments of exchanged murmurs. Then he looked at Logan Sumner and shrugged. "Change of plans for me, I guess. These fellas say they're willing to pretend for one afternoon that they don't think I'm really a white man. Their brother across the harbour sent them to borrow my hammer and saw again. He lost his own. He says they can bring the carpenter too this time, if he don't mind using his fancy tools on a real Indian's boards."

Zak turned to the nearer of the two men again. "Hey, maybe you want my *tyee*-boss instead? He's been hollering at me how he wants to take a good close look at them buildings over there, to see how you make them. He hasn't got nothing but centuries of European designs to copy from, so he wants to see if he can copy from you instead."

It was true that Sumner was interested in the simple construction of the older lodge-houses of the Indian village made of cedar planks fitted to a skeleton structure of posts and beams. Several times he'd rowed across the harbour and been shown around by some of the friendlier women; he'd taken measurements; he'd even taken certain walls apart and put them back together again. But being impressed with the principles of the design, and with its suitability to this place, was not the same as finding a way of making any part of it acceptable to clients in town.

It seemed a great effort for the two young men to look at Sumner. Both shook their heads. He would not be welcome this afternoon, even if he had wanted to come. Even if he'd been free.

Before going off with them, Zak looked back to where the race-horses were being led away and money was exchanging hands and Horncastle's voice could still be heard above the others. "Why does that man think his missus will still feed him when he gets home? Mary One-eye says some woman's come to claim him." Up in the branches of her oak, Mary One-eye put a hand on her little crown and grinned. The two men from across the harbour kept their eyes averted – the people of their village considered her to be some kind of dangerous witch. "If that was me in that trouble," Zak said, "I wouldn't go racing my horse around in a damn circle, I'd take off into the bush and never come back."

11

THE races were several hours behind them before Sumner's conversation with Horncastle could be resumed. First it was necessary to fetch Cleo and ride out with Horncastle to the Sheepshank farm, where the disappointing new horse was boarded. Then they were expected to join Horace Sheepshank and a few other racing friends at The Willows Hotel, where Sheepshank's farm labourers had already gathered to run the races over again and pass judgement.

Alfie Stott raised his cup of grog in a salute when Horncastle and Sumner entered. "A toast," said Stretch Halfpenny, standing to bow in Horncastle's direction. "I likes a man that knows how to lose a race! 'Tis a sign o' breedin' fer sure."

"A clever trick," said Alfie Stott. "To lose three races in a row with yer bran new 'orse from Kentucky. 'Twill throw the bettin' off fer sure the next time. Ah – I'm onto yer tricks!"

Stretch Halfpenny *haw-hawed* thunderously into the corner, spitting grog and wiping his sleeve across his mouth. Soon the entire room was convulsed with laughter at Horncastle's expense. He even laughed himself. He did not roll up his sleeves for the expected fist fight even when Captain Joshua Trumble (ret'd) suggested that this beautiful filly that Horncastle had been bragging about all over town must have been bought from the same dealer who'd sold him poor old half-blind Vicky.

Horncastle stood up on the nearest table to address the assembled crowd. "It's the truth, men," he said. "They publish my name in the papers back there, whenever they hear I'm in a mood for buying. That's so every red-neck white-trash hillbilly can drag out all the broken-down animals they want to get rid of. You've caught me out on that, I can't escape it."

"Maybe your Norah would be better at catching rats," said Horace Sheepshank. "You could retire old Vicky and maybe stop losing your shirt."

Eventually the conversation turned away from the race and onto the latest news from London. Did anyone think the Prime Minister and that tedious windbag de Cosmos would succeed in having the railroad extended to Vancouver Island as originally promised? No one did. Most agreed that a great betrayal had taken place. The whole business of confederation had been based on deceit – a poor beginning for a nation. When Drysdale reminded everyone that there were railroad companies south of the border that would be happy to send up a spur line, Captain Trumble said he'd take up arms first, and made it clear he was not averse to beginning the battle here and now. "We were a hell of a lot better off as a colony, men. We threw it all away!"

Eventually Horncastle grew tired of the conversation, and offered "young Sumner here" as his excuse for leaving – "Some business to talk about." When they were mounted and heading towards town, however, he kept silence for a long while, undoubtedly brooding over the race and the ordeal that had followed. "Damn!" he said. And, after more silence, "Damn!" It was up to Sumner to encourage him out of his sulk. "You were telling me about the lady, sir. This morning."

"What's that?"

"Your marriage. To the Australian."

"Oh." Horncastle seemed relieved to have a subject other than his recent defeat to think about, and allowed no more than a few minutes to go by before he launched himself into his story. "Well now, you've got to imagine me in San Francisco. I'd left her behind, remember. Left them all behind. So there I was, I worked like a navvy for two years in the gold-fields all over California to scrape together enough to buy that saloon. I mean in San Francisco. The Thirsty Traveller I called her – on Pacific Street, down in the damp, thick salty air near the wharfs. To one side of me there was this damned big hull of an abandoned ship dragged out of the mud and used as a warehouse. Across the street another hull – the first floor of a hotel. If a night was dark enough and the fog was thick, you sometimes couldn't be sure you hadn't strayed out into the harbour. More than one man stayed drinking at my mahogany bar trying to work up the courage to go out and face the impossibilities that had driven him in for a drink in the first place. Others, looking out the windows, believed they'd signed up and set out to sea. I slaved in that saloon for nearly two more years before I was in a position to think of supporting a wife."

"But at least you didn't forget you were married."

"As a matter of fact I sometimes did forget. Dammit – a man has other things on his mind! Building up a business. Had friends amongst the folks who drank there, and neighbourhood businessmen. Had even been approached about a life in politics, now that the Vigilantes had cleaned up the town. Had been no part of that group, of course – you may have heard they started out by avenging the death of a crusading newspaperman, kidnapped his killers from the prison and hanged them, then went on to clean up the town: ballot-stuffers, crooked judges, murderers, and bribe-taking police. Made the poor buggers walk out a second-floor window on planks. Stick their heads into ropes hanging from beams off the roof. Then pulled the planks in from under them! Saw more men at the ends of ropes than anyone ought to see in a lifetime. But now there was less chance my customers would be shot to death in the middle of a drink. Widow of a Vigilante lived next door. Fat old Mrs. Opal."

Fat old Mrs. Opal, Horncastle said, had people to her house and charged them money for messages from their dead. She had quite a reputation for surprising people. You didn't always hear what you thought you would hear; rarely did you hear what you hoped to hear. Loving spouses confessed they'd been pretending for most of their lives. (Her own appeared only once, and swore undying fidelity even beyond the grave.) Fathers accused living sons of cowardice. Departed mothers had already forgotten the names of their children. But she was popular, this big, loud, gaudy woman with the several chins and the twin titanic bosoms. She hinted that her powers had played a role in decisions made by important people. For instance, she took credit for persuading the famous Lola Montez to turn down the title of Empress of California when it was offered to her by secession-minded Southerners. She claimed to have talked the scandalous dancer into leaving the latest in her long line of husbands and keepers – a list that was supposed to include Franz Liszt, officers of the British and German armies, the Polish prince Sulkowski, some Parisian killed in a duel, and even King Ludwig of Bavaria. She even claimed to have persuaded her to come out of her Sacramento retirement in order to revive her spectacular dance for a tour of Australia. "Shook whalebone spiders from her scanty dress and stamped on them," Horncastle said. "I saw her – that was her famous dance!"

Sometimes Mrs. Opal would come in to the Thirsty Traveller at the end of an evening, visibly shaken from her latest struggles with the candid departed and the startled living, and sit at a back corner table slapping down cards. She would tell your future if pressed, but mainly just liked to stare into the cards for whatever comforting messages they might offer her. When enough people had gathered around her out of curiosity, someone was bound to suggest a seance. "Had no objection to this myself, once business hours were over and we'd locked the door to the street and pulled the double curtains closed. People drank more than usual before these sessions, to work up their courage, and drank even more while they tried to recover afterwards from the messages they received. Thought it a lot of claptrap myself, but Mrs. Thompkins encouraged tolerance."

"Mrs. Thompkins?" The road, which had followed alongside a cedar-rail snake fence separating them from fields of drying haystacks, now entered a section of woods. Shaded by firs, a series of mock-orange bushes and ocean spray crowded against one another, the stark white mock-orange flowers draped across the lacy cushions of toasted spirea foam, all entangled with honeysuckle.

"Mrs. Thompkins? Washerwoman from down the street – had her own business – but she helped me out nearly every night in the Thirsty Traveller. A dear friend of mine by this time. Pretty. Sweet-natured. Ran away from a husband that tried to kill her. She joined in with Mrs. Opal's fun every time, and encouraged our fat neighbour to make contact with her husband. 'If he answers, now, 'twould mean the scoundrel is dead and gone at last to his punishment.' But no matter how often Mrs. Opal demanded he make his presence known, she never got any response."

"I wonder would you try again," said a persistent Mrs. Thompkins. "He may be occupied, beating up some poor dead woman that accidentally got in his way." She had developed a habit of glancing over her shoulder whenever she laughed about this matter, as though expecting instant retribution.

No answer, though the little group holding hands around the table put all their concentrated effort into trying to help – Mrs. Thompkins was a popular figure, pleasant to everyone, always willing to make fun of the tragic figure her friends considered her to be. Everyone wished to see her set free. Perhaps a second marriage would not be out of the question.

"Not a peep out of him," Mrs. Opal eventually had to concede. All four of her chins shivered whenever she spoke. "Either he's still walking around on this earth, or he's hiding in some shadowy corner of eternity, refusing to answer for his villainy."

At Mrs. Thompkins's insistence, Mrs. Opal asked several of the more co-operative dead if they had seen anything of the infamous Mr. T, but, as one of them said, "Do you think we get to meet everyone who passes over? We certainly can't be expected to remember everyone's name!"

Then one evening she wasn't able to call up anyone at all for the longest time. Low Tide waited for a word of forgiveness from the man he'd shot in a Denver poker game, but got only silence. This upset him – he'd been brooding, tossing back far too many bourbons, not at all sure the jury's not-guilty verdict had been justified. Whispering Willie demanded that his former partner in the gold-fields tell where he'd hidden the ten-ounce nugget they'd found shortly before he'd died – but the partner obviously didn't want Willie to cash in that nugget on his own. Mrs. Thompkins was as eager as ever for news of her brutal husband's demise. Mrs. Opal put all her enormous bulk into straining after some answer from "beyond," but it seemed that the doors to "beyond" had been closed to her. Sweat rolled down her painted cheeks. Her nostrils flared. The great bright rings seemed prepared to fly off her whitened knuckles. No one would have been altogether surprised to see the roof fall in, or the walls buckle – the effort being exerted in that room was so great.

"I'm getting something," she eventually said. "I feel someone approaching."

The door swung open, though Horncastle had locked it himself. Before he'd pushed it shut again, yellow fog had begun to roll in from the street, and to spill across the sawdust floor of the saloon, coiling around the legs of tables, and curling up the walls to roll back on itself, to collect on the stuffed heads of deer and bear and mountain goats staring out from their wooden platters and to settle like cold, damp shawls around all their shoulders.

Mrs. Opal shouted: "Make yourself known! Who are you? Are you Whispering Willie's partner? Are you that villain who struck our Mrs. T?"

"Neither!" the voice answered in the dark – the voice of a middle-aged man. "I was not summoned, but came of my own volition." He might have been speaking from just behind the counter – but no one was there except for their own dim faces peering back at them through the bottles before the mirror.

"Then who are you?" said Mrs. Opal, who'd never encountered this sort of gate-crashing before. "By what right do you interrupt our business?"

"Septimus McConnell, madam!" Now his voice came from somewhere just above Mrs. Opal's head, in the vicinity of the chandelier, though nothing could be seen in the gloom.

"Are you the man Low Tide gunned down, come to forgive him at last? Tell me which of these mortals you wish to communicate with."

"The owner of this pit of sin! James Horncastle!"

The speaker's name had not registered with Horncastle when he heard it first. Nor had the voice seemed familiar. But he knew fast enough who this was when he heard his own name spoken. The hairs stood up on his hands. His heart stopped in his chest. All eyes in the room turned to him – he had never asked to speak to anyone, he had always been the silent and sceptical member of the little group. It had always been his role to draw the glasses of William Bull and mix the Mule Skinners afterwards, to comfort the disappointed, to make light of the whole business, to flatter Mrs. Opal with compliments on her talents as a great actress.

"And what is your message for Mr. Horncastle?"

"Ask that blackguard where he keeps his conscience," said the voice. "Ask him how he can sleep in his bed at night, thinking of those he betrayed." If they had been able to see the fellow, Horncastle knew he would quite likely be stained by textile dyes and draped with piggery entrails from his death in the Irk. "It is one thing that he promised marriage to my eldest daughter," he said. "It is another that he betrothed himself to my second, but it is a different matter altogether that he married my third, in secret, then left her behind and hasn't yet asked her to join him. Does he suppose he will not have to answer to me, eventually, if he continues pretending that contracts signed in one country are not binding in another?"

The seance was brought to an abrupt end when Horncastle pulled his hands out of the grip of the others and grabbed up a spittoon for a weapon. The player piano leapt into momentary life, as it did in times of tension, playing a few bars out of the middle of "Innocence Betrayed" before groaning back into its usual silence. Mrs. Thompkins re-lit the lamps. The fog collapsed into a yellowish dew which ran in streams down the walls.

No one would be satisfied without an immediate explanation. A wife! He was not the first man to make a success in San Francisco while a wife languished at home, but other wives did not have Mrs. Opal to defend them. "You must obey immediately, James. You must send for her. There is no telling what mischief that voice might be capable of. I sensed a desire for retribution in it! We will make her welcome here, we'll make her one of us. She will be a happy Mrs. Horncastle in San Francisco." Less eager than Mrs. Opal to see the bride arrive, Mrs. Thompkins worked silently behind the counter for a few moments, polishing glasses. But eventually the abused wife found that she had to speak out for her neglected sister – she demanded that Horncastle sit down this minute and write to that man's poor daughter.

So he did. Like everyone else, he was only trying to do what he thought was right. They accompanied him to the post office the next morning. Having given him advice on style and content right through the night, they intended to see the business to its end. Along with the letter was Horncastle's photograph, and five hundred dollars so that his young wife could set sail for the New World immediately. Some of the letter's contents surprised his friends – for he'd put in writing that he intended to sell the saloon and move north to British territory as soon as she arrived. This was something he had been thinking about for a good long while, for he felt himself an alien in California. This move, he thought, would also please his bride. Besides, news had recently reached San Francisco of the discovery of new gold-fields up the Fraser River – miners were heading north by the hundreds to make fortunes they would then deliver into the hands of the men who ran the saloons.

"I'll wager my four-ounce chunk of Sacramento gold she won't even answer it," he said, as he committed the letter into the care of the U.S. Mail.

"Low Tide was quick to take me up on the bet," Horncastle said. "So was Whispering Willie, who insisted on doubling the amount. Mrs. Opal did not approve of gambling. And Mrs. Thompkins said there would be enough lost and won in this business without our adding to it with immoral bets."

Horncastle stopped speaking for a while, and mused off in the direction of a cluster of farm buildings, until it seemed to Sumner that he might have forgotten his narrative, or begun to brood about some part of it. He withdrew his large silver watch from a pocket and consulted it. It was up to Sumner to suggest that there were still important elements missing from the story. For instance, did Horncastle ever receive an answer to the letter he had spent an entire night preparing?

"An answer?" He smiled, and flicked the reins to encourage a little more exertion out of his horse. "Oh yes. Received an answer – of sorts."

Naturally, when a letter arrived from Manchester a few months later, he did not open it until he had called together the same company of friends who had helped him make this contact with his almost-forgotten wife. Mrs. Opal insisted that the Thirsty Traveller be closed to the public, and pulled curtains to block out their view of the street people and the warehouses and hotels made from the hulls of abandoned ships. She turned the lamps low, in case his father-in-law wished to convey congratulations from beyond. Whispering Willie snatched the envelope from Horncastle's hand, sniffed it, held it up to the light. "My darling sweetheart," he pretended to read. "I and the six children were delighted to hear from you, but we spent all the money on booze. Please send more." Mrs. Opal snatched the envelope away, held it to her broad forehead, and closed her eyes. "I am on my way, my darling. Please heap rewards upon that wonderful woman who encouraged this reunion, God bless her!" Mrs. Thompkins declined an opportunity to give her own prediction of the contents, gruffly demanding that they open it and get this business settled fast. Low Tide, still unforgiven by the victim of his blazing Colt revolver, took one of his weapons from its holster and laid it on the table: "I'll fill us all with lead, and myself last, if she is not ecstatic."

"Lord, son. He almost did that too. When I opened the envelope and displayed its contents, he raised his gun and would have blown my brains out if Willie hadn't thrown himself on the fool. My own shock was too great, I couldn't have saved myself. Mrs. Opal had fallen back into a chair, affecting a faint, but quickly revived with a scream when she saw that Low Tide intended to send her off to join the voices on the other side. There was no letter, you see. The envelope contained nothing but my photograph, which fell out onto the shining counter in a thousand pieces."

"She had freed you then!" This seemed good news to Logan Sumner. Now surely everything else became irrelevant.

"Seemed to everyone in that room that she had freed me, as it does to you. No other interpretation could be put upon it, without straining our brains more than we wished. Low Tide and Whispering Willie were stunned, as though they had been rejected themselves. Couldn't understand why I didn't do myself in. Mrs. Opal suspected mischief, and pledged to discover whether the dead had the power to interfere with the U.S. Mail. Mrs. Thompkins was as pleased as I would have expected her to be – she pulled back the curtains, opened the door, and hauled me out into the street where the whole dark, whispering world of merchant sailors and demi-monde ladies and ships converted to landlubber purposes could witness her happiness, and there agreed to accompany me north to a new home. You know her as Mrs. Horncastle, of course, but Mrs. Thompkins was how she was known to her friends at the time."

"Mrs. Horncastle was 'Mrs. Thompkins'?" Sumner felt stupid to be asking this, but needed to hear it again. Mrs. Horncastle had been the centre of his greatest concern in this matter. Was he to discover that his sentiment was based on inadequate information?

"That's what I'm telling you, lad." He was laughing at the young man – had done this on purpose. "She'd left a drunken Mr. T behind, remember – unfortunately still alive the last time she'd seen him in County Cork."

"But did Mrs. Horncastle accept the invitation immediately? Mrs. Thompkins, that is? After standing by and watching you send for your wife?"

"Dammit, Sumner, sometimes you are thick! The woman had been living with me for more than a year by then! Why shouldn't she accept? In the eyes of herself and many others, she was already my wife. Like me, she accepted my letter as an unavoidable responsibility – good manners! – but she'd also prayed for a rejection.

Began to pack her bags the minute the fog of uncertainty lifted. Could wait to be properly married, she agreed, till we set foot in our new country." Horncastle ran a finger across his moustache, chuckling softly to himself. "You may have noticed that, though she is a pious church-going woman now, with no time for this current interest in spiritualism, she has nothing but gentle words to say about those who practise this mysterious art – recalling the kindness that was indirectly done her by our dear old fat Mrs. Opal."

Sumner felt stunned by all this news, and everything it implied. They travelled in silence together for several minutes downhill between the rows of grand houses whose lushly blooming gardens competed for his admiration. But eventually his curiosity about the torn photograph made continued silence impossible. "I still don't understand how your, uh, first wife can expect to hold you to that contract when she sent you such a clear message in that envelope. Surely she can't expect you to have reacted differently!"

Horncastle lifted his hat to the Pinches, father and son, travelling home from town in their dogcart, back to back. Sumner touched an imaginary cap. "Ah – there's the problem, you see. We interpreted the clues badly, being poor detectives. O'erhasty, to say the least, to assume that it was Katie who tore up the picture and sent it back. Katie McConnell didn't even see my letter. I learned this only last evening, from the lady herself. During those years of waiting, it was natural that sooner or later Lilian would grow tired of seeing Susannah admiring the ring and make an announcement concerning her own expectations. Kate waited until Susannah's understandable fit of passion had run down – three or four days. And waited, too, until Lilian had grown accustomed to her new role as the one who gloated. Before showing them both her certificate of marriage. By the time my letter arrived, Susannah and Lilian had become friends again, having discovered themselves to have shared an enemy. And it was

Susannah, unfortunately, who was in the habit of collecting the mail. When she saw the California postmark on a letter addressed to her least favourite sister, she suffered not a moment of indecision before opening it. Read the letter, then burnt it. Kept the money for herself, deciding that it was the very least that was owed her. Stared at my photograph until it made her sick, then tore it up and put it in a new envelope which she addressed to me, without comment. None of this did she tell to the others until years later, long after Kate had been forced to conclude that I'd abandoned her, and she'd moved with the others to Australia."

"Where the sisters continued their warfare," Sumner said, "as I already know. Lord, my head spins! So our mysterious woman in black has a claim on you after all – or seems to – and cannot be simply dismissed."

Now they were within sight of town. At the foot of the long slope ahead of them was the congregation of white and brick-red buildings, of steeples and chimneys and masts, collected in sunlight. Christ Church. The Driard. The Customs House. Pendray's Soap Works. The Bird Cages. St. John's. Because the American mountains had disappeared behind a purple haze that blended sea into sky, the city might have existed at the absolute end of everything – time, the world, the universe – a tiny, huddled, isolated fragment of civilization flung down amongst great humps of rock, assemblies of shiny green oaks, and stands of enormous firs. From this distance, it was not difficult to believe in the expectation shared by nearly everyone who lived here, of some day becoming one of the world's great cities. Another Singapore. Another Tyre. A northern San Francisco at the very least. Once the next boom arrived.

More than seven thousand men, women, and children were down there waiting for this miracle to take place. In the meantime they mended the streets, sold hindquarters of beef, sewed bonnets, filled out mortgage papers, accepted invitations to dinner. Germans, Norwegians, Italians, Chinese, Scots, Australians, Irishmen – an unlikely nesting of disparate fowl – had left home and family and often even identities behind in order to work out their dreams in this tiny city of exalted hopes. How strongly did they believe that any of their dreams would come true? From up here, Sumner had no difficulty imagining the great city of towering splendid buildings they waited for. He saw it already – soaring spires of blinding white marble, massive opera houses of blood-red stone, museums surrounded by solid statuary, gabled mansions and tree-lined avenues and sprawling terraced hotels of glass and pillars and archways and domes, going down to the sea – all waiting to come into being. After a light rain, it would be all shining, like a city of precious stones beside the glistening strait. It was equally possible to imagine none of this here yet – only the water, the coastline, the oaks and arbutus trees and grassy clearings, a few Indians along the shoreline, as the Greek sailor Juan de Fuca must have seen it as he sailed past in his Spanish-American ship. What was not so easy to imagine, as Horncastle's revelations had just demonstrated, was what was happening within the hopeful hearts of those Norwegians and Germans and Irishmen who were going about their business in the little city. If all of them kept hidden, like Mrs. Horncastle, startling secrets concerning their pasts, how was it possible to fathom what other mysteries lay hidden within their hearts? Was a person doomed to live his life amongst incomprehensible strangers?

"Something just occurred to me – dammit!" Horncastle said. "I really won that wager after all – delayed by a few years! No chance of finding Low Tide and Whispering Willie now – to get back what I paid them and collect what they owe me as well."

They followed the road between the two facing rows of grand houses with their towers and fretwork verandahs and large bay windows challenging one another across the intervening street. A carriage overtook them from behind and went on past, apparently in too much of a hurry to care about the dust that others would have to taste.

"Now tell me, how much of this – how much of your story was known by my Uncle Charles?"

"None of it! None of it, of course! Good lord! Charles was as easily upset as you are, when things were not consistent with appearances. Would not be friendship to tell him any of this, since he would only have been confused. Nor did I think the day would come when I would be forced, by circumstances, to give this account to his nephew. But come, Logan Sumner, I would like to believe that even he would have seen the humour in it eventually – as I would like to believe that you can too, if you try."

"And how do you explain the father-in-law's voice from beyond the grave? Were there some in the room who knew and –"

"Took me years to think of it. Fat old Mrs. Opal! Her husband must have got enough of the story out of me. Perhaps when we were drinking together, after the Vigilantes had dispatched one more crooked politician to the next world. Must have been a celebration, at my insistence – since he was making San Francisco fit for decent people like myself and my customers. Must have told him just enough, and he must have repeated just enough of it to his wife – while he was still alive, of course – who brooded about it for a while, then later took it upon herself to see that I was forced either to separate her friend Mrs. Thompkins from her hopes once and for all, or to make her my proper wife."

"Wherever your Mrs. Opal is now, she should be sent for," Sumner said, "and instructed to utilize her powers to bring about a satisfactory conclusion to this unhappy mess." However comical he and Horncastle might decide to find this business of suddenly having two wives, there was still the former "Mrs. Thompkins" to be saved, once again, from profound disappointment and shame.

AN ACCOUNT OF TWO

DISSIMILAR COURTSHIPS CONDUCTED

DURING THE SUMMER OF 1881

12

HAVING delivered this troublesome woman to the city's doorstep, the world again withdrew, and seemed to be farther away throughout that turbulent summer than it had ever been before. Even the great blue jagged wall of foreign mountains which sometimes hovered too close had faded away until it was hardly noticeable except as a scribble of snowy peaks above the haze that obscured the far side of the strait. Could it really matter to anyone here that far away the desperate Greeks were giving away large pieces of territory to the Turks? Naturally everyone was appalled to learn that a disappointed office-seeker had shot the President of the United States, wounding him in a manner that would almost certainly lead to his death. But, like other reports, this might have been a dispatch from a distant planet, with no real interest for people engaged in watching the manoeuvres of a wronged woman determined to achieve a sort of justice for herself – especially since they were also preoccupied with watching the volatile little hotel owner's attempts to dodge her efforts to get him back.

Rival saloon-keepers hoped for the worst. "He's got as much chance as a mouse mesmerized by a snake. Just watch her gobble him down."

"Und she iss only the first." Samuel Hatch (born Samuel Zeltstange in Mainz) suggested to customers in his Yates Street premises that there would be a woman from Kentucky next, another from California. "Ziss man, you see, he gafe a phony marriage licence instead of money to effery whore he shared a bed vith all aroun' d'vorld!"

The new owner of the Bottomless Saloon could not imagine why the woman wanted him back. "A fine-lookin' lady like her. Don't she know how lucky she was to *lose* him?"

Naturally, friends and supporters refused to believe the woman had any real claim. "Somewhere she has a husband manufacturing fake marriage certificates, sending her off to blackmail one poor fellow after another that she happened to meet just long enough to get his name. She must think he has money." But even amongst Horncastle's friends there was some grudging admiration for the invader. You couldn't help respecting a woman who'd gone to so much trouble to get what she wanted. "Halfway round the world with two little children! She deserves to be given a chance."

In some of the better drawing-rooms this spectacle of a resolute woman taking extraordinary steps to reclaim her husband was acknowledged to be amusing, but only reluctantly admitted into conversations amongst those who considered themselves above gossip. "Still, you see how it demonstrates the old maxim, that water never rises above its source. Manchester, after all!"

This dismissive comment was made on the terrace outside Lady Riven-Blythe's drawing-room, after tennis. Wives sipped at cool drinks and admired the rose gardens at their feet, while the husbands stayed below to recover from their exertions in the stippled shade of the arbutus trees that grew along the shoreline of the narrow saltwater arm.

"And proves again how dragging yourself through the rougher corners of the Empire will only scrape away whatever breeding there might have been in the beginning."

"Though she has been seen in church," said Lady Riven-Blythe into her sparkling glass.

"Not Christ Church! She isn't 'high'?"

"St. John's of course. The very picture of piety. She prays more rigorously than anyone else in the congregation. And praises the Reverend Trodd to his face far more than he deserves."

"Which is precious little, heaven knows. So she is not only vulgar but a hypocrite as well."

"But whether she is praying or praising," said Lady Riven-Blythe, "she never entirely removes her gaze from the Horncastle tribe. The backs of all their necks must be thoroughly scorched."

"Not *his* neck. When did he last enter a church? That poor wife has to drag their parade of brats behind her like a mother duck, alone, wherever she goes."

"This woman, whoever she is, could not have found a more devoted wife occupying the position she claims for herself. This ought to be a battle worth observing."

"Though not *discussing*, now that your husbands show signs of rejoining us."

"One watches nevertheless. For fear of missing the very moment she moves in for the kill."

A returned husband, mopping his brow, suggested that it was the woman herself who was doing the watching. "You see, our conservation was not so very different from your own. We have decided that she is looking us over – all of us, and not just that little fellow from the hotel. One sees her here and there, observing, like someone from Scotland Yard."

"Asking discreet questions at the bank. Of course, one is not at liberty to report what."

"And uncommonly curious, for a woman, I should think, about the price of properties. The market value of various hotels, for instance. She would have us estimate their profits for her!"

"Her dead husband, if he existed, was certainly a failure in one regard. No one seems to have instructed her on the sort of behaviour one expects from a member of the gentler sex."

"I came upon a mountain lion once – a cougar – which gave me much the same feeling: cold shivers down my back."

"Oh, Rupert, now you're being the poet again!"

"Not at all. This was while I was out in the woods for some shooting. It lay motionless along a tree limb, almost invisible, waiting for some deer to wander innocently by and provide it with dinner."

"How terrifying," said the poet-huntsman's wife, allowing a visible shiver to run down her back. "But we must change the topic, or I am certain Lady Alice will cancel her annual tennis party in future, thinking our conversations have plunged to the level of our rude surroundings."

Logan Sumner began to hide out in the church. That is, he began to go every day for the noon-hour practices which had been granted as an occasional privilege by the Reverend Mr. Trodd to the strongest voice in the choir. "I shall lift up my heart unto the hills," he sang, "whence cometh my help." But there was nothing of King David's confidence in Sumner's heart. None of the help which cometh from the hills could be found in the Holy, Holy, Holy above the altar, or in the redwood panels, or in the coloured stencils painted on the walls.

He ached to think of the pain this business must be inflicting upon Mrs. Horncastle, always the perfect wife, proud of her family, secure in her marriage to the popular little hotel owner. He could hardly bear to think of Adelina, who, of all the adopted children, would be the most affected by this catastrophe – yet he didn't know whether she would be expecting him to rush to her side or would prefer that he leave her to absorb this blow in privacy. But (how does such a thing happen?) he could not prevent himself from thinking at the same time of that poor deserted bride in Manchester, that young woman faithfully waiting for her husband to send for her. He saw her youth begin to fade, her rosy cheeks begin to pale, the spark of hope die out of her eyes as she was finally forced to admit that she had waited long enough, and then to agree to emigrate with the rest of her family, like felons, to the underside of the earth. How could the heart of an abandoned orphan and lonely widower not respond to this unfortunate woman's plight? Life must be so much easier for those incapable of sympathizing with two opposing circumstances simultaneously!

Noon-hour rehearsals at St. John's did not always lift his spirits. Instead, the great iron church soon began to magnify anxieties much as it magnified sound. The occasional gusts of wind which got caught in the gables and went howling around the corners of the building only made things worse.

Obviously neither the designers nor the builders nor the wealthy heiress who financed the building had imagined the ex-tremities of Pacific Coast weather when they shipped these cast-iron sections from England around the Horn in pieces to be reassembled here – transporting the fragments round the world, like the religion it represented, with an uneasy confidence that someone in the barely imaginable receiving city would have the knowledge to put it together properly, and the will to maintain it, and the heart to make it serve its intended purpose. They would not be able to imagine that there might be competent builders already living here who could have designed and erected a church. A mere Sumner would not possibly do. And so they had not been able to anticipate that the drumming of a rain storm on the iron roof, for instance, would have the effect of entirely drowning out the words shouted from the pulpit, or that an electric storm would convert the church into an intolerable chamber of auditory horrors. Even the mildest shower, if it went on for any length of time, would eventually find its way between the joints in the pre-fabricated roof to drip on the heads and hats of the seated congregation. And they had not imagined either, those far-off dreamers, that the occasional summer wind off the ocean, howling around its metallic joints, could cause a soloist to believe the Pacific itself had broken in through his ear-drums to go roaring around in his brain.

On the Friday that ended his first week of daily practices he eventually decided that the situation was hopeless. His voice had never been so unreliable, the wind had never been so persistent. But just as he was about to leave for his Wharf Street office, he was intercepted by the Reverend Mr. Trodd, who came out of the vestry in shirt-sleeves with a book in his hand. "Don't run away, Mr. Sumner. Not yet. For some reason, hearing your voice today reminded me that I still possessed this book your uncle once lent me."

Sumner preferred to come and go without drawing the attention of the rector, who was not content to confine his preaching to Sundays, but he could not help showing some interest in a surprise relic of his uncle's.

"He suggested I would find a sermon in it, I remember. I did not. Indeed, I had even forgotten I had it – years now! But since I have thought of it now, I should give it to you, having no use for it myself."

He waved the book about but did not put it into Sumner's hand. The Reverend Mr. Trodd did not willingly relinquish an opportunity to hold an audience. "William Law. An English clergyman of the last century. A mystic! Your uncle's reading habits were altogether too eccentric for me."

"He liked to wrestle with ideas."

"Ideas?" The rector found the very word amusing here. "Let me give you the sort of thing this gentleman would have us consider."

Driven to the front pew and pinned there by the Reverend's powerful gaze, Sumner could only hope this would not take long.

"Now listen to this." He seemed eager, already chuckling in anticipation. Pages were turned, turned back, glanced at. The thumb was licked by a wet, generous tongue, and more pages were turned. "Hmmmm. Yes, here." The book was held up at a great distance, like a soloist's hymn-book, so that the rector might fill

his lungs. "'He is the Good, the unchangeable, overflowing fountain of good that sends forth nothing but good to all eternity.' This
is the Almighty he's speaking of." More throat-clearing. The eyes
dared Sumner not to pay attention, not to find this as ludicrous as
he did himself. "'He is the Love itself, the unmixed immeasurable
Love, doing nothing but from love, giving nothing but gifts of
love to everything that he has made; requiring nothing of all his
creatures but the spirit and fruit of that love which brought them
into being.'"

"I can understand how it would appeal to Uncle Charles. How
could it not?" Sumner had never wished to cross swords with the
clergy, but this passage seemed harmless enough to him.

"Hate nothing but unkindness and deceit," his Uncle Charles
had been fond of saying. If he was quoting someone, he didn't
credit his source; he considered all wisdom to be in the public
domain. "When we act without honour and justice, we have
become barbarians." There was unkindness in this Horncastle
business now, Sumner thought. Perhaps there was also deceit. In
the thirty-one years of his life he had never once doubted the
truth of his uncle's opinion. Honour, Justice, Duty, Kindness,
Loyalty – all wrapped up in something even larger called Love.
Uncle Charles tended to capitalize such words, but never went so
far as to warn his nephew how much trouble they might cause.

"This is sentimentality, don't you see," said the Reverend Mr.
Trodd. He adopted a facial expression suggesting irony. "'Oh, how
sweet is this contemplation of the height and depth of the riches
of divine Love! With what attraction must it draw every thoughtful man to return love for love to this overflowing fountain of
boundless goodness.'" Here he paused, and chuckled. "The man
was more poet than theologian, and not much of a poet at that.
St. Paul's 'charity' shall have to continue to do."

The book, found wanting, was slapped closed and delivered
into the punishment of Logan Sumner's hand. "You will find a gap
for it, somewhere, in his library."

"Perhaps Mrs. Horncastle would be interested in the book," Sumner said. "If what you've read is representative, I can imagine her approving."

The Reverend made a sour face. Mrs. Horncastle, who was known to be a careful and thoughtful reader of the Bible and of countless religious books and pamphlets received in the mail, was not always prepared to allow the Reverend to impose his own interpretation upon his flock unchallenged. It would be better to have kept that book himself – Sumner could imagine the Reverend thinking – than to let it fall into the hands of Norah Horncastle.

"Return it to your uncle's shelves," he said. "With so many children to attend to, and a hotel to run, that dear lady should not be encouraged to waste time better spent baking bread and mending the sheets."

The sound of the great entrance door opening and then swishing closed against the wind saved them both from any need for a further exchange. Both men watched in silence as the Australian widow entered the church, a child on either hand. Having deposited the children, with whispers, in the back pew, the lady herself strode down the aisle to very near the front before taking a seat, apparently unaware of the two onlookers. Here she knelt briefly, head down, in silence. Then, amidst the rustle of skirts, she sat back and tilted down her head with eyes closed, as if lost in meditation or less formal prayer. She wore the same small, almost masculine hat atop her mound of copper hair that she had been wearing the day Sumner first encountered her in the cemetery. The gown and shoulder cape, he thought, made an even more attractive dress than she had worn that day, with dark ribbons and an ivory brooch at the throat.

Mr. Trodd, Sumner noticed, had brightened at the woman's entrance, but seemed almost disappointed now to see how he was being ignored. "Mrs. Jordan," he whispered, nodding wisely to Sumner. "I shan't keep you any longer, then."

Sumner was willing enough to leave unnoticed, but the rector's whisper caught the woman's attention – as it may have been meant to do. She looked up, she smiled, she stood up and made as though to approach them. Of course, two gentlemen must get themselves over to her first.

The broad smile displayed perfect teeth as proof of her satis-faction – Sumner thought of the hearty laugh which would not be far away. (His first glimpse of her, after all, was of a woman spinning like a carousel, roaring hilarity.) "Twice the expected pleasure!" One hand was given to either admirer. "The gentle-man who knows more of my situation than any other here." This was Sumner, given a sidelong flashing look. "And the gentleman who knows more of my soul." This was the Reverend, given a shallow but solemn bow.

"You wished a private interview?" the Reverend suggested.

Mrs. Jordan had not yet relinquished the great wide smile that promised laughter. For a moment, Logan Sumner was given her full attention: he was meant never to feel unappreciated again. One woman knew his worth. The Reverend Mr. Trodd was then looked upon as one looks upon a stern parent – with an almost apologetic hope of being further understood. "I am a newcomer here, I am a *stranger* here in this city –"

"And have found us not too unfriendly, I trust," said Mr. Trodd.

"– with critical decisions to make."

"Naturally, if I can be of any –"

"Of course, I've come for guidance, but thought I would look to the Father first – give Him an opportunity to offer His wisdom – before making a nuisance of myself to His servants."

Though Sumner found nothing especially comical in these words, he was as willing as the others to burst into laughter. One of her hands rested lightly against the Reverend's sleeve, as though to request that he not think too unkindly of her for this irreverence; the other slipped down and – unless he imagined it – clasped Logan Sumner's elbow, just briefly. As a man might do, a friend. Inviting him to – what? Consider himself somehow her ally? At the moment his head spun with confusion. Where did a solitary woman learn such boldness?

"Well," said the Reverend Mr. Trodd eventually, "we would not wish to interfere with communication of *that* sort. Young Mr. Sumner here was just about to leave, and I may be summoned from the vestry whenever you wish."

Dismissed, Sumner made his way up the aisle with Uncle Charles's spurned book beneath his arm. Walking was suddenly an unnatural act, requiring effort, when you thought the woman might be watching. Two sullen children's faces regarded his approach, a boy and a girl, and did not respond to his uncomfortable nod. It was a relief to pass them by – children, being unfathomable, were particularly dangerous. Even the wind outside was preferable.

Across the street, a figure emerged from the doorway of the little stationery shop. Sumner paused and narrowed his eyes, as he did here every time he came out of the church. No, that was no longer a stationery shop on the corner, that was the great stone-walled city hall which he, or someone, would one day build on the site. He had no trouble seeing its great arched entranceway and, directly above, the tall square tower with its broad round clocks. He saw the rows of tall windows behind boxes of flowers, a long balcony from which proclamations might be read, sharp peaks on the dormer windows in the mansard roof – something to rival the pictures he had seen of palaces in Vienna.

But here was a flustered Lady Riven-Blythe tilting across the street beneath a hat in the shape of an enormous platter, heaped with a battlefield of slaughtered pheasants. She leaned and swerved in the wind as though she had little control over the direction she might travel.

One of her tiny gloved hands held onto the hat; the other fluttered in greeting. "Oh, Mr. Sumner!" As though she were a little confused by his sudden appearance where she had expected to find only an inanimate building. She took hold of his arm and held on – perhaps he could be the anchor she'd been looking for, to keep her from flying off in the wind. She forced herself to haul in deep, long breaths, in the manner of someone engaged in a tug-of-war with her lungs, and allowed him to lead her into the shelter on the steps. "Foolishly . . . I have strayed too far . . . from my carriage. This wind was nowhere suspected when I set out to visit my –"

She stopped speaking. Her lips tightened as she let her gaze rake over the door to the church, as though she had only now realized where she was. "I've never felt entirely comfortable in this building," she said. "It is as though they left something behind. Or lost pieces of it off the coast of Chile." The door hinges seemed particularly guilty. "It is Canon Blackstock who is missing. The vicar out of my Weymouth childhood. I am not amongst the Reverend Mr. Trodd's admirers, nor is he amongst mine. He has too much love for the rules and too little for God."

Lady Riven-Blythe adjusted the angle of her pheasant battle-field. "But since we have met like this, I must tell you what I have learned: something terrible has happened. Brace yourself, since you are almost a member of that family. I have heard it this morning from my maid, who heard it directly from the chamber-maid at the Driard, that – oh dear – last night our Mr. Horncastle paid a visit to the Australian woman's room!"

Sumner resisted making any comment that might betray his alarm. Lady Alice had taken such a fierce hold on the sleeve of his coat, pulling it down to her level, that his hand had altogether disappeared from sight. "No doubt," he said, "the meeting was arranged to discuss some business matters between them."

A derisive snort from Her Ladyship. "Apparently the man *thrrrrrew* himself on his knees!" She lifted her heels for the crucial word. "*Thrrrrrrew* himself!" And dropped her heels smartly together on the step. "And begged to know what plans she had for him! He trembled all over – he shook." She was shaking herself, just to report it. "You see – he knows that he has not acted the gentleman in this matter, and that the woman has all of morality on her side."

Sumner did not say that the pious lady was only a few feet away at this moment, consulting the Almighty. (And keeping her secret: why she had squeezed a gentleman's elbow like a male conspirator.)

More heaving and breathing now. Then Lady Riven-Blythe plunged on: he'd begged the woman to leave town, he'd begged her to allow him to go on living his life as he had been living it here. (Horncastle begging!) But the woman would not let him off so easily. "Not only that – oh, my heavens, I am beside myself! He said *nothing*, made no protest at all, when she suggested that he abandon our Mrs. Horncastle altogether, to set things right." Though it meant reaching up, for such a diminutive woman, she had let go of his sleeve and gathered the lapels of his coat into her grip; she would make him quite breathless as well, by severing his neck. "What does it mean? The world spins under my feet!" They stood breathing – up and down – into one another's face.

"As it does under all our feet, Lady Riven-Blythe." He would not show how anxious he was to hear Horncastle's answer to the woman's demand – Mrs. Horncastle's fate! Nor would he suggest that they step inside and confront the woman for an explanation! He had a business which had been neglected too long. Taking Lady Riven-Blythe by the arm, he pushed out into the wind – which had the boiling-potatoes smell of the opium factories in it, as well as the stink from the mudflats. He suggested they wait for a satisfactory explanation from the Horncastles themselves. "Perhaps your servant's friend has misinterpreted. She has been mistaken before."

"But could not misinterpret the physician!" she cried. "You remember the gentleman from San Francisco –"

"To whom your chambermaid had issued a detective's licence the last time we spoke of this. Let's hope it was not your maid's friend who gave him his medical certificate as well, before putting the surgeon's knife in his hand."

A lumber-wagon clattered past, giving the wind more ammunition to throw. A ridiculous place to be conducting a conversation, engulfed in swirling clouds of dust. The figure of Queen Victoria passed by, in her local manifestation as Mary One-eye – tilting and half-running, carried along by the wind which had stirred up her veils and skirts into a turmoil. He drew Lady Riven-Blythe into a recessed doorway, where she turned up her tiny powdered face to blink away the grit that had settled into her eyes, collecting it onto the point of a folded lace-trimmed handkerchief.

She had not been distracted from her narrative. "He waited – the medical man – on the staircase, for Mr. Horncastle to come out of that room where he ought not to have been in the first place, and tried to block his descent. He issued a challenge! A *duel*! Of course, Mr. Horncastle pushed right past and did not answer him. The physician was scandalously drunk."

"While the second suitor – the long dark one – has no role to play in this?"

"He stands in corners, Mr. Sumner, just watching things." Lady Alice seemed to have noticed only now that there were corners and recessed doorways on this very block where an unpleasant foreigner might stand to watch. Even the dark figure of the iron church was not entirely free of suspicion. She shuddered. "One fails to imagine why it is that this woman is pursued by two gentlemen! Perhaps she inspires their male sympathy for a widowed mother? They wish to protect her, perhaps."

"I doubt that," said Logan Sumner. "She is a handsome woman. And I am afraid she has some of that mysterious quality that men find attractive without ever quite knowing what it is – even when our lives are made miserable by it."

Lady Riven-Blythe looked at him as though he had suddenly taken leave of his senses. Clearly his explanation sounded like nonsense to her. He had begun to suspect that even Uncle Charles, if he had known no more than Sumner did, or Lady Alice, might have suffered an ambivalence similar to his own.

"We must wait," Sumner improvised, "and trust Providence to provide the wronged lady with the means of rectifying matters to her own satisfaction without causing harm to others."

Though Lady Riven-Blythe bowed her head, confronting him with the carnage on her hat, he quickly turned away so that she might not suddenly look up and discover the uncertainty that was surely evident in his eyes.

13

INDEED, the world continued to spin, as Her Ladyship claimed, beneath their feet. So did the air around Logan Sumner's head, and sometimes even the matter contained in his skull. He no longer knew what to think, he no longer knew how he felt. His nervous habit of playing with his uncle's folding yardstick had accelerated to the point that he seemed to be never without it in his hand. He found himself taking the measure of everything in his world without really caring what they might be: the width of St. John's doorway, the length of Cleo's nose, the distance from his office desk to the window which overlooked the harbour – though no yardstick could measure the unpleasant smell from the mudflats which seemed to have settled into the summer air, mixing with the odours from the opium factories and the cattle-yards as though intending to stay.

All this indecision and uncertainty only served to feed the relentless energy of the legend growing down the length of Sumner's tombstone. He'd stopped visiting the cemetery himself, but made one of his employees responsible for riding out to add new words to the already granite-fixed sequence of altered convictions whenever they could not be resisted. What he wished to say was, "Smash it up, throw it in the sea, I don't care." But new thoughts, once they'd presented themselves, could not be ignored. If he were to throw the stone into the sea, he would soon be compelled to start a new one. Instead, the legend continued to grow. Sooner or later a third piece of granite would have to be added. Stone that might have been used in some beautiful building would be hauled out to the graveyard instead, and erected where it could provide him with an ever-lengthening tablet on which to record his thoughts.

The trouble was that, soon after inscribing an enthusiastic tribute to his relationship with the Horncastles, a psalm of praise to friendship, he'd realized that it could not be allowed to remain the final word. Bereft of parents, family, and wife, he might soon be bereft of this particular comradeship as well, since the Australian woman had driven an invisible wedge between them. Bitter about this, and aware of having been deprived in every direction of what one might call a natural history, he decided to give the world an array of imagined possibilities from which to choose. Perhaps he had been conceived in Singapore, one line of dignified letters suggested down the backside of the columned stones, the illegitimate son of a poor rice farmer; he was also descended from a long line of tribal chiefs in the Carolina swamps, set adrift in a hollow tree by an octoroon mother and rescued by a ship passing by on its way to the Horn; he was the child of a hanged Scottish cut-throat; he was an heir to the Russian throne, a child of the murdered Czar. Since life seemed determined to mock his assumptions, it seemed only right that he be the first to acknowledge the scorn. He was someone, after all, who had never seen his father, who had heard almost nothing of him from a reluctant uncle, and who had only the memory of a mother's singing-voice to link him to any life before the start of his own.

Zak did not hesitate to offer his opinion of this fantasy. "I guess if you weren't doing this crazy thing the stone would be doing it herself. All the rocks in the earth must want to get even with you, for what you put that first little piece of granite through. *H wah!* Forget it! We got better things to do."

By "better things" he meant another trial flight, this time for a slightly improved version of their flying machine. "You thought I was sick at home? I been working night and day in that barn. It's time we entered history, boss! You can tell your grandchildren you saw a miracle."

Before Sumner could witness this miracle, however, it was necessary to listen to Zak's account of once again spending a night in the city jail, again for committing the crime of saying a word. This time he had been heard informing a curious visitor from Boston that the tree with the reddish-brown bark and the shiny leaves all up on the ends of its limbs was a *lahb*. Mr. Piquette, who had been close enough to hear this, corrected him. "An arbutus," he explained to the confused visitor. "This fellow is having some fun with you, I expect. He knows that what you are looking at is an arbutus." Zak did not take kindly to being corrected in public, and the argument that ensued might better be described as a verbal brawl. Minor fisticuffs resulted, a policeman was called, and the official charge was once more "disturbing the peace."

"So all right, *tyee*-boss," Zak said. "This tree, what is the name a person has to use if he don't want to be tossed in that skookum-house again?"

Evidently Zak had decided to play stupid again. This would have to be got through before they could proceed to anything else. "You know what it is. And keep your voice down – I don't want them to throw you back in there again so soon. One of these times they may decide to keep you, to save wear and tear on the soles of your boots, going in and coming out so often."

There was not much chance of being overheard in Sumner's backyard, where Chu Lee had been instructed to serve Sumner and his guest their dinner. Here they were separated from the world on three sides by a great, tumbling, forward-leaning wall of leafy bushes – a house-high wave about to break, of crammed-together overlapping ocean spray and huckleberry and serviceberry and wild roses and salmonberry and snowberry and Oregon grape. The cascading pattern of varying shades of green surrounded and lapped against and apparently held upright a few thick coarse-barked trunks of soaring firs, as well as a half-dozen of the reddish-brown trees whose name was currently in question.

Zak may have been staging this conversation for the benefit of Chu Lee, who passed in and out of the house with their food. "The policeman says it's 'arbutus.' My uncle says it's '*lahb*.' He says our people have been calling it *lahb* for many years. So why isn't it *lahb* any more?"

"Lord, Zak, you've been doing this to me all my life. I'd learn one thing at school and then you'd tell me something else and then Uncle Charles would tell me we both were wrong. This tree that earned you a free night's sleep behind bars reminded them of something called a strawberry tree over there in Europe, so they decided it must be a cousin. '*Arbutus menziesii.*' That's Latin. You could read all this for yourself. Chu Lee could have told you that."

Chu Lee, passing by, bore an expression that suggested there were many things he might tell if he had not decided there was almost nothing he would.

"You ever see one of these strawberry trees?" Zak pushed his soft wide face too close into Sumner's own, his eyes squinted down to mere slits.

"They grow in Europe."

"You ever see one?"

"I've never been over there. I was born right here, like you."

"Then how do you know they exist? Maybe those trees over there in Europe aren't strawberry trees at all, maybe they're *lahbs*."

"Maybe they are."

"Something else. Why do the Yankees call the same tree something else right over there across the strait. 'Madrona.' Whose cousin did *they* decide to name it after?"

"Some Spaniard down in California did it. I suppose he was more of a romantic than a botanist."

"Maybe he had a cousin over in Spain with that name. He didn't know about this strawberry bush that nobody ever saw and nobody knows if it exists."

"I suppose he didn't. Maybe he was born on this continent too, and thought he had the right to name the things he saw. He had probably never even heard of a strawberry tree."

"So – the big white Queen waved her wand and things aren't any more what they used to be. Is that right?"

"That's right."

"And that's why I ended up in the calaboose for calling Mrs. Gristle a squaw. That old King-George-klootchman, the Great Mother, she says Mrs. Gristle is a lady, not a squaw. But she still hasn't decided if Mary One-eye is a lady too."

After they'd eaten, they rode through the woods to Zak's little farm and dismounted to walk through the dozen beautiful ring-necked pheasants that strutted about on the grass outside the barn, dragging their long, splendid tails – all of them descended from Uncle Charles's pet, gone half-wild now in Zak's indifferent custody. Inside the barn, Sumner saw that this latest flying machine had used up little of the company's lumber – the thinnest of pine strips formed a flimsy skeleton but it looked almost as much like an enormous insect as its predecessor. Perhaps a butterfly: slimmer in body than the horsefly, with wings that stretched out as wide as a house, resting on the wheels from Mrs. Carey's

English perambulator. "An improvement on du Temple," Zak said, though he left it to Sumner to understand what was said in the magazine articles about the famous Frenchman and those other inventors in Europe.

They waited until just after sunset before taking the machine out of the barn. Instead of boulders, however, this time the experimental passenger was to be a frightened piglet – Zak scooped her up out of a pen, squealing and kicking, to tie her four dainty ankles together with a piece of rope before placing her carefully inside the butterfly's belly.

"Found her lost on the road. She was grateful to be given a ride."

"But she's decided she'd rather walk, I think. Maybe she doesn't share your envy of the birds."

"She just don't know how lucky she is." Zak untied his horse and led it closer so that he could attach one end of his coiled rope to the butterfly's nose.

"Maybe she's already calculated that the grass out there and that ocean are not on the same geometric plane. She'd rather go back to her pen where there aren't such sudden differences in elevation."

Zak mounted his horse. There would be no reprieve for the pig. "But she'll be famous."

"Amongst the fish, maybe – their very first taste of pork."

It was just barely light enough so that they would not smash into trees and break their necks, yet dark enough so that they could be fairly certain of being unobserved. "It's not easy," Zak said, "to keep your genius secret in this nosy place." He towed the awkward butterfly past the white-stone Indian cairns and high up the grassy deserted slope towards the summit of Beacon Hill. Far below, waves crashed and sprayed at the base of the cliffs.

The strength and speed of Zak's remarkable horse gave the machine its start, pulling it down the grassy hill until, like a kite, it left the earth on its own. Already it looked as though this one would consent to glide. Once horse and rider had reached the edge of cliff, wind and the mysteries of air would have to take care of the rest.

Remarkably, the little machine with its porcine passenger did not merely topple off the world and make a Newtonian journey to the rocky beach, as its predecessor had done. For a moment it seemed as though it might actually rise into the wind and sail out – who knows how far? – across the strait or over the Pacific or around the world, if Zak should decide to release the uncoiling rope. Sumner was glad to be there, if only to see the look of wonder on Zak's face, the splendid white grin – perhaps he hadn't believed in the project quite so confidently as he would have Sumner think!

After only a few seconds of this astonishing success, however, the miracle decided to cancel itself out, the giant butterfly teetered, rocked, and tilted sharply, to angle downward into the waves.

Zak seemed to feel there was some kind of triumph in the fact that the machine had not flown apart on impact with the water, and that it in fact was floating. If the piglet was not to enter the history books, it seemed she might still have a chance to re-enter her mother's pen, and wait to meet her fate on another occasion. The prospect of rescuing a live survivor of this almost-successful experiment sent Sumner scrambling down the cliffs behind Zak, to leap into the prow of his boat.

They were not long in reaching the floating butterfly and its passenger, whose squealing was even louder now than before she'd found out what this ride could be like. Residents of nearby James Bay would think someone was being murdered. But when the boat reached the shoreline again she ceased squealing, recognizing the more familiar elements of earth; Sumner carried her under his arm as they climbed the steep trail up the cliff.

Behind him, Zak stopped to collect more pieces of broken boards from the beach. "I'll soon have every crack in the wall covered up if these things keep washing in." *Crack Proof Rubber Boots. Arancia. Canvas Leggings. Rosé.* Climbing the steep trail behind Sumner, he was forced to look into the pig's accusing eyes. "You'd think she might show some gratitude, eh, *tyee*-boss. How many other pigs get a thrill like this? At least it wasn't a butcher that rescued you off the street. You could be going snout-first into the grinder at this minute."

"I guess she'd rather wait until your invention is perfect, Zak. Then she can pay her money like somebody getting on an omnibus. You might not even have to tie her legs together for that."

When they reached the top of the cliff, Zak untied his waiting horse and mounted, using the tow rope to pull the dripping and lopsided wounded butterfly up the face of the cliff and back to the barn beside the little shack which Zak had encased with his col- lection of wooden words. Sumner carried the piglet. "Next time you visit your Miss Horncastle over at the muckamuck house, you can tell her you've been playing white knight to a squealing hog. Maybe it'll give her some hope – her turn could be next."

"God help me, Zak, I haven't gone anywhere near her since this business started. I haven't the nerve to face her. I don't know what I'll find."

Zak threw back his head and rolled it from side to side, "*H wah!*" He said some other words that Sumner did not understand. "Okay," he said. "It isn't too late yet. That's what we'll do. We'll go over to that Horncastle place and find your lady and tell her you can't stand it any longer."

"Now?"

"Tell her *I* can't stand it any longer. That's okay – I'll carry the pig if you don't want her to see you with it. We'll ask around – see if we can't find out who owns her, so we can give her back."

"Some other time, Zak. I'd rather just go home. A game of chess, if you want, before you go."

"No chess tonight. We'll celebrate. Drink to our almost- success. Well, you *saw* how long she stayed up! We can snoop around a little bit while we're there. Find out what your ladylove is thinking. I can't stand this European courtship business any longer. Why don't you just invite her out in the bush for a couple of hours – then you can tell her what you just did means that you're married now. That's what I did with that Haida woman. Remember her? Big nose, big hips, three big sons that came looking for her? She didn't stay around very long."

So much had Sumner been dreading what he thought he would find at the Blue Heron – scenes of anguish and anger, recriminations and threats – that he'd failed to imagine any other possibility. But the moment they set foot in the building it was clear that the news of this family disaster had had quite a different effect upon the atmosphere in the hotel.

The foyer was crowded – a person in every chair, many standing. Sumner overheard Mrs. Helm tell someone that she had just dropped in to see if the new Brussels carpet was as fine as it was said to be, "and by coincidence found Miss O'Reilly already here, drawn by rumours of this splendid new wallpaper." Several people appeared to be hotel guests who were reluctant to retire to their rooms or go out into the town on whatever business had brought them here, lest they miss something. What did they hope to witness? People spoke to one another but their eyes were continuously checking doorways. Did they think they might get a glimpse of the threatened wife, bravely holding up her head? Did they hope that the Australian woman might enter, and that a scene between the two principals might take place before their eyes? Better still, a scene involving *all* the principals. Carrie Clover looked as though she cherished hopes for a brawl between the wives, with scratching and screaming and hair-pulling to determine which should get to keep the husband – the sort of battle she claimed to have witnessed often while she worked as a "hurdy-gurdy girl" up in the Interior gold town of Barkerville, before she'd come south with an astonishing amount of gold-dust hidden in her corsets. No one seemed to find it peculiar that one of the two men passing through the hotel foyer held a piglet beneath his arm.

And the foyer was not the only part of the hotel to be over-crowded. They could see at a glance that the poolroom had no space left for newcomers either. Even the bowling-alley held far more people than could possibly play in one game. "It's almost irre-sistible," Zak said. "The temptation to let her loose in here. But we don't want anyone to treat her worse than a flying pig deserves."

They found Horncastle in the saloon bar, a busier man than he'd ever been before, apparently delighted with himself. Here was a former mayor demanding another rye. Here was Piquette from the newspaper, sipping a beer and obviously hoping for some insight he could develop into a story. Here were the Pinches, father and son, staring at their narrow reflections in the mirror. Even old Sam Hatch had swallowed his antipathy in order to patronize his most despised competition. Indeed, it seemed that most of the city's male population was crowded inside, with strangers enough to suggest that all the other hotels had been drained of their guests. While his hired help rushed back and forth amongst the tables, and Red Parker kept everyone happy at the bar counter, Horncastle contrived to be everywhere at once – visiting here, adding a comment to a conversation there, making sure these people were being looked after, delivering special orders to his bartender. With his sleeves rolled back to the elbows, his yellow satin waistcoat unbuttoned, his nugget collar-pin flashing gold, and his face the colour of the rose he had somehow entwined in his watch-chain, he might have been a man who had won an election, or seen his horse triumph in an important race, or learned that investments long ago forgotten had just made him wondrously rich. There was even a certain air of pleased secrecy about him, almost an uncharacteristic coyness. Yet he would not be drawn very far into conversation about the topic that had brought him so much trade.

"My secret? Why would you need to ask? It's obvious – I'm the most desirable man in town."

Though Captain Joshua Trumble (ret'd) had drunk himself into a state of open-eyed unconsciousness against one wall, his great wide grin suggested that he enjoyed the situation even while unable to contribute to it. Beneath his table, Horncastle's fox terrier Vicky lay at his feet, idly chewing on the cuff of his trouser leg.

The Sheepshank labourers, democratic in their desire to spread their patronage equally to every drinking establishment in and out of town, held down the corner table. "'Tis Mr. Sumner Construction and his right-hand man!" Stretch Halfpenny rose to his feet but quickly changed his mind when a neighbour's elbow prodded him in the ribs.

"Ye'll set down, Mr. Sumner, and take a glass wi' us?" said Alfie Stott.

"I will not at the moment, gentlemen, thank you. We're looking for someone who doesn't seem to be in the room."

"Aye, and so are we all!" shouted Jock MacCrae. "But the red-headed Australian is playin' hide-'n'-seek tonight. We've no' had even a wee peek at her yet, to see what she's worth."

"Fool!" Alfie Stott slapped the cap off Jock MacCrae's thinly populated head. "D'ye think Mr. Sumner cares a fig about a man's old forgotten wife when the same man's lass is 'idin' on 'im somewhere beneath this roof?"

"What he meant," said Zak, "is that we're looking for the owner of this pig. Found lost and worried in the streets. She might have gone on a long journey if we hadn't rescued her."

"Haw haw!" snorted Stretch Halfpenny, spraying his grog into his hands.

"What's this?" laughed Alfie Stott. "That ain't nobody's pig, that's Halfpenny's daughter." He kicked his boot at the rungs of Halfpenny's chair. "Look 'ere! That brat that run away – she's been found! I c'n tell it's 'er, 'cause she looks so much like yer wife."

"There's a table emptying in that other corner," Sumner said hastily, as Halfpenny's fists came up. "We'll have a quick drink and move on."

"No we won't," said Zak. "Not yet. Not until we've found the daughter of the house. Off to the family living-quarters we march – unless you want me to stand up on that counter there and ask them if anybody knows what she thinks of Logan Sumner."

Back in the foyer, Mr. Callow, the young Customs man from Ottawa, recognized Sumner and raised a hand as though to detain him, a sort of "Stop where you are" gesture which Sumner supposed came natural to a man in his profession, then proceeded across the carpet to shake his hand. That he was still resident in the hotel was his way of letting the world know that he was still waiting to be posted to Somewhere Better – in case they should presume to think him one of them. He shook Zak's hand as well, when it was offered, but did not comment upon the watching pig. Perhaps he thought it was usual for people with darker skin than his to carry livestock under their arm. "It may be that our friend has hired this woman to cause a scandal," he said. "Business could be no better if royalty were under the roof."

As usual, Mr. Callow moved on before any sort of real conversation could develop between them, and before he could begin the blinking and twitching that set in whenever an exchange lasted beyond the sort of opening civilities he could handle with the cool control and arrogance of his office.

Of course, there was no sign of Mrs. Horncastle anywhere. Or of Addie. A hired youth was standing guard at the reception desk. New arrivals would think they had chosen the most popular hotel north of San Francisco, certainly, or else had arrived in a city with a great shortage of space for sleeping, drinking, and visiting! None of the family was in sight, though. If Sumner was to complete his mission, he would have to intrude upon the living-quarters, and hope for the best.

Zak had turned away, to allow the former hurdy-gurdy girl to make a fuss over the pig – stroking its ears and making kissing sounds in its face. But Sumner's progress into the family quarters was impeded by Jerome, who came out through the door at the end of the hallway and promptly launched a physical attack on Sumner – punching his shoulder, throwing a tight headlock around his neck and trying to drag his head off – which was the customary sign of his pleasure at Sumner's arrival. But Jerome would not recommend that he go any farther into the family domain. "Addie will not be pleased to see you. Mama will not be pleased to see anyone. When they aren't exchanging cross words, they are horribly silent. They go off to separate rooms without explaining a thing to me."

Sumner retreated, with both regret and relief. Though he had failed to carry off the "visit from a family friend," the coward in him was pleased to postpone the inevitable pain of confronting those two women. "Let's go, Zak. This was a terrible idea. I don't know why I let you do this. Uncle Charles told me never to forget who's the boss, but you were always able to get me confused about almost everything."

"That isn't hard. You were already confused the day your uncle brought me home, you thought I was somebody's slave that wanted a little white boy to take orders from. You're still confused. You still haven't figured out what I am."

Instead of going out through the foyer and onto the street, Zak led them down a hallway and through the poolroom and out across the garden towards the back alley. "Just hold this pig while I water the horses. I'm ready to burst."

But before Zak had found shadows suitable for relieving himself, it became apparent that they did not have the rear portions of the hotel yard entirely to themselves. A voice on the far side of the shrubbery growled a protest. "Thought it was understood you were never to come here." Horncastle's voice.

Sumner froze. So did Zak, who had not yet had time to perform the act he had come for, and now stood in an agony of indecision.

"You didn't come, as you said you would." This was Mrs. Jordan. Had they stupidly got themselves trapped in a "boys' adventure" episode? "I warned you of this, I *warned* you – that I would come to you if you did not come to me. Now why don't we go inside? When I sent that little boy in with my card, I didn't expect you to come out and herd me into these bushes! I'd hoped to be invited in."

"I'll come. As soon as I've closed up for the night. Can't expect me to leave before then."

"I should have walked in through the front door like anyone else, I should have *marched* in if I had known you would treat me like this. I should have confronted you before an audience."

"Don't worry. Shall have something to offer you when I come."

"What sort of an offer?"

"A house."

"I've said nothing, I've said *nothing* about a house. What good is a house to me?"

"Offered to purchase it. The owner is moving south. Just a few blocks from here, up Yates."

"And so what are your plans, what do you plan to *do*? Give the *hotel* away? To your washerwoman perhaps, while we live happily ever after up the street – in poverty?"

"The house is for you. Only for you. It's inconvenient now for you to become my wife. Will furnish it as handsomely as you wish. Shall visit as often as you please."

"Visit! Let me understand this. You are offering to treat me as though I were merely your mistress?"

"Best I can offer now, though frankly I'd prefer that you simply go away."

The woman's rich laugh rolled out into the night. "And so you would 'visit.' I ought to have guessed that you would seize this opportunity to shower yourself with benefits!"

"If you go back to your hotel, I will go in and – *What the blazes is that? Who's there?*"

Sumner and Zak leapt at the same moment into flight. The piglet had betrayed them, having grown discontented with being squeezed against Sumner's breathlessly immobile rib cage. One squealed protest was enough to explode the entire shadowy yard into action. The two interlopers ran like schoolboys surprised in the girls' toilet, and did not stop running until they had left two full blocks behind and found a doorway deeply enough recessed for a noisy collapse and only gradual recovery.

"*Inconvenient!*" Fat puffing Zak was the first to recover, only to be overtaken again by laughter. "He finds it *inconvenient* right now to make her his wife! I guess he does, since he's already got one, upstairs in his bed."

"Lord, Zak. This isn't funny. We're behaving like children, but this isn't funny at all."

"Oh, you're right, this is no ordinary wife who's come to claim him, *tyee*-boss. This is an aristocrat of wives! You watch – she'll bring him to heel before the week's out. Damn – I still need to piss. Is anyone coming?"

"No one. This gets worse every day."

"And she'll do it with her tongue as her only weapon – unless you count the look in her eye. You see how it's done? That woman isn't bothered with European courtship rituals like you, she just takes what she wants. If you had even one drop of Indian blood in your veins, you would climb in one of those windows and go upstairs and find the girl and tell her: let's get the hell away from this madhouse. But your blood is all your uncle's blood, so you'd better go home where you can suffer some more and wonder what to do next."

14

SUMNER hoped to see nothing more of the Australian widow until the matter had been settled one way or the other. But the day after the incident behind the hotel, while he was substituting for an absent player in a cricket match between Horncastle's team and the team from Colwood, she and her two children stepped down out of a hired hack and crossed the grass towards the spectator benches. He could not escape, of course. Naturally she joined him. The children sat a short way off with an air of resignation, willing to watch the game but determined not to betray any interest. They had been threatened, he suspected. They were being paraded about in their sailor suits for the purpose of impressing someone.

She removed her gloves slowly, in a manner that made him feel almost as though he should not be caught watching. The extraordinary thing was to see those long, pale wrists so gradually revealed, sprinkled as though with brick dust. The gloves were quickly stuffed inside the great blue carpet-bag of Oriental birds which she had set down on the bench beside her, while she made exclamations about the morning's rain shower. "For a short while, everything smelled so fresh!" Her own scent was not something he recognized, though he imagined a large, violently coloured tropical flower with properties considered to be mysteriously dangerous. She would not stay very long, she said, but she had not been able to resist coming, "since he was so confident he would lead his team to victory."

"Even without the expert help of Mr. Tillman Bond, a fine spin bowler whose place I am pretending to take. He has been discovered to be a fraud – actually a certain Mr. Samuel Hutchins, wanted for a bank robbery in Montana. And has gone home to see if he can clear at least one of his names."

Indeed, Horncastle's team was on its way to victory, and Horncastle was, as usual, the star of the day. In fact, the Colwood team, having been dismissed for 150 runs, had been kept out in the field for the past three hours while the shadows of the Douglas firs lengthened across the grass, and while for most of that time the partnership of Horncastle and Horace Sheepshank had remained at the crease, with Horncastle consistently hogging the bowling. When Horncastle noticed Mrs. Jordan's arrival, he raised a hand in greeting but without any show of emotion which Sumner might interpret. She waved a glove in return. Obviously there must have been some further conversation between them after last night's overheard confrontation.

"He promised not to get into a shouting-match with an umpire, not to get into a *scrap* while I am here."

"Then your presence must be very important to him. This will be more constraint than I've ever witnessed. His own family isn't here, you'll notice – long ago embarrassed by his excesses."

She laughed – the hearty, relaxed laugh he had first heard in the cemetery, of one who not only enjoys the humour of things but takes real pleasure in the act of laughing itself – but she made no further comment on his observation. They watched in silence while Horncastle took two or three short skipping steps towards the approaching ball, to connect on the half-volley and to drive it deep into the field. The children showed a little interest while Horncastle and Horace Sheepshank raced to make three runs, but otherwise seemed intent on some private disagreement conducted in whispers.

"I know nothing about this game," the widow leaned close to confess, "but I find it agreeable to observe gentlemen absorbed in activities which give them pleasure. It doesn't really matter what happens to that ball!"

Of course, she wore the black dress of a recent widow, though the Paisley shawl she'd draped over her shoulder contained tear-drop shapes of a pale gold, a colour that was repeated in the gloves she'd put in her bag, and in the opal ring she wore on a middle finger. Sumner suspected that she could be out of the black altogether if she wished, free to indulge in all but the most vivid colours, but had chosen otherwise. Undoubtedly she knew how handsomely her pale complexion and red hair were shown off, but it was quite likely she had established in her own mind a date and an occasion for shedding the widow's weeds in favour of the greens and blues she almost certainly wore to advantage in the past. It would be, he thought, a spectacular transformation. He thought of her in pale-green silk, a young redhead going home to Manchester in her carriage, a smiling secret bride. He thought of her waiting in pale-green silk through all those years when no letter came, the youthful vigour in her hair and eyes growing duller, fainter, each time the postman went past without leaving her the long-awaited instructions from her far-off spouse.

Apparently Mrs. Jordan's attention was not entirely captured by the unbeatable Horncastle-Sheepshank pair. She spoke on quite another topic altogether. "I'm sure you have heard a good deal of talk, a good deal of *gossip*, since our conversation at the Driard." She raised both eyebrows and widened her eyes just a little. "Inescapable, I imagine." The laugh that followed was at everyone concerned – victims and perpetrators alike.

He decided this time to ignore the invitation to join in the laughter. "And painful as well, if one wishes to believe the best of one's old friends as well as new acquaintances."

And, indeed, she was as capable as he was of treating this matter with seriousness. "I've come as a victim of an injustice, Mr. Sumner. As you *know*. And with a belief, a *conviction*, that in a civilized world such matters can be set right by people who value integrity and honesty and virtue. It is our duty to the Almighty, I believe, to make the attempt. Unfortunately, the attempt may sometimes stir up idle tongues."

"I was raised myself by someone who believed we would be barbarians otherwise. But we must achieve this without hurting the innocent."

"You shall get no argument out of me over that!" She threw up both hands in surrender. "I would hate to think that my happiness had been won at the expense of someone else's. No, Mr. Sumner. I have far too soft a heart. I have always been incapable of inflicting harm, even when it might seem justified, having been myself too much the victim."

"I'm happy to hear that," he said. And indeed he felt much of his anxiety about this matter fall away. But not all. "Since I am thinking of a woman who has done no one any harm in her life, but who is in danger of being badly hurt by your efforts."

She put a hand on his arm. "A kind man! How I admire that in you. You are thinking of the woman who calls herself Mrs. Horncastle."

"I am."

"And so am I, and so am *I*! But we must not be guided by sentimentality, Mr. Sumner. Loyalty would make fools of us if we abandon clear thinking."

"Would you call it sentimentality to hope that a loving soul is not harmed?"

"Think of why we have laws and licences, Mr. Sumner, and legal marriages!" She was the older and wiser person now. "Otherwise, we would live in chaos." For a moment they both watched as Horncastle and Horace Sheepshank ran from wicket to wicket; thanks to some confusion amongst the fielders they succeeded in scoring four runs, and made no effort to hide the pleasure they took in this, and in the applause. "Sometimes people may get hurt, unfortunately. No one regrets that, no one *dislikes* that, more than I. But it is because they have chosen not to abide by the rules of civilization. You mustn't fear that I will play Madam Mephistopheles here. Your lady is safe enough." Here she paused and watched the activity on the field for a moment. "But she is only as safe as she has made herself from the law. This cannot be helped."

"Then there is nothing to fear," he said, "since Mrs. Horncastle is incapable of anything but good."

"The man is my husband. It is as simple as that. He signed a paper, he made promises, and now he must keep them. I have seen enough, since I arrived, to know that he has much he is giving to others which ought to be mine."

"I'm sorry," said Logan Sumner, "but it's all too confusing for me. I'm not accustomed to such a blurring of things."

"Have you come to this conclusion, Mr. Sumner, based on the size of my hand?"

Of course, Sumner had long ago taken his uncle's folding ruler out of his pocket and had idly taken the measurement of his surroundings while they talked: the width of the bench on which they sat, the length of his own right hand, his thumb, the distance between himself and Mrs. Jordan. But he had been doing it without thought, and was embarrassed to discover now that he had laid the ruler alongside Mrs. Jordan's ungloved hand, which she rested on the boards between them, and had even been wondering how its length compared to Adelina's. He quickly folded up the varnished wood and stuffed it away in his pocket, apologizing for his silly habit, but she was already laughing, and had put the hand on his in a manner that clearly invited him to laugh as well. He tried, but was not convincing.

Yet he found himself to have been captivated. This Kate Jordan was, unquestionably, a most attractive and intelligent woman, much more appealing in the flesh than as the subject of second-hand reports. It would not, he realized, be easy for a man to send such a woman away.

They almost missed Horncastle's downfall. Playing to the crowd as usual, he had evidently decided to win the match in style – with six runs needed to win he decided to hit the ball back over the bowler's head and send it flying over the boundary for a dramatic six. Unfortunately, the temptation to show off for a not-indifferent spectator did him in. A fielder standing on the boundary calmly caught the ball and ended Horncastle's career for the day. Nevertheless, with the game as good as won, he strutted off, waving his bat to acknowledge the applause, accepting compliments from team-mates and enemies alike and from the assembled spectators. At least he'd gone down in his accustomed manner, with flair.

When he approached the bench, he might not have been aware of Sumner's presence. "Surprised to see you here," he said to the woman who claimed to be his wife.

"But you told me about it yourself. Obviously, you wished to be admired."

"Thought you'd be busy packing your trunks."

"If you thought you had persuaded me to disappear, you were mistaken. I am *here* – and must be dealt with here."

Sumner would rather not be a witness to this, but he could not simply walk off. Horncastle's face grew long and serious and red, except for his small beak of a nose, which turned white. His fingers stroked his moustache. "Can't talk here." He meant before the children and this other person – Logan Sumner. "We'll walk." He angled out his elbow as an invitation for Mrs. Jordan to take his arm, but she ignored it. Her children watched mutely. "Last night I thought you'd agreed – to return to Ballarat."

"Then there is some problem with your ears, Mr. Horncastle. Now come, Laura, James, and say good evening to Mr. Horncastle. The four of us shall walk through the park while there is daylight. Perhaps the raccoons will allow themselves to be observed again. The children have seen *wild animals* peeking out from under the trees, Mr. Horncastle. And have also discovered secret places they would like to show you. Is that not right, James? Laura?"

"Yes, Mother." The children exchanged commiserators' glances and reluctantly followed the adults. Team-mates and opponents trooping off the field at the end of the game paused to watch an uncomfortable Horncastle walk with Kate Jordan's little family towards the less civilized portions of the park in search of raccoons and secret places. No one in the group thought to look back at Logan Sumner, abandoned in his borrowed white flannels at the bench and more confused than ever by his own alarming thoughts.

15

I<small>F</small> even Uncle Charles might have had difficulty giving advice to someone struggling with mixed feelings about James Horncastle and the woman in black, he certainly would not have hesitated a moment before advising a man who had discovered himself in love. No thinking was required in order to determine the proper procedure in such a circumstance, since centuries of tradition had laid out the required path. Sumner had long ago made his feelings clear to Mr. and Mrs. Horncastle, who had already guessed his intentions and teased him only a little before making it clear they would bless the union if he ever got up the courage to approach Adelina – who might, they suggested, be more surprised than they had been themselves.

What would Uncle Charles advise in these drastically altered circumstances? Certainly not silence, withdrawal, the face of indifference. He would recommend, Sumner felt certain, that his nephew make his intentions clear to the young woman as soon as possible, so that she might understand in this time of turmoil that she had a friend to whom she might turn for sympathy and strength.

Uncle Charles on women: "A woman is a more sensitive, more delicate creature than a man, and of course more spiritual – closer to the angels, in fact – and must be treated at every step with courtesy, kindness, and a gentleness of spirit." Subtle flattery, exaggerated compliments to their appearance, and gifts to satisfy their possessive instincts were quite acceptable, of course, so long as one never lost sight of one's own role in a courtship – "to pursue an elevation to the status of her protector, provider, and undesisting adorer."

He stroked the tiny head of his gorgeous pheasant and spoke to the young Sumner of a need for a mistress in the house, and of his own sad failure to acquire one – despite an extended journey Home for that very purpose. The problem in this city was, he said, that too many women were far too quickly swept off their feet by the rougher sort of fellow the climate produced. "One mustn't stoop to imitating them, of course. One is simply more patient, and must set one's sights on the young lady who has not yet been corrupted by the local tendencies." It was Uncle Charles's idea that a man must imitate the upper classes in this, as in other matters. "This is how the race improves. Others in town choose to imitate the lowest sort of examples, but you and I cannot do likewise without inflicting terrible damage upon our immortal souls."

The awe with which Sumner had learned to look upon the female of the species had rendered him almost incapable of speaking to women for a number of years. Fortunately, Uncle Charles had long before his own death made the preliminary arrangements for Sumner's marriage to Julia Morrison – her family had been his close friends – and there was little for the two principals to do themselves beyond discovering their willingness to go along with the plans. But within a month of their marriage his bride, who had been raised to expect precisely the sort of treatment Sumner had been raised to give, had drowned in a boating accident when Sumner was only beginning to discover her to be more

than she appeared – more complex, more mysterious, more intelligent, and far more unpredictable. In the years since, with
neither his wife nor Uncle Charles as his guide to the world of
women, he felt himself to be an explorer trusting his life to what
he suspected was an unreliable and perhaps outdated map.

So Sumner was somewhat relieved, that afternoon, to find
Addie behind the reception desk of the Blue Heron, with neither
parents nor brothers and sisters anywhere in sight. Never before
had she looked so pretty, it seemed to him, or so hospitable in her
role as receptionist. Was he interested in signing up for a room,
she wanted to know, addressing him as though he were a total
stranger. She turned the registration book towards him on the
counter and offered her pen. For a moment his heart stopped. Of
course he was not about to risk disaster. "Not today, thank you,"
he shouted, perhaps a little too jovially. "But would a young lady
be willing to abandon her post for a sunny afternoon of boating?"

She abandoned the desk with pleasure. "Moira is perfectly
capable – if I can find her."

But of course Jerome must be found as well, and asked to accompany them, as he had on many other occasions when her
parents were unavailable. Fortunately, though Jerome considered
his own attentions to be every bit as important as his sister's to
Sumner's well-being, he had little interest in riding in a small
wooden punt and preferred to throw a fishing line in the water
from the edge of the pier. Sumner had to promise that when
Jerome joined them later at Lady Riven-Blythe's gardens farther
up the Gorge, they would talk seriously about the possibility of
Sumner taking him on in his firm – this despite his father's refusal
to let him quit school. Jerome had made it clear on a variety of
occasions that his ambition in life was to put himself in a position
where he would be taking orders from Sumner even while giving
Sumner brotherly advice.

Having made up his mind to state his intentions before the
afternoon was over, Sumner had no patience for waiting until

some appropriate moment. If he hesitated now he would be silent forever. A harbour seal accompanied them, watching with its great round eyes, as though it knew of Sumner's resolve and intended to make certain he acted upon it. They passed between the gardens and tennis courts of several great homes while he gathered his courage. Herons along the shoreline paid no attention, interested in nothing but movements which promised food beneath the water.

"One of the prettiest spots on earth," he suggested, pausing with the oars above the water. "Perhaps there will be people like us in one of those novels you said you wanted to write, boating here on a sunny afternoon. And those arbutus trees along the bank, with their flowers turning to clusters of berries. And that kingfisher waiting on the dead cedar."

She made a face. "Don't be silly. There will be rills and dells and ferny glens in my stories, not *this* old salty thing, with creatures crawling along the bottom, and smelly seaweed!" She shifted her parasol and tilted her head to examine their unworthy surroundings. A pair of mallard ducks was following them. "There will be sweet-smelling rivulets, and mossy vales. And thrushes singing in the hedgerows."

"Will you put your sisters in it, then? And Jerome? Will you put me?"

She looked at him directly and laughed. "Don't you ever *read* anything, Logan Sumner?" Perhaps her mouth was the most perfect mouth he had ever seen. "If anyone ever put us in a book, we would be just the people passing up and down the streets, or eyes looking out from the woods. A person couldn't write a story about us, we just aren't right for books! The main characters would go Home and forget they had ever seen us."

He was astonished all over again each time he discovered how very pretty she was when her dark eyes flashed at him. "But they will be love stories, surely? And will the young gentleman not take the young lady boating when he wishes to propose?"

She pulled a face. "On a lovely stream, perhaps – not *here*! A stream with swans. No – in my stories they will be guests at a ball, at a country estate, and will fall in love while they're dancing. And he will propose marriage while they're strolling the next morning across the heath, or – no – over the moors, or – no – walking along the strand."

"The strand?"

"The beach, of course."

"But you have never even seen a heath. Or the moors! Or a hedgerow or a mossy vale."

It was clear that there was no way to approach his topic gently. They travelled as far as the first turn in the narrow waterway in silence, while Sumner convinced himself to abandon evasion and get on with his purpose. While they passed through the shadow of an overhanging maple he swallowed hard and then inade-quately tried to express the manner of his regard for her. Neither of them would later remember precisely what he said – a stum-bling succession of half-sentences and embarrassed phrases, an "unwarranted hope," an "astonishing beauty," and a "never enough of your companionship." Words that he had all his life been using freely and without much thought now sounded so foreign and curious they might have just arrived in a packing crate from India, without either labels or instructions. The seal's round head, like a floating ball, moved around to the opposite side of the boat, perhaps for a better opportunity, to see how the lady was taking this.

The young lady seemed to find nothing surprising in Sumner's clumsy words. Having broken the ice, and wanting to get this over with as soon as possible, he went on to outline his hopes for the future in a most indirect manner – stumbling over his words, in fact, and not at all certain he was saying what he meant. As he might have expected, she blushed while she heard him out, keeping her eyes lowered, but did not look as confused as his inad-equate speech might have justified. Without raising her attention higher than the pretty toes of her shoes, she thanked him for his sentiments, "which your behaviour has made much clearer, thank goodness, than your awkward tongue seems capable of doing."

He stood, and used one of the oars to push them through the speckled shallows beneath a row of willows. When she looked up at him again, she held out her hand so that he might hold it and press his lips to her fingers. Then she promised that she would tell him what was in *her* heart very soon. She was already quite certain of her feelings, she said, but knew the danger in putting things to words – since words that have been spoken could not be easily revised without causing pain. And pain, she said, glancing off in the direction of the leafy woods, was something she hoped never to cause anyone in all her life.

This was perhaps her longest speech of their acquaintance – breathlessly delivered as though she were desperate to hold off some rushing advance. Meanwhile, he held that hand. The seal, perhaps embarrassed, had disappeared beneath the water. When the unattended boat drifted against the bank, his balance was abruptly unsettled by the collision, and unsettled further by the rocking motion as the boat slipped away from shore. Rather than fall into the water, or collapse on top of Addie, he reached up and grabbed hold of a willow limb – but this meant that the boat, now caught in a current, slipped out from beneath him. Addie could not be blamed for laughing at this fool who was left dangling by one hand from an elastic tree-branch, swinging this way and that as he tried to reach up with the other hand for a firmer grip on the bouncing limb, his toes dangling only inches above the water.

Now the seal had resurfaced to watch this latest proof of human unpredictability from a safer distance. It seemed a damnably long time before Addie grabbed the oars, took control of the boat, and rowed it back to insert it in the space beneath his dangling feet. There was no point in trying to recapture the earlier mood of the afternoon now, with her bursting out in giggles behind her hand one moment and then trying too hard to achieve a sober

face in order to apologize the next. Nevertheless, she allowed him
one short kiss on her right check as he helped her out of the boat
onto the little wharf at the foot of the Lady Riven-Blythe's
gardens. Next door, a woman looked up from picking an armload
of ruby peonies and smiled.

He might have felt convulsed with embarrassment just to
think of the incident on the water if he had not recalled that suffering was a well-established part of the ancient ritual – at least as
it had been interpreted for him by his uncle. Though he would not
likely be presented with actual dragons to slay or dangerous journeys to take, he would perhaps be required to suffer and overcome
the slings and arrows of humiliations brought on by his own foolishness, as though these were the tests he must pass.

Nevertheless, even with so little encouragement he could
already taste the life that would be his on the far side of the tests he
would eventually pass – a quiet wedding, apple blossoms, happy
in-laws welcoming him into the family, gentle but tempestuous
love-making in the stateroom on their honeymoon trip, sitting
down to dinner together at Uncle Charles's table, discussing plans
for the house he would build her one day, thinking even of children.

It seemed that all the town was there before them in the
gardens, which Lady Riven-Blythe threw open to the public on
Sundays. Elderly couples sat at tables up by the house, taking tea
with its owner – who waved her greetings to the new arrivals.
Families strolled amongst the flower-beds, their children more
interested in chasing one another along the pathways than in
admiring snapdragons or wallflowers. Sailors walked with their
girls amongst the rhododendrons. Ahead, one young woman had
two sailors to herself, one on either arm, though it seemed that
they needed all six legs in order to stay upright – the sailor on the
left leaned in against his friends but possessed feet that tended to
wander in the opposite direction.

"Father and Mother used to bring us out here on Sundays," Addie
said, "if we weren't picnicking elsewhere, with the Sheepshanks.

But they haven't brought us lately at all, and we haven't picnicked with the Sheepshanks since last year's Twenty-fourth of May."

She allowed him to hold her hand, just briefly, as they passed through the rose garden, then retrieved it. "Why haven't you been to see us – until now?"

"Work," he said, though he was uncomfortable with even the smallest of lies. "I had no way of knowing how much your father's crisis has affected the family's life. I thought you might prefer not to see any outsiders."

"If I am not mistaken, you have just this afternoon spoken as one who wishes to be an outsider no longer."

"I feared walking into a melodrama. I'll confess it. I was not certain I would not discover you and your mother and sisters tearing out handfuls of your own hair and cursing mankind."

"Mother does not tear out handfuls of hair." She smiled. "She believes in a Divine intelligence which, if appealed to, will adjust all things in the direction of a natural good. The rest of us mill about in confusion."

Ahead, there was a woman's scream. This was the girl with the two sailors, they saw, who stood back with both hands over her mouth while the bluejackets directed blows at one another which seemed delivered in slow motion, seldom connecting. One did connect, however, and the struck sailor dropped to the ground. He lay back, stretching himself out, as though he had been hoping for this excuse to take a rest. When his companion started to kick him, however, he rolled away down the trail, and waited while the girl put a stop to it with a long, piercing scream which had them all slapping hands over their ears, including strangers who appeared from behind the lodge-pole pines.

When the victorious sailor had helped the other to his feet, and stood supporting him, the girl began to cry. She would have nothing to do with the sailors, but allowed a stranger, a woman, to offer a comforting shoulder.

Addie started down a trail that led into beds of shasta daisies and away from the commotion. "Men are sometimes barely human."

"They were sailors," Sumner said. "And drunk."

"You must promise me. You must promise you will never never never behave like my father, you must never abandon us."

"But your father has not abandoned you."

"You will! I will find out when I am fifty that you have had wives all along. Strange women will knock on my door and claim you for themselves. I will never, never, allow myself to depend on a man. Oh, you *must* promise!"

"But it is unnecessary, I assure you."

"You will abandon me. You don't even know it yourself. Your promise means nothing."

Suddenly Jerome was with them. "I know what you're talking about."

"You do not," Addie said. "Let's go to the boat immediately. Moira will be anxious for me to relieve her."

"Please talk to Papa," Jerome said, tugging at Sumner's sleeve. "You know he respects you, even though he laughs behind your back. Tell him to get rid of that woman. Tell him to make things go back to the way they were."

Jerome had always believed that Sumner could do anything, but this time Sumner must disappoint him. "I recommend patience." He felt himself to be a hundred years old. "Trust your parents to work this out between them, with your happiness in mind."

Addie laughed – a cruel laugh, Sumner thought. "Sometimes you seem more innocent than Jerome!"

"I shall go south, and work on the Panama canal," Jerome said.

"And die of malaria?" Addie said. "Like Andrew's brother."

"I shall sign up to serve in India, then." Again he tugged at Sumner's sleeve. "If you can't make things right, will you ask him to explain? He won't speak to us. He won't tell us a thing."

"Baby!" Addie said. "Do you think Mr. Sumner can make anything different?" She seized a pink Chinese rose and wrenched it so violently from its stem that it came apart. Petals fell at her feet. "This gentleman will abandon us too, for all his promises." She shook the few remaining petals to the ground, and stood looking into the green sepals in her hand, a naked star. "He will play the man's game, too, and leave us to wonder what we have done wrong."

How should he answer, when it was clear she would believe nothing but what she had already decided? It seemed he was left to steer himself through these perilous waters. And to wait, when he wished to have instant happiness. The heart longed for the opportunities of the ancient knight, but the viscera hoped for a quick and easy triumph. He was, he could not help knowing, too timid a lover by far!

16

"SHE has been asking more questions of bankers," said Mr. Cyrus Fletcher, who asked questions of bankers himself in pursuit of his land-development schemes. "She has become acquainted with Mrs. Hatch," reported Lady Riven-Blythe, "who is a one-woman storehouse of everyone's private business, provided it is unflattering enough."

She was observed sitting in a window across the street from the Blue Heron where for hours she watched the guests come and go. No doubt she had already calculated Horncastle's weekly profits, and estimated the total wealth of his guests from the quality of their dress.

From his position in the choir, Sumner saw her enter St. John's and pause for a moment at the head of the aisle while she looked over the congregation, found the Horncastle family in its accustomed row (without Father – did she take this as a hopeful sign?), and then positioned herself where she might keep them within her field of vision even while she appeared to be gazing with rapt attention on the Reverend Mr. Trodd. He could not get away afterwards without hearing from someone who presumed to know precisely what the woman had been thinking during the service. "She is deciding whether she will take the children as well."

She had also won a sort of modest social triumph, it was generally known, having been invited more than once into the Cyrus Fletcher home. Mrs. Fletcher had been intrigued enough by the woman when they shared a table at the church lawn party to invite her for tea where she might be introduced to Mrs. Fletcher's intimate friends. Here Mrs. Jordan proved to be such a successful guest, keeping the ladies in stitches with the hilarious adventures of four innocent sisters running a boarding-house in a rough colonial town, that she was even included amongst the guests at a small dinner party when Mrs. Bold was unable to come at the last minute because of a fit of sneezing. Here, at the dinner table, she was even more of a success with the husbands than she had been with their wives. Perhaps it was her colourful tales of outwitted bush-rangers that won them over, or her amusing account of how she married Mr. Horncastle right under her sisters' noses, or her exuberantly acted-out report of the panicked councillors racing their carriages all up and down the Ballarat streets in search of the Duke of Edinburgh. At any rate, Mr. Bold and the Percival Fosters stayed behind once she had returned to her hotel, in order to exchange opinions, and they agreed at once that, though she was a little too rough and direct for their taste, in the usual manner of her countrymen, and altogether too secretive as well when it came to letting you know what she really thought about things, she was charming enough, a charming woman, and very good company. Since she'd already had their sympathy as a matter of principle – a woman treated badly by a man – they'd been relieved to discover her to be such engaging company as well.

Mrs. Foster had one small reservation, however. "Behind her stated Cause I detect another, awaiting its turn. You heard the sort of questions she asked. She has designs upon the upper crust! I should imagine she would drop us in a moment if her hopes should ever be fulfilled."

"Then she has much to learn about life," proclaimed Mrs. Fletcher, who had at one time entertained similar hopes. "Do you see her at Lady Crease's table? Can you imagine her at Cary Castle? She will discover that she has already overreached herself and has only poor Lily's runny nose to thank for it."

"Still watching, though – what? Still looking us over. The waiting cougar."

"And one begins to understand why she is trailed everywhere by two unwanted suitors. A remarkable thing!"

"Not any more. Whatever evidence she has been weighing since she arrived, she has made at least one decision. She has shaken off the one-eared cattleman, who has been told that his advances are no longer welcome."

How the long slim drover was given this information was something Amelia Fletcher was soon able to report all over town, having witnessed the encounter that separated that particular man from his hopes. "She was dining alone at the Driard, with her children. Cyrus and I were dining there as well, only a few tables away – the anniversary of our marriage."

The woman was eating a roast chicken, Mrs. Fletcher reported, and the children were having roast beef. The Yankee-Australian came in and crossed the room with his great long strides and did not take his hat off until he'd reached the table. He made as though to sit with them but she shook her head. They exchanged words. He pulled over a chair from a neighbouring table and sat, but she continued to eat her dinner as though he were not there. The children were instructed to imitate her.

The room had grown quiet enough for Amelia Fletcher to hear a few words: "persistent" and "tiresome" and "unreasonable" from her; "time enough" and "ridiculous hope" and "making a fool of yourself" from him. Eventually she raised her voice so that anyone might hear: "You are to understand, Mr. Hawks, that I have made a decision, you are wasting your time with this relentless pursuit." The man stood up and raised the hand that held his hat as though he intended to hit her. The little girl started to cry. For a moment the cattleman and the woman stared at one another, and then he said, "You'll be sorry." She said, "Please leave," and he swung out with his hat and knocked over the little vase of daisies in the middle of the table. All three of the diners jumped back from the spilled water, and the man tugged on the cloth just hard enough to pull some of the cutlery and one or two pieces of china off onto the floor. She stood up, suddenly, as though this last act had transformed her into someone else altogether, and slapped him across the side of his face, and then cried for someone to take this monster out of her sight. "You should arrange to sail home immediately, Mr. Hawks, for I do not wish, I hope *never* to see you again. I shall call for the assistance of the police if you even speak to me in the street." Then, reported Amelia Fletcher, she turned to address the room: "Mr. Hawks claims to have a fortune stashed in a Melbourne bank for the woman who will have him, but he is a stupid, evil man, who consistently smells (as my daughter has pointed out) like rotted fruit."

"There you are," said Cyrus Fletcher. "She will not have anyone but her Horncastle. She's the sort of woman who would row her boat halfway around the world to take back a foaming distempered mongrel dog just because it was *hers*. And if the dog is being petted and made a fuss over by everybody that likes a dog with a little spirit, then she's just got to have it back no matter what she has to do to get it." He might have stopped there, but was pleased to discover that his conceit might be developed even further. "And if that dog has got itself a nice hotel that looks as though it could make money in a boom time or another gold rush, then she'll fight tooth and nail to get him back so she can crawl into his doghouse hotel and be looked after for the rest of her life. Naturally she's not interested in those two other hounds that came with her on her rowboat."

The drover, however, did not sail for home immediately. Sumner saw him a few evenings later in Horncastle's bar, drinking with the labourers he was now working with at Sheepshanks' farm. He kept his wide-brimmed hat on his head and leaned back against the wall with a smile on his face that suggested he found his companions amusing in ways they would not understand themselves. Horncastle stood talking by the table.

"Anything at all?" said the cattleman. He looked to his companions for confirmation of something Horncastle had said.

Horncastle appealed for confirmation himself. "Am I not telling the truth, gentlemen?"

"Aye," said Horace Sheepshank. "I've seen Horncastle lay down money on the length of time it would take a blade of grass to grow."

"You see," said Horncastle to the cattleman, "and that does not include the horses, or the ratting dogs, or the sort of thing we bet on here on a Friday night."

"There ain't a sporting man in town like our friend Hornswoggle here. There ain't a man within a thousand miles more willing to stake his money on a good bet, provided it's interesting enough."

"But I bet he's turned down invitations," said the cattleman.

"Not if there's a penny to be made," Sheepshank insisted, "and not if there's any sport to be got out of it."

"And not if I find the offer original enough to tickle my fancy. You sound like a man that's working up to an offer. Let's hear it. Come on. Let's have it so we can take your money from you and make you wish you had never brought it up."

The cattleman looked with amusement at the farm labourers around his table, who had gone silent in the whirlwind progress of the conversation. Then he looked up at Horncastle and took off his hat. "I can't do it. For you'll have to turn me down, and feel the fool after all yer braggin'."

"Try me, man. Never turned a good one down if it was original enough. Just not capable of saying no to something that tickles my fancy. If it's something I feel uneasy about myself, at least I'll keep the book."

"Very well, then. Will you bet or keep book on this? My money says" – he laid out several ten-dollar bills on the table, and placed a hundred-dollar bill on top – "that the lady who calls herself Mrs. Jordan gets her first husband back, and has him legally into her bed before the summer is out."

"*My God.*"

This ejaculation came from a neighbouring table. No one else spoke. Horncastle looked at the pile of Hawks's money and grew pale. He looked at Hawks, whose grin had slid up farther on one side of his face, in the manner of one who has contempt for every-one he deals with.

"There you are, Horncastle," someone said. "You never bet on nothing like that before."

"Nor ever will," said Horace Sheepshank. "Mister, you better put that money away."

"Not at all," said the cattleman, without relaxing his grin. "This is a chance for your most celebrated betting man to take on a wager that's more interesting to him than any he's had before."

Horncastle turned and walked back to the bar where he placed his hand on the polished surface and looked down at his toes for most of a minute; then he turned and walked back to the table and stared at Hawks again, while he bounced just slightly on his toes and his fingers repeatedly stroked his moustache. His eyes seemed to have shrunk to tiny hard seeds. Around the edges of his emerald-green satin waistcoat the material of his white shirt showed the darkened stains of new sweat. It must have been obvious to everyone in the room that the man was in a kind of agony over this. "Trying to decide if I throw you out on your ear."

The cattleman kept one finger on his money, ready to withdraw it or to push it forward, but still did not relax his grin. "My money says the widow gets 'im," he said. "Whose money says the lady upstairs will keep 'im?"

"You see!" Horncastle jerked forward and grasped the edge of the table. "Cannot take part in a wager that would insult the lady upstairs."

A sigh around the room. Perhaps Horncastle had passed a test.

"Does that mean you'll have nothing to do with it at all? How will you stand in this bar and brag about yerself in the future, when everyone knows the town's great bettin' man has turned down the most interesting bet that's ever been offered him?"

Again Horncastle paced. He would look at no one. The walls, the ceiling, the floor were stared at. "By Jove!" He went out of the room and was not seen for a few moments and then came back and crossed the bar and stood before Hawks's table. "By the lord Harry I'll keep the bloody book. You forced me into it, you bastard, I don't like it at all but you hardly left me a choice. You can bring your money to me behind the bar and I'll record it but you'll never get me to talk about it or place a bet myself."

It appeared to Sumner that there was general approval in the room. Horncastle had kept himself clear of something that would have made him look bad, but at the same time had not betrayed his reputation. Of course, Sumner was dismayed to realize, Horncastle would have to keep out of it now, whatever he might really feel about the matter. Being a sportsman, he could not allow himself to affect the outcome, once the bets had been made. Whether he was aware of it or not, he had put himself in a position where he could not be seen to favour one wife over the other.

He could only sit back and let what happened happen. There was nothing any of them could do now but wait to see what the Australian woman did next.

In fact the lady seemed to have decided that the old tactics were not going to work with James Horncastle and that something more drastic would be needed. What that was to be, Sumner discovered the next morning when he took the plans for Horace Sheepshank's new barn down to the Red Geranium Café, where he had arranged to meet Sheepshank in order to talk him into a steeper roof grade than what he'd been asking for. The café was nearly deserted this late in the morning, except for the proprietress, Carrie Clover, and a pair of travelling salesmen (farm machinery on one side of the table, shoes on the other) arguing the relative merits of San Francisco and pre-war Atlanta. Mrs. Piquette sat by herself at the window with a pot of tea, gazing out across the street to the activity in the harbour, where the steamship *Idaho* was setting out for Port Townsend. Sea-gulls, screaming in its wake, decided to follow it across the invisible border. A family of Indians beached their canoes and came up to the street with baskets of fish to sell. Hotel employees had begun to congregate along the docks, to compete for the custom of whatever travellers might be arriving on the *Western Slope* from New Westminster.

He hadn't argued with stubborn Horace Sheepshank for half an hour when the Australian widow appeared at the window. She peered in, with a puzzled expression, then opened the door and stepped inside. You could not avoid noticing how tall she seemed, perhaps because of the erectness of her posture. She wore a piece of white lace at her neck, and a sprig of tiny white flowers.

She seemed pleased to have spotted Sumner, and immediately advanced, holding out the hand he was expected to grasp and bow over. "Perhaps you could tell me why the newspaper office is closed?"

Having risen to his feet when she entered, Sumner continued to stand, while everyone looked at the editor's wife at her window table, who appeared somehow offended by this intrusion.

"I've been 'elpin' me man all mornin' and was only takin' a break," Mrs. Piquette defended herself. "When Mr. Piquette 'as to go out, he'd rather 'ave me behind the counter than Miss Marklin, but I will not go without me mornin' pot of tea."

Mrs. Jordan moved towards the woman at the window table, reaching all the while into her awkward carpet-bag with the impossible birds embroidered into its pattern of flowers and trees and vines. Eventually she brought out a small piece of paper, which she consulted for a moment before speaking. "Would you arrange, would you make *arrangements*, to have this published in tomorrow's paper?"

"Sit down and 'ave a cup," said Mrs. Piquette. "We'll go back to the shop directly. I've more than 'alf a pot yet that I don't intend to waste."

Mrs. Jordan did not sit, but pushed the piece of paper at the seated woman in the manner of an impatient duchess sending off a hired girl on an errand. "I have other matters to attend to, I have things to do. Perhaps if you opened the office briefly you could then return to tea. Or I could simply leave it with you here."

It did not take Mrs. Piquette long to read whatever was printed on the piece of paper. It took longer for her to recover her composure – her face coloured, she looked out the window, she looked at Sheepshank, she looked at the salesmen, she looked at Logan Sumner, everywhere but at the woman standing across the table from her. "This cannot be printed," she said. "I'm sorry."

She pushed the paper back to Mrs. Jordan's side of the table, but Mrs. Jordan did not reach for it. "It is startling, I grant you. But I am afraid it is necessary. Please tell me how much I must pay and I shall leave it with you here."

"It is himpossible," the editor's wife insisted. "Me 'usband would throw a fit."

"What can be so terrible?" said the farm machinery salesman.

"This is a big mistake," said Mrs. Piquette. "Maybe you don't understand what you're doin', missus."

"Read it to us," demanded the shoe salesman.

"I shall read it to you myself," said Mrs. Jordan with impatience. She shook out the folds in the paper and held it at arm's length. "I don't see why anyone should be afraid of a few words. Here it is. A piece of information to put before the public, that is all."

Yet she did not read. She looked up and found Logan Sumner's anxious gaze and held out the paper to him. "Please, Mr. Sumner. If you would."

He had no choice, of course. And he was as curious as anyone there. The handwriting was small, in a light-blue ink, the progression of words straight and tidy. "'This is to advise . . .' Excuse me. 'This is to advise the citizens of this city that the woman who calls herself Mrs. James Horncastle, much admired and respected here, is in reality –'"

His throat closed against the next words, which he had seen advancing but had not fully understood until they were upon him. His face, he realized, must be scarlet. "I'm sorry. This should not be read aloud." His foolish voice could be heard quavering through even those few words.

Mrs. Jordan took back her paper from Sumner's hand, and prepared to do the unpleasant job herself. "How can we be frightened by a few words? '– is in reality an adulteress –'" She paused for only a moment, perhaps because of the drawn-in breaths, before going on. "'– an adulteress, having been married to a certain Mr. Thompkins of Ireland when she first presented herself here as the wife of Mr. James Horncastle. In fact, she was never married to Mr. Horncastle at all –'" Another dramatic pause. "'– until just recently, when her true husband died and she dragged her companion across the line for a quick marriage in Washington Territory, both of them ignoring the fact that he was already married to someone else.'"

Logan Sumner wished that he were deaf. When she'd finished reading she raised her eyes to look directly at him, and held his gaze a moment, knowing there could be no one in the room more appalled. A great wavering sickness thrummed inside him.

"All this is the truth," said the only unflustered one in the room, still looking directly into Logan Sumner's devastated eyes. Then she looked about at the rest of them as though she had just read aloud nothing more surprising or libellous than a weather report.

"This is nonsense," Mrs. Piquette said. "Someone has misled you."

"Every word is the *truth*."

For a moment the two women looked at one another. Apparently the Australian was not the least bit uncomfortable about this business between them. Her gaze did not waver, her back did not alter an inch from its erect position, her skirts did not so much as whisper.

"Well, you *are* a sort of character we don't meet every day," said Mrs. Piquette. "Maybe you don't realize how serious this is." She took up the infamous piece of paper again and peered at the words, holding them off at a distance and squinting as though she were afraid they would explode in her face.

"Indeed I do," said the other. "And I am determined to have it printed."

"Don't you know," said Mrs. Piquette, "that you could find yourself in serious trouble with the law?"

"I have no fears on that account," said the woman, "since everything I have written here can be proved." She smiled, with that chin up and that face turned just slightly to the side, as though all the laws of universal justice had gathered themselves around her for support. "Words," she said, "on a piece of paper. Testifying to the truth."

And so, thought Logan Sumner, she would win. Outside, a sidewheel paddler which was making the necessary movements to begin leaving the harbour could come back if it wished and take him aboard as well.

She might have won if the proprietress, Carrie Clover, had not raised her husky voice. "Have you thought through the logic of this, madam?" she said. "I've seen this sort of thing myself up north. If you print this, everyone who buys a copy'll come to the same conclusion. What you've got in your hand is an admission, it seems to me, that Mrs. Horncastle and Mr. Horncastle, and you as well, are all *three* of you adulterers. Three bigamists as well! Are you so sure you want to see this in print?"

For a moment nobody spoke, so the former hurdy-gurdy girl spelled it out. "If she's a bigamist because she's married to a man who was married to you, then you were a bigamist the whole time you were married to Mr. Jordan. If there was such a man."

It seemed the Widow Jordan hadn't considered the matter in quite this light. Perhaps in her single-mindedness she had overlooked what now seemed to be obvious – or hoped others would be too stupid to notice. She wasn't grateful for the information, either. She narrowed her eyes and snatched the paper from Mrs. Piquette's hand, and put it back into her bag. Then she turned and marched back out to the street, carrying her bag as though she were some kind of lawyer hauling off her rejected evidence to a second judge. "You needn't think," she stood in the doorway long enough to say, "that the refusal of a single newspaper to publish this will keep it from being generally known. There are other ways of broadcasting news about."

For a moment they watched through the window as the woman walked down the street. Then Mrs. Piquette broke the silence by confessing that she had been a little tempted to co-operate. "Just out of respect for 'er cheek! The woman is as dangerous as a weasel in a chicken run but I can't 'elp but wish 'er success all the same!"

"And she is willing to risk everything," said Sumner. "She has not been vanquished by *this* little encounter, we can be sure of that." He looked down into the half-drunk cup of coffee which rested on the blueprints for Horace Sheepshank's barn. This little episode had changed everything, he recognized. This cat-and-mouse game had altogether shifted its nature. What they were dealing with here was much more deadly than the comic-opera romance it had so far resembled. "Of course, she will find some other way of making use of the words on that slip of paper. Nothing will stop her now."

17

LOGAN Sumner cared little for local events which neither affected his romance nor touched upon the terrible predicament that had befallen the Horncastle family. Should he be excited to hear that construction of the drydock was progressing nicely, or that the city's seventy-eighth telephone had been installed? It was of little interest to him that a new lieutenant-governor had just taken up residence at Cary Castle. When he sang up the morning world from the branches of the Garry oak, he hoped to bring up a world in which none of those concerns was of any importance, a world in which the disaster being visited upon the Horncastles and their friends had been eliminated. But he discovered every day, of course, that he had failed.

Only hours after witnessing the Australian woman's attempt to publish her infamous piece of paper, he escorted Miss Addie

Horncastle to the theatre but mentioned nothing of the new information to her – though it rested more heavily on him than anything he had earlier learned. He dared not imagine what his lovely companion must be thinking if she had learned anything of this latest development. The notion of Mrs. Horncastle as an adulteress and a bigamist was even more astonishing and incredible than the melodrama unfolding before them on the stage: Planquette's *Chimes of Normandy*.

Still, when he was not supervising employees building an extension to Tom Grebe's warehouse, or going over his plans for the commissioned new face to the Blue Heron, or worrying how he might reconcile what he had learned of his dear Mrs. Horncastle with what he had so long felt, he could think of little but the progress or lack of progress in his pursuit of Mrs. Horncastle's daughter. Though no dragons had yet presented themselves for slaying, and he had not been sent off on any epic quests, his pursuit of the lady's love could hardly be considered an easy undertaking. The latest addition to his stone-chiselled progression of emendated views expressed in Chaucer's words the difficulties of his present life: *Swich peyne and wo as Loves folk endure*. Was this a kind of reckless public declaration? If so, no one had been so brave or ill-mannered as to mention it.

When they rode out together on the Thursday evening, it seemed that she could not be ignorant of all that he had learned, for she spoke little except to answer his questions directly. Yes, she had enjoyed *Chimes of Normandy*. No, she did not think Miss Lester's voice was weaker than it had been in *Girofle, Girofla*. She insisted, when he asked, that there was nothing she wished to say to him that was causing her distress. "Honestly, Logan Sumner, you go on like Lady Alice sometimes! Let us just enjoy the summer air!"

And yet he hoped that she might transform his gloomy mood by responding to the hopes he'd so awkwardly confessed during their afternoon on the Gorge! Instead, it seemed she preferred to mock him. When he objected to the comparison with Lady Alice, she threw out a laugh to the sparrows above them and suddenly spurred Dancer ahead into a canter that quickly left him behind. A most definite challenge. He urged Cleo into a gallop, but when she looked back to discover what he was up to, she bent low and thrust the gelding into a gallop as well. This was to be an earnest race between two matched horses. North on Government Street past the head of Rock Bay, then across the bridge – the gentleman still definitely in the rear, his face in the dust. Past Deadman's Island. Alongside the water for a while, where naked boys dived off the steep banks and left fishing rods unattended. The tension that tightened his body for the contest communicated itself to Cleo, whose entire spirit transformed itself into a thundering engine beneath him. It was not long before he pulled abreast of her, but this did not signal any end to the competition. Her eyes met his and briefly locked, but she did not speak. Though she laughed, evidently finding this contest to be exhilarating, he thought there was some cruelty in the laugh, as though she would be delighted if his horse were to throw him into the weeds. She would be even more pleased if she and her gelding could leave him behind out of sight altogether. But at the schoolhouse they turned as though they were joined and thundered across the bridge with their knees almost touching.

The thrumming of the planks seemed signal enough to him that they might safely end the competition and slow for a gentler ride through the countryside. A chance to talk, perhaps. He would remind her of his patience, his impatience; he would urge her as gently as he knew how to reward his waiting. And indeed she reined in her horse, quite suddenly, at the main gate to Craigflower farm. He shot past, and must haul mightily on his own reins to bring Cleo around so that he might go back and join her.

"The end?" he said. "A draw?"

"The end," she said, nodding sombrely. "If you will open the gate."

He had not anticipated a visit to the farm. There was no one here he cared enough about to give up an afternoon of Adelina's exclusive company. Still, he opened the gate and stood back while she rode through before him. "Thank you, gentle sir," she said, stiffly. "A proper gentleman, properly trained." Still mocking! As if she weren't covered with dust from the ride! "Helen is waiting for me, to help with her wedding-dress. You may as well go home – I shall be here for hours – unless you want to visit with the stable-boys, or lean on the fence with Helen's father and discuss the price of hogs."

It was clear in both her voice and her features that it pleased her to think that he would be all at sea in such a conversation, knowing nothing about the price of hogs and being not at all interested in speaking with Helen's father. He mounted his horse and set out immediately for home.

Later, when the midnight knocking on his door became an insistent pounding, he leapt out of the hot entanglement of sheets in which he had been tossing and descended the stairs, shrugging into his robe, with the ludicrous but certain expectation of finding a distraught Adelina on his doorstep, prepared to throw herself into his arms and beg him to forgive her for her earlier behaviour. She would plead with him to marry her immediately and bring happiness back into her life. Instead of Adelina, however, he found a grinning Zak on the doorstep. "Moonlight, *tyee*-boss! Tonight the flying machine will soar like a raven right over the chuck!"

"Now? Have you lost your mind? We were supposed to make those adjustments to the propeller lengths. There's more study to be done."

"While you study the books I'm figuring it out for myself. I made the adjustments already. It'll work. You coming? History, boss – it's going to unfold before your eyes."

Submitting to Zak's enthusiasm seemed easier than resisting. When Sumner had dressed, they rode out around the perimeter of the convent grounds at the head of the mudflats and passed through the intense darkness beneath the huge firs in the park until they came out on the far side of the park in the clearing which contained, at its centre, the old barn and, beside it, Zak's little shed. Everything was awash in moonlight: the long grass surrounding the buildings, the firs and cedars and Garry oaks around the perimeter, the unpainted planks of the barn walls, the little house entirely plastered over now with pieces of debris from the wrecked ship: FLOUR, DEZASSEIS, SIDE UP, WALKING. A little house of words. The door opened, and a figure stepped out, and came forward to greet them.

Chu Lee! Grinning more broadly, if it were possible, than Zak himself.

"How has he dragged you into this?" Sumner said. Perhaps this had something to do with a desire these two employees shared, to defy him.

"Our new partner," Zak announced.

Proudly, Chu Lee bowed his approval of this interpretation of his role.

"Partner?" Towards Zak, Sumner frowned as sternly as he was capable. "You've taken money from my servant for this?"

Both Zak and Chu Lee were offended by this interpretation of things. Chu Lee was the quicker to protest. "You no say what Chu Lee do. Chu Lee go in magic machine!"

The "magic machine," Sumner saw, had already been drawn out of the barn, and was parked in the moonshadow to one side of a large oak – as unpromising in appearance as its predecessors had been, though considerably larger. A huge unpleasant dragon-fly.

Zak stood grinning at Sumner. "A pig won't do this time. It needs someone who can pedal to keep it going. You'll see. Chu Lee will be as famous as this crazy Indian when the news gets out."

"Chu Lee," Sumner said, "will be nothing but a dead Chinaman! I forbid this, of course."

Both of them laughed this time, but eventually Zak recovered enough to say, "You think a white man should be first, *tyee*-boss?

You're jealous, I think. That's all. You know I wouldn't let you ride in it because you couldn't be trusted to bring it back – you'd *like* it up there, you'd fly all the way to the moon."

Chu Lee explained that it was not Sumner's place to forbid him this pleasure. Indeed, the enterprise had been blessed by his uncle who had urged Chu Lee to become involved in it.

Sumner knew, of course, that Chu Lee's uncle – head of the family in this country – managed one of the opium factories in town, but he was slow to see what his interest might be in this foolish experiment until Zak explained: "How many boats get caught while they're smuggling opium into the United States? Those buggers across the border don't like that sort of thing. Chu Lee's uncle got all excited when he heard what we were inventing. He told Chu Lee to help me however he can."

"What has this to do with him?"

Chu Lee completed the explanation for his dull-witted employer. Unless the U.S. police were angels with wings on their backs, they would never be able to intercept an airborne delivery to grateful U.S. customers, whose government insisted on frowning upon the product of the poppy unless high import tariffs were paid.

Sumner felt profound disappointment when he recognized the connection. Of course he knew he must try to talk Zak out of letting any sort of business interests get involved in their experiments. The whole nature of what they were doing would be changed! But that battle could be fought later. First he must put a stop to this flight before he found himself helping Zak fish his cook's battered body out of the ocean. "Does Chu Lee know what happened to the unfortunate pig?"

Chu Lee giggled at this. Apparently he knew about the fate of the pig, and perhaps also the fate of the rock that had been used before that. "Machine much better this time." He also knew, Sumner could tell from the look on his face, how much this business was irritating his employer. And took pleasure from his knowledge.

Even if Chu Lee did not immediately die in the water below them – even if, through some preposterous miracle, this invention really worked – Sumner could foresee that he would only find himself eventually behind the bars of a Yankee prison. "When they capture you, do you think they'll just send you home with their best wishes? When you have challenged what they consider a perfectly sensible attitude – whatever your own opinion of it might be? Or do you imagine that all you will have to do is whistle for me to come down and pay for a lawyer to talk your way out of your punishment? It will be less expensive to find one of your cousins to replace you. Any number of them could cook a better roast of beef."

Since this did not even deserve a response, apparently, they turned away to the business of the night. Obviously there was nothing he could say that would stop them. When they pulled the machine out of the secluded clearing and into the open grassy slope above the strait, he could do nothing but stand by while Chu Lee obeyed Zak's orders to climb inside. Sumner knew he should get out of there fast, to avoid being implicated in the death of his servant. He should be looking for a policeman to put a stop to this dangerous scheme. Yet curiosity made it impossible for him to leave. He stayed to bid his servant farewell, confident that he would not see him again alive – unless, of course, he was soon to fish him out of the water like his squealing predecessor, or pass gifts from home through iron bars.

"I shall pay for a proper funeral for you, then. So that your bones may rest amongst your fellow Celestials until they are sent to join your ancestors' bones in China." Chu Lee continued to grin. "I shall also tell your uncle what I think of his role in this affair."

Before dragging the ugly dragon-fly across the grass, its proud builder looked down on Sumner from horseback. "*Nah!* Great moment, boss. You will make me your equal partner in the business when you see how clever I am."

"I would almost make you my equal partner if you were clever enough to stop this nonsense now," Sumner said.

Zak and his horse towed the machine up the grassy slope to very near the top, where the heaps and circles of white stones marked the resting-place of ancient Indians who had died in a plague. Then, turning, he towed it faster down the slope past one and then another of the isolated and tortured pines whose trunks and limbs strained in opposite directions, and across the race track. When the machine had been released and was nearing the edge of the cliff on its own, it became evident that Chu Lee had lost his enthusiasm for the moment at which he would, in one way or the other, depart from the surface of earth. He was not pedalling as he was supposed to, but was trying to stand up, though the machine continued to carry him forward. "What's he doing?" Zak shouted. "*Iktah mamook?* Sit down, you fool!" Half standing, half sitting, perhaps afraid to do either, Chu Lee teetered, and wobbled, with his arms stretched out on either side to preserve something of his balance – preparing perhaps to soar on his own if it should become necessary.

But it did not become necessary for him to test his arms' capacity for carrying him into flight. When the absurd insect was just a few feet from the cliff edge, one of the bicycle wheels dropped off, and the machine began to carve a circle in the grass. Chu Lee leapt free and set out briskly in the direction of the park, where he disappeared into the woods, despite Zak's shouted commands to stop. Sumner knew that if he ever saw him again it would be only after several days of sulking in his own rooms in the labyrinth of Chinatown.

What sort of rooms? Sumner didn't know. It had never before occurred to him to wonder. It had always been enough to think of Chu Lee disappearing into the smoky mysteries of Chinatown and pulling a curtain closed behind him. Presumably for a privacy he desired. Yet it was not possible to avoid thinking, as you heard his footsteps swishing through the underbrush, that all his life he had been putting Chu Lee away in a cupboard, like the breakfast dishes, whenever he wasn't busy running Uncle Charles's house. Perhaps this, more than anything else, explained why it was upsetting to discover Chu Lee a part of this flying adventure. Certain things would have to be reconsidered all the way to their bottom.

Sumner held his peace while Zak cursed him for allowing his stupid doubts to undermine Chu Lee's confidence, and then while Zak cursed Chu Lee for being an unreliable representative of his race, at the same time kicking at his disappointing flying machine. He did not, then, accompany the angry inventor back to his little house of words, nor did he go home to bed. Here in the open air above the strait seemed the more likely place for finding a little peace. He climbed into the Garry oak beside the Pest House ashes, and wedged himself into a fork in the branches.

(All along this headland he imagined a series of luxury hotels one day, looking out across the strait towards the Olympic Mountains – massive structures with *portes-cochères* and turrets and bay windows, with great wide curving staircases and chandeliers and orchestras playing Strauss waltzes in the ballrooms. Wealthy travellers would stay here, from all over the world, and sit out on the sunlit terraces proclaiming the hotels of Marseilles and Bath to be inferior.)

When he awoke, he was uncertain for a moment where he was. But then he saw that dawn had nearly arrived on the strait. The moon had become a weak shrunken disk in the approaching light, capable of finding only the faintest touches of colour in anything – from grass to trees to the rough wooden walls of what was unmistakably the Pest House standing before him. He heard the thin sound of someone's singing. Dear God – even as the rational part of his mind was cautioning him against trusting his mortal senses, his mortal eyes began to fill with tears, his throat began to ache. Here beside him was the very cottage he had tried so often to snatch back from the invisible past. Perhaps the terrible force of his wanting had produced it.

If he crawled out on an opposite branch he could put out a hand and lay it against the rough surface of a squared-off log. He could even press his face to the splintery grey wood as well. Even without moving he could smell the scent from the moss on the roof, the odour of long-dead, possibly rotting wood. Down through the window he could see the woman who was unmistakably his mother peer into the lamp she was lighting on the wooden table. When she glanced up and saw him looking in, she did not appear to be startled; she smiled.

"You see, it is possible after all," she said.

Or seemed to say. Perhaps mothers and sons – how would he know? – could speak to one another without sound. She turned, and set out cutlery on the table, and resumed her singing. An Irish-sounding ballad, whose words he could not make out.

"Ah, Logan my son," she said, beneath the sound of the song. "Did ye think we would leave you behind altogether? Did ye think we would never look back to see how ye were doin'? My mother's heart is breakin' in my breast to know of the sadness ye carry."

He moved closer and laid his hand against the adze-squared logs, and ran his fingers down the dusty chinks. He must climb down out of this twisted tree and go in through the door and touch her, and kiss her brow, and allow her to put her arms around him and hold him close to the great white apron that all but covered the top of her dark-blue dress.

"Now don't be a fool, son. Ye mustn't hope to see us in the world. We live, but not as ye imagine. Ye cannot bring us back, because our human histories are fabrications we've learned to disbelieve. We shed them, as that nearly naked tree beside the willow thicket sheds its bark."

The tree she meant would be the lone arbutus amongst the willows. The surface of its trunk, he saw, was already becoming a little ragged, beginning to blister and peel.

When he turned to the Pest House again, it had gone. Disappeared, taking his mother with it. Transparent air. A patch of ashes. A shivering tree. Waves crashed against the rocks at the foot of the cliffs. The sky grew lighter, the oaks defined themselves against the sea, taking on glittering leaves, and rough grey chequered bark. He climbed down and knelt to scoop up a handful of ashes, and smelled the distant fire. Forgotten smoke. Had the Pest House not really been there? Had his mother not spoken to him at all? Was he in some state, perhaps, where he was no longer capable of knowing what was real and what was not? He had no heart for anything this morning and would go home immediately, and try to convince himself that this had not happened at all, or if it had, that it could be explained by something he didn't yet understand. It was only a dream, he supposed. Otherwise, he would never find the courage again to step outside his house.

Now what was this? Had he not been alone after all? Not thirty yards away the lone figure of a woman turned from looking out across the strait towards the foreign mountains – still invisible behind a nearly colourless haze – to begin strolling this way along the edge of the cliffs. Mrs. Jordan, naturally. Without her children. Without the courting doctor from San Francisco, without the rejected drover with his coiled whip. What was a woman doing out here before dawn? She seemed unaware of being observed, and walked with strong steps, but slowly, her skirts dragging in the dewy grass, her head high and her shoulders back, her gloved hands clasped together at her waist. Her face, tilted up as though to catch the cool salted scent, was turned just slightly in the direction of the strait – not as though she were interested in the water or anything that might occur upon it, or anything that might be happening unseen on the far side, but as though she had a definite wish not to look upon the land.

As she came near him she raised a hand to her mouth and seemed to look down, or perhaps she closed her eyes. She was near enough for him to see that a frown had drawn a dark vertical line down her brow. Was she in pain? It seemed that she was suffering some sort of distress, for she suddenly tilted up her face towards the sky and moved her head from side to side.

When he thought that he must either slip away or make his presence known – or be caught out in a gross impoliteness – she put out a hand to grasp a scrub oak that grew near her path, and abruptly dropped to her knees. This was not a collapse – he resisted an impulse to go to her aid. She had assumed an attitude of prayer.

For several moments he held himself still, almost unbreathing, while she silently knelt. Was she petitioning God for His aid in breaking up the Horncastle home? Or was she, perhaps, begging forgiveness for the damage already done? One hoped she had decided to listen for guidance, and that she would receive instructions to leave the country immediately.

If she received an answer, it was not the answer she'd hoped for. She lifted herself to her feet with the aid of the little oak, making some sort of angry noise, a most unfeminine sound from her throat – not exactly a growl but rather a vehement protest, as though she were furiously resisting some hand which would push her off her path: *how dare you!* The tree was not immediately released – not until it had suffered a few good shakes. Then both hands were laid over her face.

Still Logan Sumner did not move, or do anything that might betray his presence. He only stood, and wondered at his own stupidity in not suspecting the woman of having moments of doubt. Of course she was not the Devil, even with that damning piece of paper in her hand! Yet the feeling that gripped him now was not one that offered him any sort of encouragement – far from it. The feeling that overcame him while he watched the lady walk up the slope on the trail that would take her back to town was one of fear; it occurred to him – though he did not understand – that he might, as Chu Lee was so anxious to do, have already entered some sort of foreign territory where he did not belong.

18

ADDIE was already steaming and furious when they met to ride out on roads and trails to the east of town. Again she refused to speak of whatever it was that seemed to have infuriated her. She led the way; he followed; out beyond Fernwood, out towards Cadboro Bay. At the summit of Mount Tolmie she did not even dismount; she glared furiously out over the view in first this direction, then this, then this – the blue Sooke hills, the faded mountains in Washington Territory, the long and purple San Juan islands, the low hills and gentle valleys up the Saanich peninsula. She had a grudge for them all; not even streaming-down sun earned her pleasure. Down the side of Mount Tolmie faster than was wise, past Cadboro Bay, into the woods. He followed, they did not speak; she was a fury, leading.

They left the horses grazing where she decided to leave them. They stalked through damp areas of dark spongy soil and crowded sword ferns where moss coated all sides of the trunks of alders and cottonwoods and hung like tattered rags off the branches of cedars. Then, the sea, a little cove, a rocky beach. They were facing the continent's bulk; Mount Baker floated, a pink volcanic cone, above the islands. A small, sleek otter paused in his race across the sea-edge boulders, then went on. An arbutus leaned out, glossy with rings of new leaves, already beginning to shed its curled parchment scrolls of bark. Wild sweet peas and honey-suckle grew in a chaotic hedge along the bank, though the smell of the flowers was lost in the stronger scent off the sea: salt, iodine, kelp – the world's cleanest smell.

"I suppose your famous Uncle Charles has trained you for every occasion! I suppose there is nothing for which he hasn't left you a simple code!"

She strode along the beach as though she would find some-thing on it to strike out against. Indeed, she took up a sea-washed branch of driftwood and beat at the roses, beat the pale-green newly exposed flesh of arbutus he leaned against. She strode from one side of the cove to the other, over barnacled rocks, across tide pools, along washed-up logs. Wind blew at her dark loosened hair, slapped in the folds of her skirt; she kept her head raised and seemed to be breathing it – defying it. She stood up on black volcanic rock and looked up the coastline, looked down the coastline, looked out across the strait to the foreign mountains. Then she leapt down, and struck out with her stick again at boulders that stood in her path, and beat her way through them to the opposite side. She said nothing in all this time; she did not look at him; her gaze did not seem to be taking in anything around her – only something *out there*. She climbed the bank to stand for a while on a grassy outcropping, as though she hoped for longer vision. She did not seem to find it; down she leapt again. Fiercely striking everywhere, she marched down the length of logs, she skirted boulders, she leapt over tide pools, she stomped through gravel, she strode up the slope and then, with what seemed to Sumner a savage and ferocious cry, threw herself against him.

She was no more savage than he was himself. They were a pair. Feeble protests from his greedy mouth: "Wait." The voice of Education. "We shall be married soon." Laughable words. They laughed at Education. If anything, he was even more impatient than she. They might have been two people out to destroy one another. The cries were animal cries. They might have, if they had wished, torn trees and bushes out by the roots and tossed them flying to the islands; they might have sent boulders roaring down to the sea; they might have torn arbutus flesh from the limbs above them and devoured it, if they had not been dedicated entirely to stuffing themselves with one another.

Was this her way of giving him the answer he had been waiting for? The question did not occur to him until afterwards. "Dear God," he said, looking up through branches at sky. The sea breeze chilled the sweat that covered his body. He hadn't dared to hope her answer would be delivered with such enthusiasm!

Nothing from her. She lay on her side, facing in his direction, her knees drawn up a little, one hand beneath her hair. Her gaze was not on the sky, or on him. He passed a hand down over her shoulder and then placed it upon her thigh. "We will ask your father to announce an engagement immediately. He will speak to Old Trodd about publishing the banns." His fingers lightly stroked the long, pale section of naked thigh, and slid into the hot, damp hidden crease behind the knee.

Her laugh was soft. Her shoulder barely moved. "I shall never be engaged to anyone."

"You would elope? We could cross the strait and marry in Washington. Tomorrow." This may not have been the wisest suggestion, in view of what they had recently learned of her parents' marriage, but her response had thoroughly confused him. All sense had long ago left his head.

"I will never marry."

It occurred to him that she had read too many of those novels she favoured, Rhoda Broughton's tales of strong-willed red-headed maidens kicking over the traces. Perhaps she had picked up the idea somewhere that what had just happened could be considered already a marriage in God's eyes. It seemed a brave and admirable notion, perhaps, and modern, but of course he must talk her out of it.

"But we must. As soon as possible."

Gulls arranged along a floating log complained, complained, complained to one another of life in general. Selfish, self-pitying, demanding birds – dozens of them complained, protested, on their bobbing log – then screamed in horrendous rage that one of their number had grabbed up something from the sea. Fury shot some of them skyward, flapping, but greed brought them down again to continue the endless complaint.

"Never," she said, sitting up. While sea-gulls complained, she had begun to rearrange her clothing. "No marriages for me. No husbands for Adelina. Before they adopted me my name was Croft. Did you know that? Adelina Croft. I shall use it again. Miss Adelina Croft."

"Addie, think! Think! I love you. Surely that is clear enough. I want you to be my wife. Without all this strange sort of talk. You'll be Mrs. Adelina Sumner, Mrs. Logan Sumner. Tomorrow, if you wish. Today, if such a thing were possible."

He might as well have spoken to the sea. "I shall be one of those women you see leaning against the walls in the Restricted Zone or out along Esquimalt Road."

He sat up and began, like her, to straighten his clothing. Perhaps he would be able to think again, and find the words that were so desperately needed now.

"I shall have hundreds of husbands," she said. "Dozens of husbands every night. You will be one of them, whenever you wish. Logan Sumner. My 'perfect gentleman.' But there will be others."

"Don't make light of this." Though he knew she was certainly not joking, to acknowledge anything else was to risk something he did not understand. "It's only natural that you should feel uncomfortable. But it is my fault entirely. I should have stopped myself. I shall apologize, if you wish, for ever. But we must move quickly now, and make it right."

"This has nothing to do with what we just did!" She was as fierce now as she had been while she paced the cove. "At any rate, it was I, and not you, who decided." She stood over him now. "When I am on the street, at least people will know what they are looking at, I won't hide it. I won't pretend, with signatures and pieces of paper and daily *play-acting*, like my mother, to be anything else but a whore!"

He watched with some horror as she strode off in the direction of the horses. Helpless to stop her. Unable to think of anything to say that wasn't pure nonsense. Enough nonsense had already been spoken between them. There seemed no point in following. Perhaps this business with her father and the Australian widow had driven her mad. He would never know. Nevertheless, he had behaved abominably, he had taken advantage of her weakness, and in the process he had driven her even further into that mysterious and frightening state and lost everything. "When we act without honour and justice, we have become barbarians." Uncle Charles! A barbarian had thrashed about on this beach only moments before. What would Uncle Charles think of him now? (She had sneered at Uncle Charles, at all he had taught Sumner.) "Hate nothing but deceit and unkindness," he used to say. Sumner could imagine no one, at the moment, more unkind and deceitful than himself.

And yet: "I shall be one of those women you see leaning against the walls." Was it possible for words to become so ugly? "I won't pretend, with play-acting, like my mother, to be anything else but a whore." Ugly and cruel and lacerating. Who was the person who brought *play-acting* onto this island? Who imported *whore* so that it could slash and carve? If Adelina Horncastle had been confined to the language of the sleek otter, say, or the gentle pheasant, or even the strange chesty mutterings of Zak's hermit uncle, she could not have left him felled and bleeding like this.

He reached out and put a hand on the newly exposed flesh of the arbutus – smooth as Adelina's thigh. Tattered shreds of cast-off papery bark lay at his feet – wrinkled skin of an old woman, sloughed off in favour of a new year's waiting new youth. The pale flesh beneath his hand would one day crease and toughen and detach itself and curl up to fall free as well. He placed his face against it, kissed it, moved his cheek along it, blessed it, thanked it, held on to it even while he slept. Even while the queue of bobbing gulls complained, complained of everything, watching the surface of sea for something to scream in earnest over and devour.

19

It was from Mrs. Horncastle that Sumner learned of the Australian widow's next move. He went to the hotel at a time when he knew she would be alone – or alone except for the smallest children, who could be sent from the room – in order to see if her aid might be enlisted in winning an opportunity to speak with Adelina. Without, of course, confessing the reasons for their falling out. If there was any chance at all for a reconciliation, he knew that that dear woman was his greatest ally and perhaps his only hope.

But when he arrived, he saw that her troubles were even greater than his. She sat in her apron by a kitchen window, under the row of dried bundles of dill and parsley and thyme that hung from the ceiling beam, her ironing abandoned in a heap on the table, her flat-irons ignored on a stove that seemed to have been left to go cold. One hand idly stroked the handle of the wooden chum. That broad face, so often flushed with pleasure, was pale and heavy. "The Reverend Mr. Trodd has been," she said, without turning from the window. "And it is all over now."

"The woman has given up her fight?"

"I have lost, is what I mean. When the newspaper would not publish her little piece of paper, didn't the woman go and take it with her to St. John's!"

"To the church!"

"To engage the help of my own minister! She might as well have brought her campaign right into my home." Briefly she turned her sad gaze on Sumner, then looked out the window again. "Indeed, I suppose my home *has* been invaded – since he came here to report their conversation to me immediately afterwards."

According to the Reverend Mr. Trodd's report, the conversation in the Iron Church – because a hefty rain was falling that afternoon – had been of necessity a shouted one. "He claimed to have protested on my behalf. 'One of the dearest women in the parish,' he said his opinion was. 'No one more consistently obeys the second of the two great commandments!' Of course I can tell you only what he has told me."

"Good women have been known to make fools of their spiritual leaders before now," the insolent Australian said, apparently. This conversation took place with both of them sitting in a front pew, the scandalous piece of paper between them. When he pushed it towards her, she left it where they might both stare at it instead of looking at one another.

"And that lovely family! Surely you must be mistaken."

"And you have been giving her communion regularly." Even at these close quarters it was necessary to shout, to be heard in the din from the thundering rain. "Do you see how she has made you a party to her hypocrisy? Perhaps your superiors will consider that you have become too old for your responsibility."

"Madam. Be careful. Have you no fear for your own soul?"

"Forgive me." The Reverend would report seeing tears in those eyes which would not quite rise to meet his. "In my distress, I forgot myself. But, don't you see how I have been wronged? You must order her immediately to stop living with my husband."

"Must I? Must I? Madam, it is God, and not you, who shall instruct me."

"God has already issued His instructions: Thou shalt not commit adultery! Could it be any clearer, or do you think He has recently changed His mind?"

The Reverend Trodd was not immediately grateful to have been reminded of this, he assured Mrs. Horncastle, or of the responsibility it thrust upon him. "And I failed to experience any of the sympathy which I knew this woman deserved – that all of us deserve. Frankly, I was anxious to send her on her way as fast as possible, so that I might be alone – to discover in prayer what I must do."

Perhaps the Almighty made a practice of answering the Reverend's prayers without delay. Within the half-hour he had already received his direction from Above and had found his way to the family kitchen behind the Blue Heron. Here, with similar speed, he reported his shouted conversation with the Australian. He barely waited for poor Mrs. Crabtree, a new widow addicted to doses of daily comfort and advice from Mrs. Horncastle, to collect the pies her hostess had baked for her and to leave him the field.

"I denied nothing, Mr. Sumner. And, how could I? Hadn't he been given the facts? Oh, hadn't I wished so many times that I might change the facts! 'Tis true that in our earliest days here I lived in terror of being found out. But there was nothing I could do to change the past. And as time went by I began to feel I *had* changed things. Sure now, wouldn't God understand how little choice I had! And the moment I received the news of Thompkins' death I dragged my Jamie across the strait for a wedding. *Now* I am safe, I thought. I thanked God for His patience. I tried to conduct myself so that He would never be sorry for having looked the other way. Then this – this poor driven woman with her mission.

"Can you imagine how I felt when I learned who she was? Just let her see she has come on a hopeless mission, I prayed. 'Tis a solid happy marriage she is up against. But I had never imagined that she would go to my own beloved little church, where I have always gone myself when I needed help! Do you realize, says Mr. Trodd, how you have endangered your precious soul? Do you understand what peril you are in at this moment? God knows all about it, I told him, I have not tried to keep anything from Him. He laughed! Of *course* God has known about it, you poor child, as He knows everything. But that doesn't mean He approves. You have committed a terrible sin. Week after week, you have knelt for communion knowing that you were guilty of adultery and allowed me to place the wafer on your tongue in the belief that your heart was pure.

"But we were married! Finally, we were married."

"Do you suppose a marriage between adulterous bigamists to be anything but a mockery? You must move out of his house imme-diately. We must salvage what we can."

"I cannot leave him. Not even you can make me do that."

"You must move out of his house immediately. Today. If you wish to save anything. Your reputation in this town. Your honour."

"What does a reputation matter to me if I am without my marriage?"

"Very well then. If you wish ever to take communion again in my church."

"You know I couldn't bear to give that up."

"Then you must leave. You may gather some of your things now – send for the rest later. I shall wait, if you wish, and explain to Mr. Horncastle why this has happened."

"And the children?"

"Take the children with you for now. Of course, we must consider where their welfare might best be served in the future."

"I cannot believe God wishes me to abandon a husband who needs me now more than he has ever done."

"My dear Norah! Has he uttered a word in your defence since that woman arrived?"

"You know what Mr. Horncastle is like. He knows I do not need to be fought for. I am here, where you see me. Nothing more is wanted."

"He has not said one word or committed one deed designed to preserve your marriage. He is more interested in enjoying the battle for which he will be the prize. Admit it! He will be equally happy to have either wife, so long as the thing is settled. He would have sent that woman packing otherwise, before the rest of us even heard her. Has he said one word to stop her from spreading this damning information all over the city?"

"He could not have known she would go this far. He would never have permitted it."

"I understand there are men out there this minute laying money on your chances. This gentleman you have called your husband watches each move that this woman makes with the same sort of excitement as he observes his horse on the track. It is another game – only this time it gives him even more pleasure than usual, because he himself is the prize."

Logan Sumner could not help interrupting Mrs. Horncastle's account of this conversation. "Perhaps this explains why the Reverend would have nothing to do with my uncle's book. Apparently he believes the 'overflowing fountains of goodness' have gone dry."

"Oh, but I hated him for that, Mr. Sumner. God help me. Didn't I hate that small-mouthed mean little man for saying those things. But I could not deny the truth of it either. At first I thought James was simply sparing me knowledge, of his efforts to protect our marriage. But I saw soon enough that he found it all too exciting ever to consider resisting. But still I would have defied them all. I would have fought to win him back. I would have stood up before all the righteous and the self-righteous of this town and confessed my guilt and still have fought to preserve my marriage against this poor woman with her pitiful piece of paper. But I could not do it without God. And there was nothing I could say to this man with his cruel little mouth to convince him not to bar me from the communion table.

"So they will say: What else could she do? The day is long past when she could hold up her head in this town, they will say. Sure, she can gain no sympathy by standing in the way of justice. They must be right. I have always understood what I was doing, haven't I? I must take the consequences and try to save what I can. Living under a separate roof won't keep me from loving him. Or from looking out for his interests, as I have always done. Her little piece of paper and the efforts of the Reverend Mr. Trodd can't stop me from doing that."

20

THE "separate roof" beneath which Mrs. Horncastle intended to live while looking out for her husband's continuing interests was a tall, narrow bay-windowed house in James Bay, only a half-hour's walk from the Blue Heron. After only a few days of searching, Horncastle purchased this house, which had been sitting empty since the Borzonis had returned to Italy, as the price she demanded for leaving the premises, for dissolving the partnership, and for abandoning the marriage without any more fuss. She did not intend to take in washing, as those who had learned of her San Francisco past imagined, but she would take advantage of the skills she had more recently learned, and would manage a boarding-house of her own. Already in the habit of helping in the hotel, the children would give her all the assistance she might need. Even before completing the move, she had received a request from Lady Alice Riven-Blythe that a certain room overlooking the harbour be reserved for a cousin of Her Ladyship who was to arrive quite soon from England, and who would not be entirely welcome beneath the little widow's own substantial roof.

When he learned of this latest development, the rector of St. John's made it a part of his Sunday service to offer up a special prayer for the soon-to-be-"dispossessed," requesting that the Almighty God be merciful to those who were being sent in shame from their accustomed homes to begin their lives all over again in altered circumstances. "We know your servants will suffer terrible loneliness, Lord, and will toss through sleepless nights of painful guilt as they remember their own mistakes and wilful sins; we know they will never be free from the constant fear of being reproached by their upright neighbours, and will carry the lifelong knowledge of their own unworthiness within them. Nevertheless we pray that You look down and grant Your bountiful mercy upon those in need, lest the burden becomes too much to bear."

A preacher of true compassion, Sumner might have whispered to his neighbour in the choir, if his neighbour had not been weeping. The Reverend's tone clearly hoped that God would have the good sense to let the rejected ones stew in their own juices for a while, before taking it upon Himself to answer this prayer.

"'Thy habitation is in the midst of deceit,'" he cautioned them all, with Jeremiah's help. "'For they are all adulterers, an assembly of treacherous men.'"

Sumner learned that Adelina, far from taking pride in her mother's success at protecting her own rights, only despised her further. Surely the woman deserved a daughter's admiration for the deal she had negotiated with the man who was kicking her out, and for the dignity with which she was carrying it off. Even those who saw justice being done in this business must spare a moment's compassion for the woman, so consistently kind and optimistic, always trying to make everyone's life more joyful. But "She's a hypocrite and an adulteress and now she's a fool as well" was Adelina's final word. She would not let him try to say more.

Adelina's rejection of her mother was no more distressing to him than her continued determination to make herself unavailable. Repeated proposals, he soon discovered, only irritated her. Even the most subtle reference to the intimacy that had briefly existed between them sent her into a furious denunciation of his cruelty. "Do you think that because I behaved so foolishly once, I am yours to whistle up at your will – to satisfy the animal in you?" Of course he did not remind her who had initiated the encounter on the beach. And of course he assured her, in his stumbling manner, that his interest was not in simply more of the same! But assuring her that marriage was still what he had in mind did not bring about any alteration to her attitude. She would not, she insisted vehemently, marry him. Or anyone.

At least her talk of joining the women in the brothels had ceased. Instead, she would live a life in which no man would ever have the opportunity to touch her, or betray her, or make a fool of her as her father had done to her mother. Indeed, she announced, she would be a single woman all her life – entirely independent of hated father, despised mother, unnecessary husband, or unwelcome lover.

It seemed to him that she was determined to become someone who might be found in one of those novels she read – an isolated, austere figure remaining faithful to an ideal of purity. Perhaps she even imagined that she would eventually become famous as The Unattainable. Men would one day write poems about her but never touch her, Sumner thought. Word of her would be recorded in foreign newspapers. Gentlemen, reading of her in faraway countries, would risk their lives in hazardous journeys to attempt the impossible task of winning her hand. Whether or not she achieved her goal of following in the footsteps of Miss Thackeray and Mrs. Oliphant, writing three-volume novels, history would be unable to avoid recording her visit to this earth as quite singular and remarkable. Even as an old woman, she would remain youthful and lovely and mysterious, pursued by statesmen and adventurers from around the world, admired by younger gentlemen cursing the fate that had brought them onto this earth too late, envied by an entire population of ageing women who daily wished that they had had the imagination and intelligence to have chosen a similar route, and looked up to by a whole race of young ladies who would model themselves after her for as long as family and friends allowed it.

She would eventually sail for Home, which she had never seen, where she would live alone, he imagined, except for servants, in a modest but beautiful mansion she would build in Bath or Oxford – from the proceeds of her successful books, perhaps, or from a surprise inheritance, or from gifts sent her by admirers in distant places. One day he would read of her, or hear of her, or see her passing by on the street in a closed carriage, and alone would have the satisfaction of remembering what he alone in the universe knew of the true state of the legendary beauty's famous chastity.

And what would become of Logan Sumner? Here was new and rich material for his tombstone – several blocks of granite would be needed to supply the space for this new anguish. Would Logan Sumner, too, become a legend? Was he doomed to be an ancient withered bachelor, perhaps, equally alone, equally chaste, but the object of children's taunting, the subject of jokes? "Relic of another age," people would say. "A defeated gentleman. One woman died, another gave up men altogether, now girls run when they see him coming – Old Forlorn."

No one would be able to say in the future that he had not fought Adelina's rejection with emphatic and imaginative energy. He would never understand, himself, how he came to behave in such an uncharacteristic manner. Who was this madman he became during the long week while the family prepared to move out of the hotel? Where did he find the courage to stand beneath her window at night like someone from another world, and to shout up demands for attention, and to toss up tortured letters in which he threatened to kill himself? During a loud exchange when they met by chance on Government Street, with dozens of witnesses stopping to see why this lunatic was raising his voice in such an ugly fashion to the lovely young woman, he threatened to burn his house down to demonstrate the extent of his disappointment; he threatened to join the Royal Navy; he threatened to hire ruffians to abduct the lady off the street and carry her to a secret location in the country where she would be his prisoner until she agreed to his proposal. Was the loss itself not profound enough for him, must he make a public fool of himself as well? She laughed, but the melodrama was embarrassing to them both. She was not the sort to take pleasure from seeing a man, on her behalf, reduced to lunacy.

Zak, on the other hand, who had been amongst the witnesses on the street, encouraged him to go even further. "Don't stop now, you just got started. Dress in rags and camp on her doorstep until she gives in, follow her everywhere she goes, make a nuisance of yourself until they throw you in the skookum-house." He had no end of suggestions. "Put a notice in the paper. Have yourself paddled back and forth across the harbour standing up naked in a canoe! Start building her a castle up on the hill. March into the hotel in the night with an orchestra playing behind you and go up the steps and into her room and *capture* her, and carry her away from here on a boat full of music for San Francisco! She won't be able to resist. She's waiting to see if you're finally desperate enough to forget everything they taught you."

But Sumner knew that Adelina was not waiting to see if he was desperate enough. He couldn't bear to think what pain it must have given her already to see him acting a role in public which she knew was so unnatural to him. Almost certainly an object of pity already in the eyes of the population, he was willing to become an object of loathing as well if it might do his cause any good, but he would not go so far as to intensify her suffering at this time of painful family disintegration – hardly the sort of gift for the woman you love.

And what would Uncle Charles have to say about this surprising metamorphosis? He didn't know. A great deal had changed since the days of his marriage to poor Julia, whose large dark eyes had never once narrowed at him in anger, whose soft voice had never once berated him. In that short period of their happy marriage she had never once surprised him, or behaved in a manner out of keeping with her upbringing or in any way contrary to his expectations. So soft, so quiet, so gentle had she been, in fact, that he could sometimes barely remember her now, except as a shadowy presence, like the touch of a sheer curtain brushing across your bare forearm in a gentle breeze.

What Uncle Charles would have to say about this situation was impossible to know. Something expressing his extreme disapproval, but what would be the words? He tried but could not reach his uncle's voice. Words that Uncle Charles's voice had long ago left imprinted on his brain had fractured and splintered off into unfamiliar noises he could make no sense of. Where was "Honour" to be found? What shape did "Duty" have, or taste? Where in this city could you put your hand on something that was represented by the ridiculous noise of "Loyalty," or something known as "Love"? Oh, the world had collapsed around them all, he thought – the victims of a colossal upheaval that had been precipitated by the Australian woman's arrival – and nothing meant any longer what it had meant in the past. They were all of them, all of them, losing touch with what they had once so definitely been.

"By God, you have to hand it to the woman, she knows how to get what she wants." This was more or less the general attitude about town. "Nobody asked her to come here and upset everything, life was much more pleasant and predictable before, but a person has to admire a woman who carries off a coup like that with such single-minded determination."

The Australian had proved to be quite frighteningly ruthless, it was agreed at dinner-tables, but she had a wonderful laugh which you could not resist, and besides she had justice on her side. The mistress of the hotel, on the other hand, was kind and helpful, a paragon of virtue – "Certain people would have died without her dedicated care" – but she was, after all, an adulteress. In both cases it was what came after the "but" that counted most. And even certain of Mrs. Horncastle's friends reluctantly confessed that there was some pleasure in discovering that the woman was not, after all, so perfect. She had only got what she deserved.

At the table of Mrs. Cyrus Fletcher – wife of the far-sighted and ambitious land developer – the Australian was considered, with some reservations, to be a natural champion of sorts, a woman who knew how to win. After all, it was at the Fletcher table that she had charmed so many of the Fletcher friends, bankers and successful merchants, with her enthusiastic tales of life in Australia. There was a great deal of satisfaction in seeing the colourful foreigner win out over the dull and heavy local housewife, too busy raising that brood of adopted orphans to put any effort into entertaining.

"The Australian," said Mrs. Fletcher down the length of the table, "is not exactly refined by any means – rather coarse, in fact – and not at all so original as she likes to think, but she just may be able to create a social life in that hotel, and bring a little needed colour into that part of town."

"And on top of everything else, there is a bonus we have overlooked," said Mr. Bold, the banker. "Some people will make a tidy profit out of this, if they had the sense to put their money on the successful woman."

And now the inescapable. We see Mrs. Horncastle moving out of what has been her home for nearly twenty years, and out of the hotel she has daily helped her husband to run. Of course she leaves with dignity. Of course she takes the children with her. At nine fifteen in the morning she appears at the front door of The Great Blue Heron, her travelling-cloak around her shoulders, and pauses on the step just long enough to exchange a few words with the children. There is some general but subdued complaint, some laughter from Jerome. Then, holding hands, they set out together in a southerly direction along the boardwalk, a party of six, to walk the several blocks that separate the hotel behind them from the boarding-house that will be their new home across the muddy bay. A number of trunks have been left behind in the hotel foyer, awaiting later removal by wagon.

Addie has already left, having found lodgings elsewhere for the time being. Refusing to live any longer with the mother who has disappointed her, and having turned down the offer of a separate allowance from the father she now despises, she has arranged to pay for her board by helping a Mrs. Elmira Zimmerman, recently of Vienna, to run her boarding-house on Michigan Street – competing, not incidentally, with both her mother's and her father's businesses.

As soon as Mrs. Horncastle and the children have passed from sight, James Horncastle, dressed smartly in his morning suit, with a white rose from the hotel garden in his lapel, steps out onto the sidewalk where his pair of shining black horses and his carriage have been brought round by a servant from the back. He is as excited as any young bridegroom might hope to be – grinning broadly, stroking the horses, laughing with the servant, taking time to lay a bet with his tobacconist neighbour (out on the sidewalk in front of his shop to watch these events unfold) about the length of time it would take him to fetch his wife from her hotel. Off he clatters, singing. What is he thinking? Is he doing his best to put a good face on things, to be a good sport, or is he really as pleased as he looks? Mrs. Horncastle has been careful not to make this difficult for him, but would she have wanted to succeed so thoroughly as this? Around the corner he goes, tipping his top hat to people on the street. Tipping his hat to a surprised Lady Alice Riven-Blythe as well, who is thrown into a muddle of indecision about whether she ought to respond.

Up Broad Street proceeds the singing bridegroom behind his strutting horses, and pulls to a stop before the great entrance doors to the Driard House. Down he climbs from his carriage, tilting his hat to the passersby who stop to watch. In through the doorway steps the little man, nods to the proprietor, who comes out from behind his desk to greet him on the red plush carpet of the foyer, near the foot of the staircase. The lady, announces the current replacement for the late Monsieur Driard, has been sent for. In fact, the lady's possessions are all around them now, in steamer trunks which the hired help have begun to transfer to the waiting carriage.

And now we see the smiling bride coming down the staircase. Having triumphed, she makes a victor's proud descent, enjoying every moment of the admiration she sees in the masculine faces below. The widow's weeds have been shed; she is dressed in lighter colours now – pale-green and white, with tiny embroidered flowers. Since no seamstress in town has been heard to boast of having made this dress for her, and no local yard-goods shop carries material with just that delicate pattern, the gown must have arrived in her trunks from Australia, awaiting this day! An enormous cream-coloured hat surmounts her magnificent copper hair, richly burnished by light from the chandelier. How happy she clearly expects to be from this day on. And how proud! Having conquered an army of forces allied against her, she obviously sees a future as clear and uncomplicated as the carpeted steps beneath her. A prosperous and satisfying future for the two children as well, who cling to her white-gloved hands as they descend the staircase, preparing to join with the man who will be, from this day forth, their father. No wonder she pauses on the landing and laughs richly, mightily, to show how much she is enjoying this, how satisfied she is to have effected her triumph!

When the proud bridegroom extends his arm, she leans close to whisper something in his ear. For a moment he looks startled, uncertain, almost displeased. But he recovers his mood and accompanies the smiling hotelier to the reception desk, where he makes arrangements, in writing, for the payment of the lady's entire bill.

There is some applause from the street when they step out through the hotel doorway. The bride acknowledges this with a small smile, but does not allow herself to look directly at this random collection of citizens. Horncastle, however, takes the time to bow in all directions, as though it is he and not his lady who has executed a triumph here. The children, perhaps confused by everyone's behaviour and eager to get their new lives under way, carry their mother's carpet-bag between them and climb into the carriage, where they sit as low and small as they are able while they wait to see what life is about to deal them. Their mother, having gained her seat with some assistance from her husband, takes their hands and whispers encouragement. Again, when Horncastle picks up the reins and urges the horses forward, there is scattered applause.

Laughter breaks out, now that they have gone. How happy are those gentlemen who, thanks to their astuteness in predicting the woman's success, discover themselves to be a little richer today! How happy are those married women who, having endured some marital humiliation of their own, have the satisfaction of seeing an old wrong made publicly right through feminine persistence. How happy are the pillars of the church, who have the satisfaction of seeing a sinner expelled from her unlawful place and the righteous properly rewarded. How happy are the town councillors, to witness this latest evidence that even here, so far from the centre of Empire, the fabric of British morality has been protected from rent or tatter. Happy are the representatives of the federal government, to see that the dedication to certain principles important in the eastern provinces is being upheld with equal fervour here in this new and still-untried portion of the west. Happy is the Prime Minister, the Right Honourable John A. Macdonald, in Ottawa, as he pours himself his fourth nightcap of the evening in complete confidence that all is well with the people he has been elected to represent but has not yet got around to seeing with his own eyes. And happy, too, is Her Sleeping Majesty, Victoria, far off in her royal bed in London, upon hearing in her dreams the clatter of horse and carriage transporting the reunited husband and wife to their home, knowing that even in the farthest, tiniest, most peculiar corners of her Empire, where residents sometimes forget that they are every bit as important to the larger scheme of things as every other part of the seamless whole, the moral standards of the age have once again been recognized and stoutly defended and applauded and finally rewarded with a general sense of satisfaction amongst the population. It is of no interest to her that one confused and unimportant builder amongst her loyal subjects, out walking, walking, walking, along the cliffs above the sea, is not so certain as he would like to be of this, or of anything.

LETTERS FROM A HAPPY BRIDE
TO FRIENDS AND RELATIVES IN
THE DISTANT ANTIPODES

21

Editor, The Ballarat Courier,
Ballarat, Victoria, Australia,

August 12, 1881.

Dear Sir:

Allow me to use the pages of your newspaper to send greetings to all those friends I left behind when I sailed, only months ago, to take up my new home in Canada. I recall a letter from Miss Josephine Carter published in your pages after she had moved to Auckland, and was grateful at the time for the opportunity to read of the good fortune she found in her new home. Those who have not forgotten the author of this present letter will remember a hopeful heart setting off in search of a happiness which had eluded her through many difficult years. Those who have lost their faith in happy endings may find here some reason to rekindle their trust in Providence's habit of rewarding the patient and hopeful heart.

After a long but pleasant voyage, in which my children and I were the recipients of unlimited kindnesses from the other passengers – including one of our own countrymen who made it his business to attend to my every need, and an American physician who watched over the health of myself and my dear children – we arrived safely and full of expectation in this lovely city, where we were made to feel extraordinarily welcome by an hospitable

population which seemed dedicated to overwhelming the newcomer with their generosity. Though the pleasure of this welcome
was somewhat marred by the discovery of the recent death of my
dear brother (a gentle man for whom I held fond memories, and for
whom I had felt the greatest affection despite the wide distance
which separated us all these years), the enormous friendliness of
the open-armed populace soon filled the gap created by this
sorrow and reassured me that I had made the correct decision in
coming here.

Consider my happiness when one of the first to bid me welcome
was a man who introduced himself with the name of someone I
had not seen for more than twenty years – the one true love of my
life! It is impossible to describe the joy which suffused his face
when he set eyes upon me, realizing that our unhappy separation
had finally come to an end. My heart, as might be imagined, fairly
raced within me to experience his joyous welcome. For this, you
see, was the gentleman who first won my heart and proposed marriage to me when I was little more than a girl, whom I had not
seen since he sailed from England for California – neither of us
then suspecting that forces dedicated to destroying happiness
would prevent him from returning to me – despite his many
attempts. I assured him that I had come to him with all my lifelong sorrow and hope in my breast, and would happily die, if that
was to be my fate, now that I had found and seen him at last. He
clasped me to him when I uttered these words, and he swore that
now we had found one another he would not be able to live
another minute without me at his side. Citizens of the town,
happy to see a love story unfold before their eyes, have made
unusual efforts to offer me their friendship, along with every assistance in achieving a permanent reunion.

Of course it is not blind chance that has reunited us. I had
learned of his presence in this city from a casual reference made
by my brother in one of his letters to me. This was the first
glimpse of hope in a story that has been filled with incidents of

deception. A sister intercepted his letters, and made me to understand that he had deserted me. In fact, my dear love has never married in all these years, keeping himself unattached in the hope that we would one day be happily reunited. "How could I fancy any other woman," he said, "when memory of you has never left me for even an hour?" Oh how wonderfully it has all come to its proper end! I had never suspected such joy was possible. He has taken me (and the children) into his generous heart and into his lovely home and has made me the happiest of all women in the world.

It appears that all this city has been blessed by my arrival here, for everyone rejoices. Friends, neighbours, even strangers greet us with happy faces, considering themselves to be privileged witnesses to the proper end of an otherwise tragic love story. That the heartbroken girl has been rewarded with riches (my love is the owner of a most splendid hotel) and with social position (he is known and admired amongst the best people here, who have also taken me to their bosoms) reminds everyone of the rewards awaiting the patient, the true, the truly loving heart. Yet I would be this happy even if I had found him the owner of no more than a filthy hovel, the friend of no one – I would be willing to beg with him on the street so long as we could be together.

Though there is one resident of Ballarat who will be dismayed to hear of my happiness, I know there are many others who will rejoice with me. And it is my belief that the general population, ever thirsty for news of justice and happiness wherever it can be found in the world, will welcome my letter as one more proof of Providence's care for those who do not lose faith. In gratitude I shall serve my husband and my Father all my life.

A friend abroad,
(Mrs.) Kathleen McConnell Jordan Horncastle.

August 12, 1881.

Dearest Annie,

Greetings from your happy sister in this prettiest little corner of the earth! Of course you will soon read of my joy in the Courier, like everyone else in Ballarat, but I did not wish my dearest sister to learn of my happiness from a *newspaper*! You shall learn it, dear Annie, from my own pen. I am sitting at *his* roll-top secretary, in the living-room of our home, which is in a wing of our hotel, with my dear dear James not three feet away, arguing with a newspaper and occasionally stroking the head of his poor deaf terrier Vicky at his feet – a dog who has grown too old, it seems, to understand anything of what is going on, perhaps the most irritable dog in creation! We can reach out at any moment and touch hand to hand, husband and wife – and shall do so now. There! My darling asks me to relay his fondest regards, though he remembers you as the tiniest and most demanding child, always with food smeared across your face! Oh, he is the kindest of men, Annie, and never ceases to tell me how happy I have made him. His life, he says, was empty and meaningless during all those years we have been apart, made bearable only by his constant dream that we would one day find one another and live as we were meant to live – together.

(You must not share this or any letter between us with Susannah! Let that woman read about me in the newspaper like anyone else! How I wish I could hear the gnashing of teeth! You must write and tell me how much I have enraged her by advertising my happiness in such a public way. She shall decide that I have acted only to spite her. You must report every *word*. Does she refuse to go out into town, where her few sour friends will have learned of my reward and my joy? Does she regret, at last, her horrible behaviour in intercepting my letter, now that knowledge of her crime has been made universal? She probably regrets nothing except that she did not strangle me in my sleep while it was within her power to do so!)

Perhaps there would be no harm in telling her something of the manner in which our reunion has been celebrated. I was forbidden to help with the preparations. Hotel employees were assisted by temporary servants hired for the occasion. Invitations went out for the following Saturday with the news that the entire hotel would be turned over to this happy event! The Lieutenant-Governor and his wife received an invitation. So did the premier, a man by the name of Walkem. Leading families were invited to meet the newly arrived Mrs. Horncastle – the Tyrwhitt-Drakes, the Pearses, the Pembertons. Even titled folk – a Lady Riven-Blythe, a tiny little wrinkled soul no larger than a child, with genuine jewels hanging off her like a Christmas tree. Mr. Noah Shakespeare was invited, a fine gentleman who has announced he will be seeking the mayoralty chair at the end of the year. Invitations went out to the two local Members of Parliament (our representatives in Ottawa) – one of them no less than the Prime Minister of the country himself (who was unfortunately out of town) and the other the strangest little man, whose improbable but apparently legal name is Amor de Cosmos. He was, I am told, influenced by a spell in California like so many others here, and is famous for fiery speeches denouncing this and that. Amongst other things, he would clean out the Chinese from our midst before we are overrun with the heathen. You can see that in some respects I have exchanged one Ballarat for another! Our slant-eyed Celestial brothers are encountered everywhere here, though their living-quarters are confined to a few city blocks where they produce opium for the Yankees and entertain at Oriental games. Murders have occurred, perhaps because of the almost total absence of women of their own sort. The policies of the Rev. Potter (who would force the Chinese to move five miles out of Ballarat to protect our morals, remember?) would find a welcome audience here.

Though the first families and politicians were unfortunately unable to attend, having already accepted an invitation to a tennis party at the O'Reilly home, gracious regrets were sent on the most beautiful cards. Despite this unfortunate coincidence, we were joined for the festivities by a large crowd of well-wishers. The hotel's entire dining-room was made over for the occasion, and appropriately decorated! Of course there were a few of the merely curious amongst the guests, and some who had been less than friendly with my James in the past but who wished to discover for themselves what sort of woman was now mistress of The Great Blue Heron. I disappointed no one, you can be sure, being as capable of acting the gracious hostess as anyone. The bejewelled little Lady Riven-Blythe watched everything from the sidelines, without participating, as though she were in the theatre! James made a speech that had everyone falling out of their chairs with laughter. (What an exuberant wit the man has, a virtual stage comic, though I didn't hesitate to reprimand him sharply when he began to tell jokes at the expense of my former home – which he would portray as a country of convicts! You can be sure he will not refer to me as his "convict bride" again before witnesses, however lovingly he might say it, however much I have not minded hearing him call me that in private, knowing he meant it only as an endearment!) He immediately proposed a toast to his lovely long-lost bride, now returned to him so that the world could go on in its proper course as it had been prevented from doing for so many years. (Her bejewelled Ladyship commenced a coughing fit towards the end of James's speech, poor thing, and excused herself. I suppose this attack was a serious embarrassment to her, since the sweet little woman did not return to the table at all but left immediately for home. I have made certain that an appropriate card has been delivered, insisting that we shall become the dearest of friends. It has been rumoured that she has family connections at the Court of St. James.)

I had not anticipated the pleasure of being out of the widow's weeds. Green is still my colour, as you have always known, and brought such compliments at our feast as make me blush to remember! A fine old friend of my husband's, Captain Trumble of the Royal Navy, proclaimed within the hearing of the entire assembly that "this fine lady from the underside of the earth is the most attractive woman presently in the city." Much applause as he raised his glass again and again to my singular attractions. After the fourth toast I asked Mr. Horncastle to silence him, lest it occur to the others that the Captain had spent so long at sea that he'd lost his judgement altogether and said the same of every woman that swam into range of his telescope!

But green is not the end of everything – I have not allowed a few compliments to persuade me to give up one slavery only to take up another. The prospect of choosing a frock from my wardrobe gives me more joy than I suppose it should. Yet, how wonderful it is to hear "Oh, what a delightful pattern there is in that material, Mrs. Horncastle. Did you bring it with you from Australia?" and "I am sick with envy at your daring – that hat with that dress – a huge success!" With James's encouragement, I have ordered several items from a seamstress just around the corner (one of 33 within walking distance of my door!) who does not object to the original touches I suggest. A dolman of three-quarter length is to be ready first, ginger in colour, with a great deal of fringing, tassels, pleated satin ribbons, and jet headings. Of course it will be shaped at the back, not for the bustle – though we have been told it will soon be enjoying a revival – but to accommodate the lower drawn-up backs to the dresses I have ordered made – a plum silk, with seven *volants* of pleated tulle and blue trim, and day-dresses of pale-blue and grey wool. I shall enclose my clumsy drawings of their design. You will not be surprised to learn that women here wear fashions similar to those in Ballarat – roughly the same distance in time behind society in London, we are told, but via San Francisco rather than Melbourne!

It is a heaven I have found here, Annie. Everyone overwhelms me with kindness. Even when Dear James must attend to the hotel, he does not neglect to rush to our living-quarters several times in the day, to remind his delighted "convict bride" how passionately he loves her! And how energetically and inexhaustibly he expresses his love! I must remind him often that the hotel and its guests will feel neglected while he lavishes all his excellent attentions on me.

If anyone can imagine how I feel to have accomplished such a triumph, Annie, surely that person is you. No one knows better how I suffered at Susannah's hands. No one knows better how imperfect was my marriage to Mr. Jordan. No one knows better how desperately I endured the hardships of impoverished widow-hood, or how dangerously close I came to accepting second-best, or how vehemently I insisted that a Divine justice would someday reinstate the happiness of which I was so cruelly deprived. No one knows better than you how I have always wanted only to know what is the right thing to do, and to do it. We have been partners for years in every confidence and in every secret kept from the rest of the world. You should have no difficulty, then, in imagining my present joy – how my breast is filled with glad singing, with splendid gratitude. I have *made things right again*. Still, my mind is awhirl with anticipation of the bliss which still lies ahead. I shall use my success as a foundation on which to build an extraordinarily happy life. I have not been accorded justice for nothing!

You see how I go on. James accuses me of writing an encyclopedia. I could cheerfully provide you with an encyclopedia of the various joys which have greeted my new status as James Horncastle's wife and mistress of his hotel. But my darling has yawned several times while I have been writing. I shall close now, and sit on his lap to ruffle his hair! It is a white head of hair now, but still almost as thick and handsome as when it was dark and youthful so long ago in Manchester.

The children are well, and happy to have a father again. My husband speaks of boarding-schools, where they will be properly educated for the future.

I wonder if you will ever visit me here, and see what happiness I have found. I shall pray for this to happen.

Your happy sister,
Kate ("Mrs. Kathleen Horncastle
of The Great Blue Heron Hotel").

September 22, 1881.

Dear Annie,

Of course there has not been enough time for you to respond to my last letter but I shall continue to inform you of my life here in paradise. I have never fallen into the habit of keeping a diary, but understand the need some people feel to do so. You shall be my occasional diary, Annie – my confidante, my secret ear, my private listener.

James is not at home today. He has abandoned the hotel to me and the help, having found it necessary to meet with some fellow named Hatch in a mysterious dispute involving his irritable little Vicky. I know none of the details, and wish to hear none, since I suspect that this Hatch fellow is merely some farmer whose cow has got onto the road (as they all seem to do here) where Vicky has given it a nip on the heel. He did not tell me how long this business might take, so I have decided to fill up his absence with writing to you. Thank goodness he did not ask me to accompany him! You know how I dislike disputations.

A horrid racket accompanies the progress of my pen. Outside, a new face is being erected across the front of the Blue Heron. A new verandah is going up, with stout aristocratic pillars and an upstairs terrace. Our guests must come and go by a side door, and apparently will have to do so for several weeks, on the insistence of the man who is supervising the work. The discarded suitor of an unfeeling woman, I am told, he is already becoming a local legend for his desolate eyes, his defeated shoulders, his refusal to look at another woman, or to speak unkindly of the cruel young lady who spurned him. He has my sympathy if that is what he wants for the role he has chosen, but it seems that since his rejection by the hard-hearted maiden he is much intimidated by women. Perhaps it is only married women who frighten him! When I praised the energy with which he approached his work he looked pitifully grateful for a moment, then abruptly turned gruff and resentful, as workmen who aspire to the title of gentleman will so often do, being uncertain of what is expected of them. He is someone for whom Lady Riven-Blythe has an affection, I understand, so I must make an effort to cultivate him.

He has been far too well brought up to turn the grief and anger of a rejected lover into an excuse for becoming an outrageous public oddity – he has not become a drunkard, that I know of, nor does he spit on the street at the approach of women, as you may remember Swampy Nicholson doing – but he has his quiet eccentricities all the same. He dresses in ancient, drab, ill-fitting clothing, as though he forgets to take them off at night and sees no point in buying new trousers or shirts now that he has lost his lover's hand. He will find a conversation not to his liking and suddenly bury his nose in one of the books he carries with him, as though he has forgotten his companion's existence, or considers the other of little interest. And he has had for a long time the most peculiar habit of recording his changing thoughts on his own tombstone – which has grown into something of a monstrous cairn offering a running commentary on the shifting state of his soul! Not only that, this growing monument records a totally false biography. According to the stone, he has designed and built a magnificent variety of splendid buildings around town, including a glorious cathedral with a gleaming spire of white marble, with Byzantine archways and baroque domes, and with fifty-seven stained glass windows brought from Italy, high on a certain hill overlooking the city, on a location which anyone can recognize as the site of Peterson's pig farm! According to the tombstone, he has designed and erected, near the corner of Quadra and Fort, a magnificent Opera House with gleaming domes and elaborate arches, trimmed with gold and river-jade and flanked by a host of marble statues of famous musicians. Yet if you go to the corner of Quadra and Fort you will find the site to be occupied by the same little grog shop which has stood there for several years.

Challenged by city councillors to explain this peculiar business, he protests that he is merely recording his life as it would have been if these had only been more prosperous times. They accuse him of forgetting who he is, of forgetting *where* he is, but he pays no heed. Citizens gazing upon the modest wooden plank façade of Mansell's Shoes can now imagine that it is mere illusion, occupying only in legal fact the actual location of Logan Sumner's lovely towering glass palace, a tall conservatory for the display of lush plants and exotic birds collected in the jungles of the tropics, discharging a rich moist heat and a sharp riotous noise upon those who pass by its doors.

Meanwhile, he works in the more real world upon The Great Blue Heron, and does not seem to realize that people have begun to make special visits to the cemetery in order to read his latest instalment, rather as though they subscribed to one of those London magazines which print stories even as the author is still writing them. Some go to laugh at a fool, some to smile over the peculiarities of an amusing friend, and some to sympathize – knowing only too well, I suppose, how impermanent are their own opinions on life.

I shall leave the exterior renovations to the men and concentrate on improvements to areas within my own confidence. I am anxious, for instance, to replace most of the furnishings in this parlour. Oak tables are too heavy and dark, the horsehair chairs too homely, the lithographs and etchings on the wall too sentimental. (Galloping horses, mail coaches, hedgerows, and the rolling fields of England. An example: "False Alarm on the Road to Gretna – 'It's only the Mail!'") The striped wallpaper lacks interest – everything reflecting some other taste in another time. There is a furniture factory in town manufacturing modern designs which are more to my liking. I have already put an end to the habit of filling a residence with flowers – I've always disliked flowers inside a house, as you know, and yet people here insist upon placing bowls of them in every room. Leave them in the gardens where they belong! I have collected a dozen – no, more than a dozen – ugly vases and bowls for flowers, and have hidden them from the help so that we may eventually leave the habit behind us.

I have already ordered a new, more colourfully embossed covering for the wall panels of the large banquet room – The Heron's Nest – which is rented at regular intervals by nostalgic immigrants for meetings and banquets, with speeches and laughter and incomprehensible singing. Germans come noisily crowding in every first Wednesday, to roar out drinking songs. A few Spaniards have their day as well. Fewer Belgians. Swedes. Norwegians. A company of Scots pays in advance for the certainty of damage done the furniture. Americans still ambivalent about their decision not to go home in 1871 when this province joined the Dominion meet to sing "The Star-Spangled Banner" and listen to patriotic speeches. Leading citizens are amongst them: Clyde Munro, a vehement annexationist, and Sturgess Hogan, who delivers stirring speeches in a Louisiana accent. Sometimes James attends, when he finds himself feeling some affection for California. Those who are still Americans in their hearts have been in particular need of cheer lately, stricken as they are with grief for their President, who has finally died of the assassin's bullet which brought him down in the summer. They petitioned energetically for lowered flags, and have persuaded more than one or two residents to dress in mourning, and have filled The Heron's Nest (James reports) with loud and emotional calls for seizing the moment to offer this province as a gift to the Great Republic in its time of mourning.

Married life with James continues to be a joy – though you will laugh to hear that there is a great wide red-faced Irish peasant woman in town who has decided to use the name of "Mrs. Horncastle" herself, and who encourages her huge brood of unpleasant children (every size and shape of ruffian) to use the name as well! She is quite obviously one of those women who have called seventeen different men "husband" for brief periods in her life but never signed a paper with even one. I have suggested to James that he speak to her, to convince her that there are many other pleasant names she might adopt for her purposes, but he has only laughed and called me an old snob! What difference should it make to me, he says, if there were forty-five women in town all calling themselves "Mrs. Horncastle," so long as I remain the only one with a "Mr. Horncastle" on my arm? Of course he is right. There is nothing gives me more pleasure than to be out walking on an evening with him and to hear people greet us with "G'd evening, Horncastle, g'd evening, ma'am," as they tip their hats and smile.

No, there is something which gives me even greater pleasure than walking out with Mr. Horncastle. I am become famous, dearest Annie, for my conversation. We have become sought-after as guests, and dear James insists that this is due to their fascination with me. They cannot hear enough of Australia, it seems – though every second person in this town appears to have spent some time there. Will you mind if I confess I find it very easy to satisfy their desire to hear negative comparisons with life here?

Indeed, I have no difficulty praising the gigantic trees one finds in the forest here, wide and straight and tall, or comparing them favourably with the scrawny gum. Similarly it is a simple matter to sing the praises of those who have chosen to live in this town, a polite, gentle, quality breed of loyal Britons in large part, and to dismiss the sort of rough colonial riff-raff one finds passing through the streets of Ballarat. They even swell with pride to hear me praise their Indians – as though they had chosen them! – as a more colourful and enterprising race than the blackfellows. And am I wrong? There are several of their Indians to be seen selling fish on the streets and paddling their boats in the harbour. Though I have never spoken to any of them, of course, they seem to have survived at least, and perhaps even adapted, while the primitive Aboriginal in Australia cannot even be found, having either fled the challenge of European civilization or died of the attempt to adapt. I regret I have no anecdotes to tell about them, never having even *thought* about them while I lived in Ballarat. If you hear any tales, do pass them on. You can be sure I'll be the centre of attention when I relate them to our new friends.

But I hear my darling returning. He has stopped to report to the builder outside. I can hear their voices through the window, though not their words. I wonder if the laughter means he has been winner in the dispute.

Write! Dearest Annie write! You cannot imagine how anxious I am to hear from you. It is most important that I hear news of your own happiness soon. And of course I am anxious still to learn how prominently my letter was displayed in the newspaper, and whether certain people read it, and how those same certain people have responded to news of my success.

As always,
Your loving sister,
Kate.

December 5, 1881.

Dear Annie,

How wonderful to receive your note yesterday, though I am sorry that my letter was published before you received word directly from me. Surely by now!

Of course I am not surprised to hear that Susannah, upon reading my letter in the *Courier*, did not visibly react in your presence except to "smile, as one who knows better or has some foreknowledge of satisfaction." She knows nothing, except that the fury in her heart will eat her alive, but she is an expert at deception, masking the truth in order to bring about the desired effect in others.

Yesterday my James came home from the races with a bloody nose! His pride would not allow him to explain the details to me but I am certain he was kicked by a horse. Perhaps he stood where he oughtn't, and feels foolish about it. How brave he was as I nursed him. And how we laughed together at the comical sight that looked back at us from the mirror!

Helping James to manage this hotel has meant a little more work for me than he ever intended me to do. You must not, of course, inform Susannah of this. She will only laugh at her own interpretation of it. The fact is, dearest Annie, that though James is dismayed at the sight of his wife working like a servant, this dear soft-hearted man at the time of our reunion found it necessary to mortgage the hotel in order to honour an agreement with someone much less fortunate than ourselves. I have the comfort of knowing that another has been enabled to live respectably because of his remarkable generosity. He hoped, of course, that this would not affect our life – indeed, that I would never even have to know. But I do know, and it is the least I can do to lend a hand during this time when we cannot afford to have as many servants as an hotel of this size demands. I console myself, when my hands are up to the elbows in the wash water, with the knowledge that I am doing this so that someone's children can have a roof over their head. And it shall not be like this for long. James assures me that when the next boom comes – when gold is again discovered somewhere up the island or somewhere in the province's Interior, as it is certain to be – we will, like others in similar businesses here, make our fortunes so fast we will not have the time to count our money. "We will not need to go off, like pack-horses, to dig for the gold ourselves," he says. "We will let the others go and break their backs for it and then – in the name of service and hospitality – we will take as much of it as possible away from them. And you can be certain they'll be *grateful* for it too!" This seems to be the prevailing attitude in the town – all waiting for a tidal wave of diggers to wash over us, every one of them willing to be parted from his money for equipment or comfort or a dry bed beneath a roof.

Here is an incident so peculiar that I am sometimes not entirely certain I did not dream it. I was speaking yesterday with the young man who is responsible for putting a new face on the Blue Heron – you will recall that I described him in a previous letter – and we were joined by a red Indian he introduced to me as his friend. I was surprised to hear that this Indian had a name, though I suppose he must – I had simply never considered the possibility before. What was even more remarkable was to learn that this fellow is not only a carpenter employed to work on the hotel (how had I missed him?) but an inventor as well! Perhaps he has invented a new rain dance, I thought, or a modern device for catching more fish! Though I am happy to say that he did not offer to shake my hand, he did shuffle around kicking his toe in the soil and grinning and acting as though he expected me to toss him a few pennies from my purse, and within my hearing did not utter a single word of understandable English – capable, I supposed, of speaking nothing but his mother tongue. I shall be sure to look for him tomorrow so that I might describe to you the peculiar vision of a red Indian aiming a carpenter's hammer at a nail!

The astonishing thing is that these two young men are trying to invent a *machine that flies*! You have read of these mad people in the newspapers occasionally, of course, risking their lives to imitate the birds. Eventually they end up with broken necks or broken hearts, and I have no doubt that these two will be no different from the rest. Of course, their enterprise has been kept secret from the public, but they assumed I already knew about it, since James had somehow learned of this undertaking and had persuaded the builder to allow him to observe a "demonstration" of the latest invention. The Indian (who can speak a little English after all!) suggested that I accompany them, which I did, this morning at dawn, feeling myself to be the most foolish woman in the province. Oh, it is impossible to know which of those males demonstrated the most ridiculous pleasure – the strutting inventor, the proud friend, my excited husband, or *the Chinese cook who would ride in it*! And all this strutting and puffing was for a machine which may possibly have been the most comical vehicle that has ever been made. A perambulator for giant babies is what I thought of, overshadowed by the great black wings of a flying fox! And yet, out on that cliff, you would think we were about to witness a miracle. What was more likely, I thought, was the tragic end, all in a terrible moment, of one Indian's hopes and one Chinaman's life. Yet I believe that not even I was more surprised than the inventor himself that the thing actually took to the air, once it had left the cliff! No bald-headed eagle ever soared more confidently. Wind caught it up, and pushed it forward. The wings dipped to the left, dipped to the right. We watched amazed. But eventually it slipped lower, and slipped lower, and finally came to rest on the waves, perhaps a mile out from land, and must be rescued by the Indian in his boat.

Of course, when he learned that someone in the opium business was contributing money for this invention, James (who hates to be left out of anything with an element of risk in it) insisted on contributing himself from a small amount he had recently won in some wager. If this redskin should succeed, he says, we shall all be rich! When they learned of this new source of support, the Indian and our young Sumner behaved like a couple of laughing school-boys unable to believe their good luck. Though all this occurred only this morning, I am already beginning to doubt that I witnessed, with my own eyes, this amazing episode.

(I ramble on too long, but I remember that you have always been fascinated with stories of the tribes which once had this continent to themselves. I doubt that any of your books included Icarus-redskins afflicted with the desire to conquer the sky by means of winged contraptions constructed out of bits and pieces found in the rubbish dump!)

Thinking of those cliffs where the trial flight took place has reminded me of a tragedy which occurred here recently. I believe I have not mentioned to you a certain Dr. M who came aboard the *Sardonyx* in San Francisco during my journey. Before we came ashore the man had allowed himself to become unreasonably infatuated with me, to the point where he proposed marriage several times. However, when I assured him that my heart already belonged to another, he retired from the contest like a gentleman and dedicated himself to serving the sick in the little towns of the Cariboo region. Last week I came down the staircase to the hotel foyer and found him standing with hat in hand, watching my descent.

"I was afraid of this," he said.

"There are no surprises here," I said. "This is precisely what I predicted."

"I could think of nothing else but you," he said. "Who knows how many wounded men received inadequate attention because of my obsession? How do I know she did not change her mind at the last moment, I wondered. How do I know for certain that Mr. Horncastle did not abandon her? She may at this moment be in need. So I packed up, quit everything, and moved back, to see for myself."

"And what you see is a woman happy in marriage!"

"As you say."

With that, he bowed and withdrew. I would never see him again. I later learned that he found his way to our William's former saloon, where he drank too much. When they encouraged him to stop, he shot the proprietor in the shoulder and ran away, thinking, I believe, that he had killed the man. By the time the police were roused to follow him, he had found his way through the park and stood at the edge of the cliff, apparently, where he shot himself in the head. His body toppled to the beach below! The poor man suffered from his own tendency to exaggerate whatever small hope I may have at one time allowed him to have.

Preparations have begun for Christmas. Though they will not be very much different from preparations in Ballarat, a large dinner with roast goose will seem a little less incongruous here to an English-born lady than they seemed in Ballarat at the height of summer. I wonder if, perversely, I shall miss the after-dinner ride in the open air, the bathe at the lake, the evening picnic. I expect we shall entertain a large gathering, and I shall be asked to make them laugh with stories of wiping the perspiration from our brows, etc.

You ask about the children. I know it gave you pain to part with them and they refused at first to understand why Aunt Annie was not accompanying us on the voyage. Laura is content in a boarding-school, where they labour to make a lady of her. And James has sent little James to a school in San Francisco, where he lives with a Horncastle cousin and plans soon to come home for Christmas. Occasionally I miss them very much but never for very long. You know I was not made to be the mother you were meant to be – and may be yet – and I am quite content to have my home and my James all to myself. When I am not helping to run the hotel, I try to dedicate a few hours each week to works done for the poor by the church. Reverend Trodd presides over a host of women who, like myself, wish to share their good fortune with others. No great friendship has yet developed between myself and any of these women, since there is a quiet sort of reserve and sense of privacy amongst people here which you do not find to the same degree amongst Australians. Nevertheless, I have enjoyed a friendship with a Mrs. Collins from Toronto, staying with her husband at the Blue Heron for a week while he concluded some business transaction with local furniture-makers. And for three consecutive days I was the inseparable companion of the elderly Mrs. Baillie from San Francisco, also a guest with her lawyer-husband at the hotel, who insisted on taking me everywhere with her while she was here – on a shopping spree, on a picnic into the country, even on an excursion to New Westminster to visit her brother and sister-in-law who live there! Like a couple of school-girls, we exchanged histories and confidences at the ship's rail for the entire crossing, and later parted from one another with prom-ises of a great deal more should James ever take me south for a holiday in that great American city.

Write soon. I shall think of you at Christmas. A small parcel, a gift from us both, has long ago found its way onto a ship sailing in your direction, promising to arrive in plenty of time for that special day when families think of one another with love.

Your devoted sister,
Kate.

January 12, 1882.

Dear dear Annie,

The Blue Heron prospers wonderfully! (The new façade is nearing completion.) One of the busiest bars in town – thanks to the popularity of my James! A famous dining-room specializing in recipes no one had heard of here before I arrived. The beauti-fully decorated rooms (my choice of colours) have become a favourite place for guests from San Francisco looking for comfort, convenience, and reasonable prices. Even the occasional civil servant sent out here against his wishes on a good-will visit from Ottawa will think first of the Blue Heron, unless the snobs in the cast tell them they must stop at the more luxurious (and expensive) Driard. I hope you will not think me vain if I suggest that my own presence has contributed much to the hotel's success. The departing guest is rare who does not leave his compliments to Mrs. Horncastle! For such rewards, what difference does it make if I must get up at five to help with cleaning, then supervise a new cook over breakfast, then take my turn behind the reception desk, and finally assist with the clearing of the tables after dinner? Everyone agrees that it is this constant awareness of the lady of the house which has contributed most to the hotel's growing reputation. The mortgage payments are meanwhile being met, and soon we should be able to hire more help.

Of course, my pleasure in seeing the hotel's success is inseparable from my joy in being married to such a popular figure about town. He cannot go down the street without encountering five, seven, a dozen of his friends, all insisting on his opinion of this and that, all hoping to draw him into one of his comical tirades against the more unreasonable laws. He is so popular that four evenings out of the week he must be off at a meeting with his male acquaintances. He is incapable of disappointing any request for his company when he thinks his good nature is required for the happiness of others. He is far too generous, too kind. He is altogether such a happy and energetic man; what sort of wife would wish to clip his wings? In the evenings I have taken up sewing again and quite enjoy it, and sometimes I read. Occasionally his old friend Captain Trumble stops by, expecting to find James at home, and I persuade him to stay for a cup of tea and to entertain me with tales of his life on the oceans. (He has a wife in Valparaiso, Chile, but has not seen her in twenty-six years. "By now she will have forgotten she married a lonely English lieutenant stationed nearby.") Even when I am alone, however, I take pleasure in anticipating my husband's lively accounts of his adventures with his companions out on the town. The dear man has me laughing until I must wipe tears from my eyes and beg him to stop! Sometimes I think that I have achieved the happiness that is every woman's dream. He is strong and indefatigable. His debts are very small, his scraps no worse than the harmless scraps of schoolyard boys, with no lasting damage to anyone. Though he is popular enough in town to win any election in which he chose to run, he takes little interest in the plots of the powerful, or in politics – an honest man, a man of principles, and a hard reliable workman. You see that I have been aptly rewarded for my long wait, and for my long, long journey around the globe!

People still insist that I talk about dear old Ballarat, and about Victoria (yours, not ours!), and about Australia in general! I seem to have been born with a flair for entertaining! Love triangle in Melbourne leads to opera-house murder! (Remember?) Families eaten by dingoes out in the dead heart of the continent! (Were there not rumours about the disappeared Mortons?) The Queen's son shot in Sydney, but saved from death by his own suspenders! Old folks dropping in the streets from the heat! And who is to tell the guests around Emily Marsden's table that it was not *myself* who was in the carriage which was stopped and robbed by Ned Kelly and his gang just a week before they were captured, or myself who warned him to his face about the hanging that awaited him if he didn't change his ways? No harm done if occasionally in my enthusiasm (as James has later chided me) I have become more animated than I'd intended on behalf of the animals and flowers and scenery of Australia, painting a more outrageous and outlandish picture than anyone could believe, and sometimes forgetting to say (as I was used to) a word or two in praise of the local favourites, assuring them that the native Vancouver Island cedars and crows and mountain streams are far more lovely than all that I left behind.

Sheilagh Monahan of the Ballarat Monahans is "Lizzie Sheepshank" here (!) and has begged me not to tell others of her period of hard labour as a result of that "lost-brooch misunderstanding" on the part of her employer. Her farmhouse is less than an hour's ride from here, out through some of the prettiest countryside imaginable – naked oak trees and sharp, dramatic outcroppings of rock and glimpses of sunlight on the loveliest little bays. James offered to take me with him last Wednesday while he visited the racehorses he keeps there, and I did not decline. The lady of the house was most congenial while the men were occupied outside, introducing me to her special recipe for blood pudding, and insisting that I take jars of her berry jam home with me. She has a sister in Glenrowan, who occasionally visits friends in Ballarat. I wonder if you have met her – a Mrs. Christopher Jones – or remember a girl of my age with a large discoloration across one side of her face. We became fast friends, this "Lizzie Sheepshank" and myself, though she says it is unlikely she will visit me in town. "I cannot abide big cities!" she says. "Too much noise and motion!" So it will be necessary for me to accompany James on future visits to the farm if I am to see any more of her.

You will never guess who I encountered when I stepped out of Mrs. Sheepshank's farmhouse before leaving for home. Old Stonybrow! If you have noticed that he is no longer to be seen on the streets of Ballarat, or on the trails through the botanical gardens, it is because he is here! I became aware of him watching me as Lizzie Sheepshank and I walked across the front yard – he stood by the fence, in that long, loose, lanky, insolent manner of his, watching us out from under the brim of his hat. When he saw that I recognized him (and I did not catch myself quickly enough to pretend that I did not), he touched the hat brim and sort of growled a greeting. A hired hand, Lizzie tells me! He is in charge of the horses – including James's. "Mrs. Horncastle and me have been acquaintances for many years," he tells Lizzie when she introduces us. But he does not take his eyes from me. "Mrs. Horncastle and me, we have business between us that goes back a long way! Me and her *other* husband, we was mates."

Hearing his voice makes me shiver, as it has always done. "Of course, he was never a friend of my former husband, who would laugh to hear him say it," I explained to Lizzie. Since that accidental encounter, he has approached me in town. Not another proposal of marriage, of course – I should tell him to return to Australia and seek you out if he still had that on his mind! He lowered his great dark brow and glowered at me from beneath his hat brim, and seemed interested only in making certain I realized how he dislikes me. The man has gone mad, I think! "Well, you promised to follow me to the arctic if necessary," I told him, "and we have come almost that far. But you can see for yourself that there's no point in following me any farther, as I'm a married woman."

It is a grey day. Clouds have come down low and oppressive. A thin rain drizzles on everything, as though several days of heavy downpour were not enough to wring the clouds entirely dry. The street in front of the Blue Heron has become a sea of mud. A herd of cattle has just passed through on their noisy way to the slaughterhouse, leaving both mud and scented air more than a little altered in their wake! I have discovered, I think, the purpose behind those bowls of flowers in every room, and shall dig out the hidden vases at first sight of an early spring bloom! Still, I would not trade this life for life in Ballarat – where I think of you in brilliant summer sunlight now, seeking out the shade of the jacaranda and drinking cool lemonades while you slap a fan back and forth across yourself and read my letters. Lilian has months ahead of her yet of praying for an early autumn. She doesn't write, and I have written only once to her. Do you pass my news on? (I'm certain you do.) Does Susannah even ask what has become of me, I wonder.

Visits from young James and Laura enlivened Christmas immeasurably. I hope they have both written from their schools to thank you for the books. Laura has become quite a snob, and spent the holiday correcting my manners. I believe she has decided, finally, that I am beyond repair. Her Miss Trill has taught her to regard anything that is not English as barbaric, and it seems that the damage done by all those years in Australia has only been confounded, confused, and made irreparable by just six months of living in Canada. Young James has taken a dislike to my husband's cousin in San Francisco, and threatens to insist on living with us for his next year of school – or dropping out altogether. Perhaps you will write and encourage him to value learning. He is a worrier, like his father, but unfortunately also shares his father's stubbornness, which you and I both remember well enough! Both of them continue to miss you desperately, as I do myself.

> With my loving wishes
> for your good health and happiness,
> Your faithful sister,
> Kate.

February 3, 1882.

My dearest Annie,

I give you fair warning – the purpose of this short letter, dear sister, is quite simply to persuade you to abandon Susannah, to leave Ballarat, to give up Australia altogether, and to join me here in this loveliest of little cities in this loveliest little corner of the Empire. Does that shock you? You will see how I am about to make you an irresistible offer. Prepare to start packing your trunks!

No, I have not gone mad. I am more convinced than ever that I have discovered the almost perfect life. And I am determined to share it with you! The hotel, as I am certain I mentioned in my last letter, looks splendid with its new face, and is growing in popularity every month. James's own celebrity continues to grow, to the point where I must caution him against suggestions that he run for public office! Hostesses count on me to be their entertainment over dessert – urging me on to more and more outrageous tattle-telling against my former homeland. (How successful Annie would be at this, I can't help thinking.) What has been referred to as "winter" has been little more than a damp season of waiting for spring, and life here, it seems to me, grows more attractive every day. Surely no prettier town exists, and no grander surroundings. I thank God daily for bringing you that letter which inspired me to exchange that continent for this. Will you not make my happiness complete and come join us in it?

But lest you think I could expect you to give up your comfortable life in one hemisphere out of mere enthusiasm for my own, let me take a deep breath and make you the specific proposal I have in mind. Only a sister could write what follows, as only a beloved sister might be trusted with what I am about to write. My darling has proved to be as wonderful a husband as I have reported to you in letter after letter – thoughtful, gentle, entertaining, generous, and helpful. He is, in every way but one, the ideal mate. But he has suggested many times, dear Annie, in the kindliest way, that he finds conjugal life with a wife who has already been someone else's wife before him to be less satisfying than he had hoped. To put it bluntly, dearest sister, he finds me to be "damaged." Do you find this shocking? Perhaps I would find it shocking myself if it were not for something else I have kept from you. I confess that I myself find that particular aspect of our marriage to be disappointing – not at all what I had hoped. Now I am not about to announce the imminent dissolution of this marriage, which is otherwise a very happy one, but I am about to make you, sweet Annie, a proposal which you may find surprising at first but which, upon further thought, I am certain you will find irresistible. Do you remember the afternoon when you came after me and found me at Wendouree Swamp, where I had just had an encounter with Old Stonybrow? When you asked if I had accepted his proposal of marriage, I said to you, "I will marry him if you will sleep with him!" Well, I have taken up this pen, sweet sister, in order to make you a similar offer now. There is ample room in our home for it to become your home too, and there is ample room in my darling's heart to welcome a never-married sister-in-law into his life! Certainly he would not find you "damaged," as he put it. Rather than jealous, you will find me filled with gratitude. What joy, to see my husband's happiness complete! What pleasure, to be free of a certain obligation myself! And what pleasure, too, to know that the sister I love, who has mentioned so many times how much she regrets having rejected early proposals of marriage, will share with me the satisfactions of the happy wife so far denied her!

Write soon with your answer! Do not keep me in suspense! What happiness I anticipate for us all if you should agree to sail immediately! I shall hold my breath, sweet sister Annie, until I hear.

> Lovingly,
> Your fond sister,
> Kate.

> April 9, 1882.

Darling Kate,

I have made the arrangements to sail from Melbourne in May, then north from San Francisco to arrive on June 14th, if all goes well. Susannah will try to stop me but you already know that the one thing stronger in me than familial loyalty is my curiosity. I am *consumed* with interest! – enough, I think, to drive the ship at twice its usual speed across the ocean that separates us. Hold fast, dear Kate – I come!

> Your astonished and intrigued sister,
> with love,
> Annie.

A LONG PERIOD OF WAITING

IS REWARDED

22

In those days, even within the Empire, very few other cities could be counted on to react with such enthusiasm to a visit from royalty. If this were not already an established fact, there were many here who set out to make it so. All over town, news of the imminent arrival of Queen Victoria's daughter with her Governor-General husband, the Marquis of Lorne, sent loyal hearts into a flurry of plans for dinner parties, parades, civic celebrations, and political speeches. Merchants threw themselves into an orgy of decorating their buildings, to the point where the city all but disappeared behind a façade of greenery and banners. A holiday was declared, of course, so that everyone could be out on the streets to greet the viceregal pair when their parade arrived in town.

None of this excitement affected Logan Sumner, however. For him, the holiday was merely a welcome opportunity to catch up on some of the paperwork that had to be taken care of before he could turn the business over to Zachary Jack and leave town, quite possibly for ever. Thus, he was in his upstairs office when Lady Riven-Blythe – just home from an extended visit in San Francisco – stopped in at Sumner Construction accompanied by a total stranger. Sumner could not imagine what she had in mind. Even before he began to descend the stairs he could see that this attractive young woman with the great entanglement of curls the colour of faded strawberries possessed qualities he hadn't encountered in any of the women of this town; her very posture

proclaimed it as she watched his descent, her eyes showing amusement and pleasure and even some measure of delight in what she
saw. He was afraid this surprisingly open appraisal would cause
him to stumble and send him sprawling to the floor at her toes.
Rather than waiting for Lady Alice to make the introductions,
the young woman tilted her head to one side like someone considering various possibilities and stuck out her hand like a man. "I
would have known you from my sister's letters. That forlorn look
of a deserted orphan."

"Miss Annie McConnell," Lady Alice announced, as though
to say: *And look what I have found!* "We have just now arrived off
the ship and are on our way to the welcome arch for the speeches.
But we decided we would drag along a certain young man who
spends too much time at work."

Was this some sort of modern travelling-dress the young woman
was wearing? Perhaps this strange outfit was stylish in Australia
but it would not do for long here. Her claret-coloured skirt came
only to the top of her boots – enough in itself to raise eyebrows.
Worse, the red polonaise she wore over it did not hide the fact
that the skirt lacked the expected fullness, as though several
underskirts had been removed. This was no ordinary creature
Lady Alice had collected in her travels.

And rather than displaying the sort of studied shyness he
was used to seeing in a woman who had just met a man, Miss
McConnell stared hard at Sumner, almost as though she had
come in to examine a piece of cabinet work she had ordered.

"The legs may be long and awkward," he found himself saying,
slapping his hands on his knees. "And the thatch a little too thin
on top. But the joints are a tight enough fit to last for a while.
Around here we use nothing but first-grade material."

Instead of responding to this nonsense, the newcomer strolled
across to examine the confusion of lumber and sawdust and carpenter's tools around the workshop, debris left behind by the
towers and archways and spectator benches ordered by merchants

preparing decorations for the royal visit. She drew in a deep breath. "I've always liked the scent of fresh lumber – certainly better than kitchen odours."

Sumner raised his bare forearm to his nostrils. "Cedar," he explained. Then he sneezed. "The world's most innocent smell."

"Miss McConnell," said Lady Alice, "will be a guest of the Horncastles." The diminutive old woman turned up her dainty doll-like face beneath the blue feathers of a dozen savaged ostriches, and raised her eyebrows meaningfully. "A sister to the current Mrs. Horncastle." The merest suggestion of a smile. "We met on board the ship and became fast friends, and have decided she will not join her relatives until after we have been to welcome the royal party – who should be arriving any moment up the street." An anxious glance out the window. "We have also decided that she shall be presented to Her Highness at Government House, as my guest, while they are here" – like a schoolgirl pretending to regret some outburst, she put a hand to her mouth and widened her eyes – "and that the Governor-General will dance with her while I keep his wife distracted with gossip."

Sumner hoped that this young woman would change her mode of dress before meeting with the viceroy and the princess.

"But we must hurry, if we're not to miss the speeches!" cried Lady Alice. "And we insist that you join us. Of course, I met them once, at a ball in London, when my dear husband was alive. A lovely couple, devoted to one another. But this is the first time royalty has ever visited us here."

Sumner gently corrected Her Ladyship. "There was King Kamilamaka, of the Sandwich Islands."

"Ewwww!" Lady Alice fanned the mere Polynesian aside like an unpleasant smell. "Of course you know what I mean by royalty."

Addressing the newcomer, who had taken up a scrap of cedar board to smell the raw wound left by a saw, Sumner hoped that the journey had not been too unpleasant. "We heard you'd been delayed. There were even some who thought you'd been captured in the Pacific, I understand, and ended up in a cannibal's soup."

The brown eyes smartly rejected the notion. "A sorry cannibal then. He would find me all spice and bitter seasoning, hardly any meat on these bones at all." She raised the hem of her skirt to display the slender ankle of her boot. Then, with her chin raised, she tossed that great tangle of strawberry hair and looked steadily into his eyes, grinning the mischievous grin of a bold child. "When I've rented a theatre, I shall make certain you have tickets in the dress circle."

"Come! Let us go!" urged Lady Alice, already pushing the door open. "I shall never forgive you, Mr. Sumner, if you are responsible for making us late. I have been terrified of missing this wonderful event."

Kate Horncastle had all but given up hope of seeing Annie, who had failed to arrive on the steamship that delivered her trunks three months ago. Disappointed, she tried to imagine what might have happened. A shipboard romance? An elopement now would ruin everything. It seemed that almost anything was possible. Horncastle was able to learn that Annie McConnell had left the ship in San Francisco but could not discover what had happened to her since. Kidnapped? Perhaps she'd got lost in the city and couldn't find her way back to the ship. Maybe she had been robbed, left destitute, even had her steamship ticket stolen. *Or had changed her mind!* As soon as Horncastle had told her what he'd learned and returned to his work in the bar, Kate snatched up a dinner plate from the cabinet and threw it into the dining-room fireplace with such force that it exploded into countless tiny fragments which sank into the ash.

Thereafter, each day that Annie did not arrive, one more piece of Norah Horncastle's pure white crockery went flying towards a collision with sooty bricks. Kate's children were pleased to assist. "And when they are all gone, my darlings, we shall go through every shop in town until we find a new set we can bear to look at while we are eating."

An eventual letter from Annie offered a partial explanation. "An American gentleman on the ship persuaded me to attend a public meeting conducted by his mother, a famous San Francisco lecturer who advocates the abandonment of corsets and the donning of trousers by women." Instead of taking her back to the ship after the meeting, however, this Mr. Brocklehurst took her to the family mansion and tried to persuade her to adopt his mother's cause and join them both on the lecture circuit. "I've been watching you since Melbourne. You have the sort of spirited manner which is everywhere filling concert halls these days. The sort of looks too." She was not entirely surprised to hear this, since she'd already earned a modest reputation as both a public speaker and a singer in theatres around the colony of Victoria, and in fact was every bit as skilled at rousing an audience as his mother. (All of this was news to Kate, though not surprising.)

To demonstrate the truth of this, she wrote, she stepped onto the stage of the Jenny Lind Theater the next evening in bare feet and a long white dress fashioned after the dress of the ancient Greeks to sing "Silver Threads Among the Gold" for the audience of several hundred San Francisco citizens waiting to be inspired or inflamed by Madam Brocklehurst. And later, when the featured speaker had completed her impassioned performance, she strode unannounced to the podium as if she and not the older woman were the principal reason for the gathering, and addressed the crowd herself, going even further than Madam Brocklehurst in her condemnation of the tyranny imposed on women by men in the fashion industry and adding her own enthusiastic support for the idea of seizing upon freedoms of every sort, not just in clothing, in order to make the lives of women more tolerable. "Everywhere, black slaves have achieved their emancipation," she said. "Now it is women's turn." Then she went on, beyond expectations, to insist that slavery to fashion was but a symbol of a larger slavery into which men and women alike had delivered themselves – slavery to old rigid ways of thinking, chained to habits of fear, selfishness, and despair. Some members of the audience howled out their profound rage at every declaration, a few ruffians even threw leafy vegetables, but the majority rewarded her with generous applause. She'd proved to be such a great success that Madam Brocklehurst invited her to be part of the performance every evening of the following week, and then to join her planned cross-country tour, with her name just a little smaller on the posters than Madam's own. "I promised to think about catching up to the tour at a later date, dear Kate, after I have been up to consider the situation you offered. By now, of course, my ship has long ago gone off without me and I shall have to make a booking on a later ship."

A later ship. Emancipation. Slavery to fashion. Kate was not entirely surprised by any of this. Annie had always had a mind of her own, Annie had always *pushed*. Yet, really, this was going altogether too far! She tossed down the letter onto the little side-table and paced the length of the drawing-room. Barefoot! She placed her own shod foot on the open-mouthed head of James's black-bear rug. Not strong enough to crush it. Ridiculous Madam Brocklehurst! A cross-country tour! She had not realized before how much she hated the clutter in this room. Too many figurines, too many *things*. Too many little tables heaped with books and stereopticons and chessboards. Who had decorated this place? And why had she put up with it for so long? From behind, she seized the high back of the horsehair chair in which she had been sitting to read the letter – the chair in which she, and presumably the wife who preceded her, sat for reading or working on her embroidery during the evenings. Too heavy to move. She went through the hotel snatching Norah Horncastle's antimacassars off the backs of every chair and couch, and all the doilies she could lay her hands on, then carried them out onto the street, poured kerosene over the heap, and struck a match. To those who were attracted by the smoke, she explained, "I've always detested the snowflake pattern!" Her laughter suggested, as always, that there was as much pleasure in the laughing itself as in whatever she found amusing. Others smiled despite themselves. "And of course any number of unpleasant heads have pressed against them."

Now, three months after the arrival of her trunks, when all of the city had become swept up in the excitement of preparing for a September visit from royalty, the entire set of boring white serviceable crockery had been destroyed and subsequently replaced by a set of willow-pattern china which Kate had bought at a Saturday-afternoon street-corner auction – from a distraught woman who'd arrived with all her possessions from England only to discover she must still travel with pack-horses to join her husband in the northernmost part of the island. The drawing-room had lost much in the way of figurines and unnecessary furniture, even some of the horrid dark prints and engravings from the walls, and dozens of pieces of cabinet bric-à-brac from the *étagères*, though James had not yet noticed the difference.

A second letter explained the extended delay. Annie had made several more triumphant theatre appearances, earning herself front-page attention in local papers. "Madam has gone off on her tour and left me to represent her here. I have become almost the toast of the town! I have not forgotten my destination, however, and will leave very soon."

"She will never come," Kate said to James Horncastle. "You will be forced to go down and get her." She cast an accusing glance at Annie's photograph on the mantel, where it had sat since arriving in Annie's last letter from Ballarat.

"Nonsense." He seemed to enjoy observing his wife's impatience, which had become a part of every dinner's conversation. "Having some fun before she settles down. Will be all the more enjoyable company when she arrives." The expression on his face was precisely the same as when he picked up his cricket bat, knowing he was good enough to keep the game in his power for as long as he wished.

But what had she done, she thought. What had she dared to *suggest* in that letter? Perhaps that bold offer had caused Annie to lose her nerve when she was only part-way here, frightened by the audacity of her unconventional suggestion.

As for himself, James Horncastle added, this delay only increased the pleasure of anticipating the time when he could welcome his pretty sister-in-law into his home. "I only hope," he said, as he got up from his chair to kiss his wife on the forehead, "that she arrives before you've stripped the house bare and left us living in an empty hull."

As soon as he left the room, she went to the kitchen and took down one after another of the cracked and discoloured water glasses from the cupboard and, carrying them to the window, tossed them down to watch them smash against the bricks along the pathways in the garden below. Then she enrolled the aid of her children and the house servant, Wang Low, in dragging the great old faded divan out of the parlour and across the foyer of the hotel to the front door. Outside, she led the way along the street until they came to an unattended farmer's wagon whose boards were strewn with bits of straw and flakes of dried manure, and instructed them to hoist the divan up onto the wagon and position it at the front where the farmer might sit to drive the horses.

"Knowing Annie, I should imagine she's marched into city hall by now and shown them where they have gone wrong, where they had *erred* in governing their city." This was said to Mr. Callow, the young Customs man from Ottawa, who had brought his morning tea and the whole week's newspapers out onto the second-floor terrace above the new verandah to wait for the parade. "We shall hear that she has married the *Mayor* and taken over the reins of power herself, or else been thrown into the ocean for her impertinence."

Her own cup of tea had been laced with a dash of laudanum – for the mighty headache that she could sense was preparing to assault her before very long. The hotel had never been so full – every bed in town was spoken for (except Annie's), and still there was not enough accommodation for all the travellers who had poured in for the royal visit. She had spent the morning trying to be everywhere at once – putting fresh flowers in every room, checking menus, giving the new chambermaid the benefit of some smart criticism of her bed-making skills, and settling an argument between the chef and the iceman which threatened to turn violent. Since life in the hotel seemed to be under control, at least for the moment, there was no reason she should not take her tea out onto the balcony and try to relax.

She knew the young man was never displeased to have her join him. He had become quite openly a great admirer. Also, he could be counted on to comment on her choice of dress. Today, there would be something said about the new amber checks, and the bows on the sleeves. Not even Annie's evident conversion to the cult of emancipation would shake Kate's fondness for wearing fine clothes. Was she a slave because she did not wish to look like Mary One-eye, dragging her second-hand badly fitting skirts around the world?

"You make her sound quite frightening." Mr. Callow turned from the railing to sit at the little table, then stood again and shifted the second chair so that Kate Horncastle might join him. He wore a surprising waistcoat – blue polka dots – with his usual conservative suit. And had brought a bouquet of chrysanthemums, presumably to throw down upon the parade. "I shouldn't wish to meet a young woman with so much confidence."

She would prefer not to dwell any more on Annie. Strange things had lately begun to happen when she did – a fluttering in her throat, cold hands. It made no sense, when in fact she was expecting her sister's arrival to mean only a great happiness, the reunion of allies, sharers of secrets. It was all just taking too long.

Far off in the world, said the newspapers which Mr. Callow had scattered over the table, the enigmatic city of Cairo was about to fall to the resolute British attackers. A recent insurrection in Corea had left three members of the royal family brutally slaughtered. Frenzied Hindoos in Calcutta were throwing the disembowelled corpses of Mohammedan children down wells and tossing the insulting heads of decapitated pigs in after them. A great deal of this devastation, Kate thought, might have been going on inside her.

The street had been altered dramatically for the arrival of the viceregal couple, especially on this very block, where people were already beginning to gather. Every merchant and home owner except James had erected so many banners, flags, evergreen boughs, floral wreaths, and draped buntings across the front of his premises that the buildings themselves had all but disappeared. The San Francisco Baths. H. Mansell, boots, C. W. Lange, jeweller. Wells Fargo Express. Kurtz's White Labour Cigars. W. & J. Wilson, clothier. Unlike his neighbours, James would not allow his business to hide from notice altogether, since he wanted the Blue Heron to register upon the royal memory, perhaps even catch the Governor-General's interest.

Down at the intersection, carpenters had erected towers, and a platform for making speeches, as well as several rows of spectator benches for which tickets had been sold. It seemed to Kate that everything in sight was so laden with streamers and bows and banners and flags and evergreen boughs that the visitors would not be able to see whether there were any real buildings here. Her Highness would think she'd come upon a giant theatre stage, set for some childhood nursery play, and not a city at all!

Where the city had not been obscured by decorations, it had been replaced by words. Based on the assumption that neither people nor buildings could speak for themselves, presumably, banners made pronouncements in every direction. "*Lorne and Louise*" could be seen from here. "*All Our Children Salute You.*" Up and down the street they shouted their messages. "*Willing Hearts and Hands.*" "*God Save the Queen.*" "*Welcome.*" "*Loyal to the Crown.*" Some took on larger themes. "*The Paciflc Greets the Atlantic.*" "*The Orient Greets the Occident.*" "*All Hail Scotia's Son and England's Daughter.*" "*Welcome to the Land of Peace, Plenty and Contentment.*" A city had all but disappeared behind the alphabet.

James had gone off to march with his fellow members of the Independent Order of Foresters in the procession that would precede the royal party's carriages from the naval harbour and across Esquimalt, over the Point Ellice Bridge and in to town – before moving on to Government House where the Governor-General and his Princess wife would settle in for a visit that could last for several weeks. Even the children had deserted Kate at the last minute. Since moving home to attend school, they had already made their own friends and had insisted on joining the Halket family, who had tickets on the steamer *Wilson G. Hunt* – sailing out this morning, noisy with excited citizens and blaring bands, to meet the royal party at Race Rocks, and to join the other boats escorting HMS *Comus* in to Esquimalt harbour.

Hotel guests began to come out onto the balcony, bringing chairs with them. Bald Mr. Dorchester, with his sleeping parrot against his ear, established himself in a chair at the railing where he might see what he would have missed if he had not come out on business from Toronto. "They say the Princess is unwell," he grumbled, as though he considered this rumour an insult to his own person and a failure on the part of the hotel.

"I should think so!" said Kate. "Worn out from the long journey through the United States."

Dainty, sad Miss Thurlow stepped through the doorway and stood blinking, then decided that even with the sun in hiding she would open her parasol. She, too, had brought flowers.

Close on her heels, snuffling and snorting, came old Colonel Willoughby Stokes, a long-time permanent resident of the hotel who was a familiar figure about town, sleeping through the afternoons in his carriage while his horse pulled him up and down a regular pattern of familiar streets. "Of course, they had little choice in the matter – what? The damn newspapers and the politicians with all their complaining about being *ignored* out here! Had to come, didn't they!" With the aid of two walking-sticks and Mr. Callow's steadying arm, he found himself in a chair, while Miss Thurlow added: "And since the promised railway is still long miles from completion, she had no choice but to go the long way around." She directed this at Mr. Callow, who, as a representative of Ottawa, must accept the blame.

"Queen Victoria's daughter," Mr. Dorchester quite unnecessarily thundered, "could hardly be expected to travel by Red River cart!"

"Or canoe!" added Kate, happy to fuel their indignation. "Or horseback! To cross a country which she already resents even having to live in."

Others joined them. Mr. and Mrs. Mackerel of New Westminster were only incidentally in town on this occasion, having come to see their son-in-law established in his import-export business. The Basket twins, two wrinkled ladies from up-island, were so excited about this occasion that they had to close their eyes every so often, and give themselves little talks, to keep from acting like stimulated children. The silent Stackpole family from Seattle, all alarmingly fat, filed onto the balcony, putting Mr. Sumner's construction to the test.

"There is a good deal of excitement at the Chinatown arch," reported one of the Basket twins, waving to someone leaning out a window on the opposite side of the street, "where a pagoda temple collapsed yesterday. A fortune in heathen idols destroyed!" Several people waved back. One gentleman threw a gold flower, which sailed out only so far and then fell.

Mr. Callow narrowed his eyes into the distance for a moment, then looked at Kate. "Of course far less fuss than this is made in Ottawa, where we have become used to the Lornes."

Sometimes she wondered if she should not resent the fact that
he could sound so sure of himself with her, when she had seen him
blinking and choking through a conversation which included
James, or a young and pretty woman. He was so easily won over,
in the manner of certain young men, by the attentions of an older
woman, particularly a married older woman. She determined, for
the time being, to seem only a little interested while he recalled
occasions when he had witnessed the popular couple performing
their duties, but no one could feign indifference when he re-
counted the Princess's spill in the Ottawa snow. "Dragged behind
the sled for a terrible length of time."

"And wounded? I think I have heard," said Miss Thurlow.

"Went home to Mother, of course, to recuperate."

"Ah yes," said Kate. "And begged the Queen not to send her
back to rejoin her husband, amongst the ignorant Philistines in a
savage land." Had Her Highness had the opportunity, she wondered, to compare impressions with the brother who had been
shot in Sydney? Think of all the whining Queen Victoria must
listen to, from children who resented their duty amongst her less
sophisticated subjects.

"But Mother, of course, would permit no selfishness. Sacrifices
must be made for the Empire!"

Was it for that – the sacrifice – that thousands of people were
turning out to honour her today? What had the girl ever done? An
accident of birth – born to one mother rather than another. And
had probably been complaining about her inconvenient duties
ever since. Yet all these people had dedicated days to the work of
transforming their whole city in her honour, just as though she
had accomplished something in her life you might admire. They
would turn out in hordes to cheer for a girl who had done nothing
but permit a little royal blood to go pumping through her veins.
Unable, was she to suppose, to find anyone who had actually *done*
something which deserved their admiration?

"One should hope to see Ottawa one day, I suppose," said Miss Thurlow. "But I'm afraid I would find it a dreadfully foreign city."

"I wonder if the Princess will have taken up polka dots like the rest of the world," Kate said. Mr. Callow would know that she was acknowledging his waistcoat, while he had not yet commented upon her amber checks. "They say there has never been a fashion to equal it."

"I saw Piquette this morning with a dotted waistcoat," growled Mr. Dorchester, looking straight into Mr. Callow's similarly decorated chest. "And he insisted upon showing me his matching hose!"

Kate was not rewarded with a display of Mr. Callow's hose. His face suggested that he resented Mr. Piquette's success as well as Mr. Dorchester's tone, and would leave them guessing how far his own courage had been stretched. He could look, Kate thought, appallingly prim and petulant when he wished to punish someone.

You would find no polka dots on James's cousin from San Francisco, whose fringed leather jacket could be seen down, amongst the noisy spectators who filled up the street. The long-jawed newspaperwoman smoked her cigarettes while scribbling in her notebook. Did the woman realize what a peculiar figure she made? You could hear her harsh braying voice from here, even above the anonymous roar of the crowd. She had certainly advertised the fact that she would rather have covered the royal couple's visit as they passed through San Francisco, but the newspaper had decided there was a better story to be found in a royal visit when it was a visit to loyal subjects. She would make the loyal subjects look like imbeciles. No doubt she was encouraging the tobacconist George Anderson at this moment to speak about his love for a monarch he would never see. She would record Mayor Shakespeare's most pompous words. She would describe the silly hat on Mrs. Shakespeare's head as her revenge for being here when she might have been in San Francisco when the captain of the

Comus received a note announcing that his ship would be blown up the minute royalty stepped aboard. Great consternation had followed, of course, and all nearby boats had been immediately searched for torpedoes – all this reported by newspaper writers who had not been sent off on boring missions to the north.

Mr. Callow's reaction upon recognizing the familiar visitor down on the street was a groan. "Why do Californians behave as though they may be required at any moment to shoot their way to safety through a blizzard of bullets?"

If Annie were here, they would collapse with laughter over this cigarette-smoking, poker-playing, leather-faced woman. "Down you go, Kate!" she would say. "Take your six-gun and challenge the witch! Calico Kate versus the San Francisco Chimney! Make the first shot count."

What was the matter with her? There was no sense to this panic that assaulted her, this trembling down her arms, this sudden cold in her hands. Great white cockatoos gave her this feeling in the stomach, defying her from the branches of the blue gum. Did this pale little man realize how silly that waistcoat looked on him? Did he think she found that narrow paintbrush beneath his nose attractive?

"Do I hear music?" Miss Thurlow chirped, prepared to be enchanted. "A band." She made a disappointed face. "How horrid it sounds at this distance!"

"But it means they have arrived," said one of the Basket twins. "Colonel Stokes, wake up!"

Indeed, the beginnings of the parade could be seen turning the corner off Johnson Street, at the firemen's arch – built of ladders and decorated with hoses, buckets, axes, and even with the firemen themselves, who stood up on the top to form a pinnacle. Without stopping, the marching columns passed under the "We Strive to Save" banner and started in this direction, towards the crowds at the civic arch. The militia band was first, and then the marching societies in their costumes. Horses and carriages could only be imagined still, behind them.

"But look – here is Lady Riven-Blythe!" said Mr. Callow, looking in quite the opposite direction from the approaching parade.

Down the street the tiny woman could be seen holding onto her enormous hat and pushing forward with quick hurried steps, using her furled parasol to part the crowds. Barely home from a holiday in the States and not wanting to miss out on a thing!

"And Mr. Sumner with her," a squinting Miss Thurlow guessed.

And not only Mr. Sumner, Kate saw. Surely she was not imagining things, to think she recognized the young woman who was keeping pace with Logan Sumner's strides.

"Is that Annie?" she cried, rather too loudly. Was that resentment in her voice? Miss Thurlow, the fat silent Stackpoles, bald Mr. Dorchester with his parrot at his ear, all turned to her in alarm. Colonel Stokes leapt to his feet, suddenly awake, and found himself toppled against the railing. "Yes it is Annie," she said, adjusting her tone. True pleasure, true excitement had pushed everything else aside. "It is Annie, Annie, Annie, come at last!"

The military band, the Fire Department Band, and the costumed marchers crossed the intersection and came to a stop when the two carriages had pulled up before the archway. The outriders who came before and behind the royal carriage reined in their horses. More cheers went up, and wild applause, for the Princess with the large scarlet plumes in her hat and for the distinguished gentleman in morning suit at her side.

"Excuse me! Excuse me!" All but hidden beneath a great drooping cartwheel of gigantic blue feathers, the final resting-place of a dozen slaughtered ostriches, Lady Riven-Blythe did not intend to stand back amongst the half-committed. Her furled parasol went before; the others pushed through in her wake.

Kate leaned over the railing and called, but neither Annie nor Sumner nor Lady Riven-Blythe looked up. The entire population of The Great Blue Heron's balcony took up the task of calling and waving their arms but they might only have been cheering the arrival of the Governor-General and his Princess wife. Up onto the verandah of Mansell's Shoes went the three newcomers just as Mayor Shakespeare stepped under the arch and coughed into his hand. The noise of applause and cheers suddenly collapsed, leaving silence – all but one loud voice which went on as though still safely embedded in the noise of others. "By Jove, Sheepshank – look! You owe me twenty, man! She *did* come after all!"

Of course Kate recognized the voice. Those who had paid to sit under the arch chose not to hear this outburst, but snickers and murmurs rippled through the standing crowds. Was James Horncastle about to make one of his scenes? Noah Shakespeare, perhaps wondering the same, did not delay: "To the Most Honourable Sir John Douglas Sutherland Campbell, Marquis of Lorne, K.C.B., Governor-General of Canada –" The mayor's voice had never carried so boomingly. "May it please Your Excellency: We, the Mayor and Municipal Council, desire to extend to Your Excellency and Her Royal Highness the Princess Louise a most cordial and hearty welcome on the occasion of your arrival at this city."

Perhaps Shakespeare, who was rumoured to be thinking of putting himself forward for election to the federal Parliament, imagined a close friendship springing up between him and the viceregal couple once he got to Ottawa – based on the impression he made here today. "We experience unfeigned pleasure in receiving at the metropolis of this province her most gracious Majesty's representative and Her Royal Highness the Princess Louise, and would earnestly express to Your Excellency our sentiments of loyal devotion to Her Majesty, her throne and government."

Reluctant to go down and cause a disturbance by fighting her way across the street, Kate stayed where she was and hoped to catch someone's eye. From here, she could detect a stir somewhere amongst the ranks of green-clad Foresters who stood at attention between the Janissaries of Light and the French Benevolent Society. The person himself could not yet be seen, but his passage through the ranks of his colleagues could be easily detected by the turmoil his movement caused – as one can follow the passage of a small animal through tall grass.

"Annie!" This was unmistakably James Horncastle's voice, deep in the crowd. A dog had started barking as well. A terrier's yapping. Vicky? Yes, she could see James now, and the little white terrier in a confused frenzy, yapping, biting at her own master's heels, nipping at the ankles of anyone who stood in their way.

Kate's stomach knotted, to think that a scene could not be avoided. She must go down and get there before he did while Noah Shakespeare soldiered on: "We hail Your Excellency's visit with more than ordinary feelings of felicitation, but deeply regret that Your Excellency and your illustrious consort should have been compelled to travel for thousands of miles through foreign territory to reach the western province of the great Dominion; but now that actual construction of the great railway has . . ."

Down on the street, Kate pushed herself between bodies, in the direction of her sister, aware that her husband was doing the same thing. Annoyed faces strained to hear the mayor remind the Governor-General of the promise that would locate the railway's terminal nowhere but in this city.

Kate ran up the steps onto Mansell's verandah and threw her arms around Annie. "Oh Annie!" Of course they were both crying. There was the surprise, and also the relief. "I had given up, I thought you had deserted us."

When they separated, it was to grin broadly into one another's tear-wet eyes, and to fall back into another laughing embrace.

"Of course you know Lady Alice," Annie said, when they had separated a second time. "We met on the ship, and have become inseparable."

But Lady Riven-Blythe was too flustered to acknowledge Kate. "Here comes Mr. Horncastle," she cried. "And the Princess has glanced this way, to see who is causing the fuss. She is certain to have recognized me!"

Sumner's arms caught up the collapsing Lady Riven-Blythe but did not rescue the great cartwheel of ostrich feathers which bounced down the steps and rolled off through the legs of the crowd. This sent Vicky into a new round of frantic yapping, and the gentleman who innocently stepped on the hat soon felt in his ankles the needle-like teeth of a fox terrier determined to rescue it.

Red-faced Horncastle bounded up the steps, his white hair stirred up by his push through the crowd, his short arms thrown as wide as they were capable of reaching, and, whooping loudly, grabbed Annie out of Kate's arms to dance her around. In the larger scheme of things this would have to be classified as a minor public disturbance, but Kate wished it had happened at some other time, in private. Spectators beneath the arch, facing this way, would no doubt remember this shocking interruption to the day's festivities.

"In conclusion," said Noah Shakespeare, "we have only to add that we most sincerely trust that the salubrity of our climate, which is proverbial; the scenery, which unquestionably is picturesque; and the many and varied sources of quiet enjoyment which our island affords, will not only . . ."

"Oh dear," said a revived Lady Riven-Blythe, looking at James Horncastle's attempts to bring Kate into his silly dance with Annie. "That man is quite impossible."

The man's dog was equally impossible, it seemed. Instead of returning the hat to its owner, she had decided to rip it to pieces with her teeth, setting the ostriches free to fly up amongst the crowd. Feathers were snatched out of the air by laughing members of the public to become flourished banners, and the naked hat itself was eventually tossed up amidst enthusiastic applause to hook itself, as though on a rack, on the corner of the roof of Kurtz's White Labour Cigars, about the time "God Save the Queen" was taken up by four hundred schoolchildren and bouquets of flowers were tossed down from all around upon the reactivated parade. When someone from the balcony of The Great Blue Heron tossed down a bouquet of gold chrysanthemums which landed, as though by design, in Kate Horncastle's arms, she quickly passed them over to her long-awaited sister.

23

HORNCASTLE'S response to Annie's arrival was precisely what might have been expected – what Kate had counted on, in fact. Amazed at the improvements that time had made upon the person he remembered as a plain, dirty-faced girl with carroty hair in a rat's nest of knotted curls, Horncastle quickly decided that only a fool would look such a lively and attractive gift-horse in the mouth, especially when it was offered to him with the blessings, more or less, of his own wife. Once they had eaten lunch, he invited his sister-in-law to accompany him for a walk through his garden while Kate was washing the dishes. There, he held her hand and told her what a lovely woman she had become. By the time they stepped back inside he had already persuaded her to ride out with him the next morning to admire the horses, champions all, which he boarded at Sheepshanks' farm, and to walk along the seacoast on their way back. "Will have you falling in love with this place, I warn you, and wishing you had come here long ago!"

He could barely contain his enthusiasm for their new boarder. Her sister was a real blue-ribbon champion! "And you, my dear, are a remarkable woman, to think of sending for her! A great help about the hotel. Already feel like a man about to win a one-mile race!"

The children, too, were pleased to discover their aunt amongst them again. Laura threw herself into Annie's arms and sobbed, as though to suggest she'd been constantly ill-treated but had found her rescuer at last. Young James stepped back, after the polite kiss to his aunt's cheek, and proceeded to complain about the necessity of attending a local school, cheek by jowl with the children of tradesmen and recent immigrants, when he had become accustomed to something better. "You must talk them into sending me back." Annie wept and laughed in turns, and might have been persuaded to sign a paper on the spot promising never to allow a separation between them again.

But Kate had already begun to discover that, far from the compliant ally she'd expected, a spinster grateful for even a share in someone else's husband, she had imported a much more spirited and strong-headed person than she had expected. "You didn't tell me he was such a small man!" was the first indication that things were not developing entirely as planned. At the end of their first meal she whispered her dislike of his eating habits. "So noisy! How can you stand all that smacking of lips?" When she came in from the garden, she made it clear that she had no intention of rushing into anything here, a ride in the country was only a ride in the country, she would take her time and consider Horncastle from all sides before making a decision. "I shall have a good look at his teeth, Kate, as I'm sure he does with a horse he's about to buy!"

"Oh Annie! Have you come all this way just to mock us?"

Kate accompanied Annie to the room they had reserved for her, and sat on the soft covers of the bed she had herself prepared, while her sister unfolded the clothing from her trunks and put them away in the wardrobe.

"Is he always so impetuous?" said Annie. "To disregard even the good opinion of royalty?"

Kate did not resist the invitation to laugh. "A dear, funny man. He can make you feel yourself to be the most beautiful, the most intelligent, the most talented and gracious woman on earth." For a moment the sisters' eyes locked, like a held breath. How much could be said aloud of what had been only written? Annie seemed to be waiting – for permission to release something: laughter, a scream, something.

"Oh my lord, Kate, did you really intend to write the words in that letter? There's probably never been another like it in all of history –"

"It is more likely there have been thousands! Other sisters have simply taken their secrets to their grave. As I hope we will. You *have* destroyed it?"

"Not yet. Without it, I would have turned back, thinking I'd only dreamed it."

"And I thought you *had*! Turned back. While you were parading yourself upon the stage." There was nothing to be gained, now, from assigning blame, when there was so much to accomplish. "Of course, he has his faults, like any man. But they are few, they are *small*. I have never suggested he was perfect. He had fallen a little into the habit of gambling before I arrived – horseracing, some other schemes as well. Sometimes he wastes sums of money on friends who've come to depend on his good nature rather than –"

"Really, Kate!" Annie turned from the wardrobe and sat again on the bed. "I see you really *meant* it."

"You doubted that?"

"The farther I got from home, the less certain I was that I had understood you correctly. Every time I reread your letter I became more convinced that I would get here to find you had meant it only as a joke, or as a half-hearted offer to rid yourself of a husband who momentarily piqued you."

"But you could not have thought that I would jest about –"

"That was one reason for my letters from San Francisco. In case you were serious, I thought I should prepare you."

"Annie, I don't understand, I don't *know* what you are saying!"

"Oh, Kate, Kate. Did you think a woman who stood up before a theatre audience to denounce the exploitation of women would enter into such an agreement?"

Kate had nothing to say to this, because it had occurred to her only now that of course something had been trying to warn her of this. Her body had reacted to the letters while her mind had not even known why. Annie had come without the slightest intention of accepting the offer of an arrangement. Curiosity alone had driven her! An opportunity to travel! A desire to see for herself this marriage so much in trouble that it needed an auxiliary wife.

"I feel like such a fool," she said. And of course could not stay any longer in the room. "I'll leave you to finish this, while I order us up some tea."

She did not go to the kitchen, however, nor did she summon one of the hired help; she went out onto the new balcony, where the morning's chairs stood about in chaos, just as they'd been abandoned by those who had watched the parade – by everyone, that is, but Mr. Callow, who had returned to stand at the railing and look down on the still-to-be-cleaned-up litter of the street. He turned, and looked pleased to see her: "Ah, Mrs. Horncastle! A pleasure to witness the reunion. You must tell me if there is anything –"

She had turned when she saw him, to leave, but stopped to interrupt his offer: Whose hotel was this anyway? "Please leave me, Mr. Callow. If you don't mind. I was not hoping for conversation."

Evidently the young man did mind. He stiffened, almost sniffed his indignation. But he regained his good nature when it was necessary to step aside and allow Annie out through the door. "Perhaps I may introduce myself?" He seemed incapable of carrying off anything more than a mere introduction, however; his attempt to offer his services to the newcomer was overwhelmed with stutters and twitches and the refusal of words to line up together in the expected manner. He excused himself and disappeared inside.

"The man is a little in love with you, Kate," Annie said, coming forward to join her at the rail. "I could see, before he was aware of me, how his entire countenance changed when you spoke to him."

"The man would fall in love with that bearskin down there on the wall of Mr. Buttman's fur store if it only spoke kindly to him once."

Annie remarked on the fact that the bearskin had the word "Welcome" lettered on it in rawhide. "A good omen, I hope."

And the mountains, too, Kate suggested, seemed to have moved in close to greet her, with the sun on their snowy peaks – huge, a startling blue, and almost close enough today to touch. "But of course they belong to another country, which surrounds us nearly. Every merchant and civic leader in town has one eye permanently watching those peaks. Envy, uneasiness, resentment, all three at once."

"And, do I see roses on a post down there? Still blooming! They remind me of that bush that climbed all over your verandah on Ripon Street. Remember?"

"But less brilliant. Just as all of the colours here are less brilliant, except for the green, green, *green*, which is *everywhere*. Oh, I have grown tired of praising it to them!" So tired, in fact, that she surrendered herself to the nearest chair.

"But why must you, then? None of this *needs* your praise."

You could not express sufficient indignation from a sitting position. She stood again, and took hold of the railing. "I sing the praises of this little piece of earth at every opportunity because they want it from me – and their faces flush up as though they had created it themselves. The truth is, I miss the gum trees, Annie! Can you believe it? I miss the low brown hills and the paperbarks and the wonderful colour of the jacaranda blooms. I miss a sun that means real business, and foolish galahs to fly up from behind a bush with their pretty pink breasts. Does any of this compare to Ballarat?"

"I was thinking it very much like Ballarat, with the addition of that beautiful sea all around."

Kate looked. What use was there in glimpses of a beautiful sea, when the buildings around you had become the walls of a fortress. "For all the coming and going of ships there are days when I think I might as well be living in some village in Tasmania. The Port Arthur prison colony. None of this was in my letters, of course. How could I tell you honestly, how could I *admit*, what this past year has really been like, how miserable I've been? I wrote the letters in order to fool myself."

"But did not fool me." Now Annie was sitting – Colonel Stokes's chair – and standing had become impossible. Kate sat, but did not feel welcome in Mr. Callow's chair and moved to another: poor Miss Thurlow's. "Do you think I don't know you well enough to read between the lines?" Annie said. "Of course I could not seriously consider your offer, but I could recognize a cry for help. I don't know what it is you expect of me, but I shall try."

Kate put her hands to her face. "Oh lord, Annie. My head was filled with such wonderful dreams when I left you! At *my* age, still a romantic! When I arrived here I would be swept up in the arms of a man who had waited all those years with his heart filled with love, I thought, who would want only to make the rest of my life as happy as he could, to make up for all I had lost. I would be his helpmate – in the eyes of the world his indispensable partner, but really the centre of everything that mattered to him. That's what I came here to find. You see what I've found instead."

Instead of looking at one another, they watched two Indian women who stood talking at the end of the block, in the shadow of the abandoned arch, while their children raced one another back and forth along the benches. They were of little interest to Kate – two women in bright shapeless skirts, with dull pieces of what looked like blanket thrown over their shoulders. One of them was probably the woman who brought fish to the hotel kitchen door, though she was without her basket today. Evidently they were of great interest to Annie, however, who watched as though this morning's royalty had returned. "Madam Brocklehurst will expect to hear about their dress. It is curious that they don't entirely imitate the white ladies of town."

Yet imitating the white ladies of town was exactly what these two women proceeded to do, in their actions if not in their dress. They sat on the lowest bench, affecting an exaggerated primness – ignoring the noisy children who whooped and leapt about them – and politely applauded with just the tips of their fingers. Then they fell against one another in laughter, they bent forward, laughing into their own laps and shaking their heads. Then they hoisted their skirts and moved up to a higher bench, where they were even more prim and rigid than before.

The street was deserted for the moment – Kate looked. "They would be driven out of there fast enough if they were seen. We should ignore them."

But the women's laughter increased in volume when Zachary Jack approached them on horseback from down the block. He pulled in his great rolling belly and stiffened himself and bowed to one side and the other – a pantomime for which he was rewarded with more polite applause and impolite gales of laughter. Even the children joined in – running out to fall in behind his horse and become the parade, all of them tipping imaginary top hats in every direction.

"Now we must definitely not be caught watching," said Kate. "That is the carpenter I told you about, who worked on the hotel improvements."

Annie looked confused. "But I thought I had already –"

"This is Mr. Sumner's right-hand man."

"Well than, we must call him up!"

"No!" Kate all but shouted this. Then repeated the word in a more subdued fashion. "No, Annie. We will not. It would be better if they did not see us here at all."

In fact, Mr. Sumner's right-hand man had already seen them. He executed a deep bow in their direction, then turned away and directed his horse on down through the litter of the street which had not yet recovered from royalty. His audience was left to gather themselves and their children together, and prepare to abandon both the arch and their play-acting. Kate went inside and through to the back of the hotel, to her kitchen, where she opened the sherry cupboard and poured two glasses.

The Indian women had disappeared when she returned to the balcony. There were others passing down the street now – young couples strolling, a large family crowded together in their farm wagon. But Annie continued to study the deserted benches beneath the arch. "I shall find this place fascinating, Kate. I already do!"

"Then you will be happier here than I," said Kate, as she handed Annie one of the glasses and reclaimed Miss Thurlow's chair. The drinks must not be seen from the street.

Now Annie turned all her attention to Kate, all of her compassion too. "But why unhappy, when you have found everything you came for?"

"It is all the fault of one woman," Kate said. "You will meet her, the villain of the story. Your little friend with the big hat will see to that, no doubt. She is the one who still calls herself 'Mrs. Horncastle.' A fat woman, a fat Irish *peasant* who will deceive you at first – she puts herself forth everywhere as the kind and loving motherly sort of woman. She began a campaign against me from the moment I stepped ashore, and set about making enemies for me in every direction. Your little Lady Riven-Blythe was so successfully poisoned against me that she refused to invite me to any of her garden parties. She turned down invitations to dinner at the hotel, or to any other tables where she knew we were invited.

When the ladies' club was formed to prepare for the Princess's visit, she made certain that my offer to join the group was rejected. It is her fault – the fault of *both* those women – that I have made no friends here outside of the occasional guest in the hotel. And now she has apparently made an ally of my own sister – the worst blow of all." Because the sherry had disappeared in three quick sips, it was possible to end that last sequence with the punctuation of an empty glass placed solidly on the wooden floor.

"But Lady Alice was lovely to me, Kate!" Annie held her glass against her breast. Who had she found to invent such a peculiar dress for her, without any gathers in the skirt. Anyone could see half the underclothing had been dispensed with. "She recognized me from one of Madam Brocklehurst's talks, and introduced herself. And was nothing but kindness the whole way here."

Kate should have brought the decanter out, but would not go inside and get it now, lest Mr. Callow or someone think them a pair of tipplers. "Of course the woman didn't stop there. The Irish woman, I mean. She poisoned other minds against me as well. The Fletchers, who were once so friendly. The carpenter your Lady introduced you to – he wouldn't listen, he wouldn't even *consider* my suggestions for altering his design for this verandah. And of course she has had years in which to turn James Horncastle against the girl he married in Liverpool."

Why should she care what Callow or others thought of them? She desired another drink. Kate went back to the kitchen and refilled her glass and returned to the balcony, where Annie was still sitting, gazing into her own barely-sipped-from glass. "Naturally the woman knew when she insisted upon a house of her own that James would be forced to mortgage the hotel, and that I would have to work like a Mississippi slave inside it." She counted out the jobs on her fingers. "Helping out behind the reception desk, changing beds, scrubbing floors on my hands and knees, dusting, arguing with a carpenter over accounts, dealing with an Ottawa official's wife who insists that her room is not clean enough! I hadn't anticipated how a hotel could consume you. I even have to go down to the docks myself occasionally, to compete with the children hired by other hotels, shouting advertisements at visitors stepping off the boats. Safe in her boarding-house – which she acquired through blackmail – she is laughing at us both, knowing what a strain is put upon a marriage by this constant need to be always working too hard."

Listening, Annie did not look up from her own hands. Let Kate run on, she might have been thinking, and then it will be over with all at once.

"Because when he's not downstairs in his bar entertaining customers with his talking, talking, talking, as though he must keep the hotel from falling about our ears with his voice, he is off somewhere wasting money we cannot afford on gambling, wasting time at the races, wasting his affections on scoundrels and ruffians when he ought to remember that he has a wife. That woman *encouraged* him in his vices while she lived in the hotel – like the typical Irish wife treating the man she called 'husband' more like a son, whose shortcomings were to be expected as part of the world of males."

Kate had promised herself that she would not go on like this, would not complain, but if she stopped now everything would turn to poison within her. Surely a sister could be expected to understand.

"Last night he came home, once *again* came home while I was already asleep – *carried* home by his acquaintances, who left me to finish the job of wiping the blood from his face and putting him to bed. Another big wager had been lost that we cannot afford! Another defeat! This time by a horse which Sam Hatch has purchased from a New England trader, a horse which James himself had looked at but decided not to buy. Another exchange of insults and slanders followed the race, and another fistfight which will require another appearance before a magistrate whose patience is shrinking rapidly. I will be forced to stand by while he primps before a mirror, choosing the waistcoat whose bright colours can be most counted on to offend the magistrate, confident that the popular figure he cuts is worth every cent of the money he has thrown away – not to mention the time he will be absent from the hotel in order to attend the trial, while I carry on alone."

"Of course," Annie said, without quite looking at Kate, "you haven't *left* him."

There was nothing to be said to that. Annie must be the one to continue now.

"And neither have you asked about anyone at home." She stood, and started back into the hotel, her emptied glass in her hand.

Kate followed, and once again they were in Annie's room. "I don't wish to hear about Susannah." She closed the door, and put her own glass beside Annie's on the dark wood of the vanity table.

"But there are others. There's Lilian."

"Still rotting away in her steamy rain forest. With that husband."

"She is flourishing!" Annie spoke from behind a confusion of dresses pulled from the trunk and held aloft for a good shake. "She wrote us at Christmas to say she is well, and even happy. A resilient nanny has been found for her children, and she has discovered herself to be a great success in society."

"Tired, sad Lilian?" Kate sat on the bed, suspecting that she would soon be glad she was not on her feet.

"Mr. Longspur has been elected to the colonial government."

"And she has risen to the occasion. Do you suppose she foresaw this in him? I certainly didn't. I did not like him at all."

"It seems to have little to do with what she saw or did not see. She has fallen into Brisbane society."

From a Ballarat boarding-house. With Susannah's help. With the complicity of her sisters. A little deception, a little acting, a careful preserving of mystery, a wise erasing of past and family.

Kate fell back on the bed, and contemplated the ceiling.

Lilian had fallen into society. Lilian was a sought-after hostess.
The wife of a wealthy government man. Mistress of a mansion.
When her husband stood up to speak, women turned admiring
and envious eyes on her. She had done nothing but cause a
wealthy man to fall in love with her, yet had captured admiration
as well. The wives of lesser men dreamed of deserving her friendship. The wives of leaders invited her to their homes, and asked
her opinion, and made certain that she was treated with kindness
and esteem. This was how people demonstrated their respect for
those they considered to have achieved something worthwhile.
She was someone the others wished to be like.

Of course, Australians were quicker to accept achievements
and reward merit than these people were, who had brought too
much of the Old Country with them. Determined to preserve the
separations that had been established by traditions at Home. In
Australia you were what you made of yourself; here you were
assigned a role.

"They teach us that God rewards the pure in heart, but where
has He been in this? I imagine Him laughing, I imagine that He
isn't God at all but one of that old Greek crowd, working out some
horrid pattern, to make some sort of example of me." Laid out like
this, with even her shoes up on the counterpane, she could speak
like this only if she laid one hand over her eyes. The other hand
drooped off the edge, tingling. "Is there to be no justice? No
reward? I used nothing but truth, I used nothing but *truth* for my
weapon. And where is he now that said truth would set me free?
I won my husband back without a single lie, and it is not better
now than if I had filled my mouth with fabrications. I haven't
claimed so very much, I haven't cut off heads to get at a throne, I
haven't defied the laws of any country or deliberately trampled on
any of the commandments or betrayed my fellow men to seize
power, I haven't even slandered my neighbour for a pot of gold.
Why am I rewarded like the villainess of some melodrama?"

Evidently Annie did not consider this a question she should answer. When Kate lifted the hand from her eyes, she saw that her sister was preoccupied with folding and unfolding things. It was up to Kate, then. Nothing would happen without her demanding it.

"And so when does Her Ladyship expect you to visit her? Surely she has invited you to her home."

A drawer was opened. Strange clothing, folded up, was slipped inside. "She has plans for a game of croquet and insists that I come. Apparently she was something of a champion at it once, before everyone took up tennis."

Kate sat up, and grasped at her sister's nearer hand. "It has been years since I've played croquet but I'm sure it will all come back." She swung her feet down to the floor, ready for life. "If Lady Riven-Blythe is so determined to make you part of society, she will see that she must include your sister as well. You understand I must fight?"

It seemed that perhaps she did. She clasped both hands around Kate's clinging one, and smiled a familiar smile.

"With you and perhaps even Lady Riven-Blythe, I shall be able to save something. There are two of us now. Together we can't fail, we *cannot* fail. Because to let them have their way would be the same as giving up my life."

PRINCESS IN BROBDINGNAG

24

NATURALLY Logan Sumner had no reason to think he would be seeing very much of the Horncastle family, or anything at all of their visitor. He would be sailing in a week's time – for Rome, Venice, Vienna, all those magical places Uncle Charles had once seen, while at the same time he searched for a new place to settle down, find work, start a new life. Or, he might even at the last minute change his mind and sail up the Fraser River to the Cariboo and travel even farther overland into the north country until he came to the Yukon and found some fur trapper who wanted an assistant, or discovered some little snow-laden town that needed a carpenter. He forgot all about the red-headed Miss McConnell just as he tended to forget all about the Horncastles themselves now that he no longer had business reasons to think of them. To consider them in any capacity other than as the clients for whom he had done some construction work would inevitably bring up memories of better days when he had been a regular visitor, a frequent guest at the dinner table, teased by everyone, almost a member of the family.

He had not been invited last fall, or this, to join Horncastle and his friends on their annual hunting party into the mountains, a regrettable loss of something that could not be replaced – the smell of bacon cooking over a camp-fire, the rows of willow grouse hanging from long sticks outside the little colony of tents, the sound of Schinken's impatient dogs panting and milling about, the feel of the cold metal of a gun barrel laid against his face in the morning air as they prepared to leave camp. Yet he would not allow himself to spend time regretting the loss.

Of course he stopped by Norah Horncastle's boarding-house quite often – to see if she had any tasks she wanted done, to accept a cup of her tea, to admire the latest improvements she had made in her house – but he was never required to engage in conversation about the hotel or its new mistress. He could not, however, avoid hearing news of Adelina – already well on her way to becoming the legendary untouchable-spinster figure, more beautiful than ever in her reclusiveness. In Mrs. Zimmerman's boarding-house she was approached by schoolteachers who had heard she'd taken up the writing of novels, she was pursued by the visiting cousins of local families eager to take on the challenge of a steadfast spinster, she was admired even by one high-ranking naval officer who showed little regard for class differences but boasted about a large appetite for the unattainable, and of course she was talked about in every drawing-room for her habit of rejecting suitors out of hand before they even had time to show off what they could do. It was just as painful as ever for Sumner to hear about her – one good reason for leaving town – just as it was still uncomfortable for him to see her father, or her father's new wife, or even The Great Blue Heron Hotel.

But the Horncastles intruded upon his deliberate amnesia with an invitation; it was sincerely hoped that he would join them on an excursion, a riding party out to Metchosin, where there would be plenty of food, expeditions on horseback into the forest, games of tennis and croquet if the weather permitted, and an evening of songs and dancing in the Schinkens' farmhouse – all to introduce the new member of the family to Vancouver Island life. Sumner sent his regrets. He had got too far behind in his work, he wrote, and needed that day to catch up.

Perhaps if he had joined the riding party, he later thought, Miss McConnell might have been convinced of his undesirability as a companion. But unfortunately, his refusal only seemed to fuel her interest. She came in to his workshop and watched him descend the staircase. "Tight enough joints? Nothing but first-grade material? I predict that you'll soon fall apart from excessive devotion to industry. Of course it's not my business if you've decided to have nothing in your life but work. In this innocent scent of violated lumber."

"I'm in the midst of renovations to a roadhouse – The White Birches – and want to see it completed before I leave."

Nevertheless, she remained in the shop for most of an hour while she asked him a thousand questions about his work: the name of this wood, the purpose for that tool, the reason for these drawings opened out on the workbench. She wanted to know about the town as well: why it was here, what had been done with the old Hudson's Bay fort, which of the present citizens had been here in the days of the fur trade, and which of the women were the most intelligent, and which the most imaginative, and which the most likely to be dissatisfied with their lot.

Eventually, when she remembered errands she must perform for her sister, he escorted her out to the street with some relief. Her attention was almost immediately captured by a small crowd that had gathered on the next block. "Do I see the Princess in the midst of that?" she said.

"And her attendants. Visiting at each of the shops, as she promised to do." Even at this distance you could see that she paused to speak a few words to one and then another of those admirers who approached her. "Evidently she has no interest in the scent of lumber, though she seems as eager as you are to learn everything there is to know."

"Maybe this is my opportunity," she said, starting away. "I've been told she has expressed some interest in modern ideas about women's dress."

Within a few days he began to realize that whether he was in his cedar-scented workshop poring over sums and floor plans or at home reading before a fire or even out at the Porter Brothers brick-fields placing an order, the red-headed Australian with the bold gaze and the challenging laugh seemed to be always coming between him and what he was about to do, demanding to be listened to, expecting to be entertained, wanting to be told this or that about the building trade, insisting that he drop whatever he was doing to satisfy her latest whim. Never had he encountered a woman so indifferent to the accepted manner of doing things. To Sumner it seemed that she had taken for herself all the privileges usually tolerated only in eccentric old women who felt they had nothing to lose. Having so little experience with women of any sort and none at all with women who rejected their inherited roles, he was uncertain what to make of her.

There was no point in wondering how Uncle Charles might have advised him. He was barely able to recall his uncle's voice. He could remember the evenings up in the branches of the backyard tree, with Uncle Charles leaning back against a sturdy limb, a beautiful pheasant in his arms; he could remember the shine on Uncle Charles's boots, the glitter on the ruby ring as his hand caressed the pheasant's head, and even the steady rhythms of his warm and confident voice – but he could no longer bring back the words. Only splinters of sounds, broken fragments, meaningless noise, as though the man were speaking out of a fractured throat a language invented for some foreign country which had nothing to do with him. How could such splintered, incomprehensible language make sense of this phenomenon of a bold and pretty Australian woman showing up every time he turned around, when it was a situation that Uncle Charles could never have imagined himself?

Not even when she invaded Uncle Charles's own house did the forgotten voice return to rescue him – not even when she caused Chu Lee to fall immediately in love with her and to insist that she join the master in the parlour while he made them both some tea. This was at the end of a day in which the Governor-General had visited one manufactory after another in town, with some possibility of stopping in for a few minutes at Sumner Construction. At Kurtz White Labour Cigars he'd been serenaded by fifty Caucasian cigar-makers who sang the English national anthem in German; at Albion Iron Works he surveyed the two hundred men (all as unadulteratedly white as the cigar-makers) employed in making the stoves, mouldings, machines, and boilers in that shop; at Sehl's Furniture he chatted with the proprietor in German and learned that native woods were quite suitable for local furniture; but his time ran out before he reached Sumner's shop, where the civic officials who accompanied him would undoubtedly have been disappointed to notice that Sumner, unlike so many of his fellow employers, did not seem alert to the inadvisability of hiring men of certain other races. Made irritable by the strain of waiting for the visit which did not come off, Sumner had little patience for Chu Lee's whimsical hospitality, or for the lady's bold persistence.

"Why are you here?" he said, instead of a greeting.

"My sister's unhappiness. She includes you amongst her enemies. I intend to see if she is correct in her estimation."

He laughed. "But you must have seen for yourself that I'm harmless. The sort of enemy most people would be happy to have."

She sighed. "I'm afraid I am less help to her than she'd hoped."

She expressed curiosity about the great mess of unrolled drawings all over the floor, the opened books stacked up all around. "Dreaming," he confessed. "The owner of The White Birches intends to build a three-storey hotel near the harbour. If he's pleased with our roadhouse renovations, he may award the contract to us. As you can see, I intend to offer him something rather splendid."

"But you will leave anyway?"

She could see for herself that his house was ready for his leave-taking. The furniture only hinted at its original shapes from beneath the white shrouds Chu Lee had thrown over everything.

"I shall give the plans to Zak, you see. This will be something I can leave behind."

She closely examined several of the drawings. "Splendid indeed. Rather like the fantasies which I've been told are recorded on a certain tombstone?"

He closed his eyes. "My famous embarrassment."

"Which I'd hoped you might show me."

As a matter of fact, he had been intending to visit the cemetery this evening, where some serious changes had just been completed. "I suppose – when you've finished inspecting those – you may accompany me."

The column of interlocking granite had grown so tall that it now seemed to have thrust up out of his still-empty grave like some sort of monstrous fungus, with the apparent intention of eventually puncturing the dark, overcast sky. If it had been allowed to continue, flying buttresses would have been needed soon, to keep it from toppling across the less ambitious stones, murdering those who had only come to read. Instead, he had arranged to expand out around the column, using archways and terraces and castellated walls to create a sort of elaborate palace about the width and breadth of a child's room, with words and sentences carved into every side.

The original words were already so high now that you might not read them without stepping back a distance, where you could see (if your eyesight were good enough) his entire story tumbling down the varicoloured structure of moisture-streaming stones: an orphan, a romantic, a builder filled with impossible dreams, a grieving widower, a betrayed friend, a broken-hearted lover, a man of shifting opinions, a man in search of something he could not even identify himself. Bits of poetry had been flung at it here and there, as well as snatches from the Bible.

By stepping around to the far side they were able to read the latest additions to his still-growing alternative biography.

Following upon the opera house and the giant conservatory and
the towering cathedral, he had recently demolished all the buildings adjacent to the inner harbour – including his own, and the
federal Customs House – and had replaced them with a connected series of waterfront terraces and hanging gardens, pergolas
and caryatides and lancet archways and oriel windows and soaring
towers of vermiculated stone blocks, places of business and places
to eat, museums and theatres and docking facilities. In that tight
space he had created a semicircle of brick and timber and marble
and gold-trimmed peaks and plateaus which were meant to
reflect and even compete with the facing semicircular wall of
gigantic foreign blue mountains that all but surrounded the city.

"Your gravestone threatens to rival the pharaohs'," Miss
McConnell said, stepping back to view the entire structure.
"Though we understand the pyramids are the same size now as
when they were first erected."

"Pyramids grew slowly if you were there to watch them. Even
slower if you were one of the slaves hauling stones. My employees
are at least earning a decent wage."

She tilted a sideways smile his way, as though she knew she was
risking offending him. "Pyramids attract the curious and so do
you. I'm told there are people who come out here quite regularly
for the latest chapter."

He smiled. "As they reach for the latest serialized novel?" He
used his fingers to comb back the hair that would only fall forward
again. "I'm aware of that. That has been some of the pleasure."

Eyebrows registered their surprise. "Deliberately giving people
an opportunity to laugh at you? I wonder you don't take up writing
for the paper then."

"Newspapers are for indignant editorials. Last week someone
wrote: 'Mr. Sumner thinks he is an Italian poet, perhaps, or a
song-maker in some Irish bog. He should realize where he is, and
who he is, and apply his compulsion for recording works to the

task of keeping his business accounting books.' Newspapers are read and then burned."

Her frown suggested she was having some real difficulty with this. "And it doesn't seem dishonest, to use one's own tombstone as an amusing distraction, like a magazine?"

He put his hand against the stone, and let his fingers run across the chiselled letters. "Most histories miss the truth, I think, but tidy histories tell more lies than messy ones. I suppose I hoped to surprise myself by stumbling eventually upon some kind of truth."

His fingers had begun to trace the sharp cold troughs of a series of letters which collectively made up – he could read without looking – the word "charity." All at once it seemed miraculous to see this familiar word here, so perfect, carved into the stone as though it were the only perfect "charity" in the world. "How has this got here, do you suppose?" he said. "This word. Who was the person who brought the word 'charity' onto this island?"

She clasped one hand in the other behind her back and adopted a thinking-schoolmarm pose. "Someone from San Francisco, I suppose, who was given it by a cousin from Boston."

"Whose grandfather brought it from Plymouth, on the *Mayflower*, wrapped up in an old shirt with the rest of his belongings."

"Whose grandmother rowed it across the strait from Calais – a whole trunkload of *charités* for the English to distribute as they pleased." Hands flew out from behind her to congratulate one another with brief applause.

"Because her own ancestors had been given – now, if Uncle Charles were here – a *caritas*? A *caritas* or two by a Rome-trained priest, not realizing what a tremendous journey he was initiating."

With nothing more to be said on the subject, Sumner could only trace his finger over the word, and feel the cold travel up his arm. It was almost impossible to think of how the stone palace had been built out of such long voyaging histories.

"And if you should ever find this truth you say you hope to stumble upon?"

"I would probably knock this whole thing down, since it would have become unnecessary."

She nodded, as though to suggest she had suspected as much. "And this is your reason for leaving, I think. Because you've been unable to build any of these dreams in the real world."

"There seems to be little reason any more to hope my sort of business will ever improve in this place. If we are all patient herons waiting for the future to swim by, as your brother-in-law insists, well, I am one who has lost his belief. There must be somewhere else, out in that world I haven't seen, where I won't feel so unnecessary."

"But this is home! I was told you were one of the few who'd been born here."

"But have listened to thousands of voices convincing me that Home is somewhere else. They live here, all these people, but they all seem to have brought along a more beautiful, more cultured, more *interesting* home with them, which they never tire of talking about. Home is Surrey. Or Boston. Or Munich. It is as though the place of *my* birth were merely an empty stage, or a blank magic-lantern screen for them to project their own remembered homes upon. I've been invaded from too many directions to feel there is anything left for me."

"Well, it isn't invisible or blank to me. I'm fascinated with it just the way it is."

"Then you are a most unusual woman, Miss McConnell. Someone else would already be suggesting how we might make this cemetery look more like the cemeteries in – wherever you're from – in Australia."

Well, if he was determined to leave, she said, looking off through the trees, the two of them must set off to explore the deep secrets of the north first – that is, to ride into the forests of the unknown parts of the island, to climb its mountains, follow its rivers, meet with its dark-skinned inhabitants, draw maps of the magical shoreline. "We will discover new lakes, and name one of them after you, one of them after me."

He laughed. She was as fanciful as he was, though she did not seem to realize this. "That is hardly an afternoon excursion. You may board one of the little ships that visit the towns up the coast. Or you may put together a pack-horse train, and go over the mountains."

She leaned forward, annoyed. "I wasn't thinking of an afternoon excursion. You will bring Chu Lee, and I will bring one of my sister's servants. We will camp at the edge of magnificent glaciers, and swim in streams never before seen by civilized man."

"I'm surprised you would waste your time – when there are so many who are more interesting company."

She turned away, and began to walk towards the cemetery gate. "I've been told that you behaved, just briefly once, like a man possessed. A wild man in the throes of a romantic fit. But I don't believe it. I've been thinking you may eventually be a little less stiff with me if I get you away from town, if you've been scratched by trees and bitten by insects and embarrassed by rents in your clothing. And tumbled, at least once, into a river."

She appeared again while he was out in the backyard of Norah Horncastle's boarding-house, helping her to rake up the season's first scattered fall of maple leaves. The grass was wet, after a light rain, the air was cool, and Norah Horncastle's children had decided watching a shipload of horses unload on the docks was a more interesting way to spend an afternoon than tidying up the garden. The royal couple had already been heard to say that they were enjoying their visit in the city so much that the three weeks they'd earlier intended to stay would almost certainly be extended.

Sumner expressed his surprise upon seeing Miss McConnell, since he did not even know the two ladies were acquainted.

"Thanks to Lady Alice, we have become good friends," said Annie. "Though a certain relative cannot conceive of it."

Sumner looked to Norah Horncastle for confirmation. "Anyone who knows Mrs. Norah Horncastle knows she is incapable of resentment," he said. He supposed his opinion of the Australian ought to have risen, to learn that she, too, felt affection for this dear woman. But he could not avoid recognizing his own childish resentment at her sudden invasion. An encroachment upon a friendship invariably felt like a threatened expropriation.

"It is a matter of forgiveness, I suppose," Miss McConnell said. "I can't imagine being so generous myself." She insisted on taking the rake from Norah's hands and sweeping a few leaves into the pile herself, elbows angling in and out of the raspberry-coloured cape.

"Ah sure, how could I be feeling bitterness?" cried Norah Horncastle, as she went towards the house. "When your poor sister is unhappy!" She called to Moira inside, to put on the kettle. "Wouldn't I help her myself if there was something I could do – if I thought she would tolerate such a thing."

"This lady wishes to be a saint," said Miss McConnell. "My sister has always strained one's good intentions. She would make herself everyone's enemy and then wonder why she isn't loved."

Your sister, Logan Sumner thought, would agree that you are an interloper here.

"Ah, forgiveness is not such a difficult thing, when you remember that your enemy is never another human being." Norah Horncastle knelt and brought up a broad yellow leaf from the grass, which she sniffed at but evidently found to be without smell. "I am so fond of the smell of rotting leaves, when you walk through the woods." She tossed this disappointing example into Sumner's pile. "My only enemy is anything in my own thoughts which would try to separate me from good." An expression that Sumner could only think of as *fierce* tightened her face. "Hatred, and anger, and resentment are my enemies. Kate Jordan never was. She couldn't be. Isn't she made like the rest of us?"

"There you are," said Annie McConnell. "More than a saint – an angel."

Norah Horncastle bent and gathered up an armful of leaves from her pile and tossed them up in the air over Annie McConnell's head.

She laughed, as Sumner did, at the young woman's surprise. "You might as well accuse me of being selfish. Haven't I seen too many people make themselves ill with their hating."

Annie shook herself free of the leaves that had attached themselves to her cloak. "Then you have forgiven the Reverend Mr. Trodd as well, I suppose."

The surprise friendship had evidently progressed beyond Sumner's conjectures for this sort of jest – otherwise cruel – to be flung out so lightly. Though their hostess's face was filled with alarm for just a moment, she quickly simulated an exaggerated grimace. "Don't ask for too much all at once. I'm working on it still."

Over tea, Sumner expressed surprise that Miss McConnell's "certain relative," as she had earlier put it herself, could allow her so much time away from the hotel. "Does she mind that you are so often away without her?"

"You can be sure that I'm doing my best to make her life a little easier for her," said the intruder, innocently. "However, I didn't sign a contract which would make me a prisoner of that building."

"Which she must sometimes feel herself to be," said Norah Horncastle, who would know.

By the time they had finished their tea, Miss McConnell, who seemed not to have sensed Sumner's resentment or ever imagined being denied a firm enough request, had persuaded him to take her with him the next morning to Holyoakes' sawmill, where he would be inspecting the lumber set aside for The White Birches, and to go on from there on a horseback excursion into the country.

Since an expedition into the northern reaches of the island was not to be thought of for the time being, she wished to see *something* of the wilder territory on the outskirts of the city.

The sawmill provided her with enough exotic scents to send her hurrying excitedly through the lumber-yard. Yellow cedar. Hemlock. Spruce. Ponderosa pine. Together she and Sumner circulated amongst the stacks of fresh-cut lumber in search of the planks and studs and floor joists marked for delivery to the road-house, with only the annoying squeal of saws through resistant logs to spoil the perfection of the morning for her.

"If this man should decide to let you build his hotel –"

"Abner Lucas."

"– you would have the opportunity to do the sort of thing you've always dreamed of?"

"With some modifications for common sense, I suppose."

"You must hire me, then, to work on it with you! You can teach me which end of the hammer is meant for the nails."

"Miss McConnell," he said, "you've already raised more eyebrows in town than your sister has. You are not about to become a carpenter."

Had no one ever denied her before? She narrowed resentful eyes. "You wait and see. I'll dress as a man and get myself hired, and even get myself promoted for my good work, before you discover who I am. Oh, I think it must be the most wonderful thing, to build your dreams out of material that smells as lovely as this."

"You seem to have forgotten. It will be Zak who builds the hotel. If it is built at all. From my plans."

The pleased expression was once again replaced with anger. "While you are poking around Paris, looking for some place that *needs* you? It's ridiculous. Paris doesn't need you, Venice doesn't need you, San Francisco doesn't need you. The day may come when *this* place needs you but you'll be somewhere else!"

"I visited the steamship office yesterday afternoon," he said, "and postponed my departure until next month. I suppose I felt *rushed*."

"I can't imagine why," she said, but in a tone that suggested she knew precisely why, even if he himself could not begin to understand a thing.

They rode for an hour, two hours, through forest. They crossed shallow streams in grassy clearings, and followed a split-rail fence where several horses accompanied them for a while through a stand of alder, whinnying and making as though to jump the fence and galloping on ahead to turn and come back. Then they crossed a hillside of long grass where a boy led a herd of bleating goats up the slant towards a shed, and followed the bank of a river through darkened canyons of giant prehistoric fern and pale leaning alder trunks trailing shreds and tatters of old-man's-beard. And finally they came out into the sunlight along a naked beach of grey sand where a colony of great jagged black pinnacles of tide-smoothed rock stood about as though embedded there after falling from some other planet, or after exploding out of the centre of the mountain that rose above them.

As soon as they'd dismounted, she removed her boots and her stockings and hoisted up her skirts to go walking in the frothy edges of the tide. "Norah Horncastle said I could do worse than make you my guide."

Then it was Norah Horncastle he must blame for this woman's interest? Or must thank, he supposed, on a glorious day like today which would otherwise have been spent poring over blueprints.

"To hear her boast, one might mistake you for her son. Naturally she meant as a guide to the landscape, but I'm more interested in what you may show me of the masculine heart."

Wind off the strait might have been trying to tear the tangled red curls from her head. How seriously did she intend to be taken? The smile she tilted his way suggested she was serious but did not want to frighten him. Sumner looked away, hoping for seals or sea lions to distract them. A killer whale might surface and save him from having to speak. But sea-gulls had this beach to themselves, except for the human intruders. "If you took this scarred and muddled heart as a model, I'm afraid you'd soon decide there's no hope of finding your way at all. Even I have discovered no map."

"Still a woman who presumes to advise other women must try to fathom the heart of men, don't you think."

"I'd hate to think that other men possess anything like it. I assume I am alone, and that everyone else is as certain of things as he appears."

She lifted her skirts nearly to her knees and took three, four, five long strides out towards deeper sea – Sumner in boots was left on the damp shore. The skirt was captured between her knees while a line of amber kelp was gathered up off the gently heaving surface and examined, a gleaming bullwhip fed through her hands, and then tossed aside. She turned, and faced him, and laughed. Then came striding in towards him, her bare feet and long, pale, gleaming legs streaming with sea water. She could not be surprised to see that he had noticed. You only hoped to discover that ankles, finally seen, would be as lovely as these.

"If the water were not so cold," she said, "I should step behind that rock and remove my outer clothing and run in for a bathe. And I should mock you until you joined me."

"Two frozen bodies would be found, washed up in Japan."

"Instead," she suggested, "we must start a fire and sit like Indians over it, while you try to tell me what it is like – to be a man whose heart has been wrung out like a washed shirt by love, and then tossed onto the dung heap by a woman."

"It is something I've never even imagined telling anyone." Gathering sticks and twigs, he could keep his back to her.

"Self-pity?"

"A sorrow as heavy as those mountains, to put it strongly. And as firmly embedded."

They both stopped, to look. Across the strait, the high wall of mountains again seemed intimidatingly near. "They have a name?" Annie said, when they had stared long enough.

"The Olympics."

"Perhaps because there are gods in those snowy peaks, then? Determining the fates of mortals over here?"

"Yankee gods, maybe. Politician-gods, squabbling and plotting our future. 'On the other side of the flood' is a phrase that comes to mind." He recommenced his search for bits of wood dry enough for kindling.

"But that was referring to Egypt. Can you imagine these waters parting, or a column of slaves approaching us along the bottom, in search of freedom?"

"In fact there was such a thing once. Though they didn't walk." He sat on a log to tell this, and she sat beside him, clutching her handful of twigs. "I was a child – this was in the days of the Colony – I remember seeing a man with a face the colour of chocolate, crossing the street at the corner of Yates and Government. I was terrified. I didn't know what I was looking at – some horrible disease."

"No one explained?"

"And soon afterwards I saw another. And another. A large number of them had arrived, my uncle eventually told me – former slaves who'd been promised that they'd be free from the old prejudices on this side of the border. They'd be just the same as everyone else. Unfortunately the Egyptians, you might say, came with them. The same boat that brought them from San Francisco also brought a number of California miners, who didn't see a mere border as a reason for leaving their opinions – or their behaviour – behind. It ended unhappily. Egyptians believe all the world to be Egypt, or will make it so."

Even as he'd been speaking, Sumner was half aware of faint scribbles of music in the air, from somewhere behind the rock pinnacles. A thin dancing line from a horn. Of course this was impossible, out here. And yet Annie was listening too. "A cornet," she said. "A dolphin has taught himself to play?"

By the time a grazing horse came into view, they had already got to their feet and set out to investigate. High on a ledge of the rock, above the sea, sat a young sailor with his uniform jacket tossed over a small bush and his horn raised to his lips. But he lowered the gleaming instrument, embarrassed, upon seeing the intruders.

"Please don't stop," Annie said. "It was lovely."

"Thank you, miss," he said, rising to his feet. "I thought I was alone. I ride out here when I'm feeling a little lonely, miss. Thinking about home, you understand."

"And where is home?" Sumner said.

"When I was a boy, I lived in a small village."

"And where is the village?"

"Nowhere any more, sir. The Prussians came in and took it. Changed its name. My family moved to England."

"Well please," Sumner said. "Don't stop your playing because of us. We'll return to our side of the rock and leave you alone."

Annie McConnell was not content to disappear so easily. When the cornet's sad music began again to snatch at the wind, she swept into a sort of dance along the white froth of the sea, and insisted, insisted, insisted that he join her, and turn with her, and make slow graceful arabesques with her on the sand which gleamed beneath the successive washes of the incoming tide.

Although he had not invited them, Annie McConnell and Norah Horncastle arrived together the following afternoon at his work site east of town, where he was supervising the preparations for an addition to The White Birches Roadhouse. A steady chill wind and occasional showers continued to spoil whatever chance there might be for an Indian summer, but once the two women had stepped down out of their carriage onto the damp grass, they took the time to admire the rich show of country colours that surrounded them: the orange pumpkins and yellow squash in the adjacent fields, the red berries on the hawthorns, the white pearls on the snowberry bushes, the yellow leaves of the willows along the drainage ditch. "Could you find a lovelier place in the wide world, I wonder?" said Norah Horncastle, heaving in a deep breath of the air.

The gable end of Sheepshanks' farmhouse could be glimpsed, in the distance, behind a stand of yellowed cottonwoods.

Annie McConnell would not allow Sumner to release their horse from the buggy or to lead it over to the trough. She would do everything herself. Stroking the horse's silky neck, she anticipated his question. "It was Norah who suggested this."

The accused displayed her innocent palms. "'Tis only that I wished to see if my young man is earning his pay. Where is he hiding from me now?"

Of course she could see that Jerome was only a few yards away, and perfectly capable of hearing her. He stood up with his arms full of splintered wood scraps – it was his job to carry it off and burn it behind the roadhouse. "Maw?"

"Too old and hard by now to give your old mother a welcome kiss, I suppose."

Jerome's mouth dropped open with alarm as she advanced upon him with her arms thrown wide. "Maw?" Perturbed, amused, unsure what to do, he tried to run away. Too late. His mother had him by the arm. He laughed and struggled to set himself free. "No! Don't! You'll make me drop it!" And indeed he dropped his armload of wood scraps on the ground. But a determined mother cared nothing for dropped scraps, she had him by the neck and would not let go until – triumphant – she had planted a kiss upon his embarrassed cheek.

"He has earned every penny since he talked me into letting him do this," Sumner said, "but he still hasn't learned not to stop work every time someone he knows comes by."

Jerome gave his mother a look that said: Do you see what humiliation you have caused me? Then he stooped to pick up the scattered debris.

"Another reason we are here," said Annie McConnell, "is that we wish to be taught important things. We wish to become experts on improving roadhouses – don't we, Norah?"

Of course Sumner had had his folding yardstick out of his pocket for some time, and had already measured his right leg, his left hand, and the width of his pocket. Now it could become a professor's pointer – though it bent and slapped aside and did not wish to be pointed at anything. In effect this construction before them would be another case of putting a new face over the old, Sumner said, like so much of the work he was asked to do. "But a new room is also to be added to the old structure, which means one section of this wall must be taken down altogether." (The gash that had already been opened up was five and a half feet wide, the ruler told him – but of course he knew that already.)

In order to do this, the men had first removed all the flags and bunting and evergreen wreaths the owner had hung up against the front of the roadhouse for the coming of royalty. There lay the decorations against a fence. "As you can see, we removed the horse trough to the side yard where your nag is enjoying herself. And we removed the cage of raccoons which were meant to occupy the children and wives of travellers who step inside for a drink. And then we pulled down the roof and posts and railings of the verandah itself. Jerome is clearing the mess away."

Today the pair of carpenters had almost completed stripping off the front wall's face of sheet iron, manufactured in San Francisco to look like a wall of stone blocks.

One of the carpenters was Zachary Jack, who threw down his crowbar to become the teacher's assistant. "*H wah!* Look at this. Behind that iron there's bricks – see? These walls got enough layers to stand all by themselves through an earthquake! You get stripping these false faces away, you start to think that some day you'll find something you could call the real one." He raised both eyebrows at the red-headed foreigner and patted his great belly.

Annie McConnell did not smile. "How would you recognize it when you saw it? The real one, I mean."

Sumner and Zak had discussed this before. "In the world of architecture," Sumner said, "you would have a hard time of it trying to determine which are the false faces and which are the real. If we got to what we might think is the original – even that would be only a sort of façade, to convince the world of what we wish them to think. This elegant house must have elegant people living in it. This unpainted old-fashioned saloon must be for the hard-working man to drink in with his friends. This roadhouse stands for tradition and ties to the Old Country. To the designer, the *real* building remains in his head." Why was he always astonished to find that the yardstick, folded up in his hand, was only six inches long?

"Which is to say," said Norah Horncastle, off in the direction of the vegetable garden in a tone that suggested this was merely the logical result of taking these men as seriously as they took themselves, "that you would have to keep stripping away until you were looking right into the heart of our Maker." She turned her head abruptly, and looked straight at Logan Sumner, and smiled. "If you'll forgive me for being so predictable."

As a boy, Sumner had given to God the face of an older Uncle Charles. Sermons had reinforced this: God was Uncle Charles's Uncle Charles. Norah Horncastle, on the other hand, had probably never made the mistake of limiting Him to even superhuman proportions.

Business in The White Birches had not been suspended altogether during the period of renovations. One gentleman had ridden up on a bay mare, dismounted, and gone inside. And while they stood talking, the proprietor had come outside carrying a small table which he set down on a level spot in the grass. His wife, following, placed a white cloth over the table while he went back and came out with chairs. "Tea in a moment," the woman said, and invited the two ladies and Logan Sumner to sit while she went inside. Her husband, Abner Lucas, stood back and allowed a grin to spread out across his little red wattle face. "Now ain't this a sight to behold! My builder taking time off from his work to have tea with the ladies! At this rate, my building won't be done till Christmas."

"You brought the table, we didn't ask," Sumner said. "And anyway, you know we're well ahead of schedule as it is."

"Oh, do we now?"

"By Christmas they'll be driving past just to see for themselves how beautiful your place has become."

Now all of Abner Lucas's six remaining teeth could be seen – most of them well to the rear. "I don't want them driving by, my friend. I want them stopping in!"

"Are you the man who intends to build the hotel?" Annie McConnell asked.

Logan Sumner did not know whether to think, "This is no business of yours," or "When did anyone show so much interest in my affairs?" He raised his forearm to his nose and smelled – cedar dust – and sneezed.

"I am," said Abner Lucas. "I am indeed. Without a word of a lie. You wouldn't mistake me for a rich man, but this business of mine has given me all I need to build me own dream. We'll give the Horncastles a run for their money – see if we don't." He winked at Norah Horncastle, perhaps forgetting the alteration in her affairs, then coughed into his hand when it seemed he might have remembered.

"I've seen some of Mr. Sumner's drawings," said Annie McConnell. "And I am sure you'll congratulate yourself when you have chosen him."

"I'm still waiting to see what sort of mess he leaves me with here," said Abner Lucas. "Without a word of a lie."

"And anyway," Annie said, "it will not be Mr. Sumner who builds it. He'll be starving in some attic room in Madrid – happy at last."

Jerome continued to come and go, taking away his armloads of debris for the fire, without betraying the slightest interest in the world of adults.

Tea had been poured but not yet drunk when out through the gap in the wall spilled Horace Sheepshank's hired hands – Alfie Stott, Stretch Halfpenny, Jock MacCrae, and the long, thin Australian-Yankee who took care of the horses. They paused before stepping down, and looked over the outdoor congregation. Alfie Stott spat his tobacco juice into the dust on the floor beside him and briefly lifted his hat from his head. "Ladies."

Stretch Halfpenny was more specific. "'Tis Mrs. 'orncastle!" He put both hands on his knees and leaned forward, mouth gaping, like someone about to leap into a swimming-hole. "Always a pleasure, ma'am, t' see ye!" He gave both knees a solid thwack. "Haw haw! I nivver t'ought I'd see ye waitin' to gain entry to a roadhouse now, did I? But 'ere ye are, waitin' yer turn."

"Only passing by, Mr. Halfpenny," sang Norah Horncastle. "Sure, your sanctuaries are safe enough from the likes of me, even when they are torn open to the elements."

"Open to the elements," said Annie McConnell, "but not to women. Rain and winds and birds have the freedom to go in and out as they please. But not even a hole in the wall makes it possible for ladies to enter without causing a stir. I am with you, Norah, if you've a mind to defy convention."

Sumner closed his eyes. There would be a scene.

But perhaps Norah Horncastle had already defied enough convention for one lifetime. "'Tis time we were going, we've kept these gentlemen from their work long enough."

"Ye have that!" growled Alfie Stott. "There's a terrible draught blowin' through the premises while they're out here jawin' wi' the wimmin. Me and the men is takin' our business elsewhere."

Annie McConnell's threat to go inside had brought her to the attention of the horseman Hawks, who leaned back against the wall and rolled a cigarette while he continued to watch her from beneath the brim of his hat. When he heaved himself away from the building to leave with the others, he smiled and shifted direction and strode close enough to mutter, "Miss Annie, a pleasure to see you in this part of the world," before striding to the farm wagon and climbing aboard.

She snatched up Logan Sumner's tube of drawings and unrolled the sheets of paper across the tea things. "You were suggesting something outrageous, I think." The White Birches, which only a few feet away displayed its gaping wound, had been transformed by pencilled lines into something quite handsome. "You wished us to believe that to a designer a building represents something perfect. I understand that much. As a work of art may do."

For a moment Sumner wondered what she was talking about, before recalling. "I suppose that's what I meant. Something like that. Buildings have their integrity, if I may say so. They tell their stories too."

"But: works of art?" Half demolished beside them, The White Birches was invoked as an obvious mockery of this preposterous idea. The sheets of paper were only paper after all, the careful geometric lines only lines.

Norah Horncastle said, "Haven't we all seen buildings which seem to be posing for their portrait – all stiff and tidy and frightened? Whole rows of them up Fort Street!"

The sheets of paper were rolled up and thrust back inside their tube, the future – or hopes for it – dismissed. Annie McConnell looked to Norah Horncastle for an ally: "He strips the false faces off other people's buildings, claiming that he's getting closer to the 'truth.' At the same time he erects a tombstone telling elaborate lies. Is there any hope of understanding him?"

Norah Horncastle did not hesitate. "Ah, he has argued this sort of thing with us before, half the night away around the table! 'Tis certain he's bored with hearing what I think of such matters."

"I could tell you from memory what Norah Horncastle thinks of such matters. She thinks that our histories and our fictions and all the rest – our buildings are included – are no more what's real than your ladies' fashions are the lady, as I understand you have been heard to say yourself."

Norah Horncastle did not dissent. "Merely dreams recording other dreams," she said. "Isn't it a fact that most of the time we live in a dream of our own making?" Perhaps the faces of both her listeners demanded proof of this. "Who should know better than I?" The look she turned first on Sumner and then on Annie McConnell was both apologetic and amused: What do you expect, it sounds mad, but I'm doing the best I can.

Then she leaned forward, grinning. "Lest we take ourselves too seriously now, let us not forget those cows chewing grass across the fence do not understand how wise our conversation is – they see three humans bundled up against the weather, taking tea at a little table set out on the grass beneath the clouds, only a few feet from a roof. What stories will they circulate about us?"

When tea was declared to be over and they had started towards the buggy, ready to leave, Zak dropped his tools and insisted on fetching the horse and hitching it up. He suggested to Sumner that he bring the Australian lady to witness the flight of the latest version of their flying machine. "Wednesday at dawn." To Annie, he said, "you'll have something to write about to the kangaroos back home."

Sumner was not enthusiastic about the idea but the Australian would not be uninvited now. Especially since the idea seemed to please her. "A flying machine!"

"With wings," Zak promised her.

Sumner added, "And this one has actually stayed up in the air for more than a minute, before crashing."

It was clear she was pleased to have stumbled into the company of the sort of madmen she preferred. "I have dreamed of flying.

Will I be allowed to ride in it? No, of course not. But, someday, do you suppose?"

Sumner and Zak looked at one another. "Not immediately," Sumner said.

Annie watched Zak walk away to rejoin the other carpenter inside the gash in the wall. "My sister tells me that marriage here with native Indians is not uncommon."

"Be careful. If Zak hears that you think he has some white man's blood he'll withdraw his invitation. The only parent he acknowledges was pure Nootka."

"Mr. Sumner, are you aware that you are measuring my foot? It hardly seems the behaviour of a gentleman. Will I find you so bold as to try measuring my calf next?"

She laughed, but Sumner quickly folded up the yardstick and put it in his pocket. "I'm sorry. It seems to take on these tasks itself!" (Her foot, or at least her boot, was eight inches long.)

"He constantly measures the world," said Norah Horncastle. "He is still trying to discover whether there is a place where he might fit."

"Or whether he is still confined to this inadequate planet," Annie said. "It is a practice I approve of. Oh, I don't mean your habit of measuring things, I mean the intermarriage of races." She was back on her topic as though nothing else had been said. "You'll find a new race being born here, like the races of South America. Strong and mysterious and very beautiful. Australians will never allow it, I know, but I understand it has already begun to happen here. My sister tells me the widow of your former governor is the product of such a marriage. Now, if I, for instance, were to bear your carpenter's children –"

She gazed boldly into his eyes for a moment, the faintest suggestion of a mocking smile on her lips, as though daring him to be shocked.

He was shocked, but only by his sudden realization of what was going on here, of what had been going on almost since the moment she arrived in town. She was interested in him, she wanted them to be friends, and more than that she wanted him to be attracted to her as a woman. God only knew why. If the great heat that rose to his face meant anything, or the indignation he felt at her threatening to pursue Zak, or the thick lava of steaming soup that choked up his lungs – if any of this meant anything, then undoubtedly she had long ago achieved her purposes without his even suspecting it. He had been so mesmerized by his own misery that he hadn't noticed until now that he'd been quite happy for several days in a row.

Of course, he handled it all wrong. He acted as though he were amused at her suggestion. "A pretty idea, but not very likely. The 'forest maidens' were quite acceptable when there was a shortage of European women, but the situation has changed. A bride ship was sent us, for instance. Lady Douglas is not a pattern for the future."

She might be thinking of resenting this, her eyes looked so steadily into his. But she turned away and got up into the buggy without speaking. Then she took something from a pocket of her cape – a rectangle of stiff white paper – and handed it down to him. "An invitation for Monday evening. The Theatre Royal. Perhaps you shall learn something – a man so old-fashioned he does not think a woman should choose whose children she should bear, or even dare to speculate aloud on the subject! Perhaps, sir, you would deny me the right to speak at *all*, on *any* subject, without first asking permission of you or some other man!"

She slapped the reins against the horse's haunch and started the buggy moving towards the road. Only Norah Horncastle looked back, and lifted a hand in a farewell gesture, and smiled.

25

FROM childhood Kate McConnell had been a person who knew, or thought she knew, the reasons for everything she did – her goals had always been specific ones, her actions always carefully chosen in order to move her towards the achievement of those goals. Her older sisters had recognized this – she had never been a mystery. But from the time of Annie's arrival at the hotel she was no longer entirely certain of why she did anything. Even in the midst of acting or speaking, she was aware that she was behaving out of some ill-defined instinct which seemed to have taken her over, propelling her towards some inevitable end. During the week that would end with the Agricultural Fair, where James would be riding in the one-mile race before the entire town and hundreds of visitors – including the royal couple and their entourage of attendants and officials – she had several occasions to wonder whether she might not, without quite understanding why, destroy them both before the anticipated day arrived.

Annie might have helped. Annie might have cautioned her against her own impatience if she had not grown into the habit of deserting her own family in favour of that sad-eyed carpenter with his silly unfolding yardstick and his aura of fine sawdust. Kate was left to stumble through on her own, as always, unaware of the damage she could do until it was already done.

To begin with, she attended one of James's courtroom appearances for the first time without first asking him what she might expect. This was another battle with the one-armed saloon-keeper Samuel Hatch, who had laid three charges against James – damages caused by his fox terrier (who'd sunk her aged teeth into Hatch's meaty thigh), assault against his person (another bloody nose in an argument that resulted from the dog's offence), and unpaid debts incurred in a series of wagers, including private bets agreed upon at the races. An impatient magistrate demanded an apology, a promise of a two-month abstinence from gambling, and the immediate payment of the debt.

So upset was Kate by this whole experience that she made the mistake of suggesting, as they walked the few blocks home from the police barracks, that it was time he considered putting Vicky out of her misery. "She has become a constant source of embarrassment to you. And she is obviously not very happy in her uncomfortable old age." He would not listen. The dog had been with him for years, he protested, a faithful companion, an important part of his life. How could he discard her now? She was only exhibiting good sense by taking a nip out of Sam Hatch's leg, she ought to be rewarded for the deed.

Kate did not remind him that his faithful dog, who had recently taken up the habit of eating the clothes of humans, was at this moment locked in his office so that she would not finish the job she started, at breakfast, on the legs of his best suit trousers. Yesterday she had destroyed a top hat that had fallen to the foyer carpet from the hand of a Bostonian banker who was signing the register.

Coming so soon after the unhappy end of his courtroom appearance, her suggestion had put him in such a foul mood that she feared bringing up anything else unpleasant. Yet she could not live with the dread that had been stirred up within her when she heard the size of his debt – their debt. Though he was in a hurry to return to his bar, she insisted that he accompany her to the family kitchen where they might speak in private. "This ugly business with Hatch, this *horrid* affair, has made it imperative that I speak to you. Now. Of something which has been on my mind. If we are to avoid disaster."

"Haven't noticed you biting your tongue before now."

"Annie agrees with me on this," she said, when she had closed the door on the rest of the world, "that your spending, your disregard for our finances, is a serious danger to the hotel."

"What! *What!*" Evidently he had never been confronted like this before. His face reddened, his mouth gaped, his hands appeared unable to decide what to do with themselves.

"If the Blue Heron is not to be lost, you must keep it safe –"

"The hotel lost? What nonsense is this now?"

"By engaging a lawyer, James, who will agree to transferring the ownership."

"Transfer the ownership to whom?"

"I have taken the liberty, I have *glanced* at the books, and there is trouble ahead –"

"You have been in my office?"

"I should have imagined you'd be grateful to think I am interested in helping. Of course I grasped little of what I saw, but I understood enough –"

"Transfer the ownership you said, but did not say to whom."

"A way can be found, I am certain – though what I am proposing is highly unusual. Of course I mean, transfer the ownership to me."

He sat, abruptly, on the wooden chair by the table, and appeared to be struggling for calm. "And Annie agrees with you, you say. Is this why you brought your sister here – to scheme and plot how to separate me from my life's work?"

Having launched into this, she refused to be frightened off. She would not think until later of the risk she was taking. "We are speaking of nothing but a piece of paper, only a *document!* You would notice no real difference."

Both palms slammed down on the table-top. "A piece of paper has already been responsible for more trouble here than anyone could have imagined. Don't 'only a piece of paper' me! I think you have gone a little mad from thinking. Stop thinking. Did not marry you for your thinking. You will have us both behind bars, or run out of town, if you keep on thinking as you are."

"But when you have had time to consider it, you will see how much sense there is to my plan."

"I will not, I will not, I will not!" He leapt to his feet and started for the door. "It will not be mentioned again."

She followed him into the hallway. "I am to be poor for ever, then? I am to scrub floors and make beds and rescue guests from the mice until I am too old and crippled from labour to do it any more?"

Down the hallway he went, ahead of her, and into the parlour, where he snatched up the newspaper. Then out into the hallway again and towards the door to the hotel. "This is only what you fought for, madam. This is what you took from another. This is what you came here for and hurt others for and ought to be happy with. I've heard enough of complaints."

"Then you will not even consider the matter?"

"My God, Kate! What sort of man do you think you have got?" He strode across the hotel foyer – which was empty, she was glad to see, of anyone but the boy behind the counter. "To hand my business over to a woman?" He waved his arms about and stepped inside his office. "Won't listen to any more of this!"

She raised her voice to be heard through the door he had closed between them. "Then you must not be surprised, one day, to find that you are handing it over to the bank, or to one of your rivals. Or to someone who has outwitted you in a wager."

Perhaps it would be possible, later, to blame everything on Lady Riven-Blythe's mood, a fit of homesickness brought on by the presence of royalty. "Once again I am planning to go Home – this time for good!" She did not at all feel like putting the usual effort into being the perfect hostess, she confessed, when her heart had already gone on ahead to sail round the Horn.

Nevertheless, she allowed herself to get caught up in a game of croquet. "I warn you, though. I always win! I expect to win. You'll have to watch me – if I see myself starting to lose I will cheat!"

Ladies who had played with Lady Riven-Blythe before assured Kate that their hostess was not exaggerating. "We play to see who will be second."

"And for the exercise, of course."

"And for the table of delicious food we will destroy immediately afterwards." (This was Mrs. Olfried Thornycroft, who had thought herself to be Mrs. Olfried Harrow until only recently, when her husband was discovered to be hiding his real identity as heir to the famous Salisbury Thornycroft family of embezzlers.)

They were not encouraged to spend time in the house – which was, Kate thought, as cluttered as an auction house. There was no room for people of a normal size amongst the superfluous chairs and sofas and tables and lamps. Since the weather had had the good sense to co-operate, they were rushed immediately out onto the lawn, where the sun, which shone down through the shoreline arbutus trees onto the vast display of dahlias and chrysanthemums, had dried the night's moisture from the grass. Kate was given a red ball and a wooden mallet with a red ring around the handle, and came behind Mrs. Fletcher in the order of things. Annie, being Lady Riven-Blythe's newest favourite, was permitted to choose blue, and to take her turn immediately after the hostess, who claimed it was a rule of the game, at least when it was played in her garden, that hostesses must go first.

But Kate very early fell hopelessly behind the others, unable to send her uncooperative ball through the second wire hoop. Again and again she tried, unsuccessfully, to launch an attack on a hoop that seemed to have thrown up an invisible wall to fend her off – while the rest of them surged ahead, finding no difficulties. Conversations soon became too distant for her to be part of, or even pretend to be part of, then moved on to become even too distant for her to hear. She and her mallet and the red ball were left to play a frustrating game of their own. She might call it "Catch-up" but saw herself falling farther back by the moment, while ladies screamed with mock envy, and squealed with feigned surprise, and roared with pretended indignation over a hostess who was as willing to cheat as she had claimed to be. It did no good to signal to Annie for aid. As Annie's helpless shrug suggested, she was on her own. Soon the others were gathered about the final hoops – someone would at any moment drive home to the winning peg. No one remembered now that a certain Kate Horncastle had even joined in the game.

She saw all too easily what it meant. There was nothing Lady Riven-Blythe would do for her. There was nothing Annie *could* do for here. She might as well have remained at home.

But as soon as she had won the game and received her congratulations, Lady Riven-Blythe left the others squabbling over who was to be second and came back with her yellow ball in one hand, her mallet in the other, to join Kate at the beginning end of the lawn. Perhaps she was not invisible after all.

"Of course, since your sister has asked this favour of me, you must join us tomorrow evening at the 'Drawing-Room.' I shall arrange for it. I trust you have something to wear?"

"I have something."

"We shall all meet on the steps to the legislature, then. And go in together."

"It is a great kindness, Lady Riven-Blythe. I am grateful to you and my sister both."

"But there is something else, since we are alone for the moment." Lady Riven-Blythe let her successful ball spill out of her hand and drop to the grass, where she nudged it with her toe until it lay against Kate's disappointing one. "I would prefer not to say anything about this pestilential affair to you, naturally." She put her foot on her own ball, and lifted her mallet. "It is not any longer my business. And for the sake of your sister I have tried not to be unkind. And, I suppose, my own dear friend would forbid me to tell you this." Her mallet struck the ball beneath her tiny foot, which in turn sent Kate's ball spinning off towards the delphiniums. "But one finds oneself simply unable to resist telling you what you

JACK HODGINS

so obviously have not even imagined." Having got Kate's ball out of her way, she leaned forward to take a practice swing at her own – for the blow that would send her back up towards the far end of the lawn a second time. Perhaps she had hopes of winning "second prize" as well.

"Please. What is it I have not even imagined?"

"That your 'husband,' as you insist on calling him, continues to visit his wife quite regularly at her boarding-house." The mallet cracked sharply against her ball, which shot off in a straight line through the hoop that had been set there to frustrate Kate. "Perhaps there are more important things for you to take care of than trying to thrust yourself into society."

She might have waited until tomorrow to confront him. She might even have held her tongue until she had gained some measure of calm – if calm were possible. But she came home from Lady Riven-Blythe's with a great howling desire to do violence. To hold her tongue through supper was almost more than she could bear. And he was reckless enough to ask, when he came into his bedroom to begin dressing and found the door open to her room: "A pleasant afternoon with Lady R and her mallets?"

"She has agreed that you and I should attend the 'Drawing-Room' tomorrow evening. With her and Annie." This ought to have been a great triumph – it *was* a great triumph – but she felt in no mood to enjoy it. "Otherwise the croquet was a boring, endless game. Lady Riven-Blythe was out of sorts – she is planning to go Home!"

"Again! Must have worn a trough through the ocean by now, with all her back and forthing. Why can some women never settle?"

A copy of Annie's handbill lay on her bed. She and Mr. Sumner and some of Sumner's employees had tacked them up all over town.

THE THEATRE ROYAL

An Evening of Theatre
With Miss Annabel McConnell
of Ballarat, Australia

Songs

A First Hand Account of
Life Amongst the Aborigines

A Few Words
on the Modern Woman

7:00 P.M.   *Monday, Sept. 25*

It was unlikely that Annie had ever seen an Aborigine, but she
would not find that a serious hindrance. All of it – the singing, the
"tales of the outback" – would be there merely to help people
grow attached to their seats before she hit them with her message:
suffrage, freedom from fashion, careers for women. Kate's suggestion of an elocutionary evening at home would not do; she must
hire a theatre, like a travelling actress.

Annie will not do me any good, Kate found herself thinking.
I might as well have left her undisturbed in Ballarat. I am alone
in this.

"Playing croquet with Lady Riven-Blythe, one learns that
there is a still more serious brand of cheat running free!"

He was never able to get his cravat right the first time – off it
came again, for another attempt. "What sort of nonsense has the
old woman put into your head?"

She was nearly dressed already – had started early, in fact, so
that there would be time for this. She stood in her underskirts,

waist cinched and laced, ready to slip her gown over her head. She took the garnet ring off; put on the opal. "What I have been the only woman in town not to know. That you pay regular visits, to that woman."

He laughed. "To visit the children, Kate! Surely you weren't surprised. Must stop by occasionally for the sake of the children."

"You care nothing for the children." This was said from inside the gown, as it rustled about and began to slide down over her. "Don't lie to me." Now that her head was free she shook out the folds of the skirt. "The children are often not even there. It is the woman you visit. In order to make a fool of me!"

No one had ever had such wide, innocent eyes as James Horncastle surprised in his guilt. "Lord, Kate. She was my wife – for years. It isn't natural to cut off all –"

"It is entirely natural, when there are ties with a legitimate wife. Please do up the buttons."

He laughed, as though she could not possibly be serious, but slipped buttons into buttonholes up her back. "But I *miss* her, Kate! You must understand that. Surely. She has such a great warm heart. A man cannot just turn his back on such kindness."

"Then, you insult me." She sat before the mirror and contemplated her hair. Though she had been careful not to disarrange it with the gown, there were stray pieces in need of discipline.

Now he seemed not only amused but immensely pleased. "By the lord Harry, I believe you're jealous. Why – don't you know? It was you who made me think there was no harm in it. When you wrote to Annie. You would give her to me as a second wife yourself. It was none of my idea, remember! If she sees no harm in a second wife, I thought, she can't see any harm in a third wife, either. So I stopped worrying about it. A man will take all the wives he can get, so long as each of them gives him something different."

Yes. She supposed he would. The fat one for mothering. Annie for his male instincts, if she had accepted him. Kate would do for making the meals, and helping to run the hotel. Were there others, somewhere, she did not know about? It was a wonder he hadn't insisted on collecting them all beneath the one roof. A man who owned a hotel had rooms for any number of wives.

"Well, you will promise me before we leave this house tonight that it will never happen again." She spoke to the red-faced little man in the mirror.

"You're mad!"

"You will never even *speak* to that woman again. You will go nowhere near her house."

"And this damn tie will drive me mad as well. Will you help me with it, Kate?"

"You should be afraid to allow me that close to your throat!" She stood in the doorway between their rooms. "Your behaviour will make it clear to everyone that you have left that marriage behind." She was panting, she could hardly breathe. "Because if you don't, I will burn your hotel to the ground."

"By God, Kate, you are hard. She is a *friend*, a dear friend. We have become accustomed to one another. Would you come between *that*?"

"Do you wish me to set a match to *her* house as well?" she said, but shut the door between them before he could respond. She would not set a foot outside this building without first doing something about the throbbing in her head. "Wang Low?" Usually the house servant could be trusted to notice her mounting need, and to stand by with something already prepared.

His "dear friend" was already sitting in one of the parterre rows when Kate and Horncastle arrived in their assigned box to the left of the stage. Fat cheeks flushed, eyes riveted to the stage. She could probably not believe she would be watching someone perform whom she had actually met. The same slack grin was displayed on the faces of her scraggy brood on either side of her.

Was it fitting that the only theatre Annie had been able to hire – once the grandest in town, it was said, though it had begun life as two Hudson's Bay warehouses pushed together – was now scheduled to be torn down within the month? They would be its final audience – Hattie Moore's English Comic Opera Company had been the last of the travelling troupes to use it, but there was nothing to show that *The Mascotte* had ever been performed on that stage, or that Signor Montegriffo and Miss Florence D'Arona had once sung Lucretia Borgia and Carmen. All scenery had already been removed, except for a red brick gable, a window, and a door. The curtain with its gilt advertisement would soon be rolled up and taken away, the gas lights torn out, the walls demolished. It seemed to Kate that the place had a deserted look about it already, as though it knew its fate and had already surrendered its soul. The accumulated perfumes of all those years were as dark and melancholy a mix to the nose as the gaslight was to the eye.

Fortunately Annie made a singular enough figure to draw your attention away from the doomed building – with bare feet peeking out from beneath the white Grecian dress, hair wildly afloat and studded with flowers, one hand anchoring her to the gleaming black piano. The entire audience exploded into applause after her voice faded away at the end of "Beautiful Dreamer." Not a professional voice, but it was sweetly appealing.

Though he applauded briefly with the others, James was stiff with indignation, still furious with Kate for the scene at home. The fingers of one hand opened and closed on his thigh; the fingers of his other hand repeatedly stroked his moustache. His great horned eyebrows scowled as they did when his horse had just lost a race or the magistrate had just begun a long reprimand. He would look to neither the right nor the left. Greetings before the show had been ignored. Young James and Laura had found empty seats for themselves in the gallery, angry with both of them for causing a row on the day of Aunt Annie's local debut.

Beneath a surprisingly discreet hat of wax fruit, Lady Riven-Blythe was in a box on the far side of the theatre. She was accompanied by those few members of her circle who could be persuaded to give up an evening for this – to expose their ears to the danger of revolutionary ideas. (What had any of them ever done to earn their place? Even Lady Riven-Blythe, who was not above cheating at croquet – what had she done to earn a title? Married a man who spent a lifetime accomplishing things – while she accomplished nothing but the feat of outliving him.)

The royal box was empty – you didn't see *them* here. You didn't see the rest of the crowd from Government House, either. Or any elected Members. Not even the Shakespeares. Maybe a few minor civil servants stirred in with the common lot. There was Logan Sumner too, of course, in the stalls below the Riven-Blythe party. No room for his long, bony thighs – his knees wedged up against the seat ahead of him. Of course, he was not sitting in this same doomed pair of converted warehouses with the rest of them – not *him* – but in some grand opera house of his own invention – with chandeliers and velvet curtains and a full orchestra in black ties. But holding flowers! How was it that a man who carried the sorrows of both orphan and widower, and suffered the shy awkwardness of a man filled with doubts, could seem at the same time to be also a child filled with *joy*? It could offend you, seeing that glad face, when you could barely remember the last time you felt genuine joy yourself.

Of course you have chosen not to leave. Annie had said this. *You haven't left him.* Why? Why had she not left him? Why not leave him now? Tomorrow. (She could even walk out and leave him sitting here in the theatre. Take the children with her.) She had only to move out of the hotel. She could insist on having a boarding-house of her own to run, like the other woman. Or take up sewing again. She could divorce and find another husband. Or return to Australia – not Ballarat, perhaps, but somewhere: Sydney, Melbourne. She was not a prisoner here.

Yet she would not leave. She wanted what she had a right to, what she had worked for, what she had earned! She would not, like Susannah, be defeated. Lilian had fallen into Brisbane society; Lilian was someone the others admired; Lilian was a woman of achievement. And Annie had her talents, and her audience – hardly the sort of people Lilian would be associating with, but nevertheless there was a crowd here who had given up their evening to pay attention. And applaud. And say, as she had overheard someone behind her say, "That young woman is remarkable!"

And what of Kate? Who applauded for Kate? Who in the world thought Kate was remarkable? Who believed that Kate had ever done anything worth admiring?

"A pleasant voice, but she can't hold these people indefinitely," said impatient James. "About time she got to the blackfellows."

And to her great feminist themes. How long before she would start demanding that they kick the boots off their feet and go barefoot like herself? Urging women to stand up for their rights, telling the men to permit them – whatever it was these women said when they got themselves wound up.

But instead of getting on with her tales of Australia she had come to the front of the stage, she was holding out a hand towards someone. Logan Sumner! He looked confused, embarrassed. He pushed his glasses up his nose, he ran a hand through his hair, he looked around as though he hoped to discover that someone else was being addressed. Was she telling him to give her the flowers? No, she raised her voice to make it clear: she wanted him to come up and join her on the stage. She wanted to sing a duet.

The applause was hardly thunderous, but apparently Logan Sumner considered it encouragement enough. Up onto the stage he went, all angles and lanky awkwardness. When he realized that he still held his bouquet of red and yellow dahlias in his hand, he seemed for a moment to be unsure of what to do with them; his hands made as though to toss them back into his abandoned seat, then to drop them onto the boards at his feet, then to toss them over his shoulder. Exaggerating the problem. It occurred to him suddenly that he might do with them now what he'd intended to do with them eventually – give them to Annie, with a small bow.

What would the tree-singer call up tonight? In church, he was confined to calling up the attentions of God – his solo voice rang out occasionally in the midst of Psalms. "Praise my soul the King of heaven; to His feet thy tribute bring; ransomed, healed, restored, forgiven, who like thee His praise should sing?" Perhaps Annie would require of him that he sing into present creation all the fury of fashion-enslaved women from around the world, past and present, to assist her in tonight's speech.

Not at all. They sang "I'll Take You Home Again, Kathleen." Annie began, high clear notes like blinking bubbles; then he joined in and laid his baritone beneath her, a warm, dark, flowing undercurrent that only occasionally rose to the surface to join her briefly before diving down to roll along the bottom. Both looked surprised – hadn't they practised together? More than surprised, they looked too pleased with themselves. Performers who are pleased with themselves did not know when to stop.

And indeed they risked a second number. Something from *HMS Pinafore*. "I polished up the handles so carefullee, That now I am the ruler of the Queen's Navee!" Sumner returned to his seat during the applause, and Annie, wisely, stepped over to stand behind the lectern to begin her talk.

An uncle, she said, a great-uncle who liked to spy on kangaroos, had interrupted a black man's walkabout and found a spear in his throat! (No one Kate had heard of.) Where Ballarat now stood, tribes of nomads used to wander in search of yams, nuts, emus' eggs, yabbies, fresh-water mussels, possums, and kangaroos for their food. "I was only a little girl the first time I tasted 'roo. I'd walked out alone one afternoon into the bush and came upon this family of blacks."

"Not an easy matter for someone living in Manchester," James said, in a voice just loud enough to turn a few heads. Kate closed her eyes and said, "Please."

"The Aboriginal woman wore little in the way of clothing, perhaps believing without knowing so that it is God who clothes the lilies of the field? Imagine this fortunate primitive woman, and consider how dumbfounded she would be to learn that the white woman she sees on the street is not so different in form from herself as she appears, but rather has deliberately submitted herself to the tortures and indignities of whalebone corsets, inflatable bust padding, bustle and hoops and high-heeled boots, Pompadourian hairpieces, and head-dresses piled high with birds and nests, with beetles, and centipedes, and reptiles – deliberately deforming the figure, impeding movement, causing discomfort, and injuring health."

"And taking half the day just to dress for tea," James said. He leaned forward against the rail and grinned at faces that turned his way, and shook his shoulders free of Kate's restraining touch. "Will speak if I bloody well wish."

"Yes, and will spoil everything."

"Everything has already been spoiled. You have seen to that."

"Do the ladies of this city wonder that the Indian woman seen selling fish on the streets or herding her children down the beach to her canoe has not yet adopted the corset or stays or crinolines of her white neighbours? Is it a mystery to you that the dark-skinned lady is never seen running off to the dressmaker with the latest issue of *Myra's Journal of Dress and Fashion* under her arm?"

"That's because she's got the sense to use it for wrapping her fish," James said. Quick snorts of laughter escaped from a few people, but otherwise lips tightened in annoyed faces. "She's got more sense than to buy the damn magazine in the first place."

"That is enough," Kate said. "What are you trying to do?"

Far from appearing disturbed by the disruption, Annie seized on Horncastle's observation. "Exactly. She has better sense.

Perhaps she understands instinctively that today's woman, who is educated, enterprising, and ambitious, is beginning to insist that she is more than a doll to be weighed down with impossible draperies for admiration, and she is more than a mother and wife to be harnessed in clothing for work – she is a woman who demands that her attire, though appropriate for work and beauty, must keep her comfortable as well. She wishes not to suffer more than necessary from the cruel tyrannies of dress."

Perhaps James Horncastle was displeased that Annie had taken his last point well. "Oh yes, she does," he said. "She would not be happy if she had no suffering to complain about." This time heads turned abruptly, and frowned at the disruption. "She wishes to draw attention to her martyrdom." He waved a hand in greeting to his tribe of children, who had turned to look up this way, both embarrassed and amused to recognize the voice. He had turned their box into a stage of his own, and would likely any moment take a bow. The children's mother kept her gaze on her folded hands, perhaps as mortified by this as Kate.

"You will stop this," Kate said. "Or you will be sorry."

James leaned closer, and spoke as though to something that had fallen between their seats, but did not lower his voice. "She has no intention of fulfilling this role you suggested she come here for. We both know that. She has come here for her own reasons."

Did he think she hadn't seen this for herself? Did he, perhaps, expect her sympathy? "How unfortunate, James! From three wives you have been reduced to one in a single evening!"

Snorting like one of his own horses, he stood bolt upright beside her. "Enough! Dammit!" This was almost a shout. "Excuse . . . me . . . madam!"

He pushed his chair back roughly, and stomped out of the box to achieve his freedom. Still speaking: "Should have had the sense to stay home and get drunk."

Heads swivelled, of course. Eyes all over the theatre watched his exit. Lady Riven-Blythe was aware. Her friends. People were

shocked, to see the featured speaker's own brother-in-law stomping out. Kate was looked at with – pity? Horror, perhaps. She
should have better control of a husband. Perhaps she was the only
one in the theatre who could see, within the gestures and facial
expressions of James's histrionic fury, the faintest traces of both
amusement and issued challenge. This is only a recess, he was
clearly saying to her, and we will continue the battle whenever or
wherever it pleases you to do so. Annie sailed on to add up under-
drawers, underskirts, balmorals, dress skirts, overskirts, dress-waist,
and belt, to conclude that sixteen layers of cloth girded the
stomach by the time a woman was dressed, all of it pulled in as
tight as possible. "Think of the damage done to the diaphragm,
the lungs, the heart, and the stomach, not to mention the
womb!" She urged women to throw away their corsets, throw
away their chemises, use cambric rather than the heavier muslin
for a single underskirt, wear suspenders, hang everything off the
shoulders instead of the waist, use as little cloth as possible in the
outer skirt, and cut the hems off four inches from the floor. Now
that she was caught up in her topic, Annie – true to form – did
not seem to notice that anything in Kate's world had gone awry.

When Kate got home from the theatre she went straight to bed
and blew out the lamp. But she was soon aware of him in his own
room next door, preparing for bed, and was not altogether surprised when he opened the door between them and came in to
stand by her bed.

"Have been fighting all day, the two of us. You and I."

She grunted, and kept her eyes shut against the faint light that
came in from the lamp in his room. She would prefer to have him
think she was asleep, or nearly. Besides, there was little point in
commenting upon the obvious.

"Shall try to stay away from the boarding-house, as you
requested."

"Why should I believe you? You have promised things before."

"But you cannot expect me to stay away from the children."

"The children can visit you here. I have never forbidden that."

She had, of course, forbidden that. From the beginning. But in his gratitude he seemed to have chosen to forget. He sat on the edge of her bed. "You're a damn fine-looking woman when you are fighting for something, Kate. That's probably why I was pleased to have you after me in the first place."

"It is only that you know you have lost the possibility of Annie and are left with no one but me."

"Nonsense. It is when the anger starts to blaze in you – the *fight*. Makes me proud to call you wife."

He was never shy about letting her know what he had in mind. He lifted the covers now, and slipped into bed beside her, and ran his fingers down her arm.

"Forgive me for stomping out of that damn theatre? Hate that sort of thing anyway – you knew that. Should not have insisted I go."

Vicky could be heard in the other room, tearing cloth.

"Ask *them* to forgive you – all the people who saw you insult your wife and your sister-in-law. Now leave me. I was almost asleep."

"But since you are awake –"

If she consented, she could be grateful that he usually devoted himself to love-making much as he did to racing horses: the idea was to get to the finish line as fast as possible. A one-mile heat could end before you'd even realized it had begun. Unfortunately, you occasionally sensed something of the cricketer as well, the champion showing off for an imaginary audience which expected to witness a superior talent in action. And the cricketer, unlike the horseman, so long as things were going well, was not necessarily in a hurry to get to the end.

Tom Jordan had been clever enough to know she could never be courted too much – with gifts of flattery and kisses and slow caresses – that she would be content to have them become an end in themselves, as they were in books. Of course, the *pursuit* could occasionally inflame her, eventually, though she had tried not to let him suspect lest he take advantage of a weakness. With James, however, the brief original courtship was meant to do for a lifetime. He had no time for trying to win again what he considered he'd already won. Perhaps he had never heard that a woman could sometimes be made to desire what he desired. Perhaps he had heard but did not approve.

"You may do what you wish," she said, sitting up, "since you have made certain that we are both awake."

He sighed – or laughed, she could not tell which – and pushed his face into her throat. "Ah, Kate –"

"But at the same time, we will discuss the future of the hotel."

"We will *not* discuss the hotel." He yelled this at her. Then lowered his voice, presumably so that the building's guests would not hear. A sharp bark from Vicky let it be known that she was available if she were needed. "We will not talk about anything. Lie down!"

"You will gamble it away, or find you have too little money left for the taxes, or wake up some morning to discover you've given it to some reprobate friend you started feeling sentimental about."

"Dammit woman, you have gone and ruined it again!" He sat up and swung his legs out to put his feet on the floor. "Might as well have stayed in my own bed." In the open doorway, he turned back to face her. "Good night, madam."

The light from his own lamp made a shadow play of his naked body inside the nightshirt. Behind him, in a heap of covers at the foot of his bed, the terrier raised her head to see what she had missed.

"It would make no difference for you to own the hotel," he said, still standing there. "You are my wife. This is the same as owning it myself. Do you know nothing of law? Or do you think, perhaps, that you are a *man*?"

"You are in danger of losing everything you've worked for. If we were divorced, and no longer married, the hotel would be safe in my name. And everything else could go on as it has."

"My God, woman, you are a strange one. Divorce, and everything could go on as it has? Do I understand you correctly? Having raised cries of immorality to oust one mistress from the hotel, you are now prepared to live in sin in order to keep it yourself?"

"I would still consider us married, as I would consider the business to be yours. The important thing is, it would be safe from your creditors, your enemies, and your own weaknesses."

"Shall pretend I've heard nothing. Good night."

"You are a beast!" she shouted. And threw her pillow after him.

Grunting, he caught it as it thumped against his chest. "It will be in my bed," he said, "if you should decide you want it back."

"It will stay there then, for the next century."

He laughed, but was drowned out by the terrier, who tumbled down off the bed and stood beside her master, yapping tentatively towards the enemy in Kate's room.

James lifted the dog in his arms and placed her again on his bed and came back to the doorway. "Will leave the door open in case you change your mind."

"I would not risk Samuel Hatch's fate by going so near your dog."

"Have given her an old waistcoat to eat – she's not likely to notice."

"Do you have any idea how ridiculous you look, standing there in your shirt?" Despite everything, she allowed herself to laugh.

"Of course I do. Just as I know you'd have it off me in a minute if you thought I would consider your demand. And have more pleasure out of it, too, than you'd ever admit." He turned, and then retreated. She could hear him climb into bed but saw nothing of him now except the peaks created by his feet beneath the bedclothes. "We've only ourselves now, Kate, and must begin to discover how much we can hope to get from one another."

She sat fully upright, and pulled her bedjacket around her shoulders. "There's little I can hope to get from you, except the drudgery and failure I have already got!" There was some pleasure to be got out of hurling answers back with gusto in an empty room. "I should have accepted the doctor and gone off to the Cariboo with him."

"Yes, or the man with the whip," boomed his voice from the other room. "Or Captain Trumble. Or the young prig upstairs, from Customs." To give him credit, he could give as well as he got. "Except that you would have found them as unsatisfactory as you find me, being only men."

"And not –?"

"You prefer to be admired and flirted with and pursued. You *invite* pursuit in all directions even while you are yourself pursuing. But you do not wish to live the life beyond it."

"The life beyond it is this." A parody of her own usual robust laughter pronounced her opinion of *this*. "A selfish husband and the tyranny of work."

"I mean the life beyond it in bed! Madam, you will not be loved."

This was an unfamiliar track he had started down, on the far side of a wall. Her roaring parody of a laugh was less convincing this time, even to her. "I have *been* loved! Men have loved me." Her voice, she could hear, had become fierce enough to pronounce this a battle to the death. "One man has even, one man has *died* for me. And a husband, do not forget, gave me children. A brother-in-law –"

"You have been *admired*, Kate, and you have been coveted, and undoubtedly you have even been lusted after, but –"

"A brother-in-law, I say, confessed that he had fallen in love with me, to the point that he was prepared to give up everything – his wife, his children, his fortune – if I would only love him too."

"Aha! And you? Of course you fled."

"Naturally I could not stay in his house."

"You would not want a man who could give up his fortune so easily."

"I would not betray my sister."

"Madam, you are talking to someone who has seen you betray your sisters without batting so much as an eyelash. You would rather have the memory of a man who wanted you than have to discover whether you could love him as well. My point is made. You will not be loved."

"Neither will I be talked to like a schoolgirl! Close the door and stay with your filthy dog."

"Door remains open, unless you close it yourself. As for Vicky, she has never even bared her teeth at me. Cannot say the same of you."

"Close it close it close it!" She got out of bed and crossed the room even as she shouted this. When she reached the door, she saw he had propped himself up in bed, and was grinning at her. One of his hands stroked the head of the dog, who looked up from tearing a shirt into shreds only long enough to bark one bark at Kate.

She stood in the doorway to say this. "Do you think, then, that when I ran off to Liverpool, when I *raced* off to Liverpool after you, I was not hoping to let myself be loved?"

"Assumed, at the time, that you did."

"And what do you suppose has happened since?"

"That is something only you could know."

"*You* have happened. Time has happened. Life has happened."

"And has not finished happening yet. To either of us." He slid down under his bedclothes. "Will blow out the lamp now, Kate. You'll be halfway between. Can find your way in the dark in either direction."

She did not close the door, and even once the light had gone remained where she was, fiercely thinking. How had she manipulated herself into a position like this, where everything in her strained to go in both directions at once?

"The dog," his voice said, "will not mind if I tell her to sleep on the floor. But she will be instructed to bite the first person who mentions ownership of the hotel."

"I shall be in my own bed," she said, "where I can be found by anyone who wants to find me. I will not be instructed what I may or may not mention." Yet she stood where she was for a few moments longer, frightened, suddenly, by the enormity of the silence in this house, the astonishing size of this building that contained her. It had not occurred to her before how terrifyingly silent this hotel could be in those rare times that his voice could not be heard talking, talking, keeping the whole thing up, preventing it from collapsing about their ears.

Throughout the morning he remained in his office with the door closed, having given instructions that he was not to be disturbed for any reason. Kate went about her usual morning duties of supervising the help in the dining-room and checking on the work of the chambermaids and dealing with the complaints of "not enough bedclothes" from an elderly woman more accustomed to the climate of India, but she also had to take the time to give Annie instructions on how to prepare The Heron's Nest for the monthly luncheon of the Yankee Club. She hoped that behind that closed door he was taking a good look at the hotel accounts, horrified at his own profligate handling of their money, and feeling guilty about his wife's anxieties. But of course she could not be certain he was not merely pouting, writing letters and planning wagers, even laughing at her for thinking he was taking her fears seriously.

When he finally emerged late in the morning for a cup of coffee in the family kitchen, he said nothing to indicate what he had accomplished that morning, nor would he be drawn into conversation about anything at all. Instead, he opened up the newspaper and made noises that indicated he would ignore her.

But he did not ignore her for long. Though reading the four pages of advertisements, obituaries, news from the world, and market prices usually upset him, today he almost immediately found something amusing he insisted on sharing with her. "By God, Kate! Have you read this?" Something had been reprinted from the London *World*, under the title "Princess in Brobdingnag." "Located us in *Gulliver's Travels* because they know their readers are more capable of finding us in a story book than on a map."

At first she only half listened to the long account of how Princess Louise was to have found her way to this remote part of the world. Chuckling beneath the words, he read that the "'linen drapers and apothecaries, who, owing to the uncommon fertility of the soil, blossom with such rankness into premiers, senators, and leaders of the opposition, have begun to quarrel over who is to play the big man on the occasion, blah, blah, blah, which in those innocent parts, constitute the acme of all mundane bliss.' By God, this fellow must have met our Noah Shakespeare!"

Despite herself, she found herself listening, perhaps because he seemed to be getting some strange sort of pleasure from it. "'The citizen who swindled his creditors in an effete European monarchy is loudest, now that he is rehabilitated in a new land and a fresh name, in declaring only high-toned personages of spotless reputation shall figure on the reception committee.'"

Before he could go on, however – as he clearly intended to do – Annie came in, flushed with obvious pleasure, bringing with her the long-jawed newspaperwoman from San Francisco. "We have just introduced ourselves to one another in The Heron's Nest. Mrs. Stark is to be their luncheon speaker."

"I'm a little early," the cousin explained, to Kate. Her leathery face was as creased as an old glove – exposed, perhaps, to even more abuse than her jacket.

"So I insisted," Annie said, "that she say hello to her relatives."

Her closest relative in the room was uninterested in saying anything, though he did offer a perfunctory greeting. The expression

on his face became a deep frown, and he shook out the pages of
his newspaper to concentrate fiercely upon the interrupted story.

Kate poured the intruder a cup of coffee and invited her to join
them at the table. Though she had succeeded in avoiding this
woman until now, she did not want to imitate James's rudeness, or
make an enemy of someone who spoke to absolutely everyone,
and wrote down her opinions for thousands to read.

Naturally Annie was fascinated by a woman who not only wore
a fringed buckskin jacket and spoke with a loud California accent
but also lit up a cigarette right before their eyes, striking her
match on a rung of the chair she sat on. "What is the subject of
your address to be?" she said. "I spoke to audiences myself while I
was in your city."

Narrowing her eyes, the cousin regarded Annie through her
smoke, perhaps to imagine what sort of audience she might
attract. "I don't take you for a temperance shrieker."

"The tyranny of women's dress. Though I did not think of
recommending anything so courageous as leather."

"They don't care what I talk about," the long-jawed Californian
said, putting the cigarette between her lips, "so long as it makes
them think of home."

"There is an Australian club that meets here as well," Kate
said. "It is much the same – mainly an excuse to use words which
have gone rusty from lack of use."

Annie said, "You soon discover, on a Canadian street, how a
Yankee's glare or an Englishman's snort will make an old familiar
word taste like something foul in your mouth."

"No 'larrikins' allowed? No 'tucker' served?"

"Only with the sort of sneer you have just now used yourself,"
Kate said, "without intending to, of course. There is a kind of
joyful treason committed in The Heron's Nest, I have decided."

"Treason?" The newspaperwoman removed the cigarette from
her mouth to say the word.

"They can speak of 'jackeroos' and 'swags' and know they will not be hanged for it here, or even frowned at. Germans close the door and shout *Guten Abend* at one another, and sing their songs with enough force to blast every other language off the continent."

James had made a great point of not listening to their conversation. "This is written by an idiot!" he suddenly shouted, his face quite red. His eyes blazed. If there were someone in the room he might justifiably punch in the nose, he would do so. Evidently the writer who was astute enough to mock the Noah Shakespeares of this town had overstepped. "Sitting in their damn London offices – what do they know about us? Listen to this! They think the reason we are so pleased to meet their damn royalty is that we have none of our own! 'The Aboriginal chiefs have princes and princesses addicted to scant clothing, loose morals, and the rum bottle. But they do not count for anything.' Damn their hides! According to them, our towns have long ago fallen to the Indians, 'who hold high carnival in the church and burn a house when they are too lazy to cut firewood.' They think we are out on the edges of the world with the savages. Will not read another word."

"I bet he'll force himself," said his cousin from San Francisco, raising an eyebrow for Annie.

And, indeed, though his face had become a dangerous colour, he did read on. "'The Princess will also meet some queer people.' That's us, I suppose. That's you and me, Kate. That's what they think of us back there. 'The half-civilized trapper is not yet extinct, while Britons afflicted with a taste for forest maidens – a malady for which there is no cure – are sufficiently numerous, though they are not likely to pay their respects to the daughter of their sovereign.'"

Now he pushed the paper down between his knees. "Does not deserve to be read. Will go down and punch the man who decided to reprint this, Kate. Will write to England and tell them what is thought of such bilgewater here."

The cousin's laugh was a coarse braying. "I'll call you on that. You'll scare 'em for sure. They're all just holding their breaths over there, waitin' to hear what you've got to say so they'll know if it's all right to go on running the world the way they want."

- Annie turned her smile away, perhaps already aware that James would not find anything to laugh at in his cousin's taunt.

"No worse than what you have written yourself, madam! Did you think your paper would not reach so far north, or that we were incapable of reading?"

"You are shouting at a guest," Kate said.

Too late. The newspaper in his hand was forgotten. "A guest of the country who should not be allowed across the line. Does not even blush to sit there at my table when she knows what she has published at home. Damn Yankees are as patronizing as the bloody English, and a damn sight nastier in the end."

Perhaps the newspaperwoman was accustomed to attacks of this sort. She drew long on her cigarette and leaned back in her chair to release the smoke slowly down her nostrils while she studied her attacker through narrowed eyes.

Though no one asked, he recalled the entire catalogue of insults his cousin had set down in black and white in her reports on the royal visit, each one making him angrier than the one before it. "Charming in our simplicity! Touchingly innocent in our faithfulness to a foreign monarchy! Almost to be envied for our childlike belief in promises from distant politicians and an invisible Queen! Sneering at us as if we were a race of poor relatives, a nation of village idiots – slow, dull, easily excited by trinkets! Thrilled by the symbols of our own bondage!"

"I think we have heard enough," Kate cautioned.

"Swore you would never set foot in my home again."

The cousin seemed pleased to hear this. "And here I am, drinking your coffee. And filling your air with my smoke." She removed the cigarette from between her lips and flicked the ash off into her saucer. "You remind me of a fellow I knew once, who got so hot under the collar about a woman beating him at poker he just dropped dead on the spot."

"Bah!" James leapt up, kicking his chair back, and made for the door. "Excuse me, ladies. Business to attend to! Tell the Yankee Club I send my sympathy." While his cousin brayed out gusts of booming laughter, he turned in the doorway. "Shall be gone for the day, Kate. Must see how much more of our money I can throw away."

He closed the door abruptly, perhaps aware that his wife would be trembling with an impulse to throw all the china off the table after him. The table too, if she could move it.

"Oh, I have forgotten to tell you, Kate," Annie suddenly blurted out. "We have been invited by Mr. Sumner's friend to be there when they fly their latest invention. Tomorrow morning, at dawn."

"An invention that flies?" the cousin said, in the too-innocent manner of one who wrote for a newspaper.

Kate hoped her look told Annie that she had already said too much – though of course it was James's own parting remark that was to blame. "This is only another of your cousin's foolish investments," she explained. "More money thrown away that could be used in the hotel." Here was an opportunity, since he had left her in this turmoil, to air just a little of her dissatisfaction before someone who might be sympathetic. "For all my pleading, he refuses to withdraw from the scheme – a ridiculous invention, a ridiculous *adventure* by a couple of impractical dreamers."

She added for Annie's sake: "Two people one might better avoid."

"If someone's invented something that flies, you better not expect me to pretend I didn't hear."

"It is all quite secret," Kate said. "You will hear nothing more from us. Annie should not have said anything at all. And here – we mustn't keep you. Your Clyde Munros and your Mr. Drysdales will be gathering soon, expecting their monthly dose of nostalgia."

Annie went ahead, at Kate's request, to make certain that preparations had been satisfactorily completed in The Heron's Nest.

"James has gone and invested dough in something that's supposed to fly?" the cousin said, as soon as Annie had left. She
seemed to find this amusing.

Kate moved the cream jug from one position on the table to
another. "Naturally it would be foolish to resent an investment of
a few dollars," she eventually said, "especially in such a romantic
venture, which *could* prove to be more interesting than we
imagine." She gathered up the cups and saucers and took them to
the sink. "But since this is only a silly scheme to help the Chinese
transport their produce across the line –"

The newspaperwoman found a match which she struck against
a rung of her chair and squinted her eyes while she lit another cigarette. She shook out the match and slipped it into a pocket of her
jacket and regarded Kate for a moment before saying: "The
Chinese? What sort of deal's he made?"

"When you see him again, you might tell him what a fool he
has been. But now, let me to take you to your audience. I wonder
if Mr. Holmstrom will be joining you today?"

"You mean Holmstrom the lawyer?"

"He comes here to shout *Jag ar torstig* with the Swedes as well.
A truly international man. He makes such a point of pressing my
hand and flattering me in the most outrageous manner that I
wonder if he hopes I will bring him some business. Is this how
lawyers acquire their clients in the United States?"

"Honey, where've you bin all your life?" said the newspaperwoman through the blue cloud of her own exhaled smoke. "That's
how those *hombres* lasso and hog-tie their victims everywhere."

26

ONCE Kate had arrived at the "Drawing-Room," she was no longer certain why she had ever wanted to attend, when it was so obvious now that this great social breakthrough would do her no good. Yet everyone agreed that her salmon-coloured satin with the dark cherry-red trim was a success – and of course she carried her ivory fan of black cockatoo feathers. Everyone agreed that James should wear his top hat more often, and admired the dash of rebellion in his blue embroidered waistcoat. They stood with Annie and Lady Riven-Blythe in the crush of people who'd crowded into the legislature anteroom, until bugles announced the arrival of the royal couple and the doors were thrown open so that the population could begin to move.

"By Jove, I'll not stand in a crowd like this again to peer at anyone! Next time His Excellency wants to see me he can damn well come to the Blue Heron like anyone else. Will tell him so myself."

"Yes, and I suppose he'll come!" Kate said.

"Sit in the foyer and cool your heels, I'll say. Wait your bloody turn."

"They'll throw you out on your ear! Now hush."

"Who will?" He was ready to fight them now, his fists were up. "Who do you suppose will try? They'll change their minds quick enough when they feel this fist in their jaw."

All this, of course, was for the sake of scandalized Lady Riven-Blythe, and for the tittering ladies behind them in the queue. And of course for anyone who might have read Kate's advertisement in today's paper, in which she begged the public not to indulge her husband's crippling weakness for betting which was turning them into paupers. They might be wondering why he hadn't murdered her yet, since they were not aware, as Kate was, of the advertisement he'd placed in tomorrow's newspaper advising merchants that anyone seen doing business with his wife would lose the good business of James Theodore Horncastle, esq., immediately and forever hereafter. Otherwise they might possibly be able to imagine the vehemence of the dishes-throwing row that had occurred less than an hour before they had begun to dress for tonight's occasion.

Eventually they were permitted inside the Assembly chamber, where James and his friends exchanged loud joking commentaries upon their surroundings. "Plenty of hot air blown about in this room over the years." "Plenty of damned treachery too!" "Listen hard enough and you'll hear de Cosmos thundering out his long, ridiculous speeches."

They worked their way up the line to the front, where they handed over their cards to the aide-de-camp, who announced them to the Governor-General and his Princess wife – standing side by side before the throne, flanked by smirking attendants. How were they chosen? Colonel DeWinton? Mrs. Bagot? Not for youth or beauty. They might be saying: What a world of difference there is between your side of this reception line and ours, but you'll not be told what it is. Kate Horncastle curtseyed to His handsome Excellency, who bowed; she curtseyed to the Queen's daughter – prettier even than they'd reported, and dainty, with shining eyes and a most gracious smile. Then Kate moved on past Lieutenant-Governor Cornwall and his smiling wife. (I have been smiling without pause since they arrived, Mrs. Cornwall might have been saying, you've no idea what it means to have those two underfoot night and day, when you would like to put up your feet and loosen your stays and doze for a minute like a normal person.) You are looking at the wrong woman if you wish sympathy, Kate thought, and moved on to join the others in the galleries.

Annie was displeased to see so much attention paid to dress but delighted with everything else – His Excellency's manners, the Princess's splendidly gracious carriage. "Freed from all this protocol, I'm certain she would be a considerable force for the advancement of women. But of course she is padlocked." She exclaimed over faces she recognized in the crowd – particularly Lady Douglas in her black moiré with a lace fichu. The fact that this old woman was a half-breed increased her worth immeasurably in Annie's opinion, who still hoped to discover the town had many others like her. But she could not hope to get any such confession out of others she admired: Mrs. Gospel wearing diamonds and a grey silk trimmed with black velvet, Mrs. Rithet in an ivory satin trimmed with lace, with feathers and diamonds in her elaborate hair, "and Miss Crease – in such a simple dress, that pale-yellow silk, with lace." It did not seem to matter that not one of them, as Kate reminded her, had attended her performance at the theatre.

Less than an hour after they'd arrived, the royal couple had already retired, having performed their duties, and the rest of them were left to look at one another, to admire gowns made by local dressmakers or (even better) by dressmakers in San Francisco or (best of all) brought around the Horn from Home, and to wonder why on earth Kate Horncastle would imagine herself comfortable at such an affair.

So it would make no difference, her attending. She knew that already, though she was no longer certain what it was she had hoped for. It changed nothing at all. That she was there with Lady Riven-Blythe meant nothing – Lady Riven-Blythe was an eccentric. Lady Riven-Blythe pushed her at people, initiated small talk, tried to make her seem interesting to these women – all for Annie's sake, of course – but they looked at Kate Horncastle as they would look at a travelling salesman who had shown up: My dear, why does that woman insist on pushing herself upon us, why does she try so hard?

"She has been given a night off from handing out room keys, I see," she overheard.

"Do Australians care very much about the Queen, do you suppose?"

They cared less about the Queen themselves now that the daughter had arrived in their midst. They had fallen in love with the girl, who had done nothing to distinguish herself except visit their shops, smile into their faces, and make public pronouncements about the beauty of the scenery. It didn't matter, she could be a simpleton, she could have done nothing in her life, she could even be keeping unacceptable opinions to herself – there were those who intended to find a way of inviting her to stay on, whose husbands were even whispering vague plots to throw off the old woman and ask the daughter to become their Queen in her stead.

Lady Riven-Blythe was dumbfounded. "Of the Empire, do you mean?"

"Perhaps of Canada only."

"Or British Columbia."

"Do your husbands realize they are talking treason?"

"Of Vancouver Island at least! She has made no secret how she loves it here. She will be a solution to everything – independence under her monarchy would mean tossing off the British, the Yanks, and the Canadians all in one throw."

What some husbands were willing to risk – so that their wives might trade in their silent, disapproving photographs of a fat, ageing chicken-hawk for a breathing young beauty they had seen with their own eyes, spoken with, passed on the street, been presented to on occasions like this and at banquets and various other affairs where Kate Horncastle could never have gained entry! They wanted a Queen they did not have to share with the rest of the Empire, or with anyone else at all who was not one of them. They would all, then, overnight, go from being the wives of solicitors and brewers and cigar manufacturers to members of the royal court.

"Damn waste of time, this whole affair," said James, though she had already heard him putting it about that the Governor-General had all but winked at him. "Knew who I was, I'm sure of it. He's planning to show up at the Blue Heron one night after hours, for a drink. But I've got a surprise for him – he won't get out of there until he's promised to bring that railway right to my door."

Out on the steps, the women turned to one another for their good-evenings while they waited for James to detach himself from friends at the door. Lady Riven-Blythe's face would not reveal whether she regretted giving in to Annie's request. Evidently her mind and heart were busy deciding which belongings were to be sold and which to be packed in her steamer trunks for removal to England. "They have brought a little magic with them," she pronounced with a melancholy sigh, looking off in the general direction of Cary Castle, "but it will not be here any longer once they have gone."

"I have no idea why we went to the trouble," Kate said, when James had assisted her up onto the seat. "I can't remember why it seemed so important."

Neither did she fully understand why it was so important that she rise before dawn the next morning to accompany James and Annie out to the cliffs for the trial flight of Zachary Jack's latest invention. Although she despised this ridiculous determination to invent the impossible, and resented James's investment of their money in the venture, she was not to be left out. She had developed an absolute horror of being alone, of being *left*, which not even the noise and bustle of the hotel could prevent. Panic would fly up in her all at once like a frightened galah out of grass, leaving her cold and gasping for a short while, knotting her own trembling hands into one another until she had got hold of herself once again.

No, she would not be left behind. And, anyway, perhaps there would be some satisfaction in seeing the experiment fail, as earlier attempts had done. What sort of men thought it reasonable to be making arrangements to fly?

On the far side of the park, Logan Sumner met them in front of the little shack that the Indian used for a home – a building

constructed entirely, it might appear to someone who had not
seen it before, out of words. *Bazaar. English Linen Billhead Paper.
Zonder. Keatings Bon Bons or Worm Tablets. Fancy Goods.* A scaly
coat had grown over the walls, of stamped and stencilled combi-
nations of letters on scraps of broken lumber.

The door was opened by a broad, dark-skinned woman, who
looked from one to the other of them in silence for a moment,
without expression, before turning away. When Zak came to the
door in his long woollen underwear, he acted as though he had
not expected company – raised his arms in a mock-surrender
manner. "H *wah!* King-George-men got-em Indian surrounded!"

Having got up so early in the morning, must she listen to this
sort of nonsense as well? "Why do you talk this silly talk?" Kate
said. "You can speak English as well as – as Mr. Sumner."

A little surprised, Zak shrugged, and put a hand flat against his
fat belly and squeezed down his tiny dark eyes to look hard at her,
as though he wished to decide how seriously he was to take her.
"It's all silly talk to me," he said. "English or Californian or Swede,
it all races around trying to do what my mother's language used to
do without any fuss, back when I was small."

Annie, being Annie, could not leave things alone. "You still
speak your mother's language?"

He shrugged. "I don't remember my mother's language any
more. A dozen words maybe. All the rest were slapped out of my
head by that schoolteacher. Now I can't even talk with my old
uncle, except in that Chinook."

They left Zak to get dressed, and walked together out towards
the cliffs. A cold wind blew in off the strait. It was important,
apparently, that there be just enough light for safety, but they
were determined not to wait so long that unwanted witnesses
could be up and about. They stamped their feet and kept their
hands up inside the sleeves of their overcoats and talked in low
whispers as though they were afraid there were people sleeping

beneath the tortured trees who might hear them. Why would there be?

Already she regretted coming. If they didn't run her down with their ridiculous machine, she would catch pneumonia from this wind. Or something worse from this wretched smell of low tide – exposed seaweed and rotting animal life. She had always welcomed the first breaths of warm air in a Ballarat morning – the dry scent of the blue gums, and her roses. Even the squabbling racket of the cockatoos might seem agreeable here, if they brought a sun with them that was capable of taking the chill from your bones.

It was not a spectacular dawn. By the time Chu Lee and his ancient uncle arrived, weak light appeared from behind the eastern mountains, as though embarking only under protest upon another day, refusing to send anything more colourful than a pearl-grey wash ahead of itself up the underside of a clouded sky. Everything beneath the clouds was made grey as well – the immense mountains, the strait, the isolated trees along the cliffs, even the grass beneath their feet.

The latest flying machine had been given the name "Blue Heron" in honour of James's hotel and in gratitude for his investment, but when Zak arrived on horseback from the direction of his barn, the monstrous contrivance that followed at the end of a rope made Kate think of some distorted and freakish moulting crow which had been bloated up to the size of a toppling cow-shed, its beak truncated, its wings sagging, its bulging eyes pushed back to sit by its tail, its entire body gleaming with the slime of having fallen into a vat of a thousand broken eggs. Some kind of joke? This was a far cry from the slender heron! The smell that arrived with it might have been from a boatload of long-dead rotting fish.

Was this what James had thrown their money at? She wondered if she were the only one here who was sane.

Zak saluted. "*Kla-how-ya!*" You would think, from his grin, that this ugly contraption had been delivered directly to him by his heathen gods, with their blessings. This time, he said, he had ignored all the impossibly intricate plans drawn up by his *tyee-boss*, who had studied too many European failures in the books and magazines. Instead, to build the "Blue Heron," he'd gone to his own people, who had never invented a flying machine because they had always been able to fly without the aid of machinery but who nevertheless had had centuries of experience inventing devices to make the impossible easy.

Taking his lead from his own people, Zak said, he'd constructed the frame for his great raven out of strips of dry, light, aromatic cedar, *canim stick*, the same wood used by his people for their canoes and whaling-boats and shelters. No more scraps from Sumner Construction – he'd gone out and found a tree, split it himself. Then, to ensure that the machine would glide through the air with the speed and ease of a salmon slipping up a river, he had stretched the hides of a dozen elk over the frame, and then given it all a coating of oil from fermenting oolichans. "If you were wondering about the smell, well there it is." Finally, though he had put the propeller blades on the nose, just as he'd done before, and had erected the great long sagging wings precisely as he had done in previous attempts, he had decided that the reason all the earlier inventions had lost their way and ended up in the sea was that he had not thought to give them eyes. This time he had mounted two large eyeballs, painted white with black irises staring ahead, one on either side and just in front of the tail. "Barrels, if you want to take a look – each with a little steam engine inside. I decided we needed more weight at the rear."

No one wanted to step into the stench of rotting fish for a closer look. Kate held a gloved hand over her nose, as Annie was doing. Even James, who would have probably liked to climb inside to play with the controls, stood pinching his nose between his fingers, scowling.

"You let me invest my money in this, Sumner. Where did it go?"

Logan Sumner looked embarrassed. "The engines, I suppose. Somebody had to build them."

Zak added: "And my greedy cousin didn't want to part with them hides."

Horncastle did not take his stern gaze from Sumner. "Your Indian thinks this is some kind of joke."

Apparently Chu Lee was not at all certain he was willing to trust his life to this savage-inspired beast with the gigantic eye-balls mounted on either side of its tail. He and his uncle walked all the way around it, exchanging words in their own language, both looking worried. The uncle placed a hand against the gleaming flank and smelled his fingers, then shook his head and pulled his face into an expression of disgust. Again the two men talked. Together they bowed their heads and studied the ground at their feet.

"We didn't come out here to watch your family prayers, Chu Lee," said Zak. "We came to fly! Now, climb in. *Kawak!*"

"Not so," said Chu Lee. "Uncle say this machine have bad spirit. There need to be ceremony first."

"No ceremony! Tell your uncle you were already inside this thing yesterday, learning what to do, and nothing bad happened. We don't have the time for a ceremony. You tell your uncle all the evil spirits have already been driven from this machine – chased up into the top of that biggest tree over there."

But Chu Lee and his uncle seemed to feel that still more muttering was necessary.

"The sooner we find out this bird can fly," said Zak, "the sooner we can start moving your opium over the border and bringing back all that nice Yankee money on the return flight."

Chu Lee and his uncle decided to put expedience ahead of ritual. "My uncle say he will take the chance. He has plenty more nephew." He climbed the ladder that Zak had laid against the side of the malodorous slimy crow and lowered himself into the cavity behind the controls. Zak climbed up behind him and for a few minutes seemed to be issuing instructions, giving orders, demonstrating how things were to be done. He pushed whatever was necessary to start both engines sputtering and trembling inside their barrel-eyeballs, boiling up clouds of smoke and escaped steam, then came back to the ground and leaned the ladder against the branches of an oak.

"Remember what I told you, Chu Lee. When you want to come back to earth you use this stick. And once the wheels have touched the ground you aim it away from the trees. Just head out across that grass. Turn off the engines. Get onto the race-track and follow that until it comes to a stop."

On horseback, Zak led the great throbbing steam-belching machine across the race-track and well up the slope, then turned it around so that it was facing the edge of the cliffs, the sea, the mountains across the strait. Then he galloped back down to join the others, and to watch from the back of his horse while his invention came sputtering down the grass and sped right past them, to lift off the end of earth and take its chances with air.

Kate gasped. For a moment Chu Lee dropped below the level of the grass he had left behind. With the others, she rushed forward to see what was happening. It had not crashed, however. It was flying just above the water's surface. It was rising a little, just a little. It lifted, its wings tilting this way, then that, it rose back up to a position higher than the cliffs, and then went on rising even after that.

She might have gone with it – something in her did. She felt, all at once, as detached from the world. As alone and vulnerable and without visible support. She held her breath, but could not close her eyes against this amazing thing.

Amongst those who watched from land there was only silence until Zak, perhaps deciding that it was not a dream he was observing, released a great joyful cry which was then echoed by them all. Chu Lee and the huge slimy bird continued their journey towards the towering mountains on the other side.

You might not have expected Logan Sumner to demonstrate such enthusiasm. He yelped and whooped like a child. He threw his arms around Annie for a moment, then detached himself to do the same to his friend and partner, who leapt down from his horse to meet the embrace, and together they danced in great leaping circles around the grass, slapping one another on the back. Their dream had come true. The impossible had happened. The preposterous hope that had kept them poring over books, experimenting with designs, arguing through entire weekends – not to mention dealing with the humiliation and frustration of several failures smashed to pieces in the waves – had finally borne fruit. Whatever happened now, they had become the first people in history to make a flying machine that had stayed up in the air for more than just a few seconds.

Of course, Chu Lee would have the honour of being the first human in history to fly, but he was still driving the grotesque "Blue Heron" through the air that separated two countries, getting smaller every minute, and no one could see how pleased he might be with his success.

"Now anything is possible," a smiling Logan Sumner said as he returned to the others. "There isn't anything we can dream that we cannot hope to achieve."

Annie caught hold of Sumner's arm and held it close against her. "That is the most beautiful thing I have ever seen – at a distance. The next time that foul-smelling bird leaves the earth I intend to be inside it."

Kate did not participate in this celebration. Breathless with the sensation of flying alone, with nothing visible or tangible beneath her, she stood where she might hold onto a rail of the buggy and keep her eye on the receding machine. But James's face was as flushed with excitement as anyone's. "Do you know what this means, Kate?" He stood before her and grasped both her arms, as though he might break into a dance.

"He hasn't returned yet," Kate said. "He could kill himself trying to come back down to earth. He could kill us all."

"But do you know what it means for us? When they start to carry their cargo? We'll get a small piece of the profits. Sooner or later we'll be rich."

"I will be happy just to see us get back some of the money you've thrown away," Kate said.

Coming over to join Sumner and Annie, Zak was all teeth. "I didn't do too bad, did I, *tyee*-boss? Maybe now those damn Indians will stop calling me a white man, when they see how I did something only an Indian is smart enough to do."

"Did you tell him how to turn around?" Sumner eventually said. "Does he know how to come back?"

Zak nodded. He looked a little more sober now. They all did – except for the uncle, whose grin had been growing broader ever since the grotesque titanic crow had begun to ascend.

"Did you tell him how long he should wait before turning around? He doesn't intend to cross the entire strait on this first flight!"

"I told him five minutes. No longer. He should have turned by now."

"Maybe he's forgotten what to do," Annie suggested.

"Maybe he's fainted," Kate said. "From the smell if not from fear."

James said, "He's going the whole distance."

"Chu Lee doesn't like to take orders," Sumner said. "Nobody knows that better than I do."

"He wouldn't," Zak said. "He knows I would kill him."

Even while they spoke, all eyes were glued to the rapidly diminishing machine. By now, the absurd inflated crow had become little more than a simple bird of some undistinguishable species.

"That bloody Celestial is going the whole distance," Horncastle said. "We'll never see our machine again. He's been plotting how to smuggle himself across the border for years, and you bloody fools gave him a way to do it. With my money. He'll join all those other Chinamen they smuggled across in boats. Ask the uncle."

Zak's excited shouting elicited no response from the uncle. Not even several minutes of soft earnest persuasion on Logan Sumner's part interrupted his evident pleasure. Only when James Horncastle pushed in and lifted the old man up by the front of his shirt, yelling threats into his face, did the uncle speak. Even then, he spoke in his own language. He seemed to have forgotten whatever English he knew – or thought he was already speaking it. Again Zak went in, asked Horncastle to stand aside, and explained patiently that it was important he be told anything the uncle knew about Chu Lee's intentions.

Kate was standing too far away to hear the uncle's answer, but she had no trouble hearing Zak's cry of outrage and dismay. He flung out both hands, whirled around, and drove a fist into the trunk of a tree. This caused him to cry out even louder, of course, and to drop to the ground.

Logan Sumner got the message from him and told the others. "Chu Lee's clothing is stuffed with packages of opium. He intends to deliver it. His uncle says they didn't see why they should wait for a second flight before taking advantage of their investment."

Perhaps the eye of every person on that headland was on the machine (no larger than a housefly) at the moment it exploded, spraying outward from itself like a small black fountain, a temporary flower in the sky. The sight was so sudden, so extraordinary, so *unreal*, that no one made a sound. The barely perceptible pieces had already begun to fall, bits of pepper sprinkled from a shaker, when the sound reached their ears: one, two, three – a rapid

sequence of *cracks*, like lightning striking far-off trees. The sky –
they all checked – was entirely innocent of cloud.

The explosion might have occurred inside her. All at once she was
without support, or any sense of being held together. All at once,
though she had thought she'd got hold of something in life she
could cling to, she knew she had really got hold of nothing at all.
There was nothing to do but fall, or fall apart.

While Logan Sumner and Zak rushed off towards the harbour
to see which ships might be talked into taking them out to where
Chu Lee had gone down, James Horncastle helped her into
the carriage. He could not see any point in chasing after them.
"Nothing I can do. Only be in the way. Let them think of how
they'll pay me back my money."

"And it doesn't matter to you that a life has been lost?" Kate
said.

"What can I do? The damage is done. Plenty have lost their
lives out there before now."

It did not matter any more what she said. "You are a fool if you
think they will pay you back your money. They'll find a way of
getting even more out of you. That is what everyone knows – that
you'll part with money for anything that amuses you, without any
regard to wife or family or the financial state of the hotel."

"I was a fool," he said, as they rode through the park, "to think
that one marriage would be an improvement over another.
Should have put you on the next boat the minute I saw who you
were. Was a fool to be flattered by your determination. Should
have realized that it was a determination to spoil everyone's life."

"And who has spoiled lives, I wonder! Who has thrown away
money? Who wastes his time with scoundrels? Who makes a farce
of marriage by visiting the adulteress, breaking his vow? You may
let me out here. I have no wish to travel any farther with you.
Indeed, I have no wish to return to your unhappy hotel."

"You thought that lawyer Holmstrom would be as easy for you to charm as that doctor who followed you here, I suppose. Or that little Customs man who slinks about the hotel, or poor ridiculous Captain Trumble."

"So Holmstrom has told you something, then?"

"Did you think he would not?"

"But when?"

"You didn't notice him last evening at the Drawing-Room? He approached me. Wanted to tell me how interested he was in observing you attempt to make one of your devoted admirers out of him. When you visited his office. Even went so far as to pretend he was willing to co-operate, he said, for the pleasure of hearing you out."

"Then the man has betrayed me."

"Who is the betrayer here? Did you think that in this town a woman might speak to a lawyer about transfer-of-ownership papers without the lawyer speaking to the husband? To question his sanity if for no other reason. I suppose you intended to forge my signature."

"I chose badly, that's all. I chose the wrong lawyer. I was certain that Svend Holmstrom would be delighted to see you taken advantage of, for your own good – even by me."

"Never by you, madam. Even my worst enemies would not take your side against me."

"Then it will never happen? I am to understand that you will never protect the hotel from yourself?"

"I should sooner cut my throat."

"Then if you will stop the horses I shall walk. Perhaps I'll not go home."

"You will sit where you are sitting. And you will go back to the hotel. And you will never again take steps that amount, as I'm sure you will admit, to a betrayal of all your vows."

A betrayal of all your vows? She didn't know what he meant. Though her ears had clearly heard the familiar sounds, her head would not receive them. A cushion of fog forbade it. Had hotels and vows been named with her in mind? She heard them now as though they'd been invented for some category of people that excluded her. They were not her words. She was not sure that she *had* any words. Her lips were dry, without sound.

In heart-racing panic, she hurried inside The Great Blue Heron. Her home. (The hotel? Was a hotel not a place for guests?) The building that sheltered her family, her children. But her children were gone – Wang Low announced that he'd sent them off to school. Employees could be heard rushing about, preparing and delivering breakfasts. She went directly through to the living-quarters. She would pack. She would leave, she would leave, she would leave! Passing by the doorway to the dining-room ("Norah's dining-room" – three words had penetrated, real words – she had still not been able to afford to refurnish it as she'd wished) she discovered that she was crying. With one hand against the door frame, she leaned forward into the room; her wet, distorted face cried back at her from the mirror above the buffet. Why? Why was she crying? She ought to be angry – furious! But of course she *was* angry, a terrible fury roared inside her. Had she thought that he was the only one who could feel anger?

The nearest chair had shown signs of weakening anyway, so she was not entirely surprised when it flew apart upon impact with the table-top. One leg flew off. She wrenched off another, and threw the entire heap into a corner. A second chair was sturdier and required two, three, four solid blows before it began to weaken. The sound of wooden pieces clattering onto the corner heap was a satisfying one. She pulled out one buffet drawer, and turned it over: linen napkins and table-cloths fell onto the pieces of chair. A second drawer, turned over, spilled someone's bundled letters, scraps of saved newspaper, a deck of cards, faded photographs. Yesterday's paper, snatched up off James's chair, quickly responded to the wooden match.

But when it just as quickly curled up and became ash, without communicating combustion to the broken chairs, she left the dining-room and followed the hallway to her bedroom, where she opened her wardrobe and brought down a box from the upper shelf. In the dining-room again, she removed the little glass lamp and placed it on the table. Removed her long ivory pipe, and the steel pin. Selected a small dark gummy wad from a tin. Then she lit the lamp and held the needle in the flame. "Thank God for Wang Low, who may be the only person who understands me." When the needle tip changed colour, she speared the gum, and held it over the lamp until it blossomed with blue flame and a bubble formed, then placed the burning pill into the tube at the side of the pipe. Black smoke. She put the pipe to her lips, drew the smoke all at once into her mouth, her lungs, and held it there, before releasing it again through her nose.

There would be a heavy peace soon enough. She would feel it creeping into the lids of her eyes. Poor Kate would soon feel this anger fade, a lovely heaviness descend, the world slide away. James slide away. Hotel slide away. These tight lines of pain in her scalp slide away. Already, already: the beginning of calm. What did anything matter now?

What did anything matter, what did James Horncastle matter? Susannah. Susannah was on the far side of the globe, and harmless. The sharp, pleasant ring of horseshoes on stone came up to her, a passing horse; wagon wheels turning, an axle in need of grease. Whispers which might have been inside the room. And sea, waves of the sea, swelling and breaking waves, breaking against the shore-line, slapping against the steamships in harbour. Somewhere, one of the Indian women was shouting – a basket of fish for sale.

From the wall closet she brought out her *Pao-Tu* carpet-bag and set it upon the table beside the lamp. It was in a time of similar futility that she had fashioned the bag for herself, but the lustrous beauty of the phoenix bird had lost whatever she had chosen to see in it then. An Empress's symbol of joy! She had lost it, for-feited it – exchanged it for the dull and awkward patient heron. Pulling almost violently at the polished brass clasp, she spread open the great jaws so wide that the birds, trees, and flowers on the outside could not be seen.

"And what do we see inside?" Her marriage certificate sat on the top of the heap. There. Come on out, let's set you on the table-top where you may be seen. James Theodore Horncastle – what a scrawl! And Kathleen Abigail McConnell Horncastle. Who was she? What sort of young fool must she have been? And where was she now – what had happened to her since the time of this foolishness? Not quite so many creases in her face yet as in this piece of paper. Yet you could breathe in a smell off the paper that took you back to that evening's walk along the dark Liverpool docks, the visit to that irascible parson, the return to the hotel. (The harbour smelled sweeter on the return journey!) Could you be certain, now, that the joy you felt then was the joy of love and not the joy a sister feels upon cheating sisters?

Never mind. One way or the other it would make as good a flame. Here's the lamp you've been searching for, and there – your corner scorched, your fibres curling. Now come, we'll use you to set this heap of rubble afire – see if you can do a better job than the newspaper did for poor Kate. Yes! A little thread of smoke, a hole bored in linen, a glow – it will spread.

Another long, luxurious inhalation. Feel the dark peace swelling, and moving now back through the chambers above and behind the nose. And what else do we have in the darkened soul of this bag? Ahhhh, Susannah, your emerald brooch! How long it took you to miss it – "Mama's emerald," you called it, but of course Mama never wore it herself, she gave it to you to wear and you chose to keep it hidden where only your eyes could see it. But you must have grown less interested, you must have forgotten, you did not notice for several months that it had gone missing. Now here it is, halfway round the world from your hiding-place, where I am about to throw it into a corner heap of burning rubble. The flames won't harm it much but it will be made ugly, and then buried with everything else beneath mud, scorched walls, fallen lumber. There! On Susannah's bosom you would only have turned cold, become venomous with age. In my bag you have awaited the day of your punishment.

And here. Third grievance. Third outrage in a stack of outrages. (And where is the lawyer who would seek restitution? Who will reduce this ugly pile?) Lilian's box! Dance cards. Hair-ribbon! Pressed flowers. Mementoes of evenings spent in the arms of the handsome young sons of the squatocracy, dancing on the wisteria-bordered verandahs of the country homes, plotting your escape while we who prepared you stayed home and affected satisfaction. Now that you have achieved Brisbane society, do you remember how many sisters it took to send you properly out into that world? Would you care to see this box, and all its contents, sail through the smoky dining-room air to crash against wallpaper and fall, spilling, into flame? And after it – where is it? Here – your husband's handkerchief, left in my bedroom the morning after the storm. How I might have avenged myself with him!

While we dig for more. There is plenty more. Tom Jordan's drapery shop, prosperous for not much more than a day – a swatch of cotton snipped from a bolt when you weren't looking, Tom, that day when I came upon you weeping and you proposed marriage. Promised a lifetime. And here, brother William's photograph – sent in the same letter where he refused to come home to the business. And what else? What else do we have –? Ahhh – first betrayal! A newspaper clipping. MILL OWNER'S BODY FISHED FROM THE IRK. From water now into flames – join the conflagration, Father. Up in smoke with the rest!

But how had this happened? Annie was in the room. "Kate? Good heavens, what have you done? What are you doing?" Annie was gone again. But came back almost immediately with blankets – one of which she tossed at Kate while she began to beat at the fire. "I had this feeling – that's why I followed. Help me with this!"

As though it were someone else and not herself who had started this fire – one of the children perhaps – she shook out the blanket and began to beat at the flames. Both of them coughed, choked on the smoke, which had filled up the room and by now must have drifted through much of the rest of this floor of the building. Not enough time had gone by for the pieces of chair to have been any more than singed.

They were singed themselves by the time they had beaten out the flames. Annie poured a milk jug of water over the remains – darker smoke poured up, to blacken wallpaper, and to leave smudges on their hands, on their faces. Kate opened a window while Annie went back for more water.

They sat, exhausted, coughing, on two of Norah Horncastle's remaining chairs, and looked at one another. Neither spoke. The flame in the little lamp had gone out. *Of course you have chosen not to leave him.* But why? Why? Had she really made it impossible? If she did not leave, all she had accomplished today was the added burden of one more expense. The dining-room would have to be repaired. The furniture would have to be replaced – more expenses they could not afford, more reason for the continuation of her enforced slavery to this business. James would have to be placated when he saw what had happened.

"Well of course I must love him, mustn't I?" she eventually said. There was no difficulty in giving her voice a flat edge of sarcasm. "Otherwise, I would not still be here, surely. Do you think I must try even harder?" She stood up and gathered the lamp, the pipe, and put everything into the box, which she carried back to her bedroom and replaced on the upper shelf of her wardrobe. "Oh, Annie, look what I have done!" she said, when she'd returned. "He will be furious. I have made things even worse."

"You have a habit of pushing too far," Annie said. "Did you learn nothing from poor Tom's unhappy end?"

"Tom? Tom?"

"You were never satisfied. Tom suffered from it."

"The laziest man on earth without someone to drive him."

"Yes, but might have lived on in better health."

"And where would *I* be then? And the children? If he had been allowed to creep at his snail's pace through life!"

"Still his wife, perhaps? Rather than his widow. Who am I to know?" Annie looked down into the smoking mess in the corner, as though thinking of starting to clean it up. "I am only saying this: I have seen you like this before, and have seen how everyone around you eventually suffers from it."

"They will laugh at me," Kate said. "When they hear of this. I shall hear them laughing at me every day of my life."

27

HARNESS leather. Sole leather. Strap leather. Unless you came to the Agricultural Fair you didn't realize that leather was not just leather. Bag leather. Calf leather. Pigskin. Here every sort of leather declared its name, beside the fourteen different types of boots and shoes from the establishment of G. H. Maynard and H. Mansell. The smell did nothing to improve the mood of anxiety that had intensified within her as the day progressed. That she was acting again at least with definite purpose did not necessarily make any of this more pleasant.

She hated being forced into this uncomfortable proximity to so many people. Had the town been emptied by an expectation of

nothing more rewarding than this suffocating closeness to one
another? Hardly a soul had remained behind to avoid being
crushed, elbowed, stepped on, breathed on, and pushed about in
this pavilion which had not been built for such crowds, the
designers never having anticipated the magnetic effect of royalty
upon the populace.

Nor had she anticipated Annie's almost immediate desertion.
But friends had been spotted – young women of the town, inti-
mates of Lady Riven-Blythe, ladies who had attended Annie's
lecture and wished to be seen with such a talented and brave
reformer.

Baldwin apples, Duchess apples, Golden apples, Russet apples,
Kings, Alexanders, Northern Spy, Winter banana, Yellow transparent, Yellow Newton Pippins. If apples could speak, the exhibition
hall would be a cacophonous riot of their shouting. Instead, they
silently thrust their names at you in a carnival of white cards.
Here Mr. Fletcher exhibited the "Wanzer" sewing machine,
while Mr. Adams exhibited the "Genuine Singer." In the wake of
the royal party, which had already passed on to admire the countless flowering plants from the nurseries of Mr. Johnston and Mr.
Jay, both types of sewing machine had lost some of their earlier
enthusiasm for laying down miles of perfect stitches across
expanses of cotton.

A small commotion accompanied Queen Victoria's attempts to
make her way through the crowd towards her daughter and son-
in-law. She was quickly apprehended and dragged away. "They
told her if it happened again she'd be put on a boat and sent
north," said one stout father to his wide-eyed children. "She'll be
on her way to the Queen Charlotte Islands by tomorrow, we'll
never see *her* again."

If the Princess were to catch sight of tattered Mary One-eye, all
dreams of persuading her to stay on and replace her mother would
be dashed. Certain ladies, and their husbands, would never
recover. Wall space had been taken advantage of to reinforce the

hope: *Welcome Lorne and Louise. Cead Mille Failthe. Willkommen.*
All Our Children Salute You.

Of course, Kate's head was already throbbing with tight lines of
pain even before she'd plunged into this horrid crowd. Thank
heavens for Wang Low, who saw to it that her little bottle was
always filled with the proper mixture – she had it with her now,
safe in her skirts. As soon as the children had run off to join
friends from school, she slipped out of the pavilion in search of
some private spot where she might administer relief.

She'd intended to visit the stables anyway, to view the horses,
who did not pass judgement. Light in stables was always poor;
the rich aroma of oats and manure contained mysterious sooth-
ing properties of its own. So did the muffled hubbub of munching
and stamping and whinnying from the stalls. The precious liquid
quickly performed its function as she had learned to trust it to
do. Thank heavens for the merciful poppy! Thank heavens for
peace. She would have taken up chewing the gum if she hadn't
thought James would be bound to notice, and of course to
object. There would be those who considered it a filthy habit for
only the weak, the wicked, the lonely Celestial, or lunatic poets.
Did they think she could have survived the year without this
sedative's friendly support?

"What? – not offering to share it?"

Hawks! Old Stonybrow had once again surprised her. Was
there nowhere she might go to escape this man? You could see in
the sly, insinuating smile on that ugly face of weathered stone
that he had noticed her fumbling to slip the bottle back into the
folds of her skirt. Well – what business was it of his?

"The races will soon begin." A statement of the obvious – but
she must behave as though she had not heard what he'd said.

He was leading Norah on a rope – bringing her across, he said,
from Sheepshanks' farm, which was just beyond the fence. The
filly pranced and danced, her nose high, her knees high, as though
she believed she was still in the Kentucky paddocks of her youth

when she could expect a happy future as a champion racer. Hawks made as though to lead the horse past Kate and down the passage between the rows of stalls, but stopped so that she might stroke the long silky grey neck.

"He insists on riding her himself," she said. *The fool*, her voice suggested.

"Hornswoggle? Jesus, ma'am, what's the matter with him? Old Harris don't ride any more."

"Harris is too fat and too old. James wishes to be seen by royalty as more than just a champion's owner. Whatever bows are taken he will take himself."

"You bring them carrots from home, ma'am? There's grooms that would object. They don't like nobody feeding them before a race."

"Well, you can see she is grateful. Aren't you, sweet Norah? I would have thought you'd be the one to feed them. Or whatever is done before a race."

"Not this bloke. I just deliver them and go."

"Not staying to watch?"

"I ain't interested in their races." For a moment his gaze locked into hers. "No more are you. Maybe you should bring your bottle and come with me." A pair of youths had taken charge of Norah and led her away into the shadowy stables.

"I would rather throw myself beneath the horses."

He touched his hat again and smiled, as though to suggest he knew better – then set off, with his great long strides, and quickly climbed over the wooden fence that separated them from one of Horace Sheepshank's pastures, and did not look back.

More banners could be seen from here, sagging across the rain. *Loyal Hearts and English Homes. God Save the Queen.* What they called an Agricultural Fair was as much an exposition of words. *Harvest Abundance in Praise of Our Queen.*

Potatoes, tomatoes, beans, corn, squash, pumpkins, cucumbers, hand-painted china, gloves, cigars, statuary from Wright and Rudge's, dressed beef and mutton from Goodacres and

Dooley – inside the pavilion again she could see long before she reached him that James was making an effort to be interested in Borde and Morely's patriotically arranged display of horseshoes – ten varieties, from the very lightest for racing to the heavy cleated shoes for the mud and snow. But he was making the effort only for Horace Sheepshank's sake. And Lizzie's. The fury that had seized him at breakfast had an obvious hold on him still.

Today's anger had naturally been triggered by the damage she had done the dining-room. Yet he had said nothing to her about it – the broken chairs, the charred wallpaper, the torn draperies, the terrible smell of scorched varnish. Instead, he ate his breakfast in white rigid silence. As soon as they'd arrived at the driving-park he had abandoned her and the children to their own devices while he strode off to join acquaintances. Still, once she returned from the horses she tried to stay close enough to observe him, and was near enough to notice that he was the only one amongst these thousands to laugh aloud when a southwest wind blew up clouds of sand and dust across the premises and toppled the elaborate marquee that had been erected for the Governor-General and Princess Louise. All in a moment it became a heap of wreckage. Everyone else, of course, had been horrified. What if the honoured guests had been under it? He thought it was funny, as though he were happy to see disaster visited upon others. Perhaps he imagined the writers of the London *World* to have been under the collapsing roof – and his cousin as well, who was somewhere out there interviewing people.

Jammed in with jostling crowds, he was almost forced to be sociable, though you could see that he found it a great effort to look pleased when old Kurtz stopped to report that the Governor-General had admired his display of white-labour cigars, and had conversed with him again for a few moments in perfect German!

What was it that Logan Sumner and his Indian friend were interrupting him now to report? His response was explosive. A worried Horace Sheepshank put a cautionary hand on his shoulder, but James shook it off and turned, fiercely, to call Kate over so that he could repeat what he had just heard. The flying machine had not simply exploded, as they had thought. It had been shot down. Deliberately. By American police who had been there for that very purpose.

A subdued and solemn Logan Sumner explained the rest to Kate, and to Annie, who had just joined them. "They came to Zak this morning, and admitted doing it. They'd discovered what Chu Lee's relatives had in mind, you see. Someone informed them. And they did what they did to prevent it."

"We'll send the Mounties after them!" James shouted. "That plane was still on our side of the border."

"No point in that," Zak said. Of them all he seemed to be taking this with the most calm. "They would deny it. They told me this."

"Then, dammit, we start again!"

Both Sumner and the Indian smiled at this, Kate noticed, but they were sheepish smiles. Zak shook his head the more energetically. "Never. This Indian ain't so crazy as that." And slipped away into the crowd. Disappeared.

"But why would they admit it?" said Kate. "Why would they want you to know?"

James was all for going after Zak. "Will start another, of course. Can't quit just because of them!"

Logan Sumner explained in a lowered voice. "They came to frighten him off," he said. James would not believe. "They returned Chu Lee – they'd scooped him up out of the water, badly wounded and nearly drowned. But whatever they said to Zak, he was very frightened when he came to my door. Maybe they threatened him, I'm not sure. Whatever they did, he will not build another."

As if Zak's mood weren't already foul enough, Sumner said, he had also been forced to spend another night in jail, this time for cursing the visiting American police in plain English. "He says he's going to stop talking at all, it's too dangerous using a language somebody else has given you. Like weapons they've put into your hands without explaining which movement of your fingers will set them off, or what sort of damage they might do."

James pushed Sumner away in disgust, and joined Kate beside Sehl's display of furniture made from local woods, where he kept a furious silence for a few minutes, while Sumner and Annie moved off together through the crowd. "That damn fool Sumner won't do anything without him. Will never have to worry about the Yankees invading us. Don't need to. Can already make us do anything they want."

Across the aisle was a display of Pendray's soap. Catholic soap. Whale-oil soap. White, blue, brown, and mottled household soap. Superior Borax. Hysolime Soap powder – "the best shaving soap in the world." She found herself counting – fifteen names for soap. It was not in her to feel sorry for the loss of the plane, or for those who mourned. Dreamers should expect such disappointments, and fools like James should not be surprised at the justice in it.

"Try not to mind so much about everything," she said. When it was safe to assume that he could be counted on to mind too much about everything unpleasant. "Shouldn't you be with the horse? They'll be starting the races soon."

He growled, but set off towards an exit. "By Jove, it's started to rain!" As though this proved something. Others had noticed as well, but he was the only one to shake his fist at the sky as he left the pavilion and started towards the stables.

Beside the horseshoe display, Annie and Logan Sumner engaged in private conversation, a profoundly solemn Sumner shaking his head from side to side as though there were nothing in the world that could lessen his disappointment. His spectacles, having slid down his nose in accordance with their habit, were not this time pushed back; the fingers that combed his pale hair back only left it in a turmoil; repeatedly he pulled his folded wooden yardstick from the pocket of his saggy tweeds and almost immediately replaced it unopened. Then Annie, flushed and apparently bewildered, abruptly broke away and pushed towards Kate through the crowd, which had now begun to move towards the exits.

Kate admitted that she was not altogether sorry to see the end of the hideous, stinking machine. "Of course we are all relieved that Chu Lee is alive – but I am still appalled that the man's life was risked in the first place."

"And it's only now occurred to him," Annie said, "to feel sad that the success of Zak's invention was achieved by ignoring all his excited research and suggestions."

"While his own dream remains unrealized – we're still in this all-too-ordinary little city he would like to transform." Kate smiled, but knew better than to say, It served him right.

Annie did not respond. Instead, she stretched to look around and inquired about the whereabouts of the children.

"With friends."

Lizzie Sheepshank was upon them now as well, having materialized out of nowhere. "But I saw them earlier, and they were not with anyone."

"I thought I saw them setting off towards your place – towards Sheepshanks' farm," said Annie. "Maybe they thought they would find you there. You seemed to have disappeared."

Laura? Little James? Had wandered off. When she had not the energy to become alarmed.

Still: "Are there animals?" To Lizzie, who stood gawking.

"It is a farm, dear. Of course there are animals!"

Even in this cottony calm, anxiety began to bubble up to the surface. Her children had wandered off. "I mean dangerous animals, of course! From the woods."

Lizzie shrugged. She might never have been a mother at all. "You mean bear? Not often, but sometimes – after a sheep. Deer wouldn't hurt them! Raccoons neither, unless the children were foolish enough to bother them. The cougar don't intrude upon civilization much."

"Perhaps not every cougar would believe this to be civilization. I must go out to find them." Outside, the crowds hurried towards the races beneath bouncing parasols. Her own kept the rain off her hair but did not protect her skirts from the splashes of mud. "They've fallen into a hole, I'm certain of it."

No voices answered Kate's calls from the fence. "Disappeared! Lizzie – point a way for me to go."

"We'll go with you," said Lizzie Sheepshank. "I know the trails and clearings. My own children would disappear, not so long ago."

The three women crossed a field and passed by the chicken run, where fat white hens scratched in the dirt ("Leghorns," Lizzie said, by way of identification), and walked in single file down a narrow lane between cedar rail fences: Lizzie Sheepshank, Kate, then Annie – the hems of their skirts collecting moisture off the laden grass. Ahead, the pathway could be seen evading a stand of yellow-leafed trees to cross a pasture on a downhill slope towards the woods.

"Poplars," Lizzie Sheepshank said. "A stand of alder there. One cedar. That's a little blue spruce by the fence."

"Good heavens, Lizzie, do you think Annie has been living on the moon?"

Lizzie Sheepshank was silent while they crossed a rough, narrow pasture. Then, when they had climbed a stile to a second pasture, she took up instruction again. "Wild hawthorn, Annie. Scrub oak. Snowberries – like pearls on the branches, I always think, now that the leaves are going. Salal. Pine – white pine. Arbutus. Could be human flesh – the colour of some Indians."

"Where are they?" Kate said. "Laura? James! Do you have open wells where children may drown?"

"They may be hiding on us," Annie suggested. "Playing a game." Perhaps Annie wondered where all this motherly concern had come from. Kate wondered herself. But there was no question the rising anxiety in her chest was genuine. She could feel the bottle against her thigh but could hardly make use of it here.

Kate held up an open hand to the side of her mouth. "James! Laura! James!"

"Fern – maidenhair," Lizzie said. "You won't find no open wells on this property, not with Horace in charge. Sumac there. That way leads straight into swamp. Willows."

"But we're heading straight into forest!" said Annie. "Look at the size!"

They were crossing a space now that had only recently been cleared. Soil had been stirred up, but not yet harrowed. Tree stumps and roots had been dragged into piles and blackened by fires that had not yet completely burned them. Some stumps stood upright, rooted in soil – ten feet high and nearly as wide – but charred and gutted. Moving along the forest edge, the trail swung left to avoid a great tangled heap of vines, each as thick as iron rods – "Blackberry," Lizzie said, gingerly testing a fingertip on a thorn – then swung right again to slip between tree trunks as wide as wardrobes. Beyond was all shadow, darkened by the dense boughs that hung their overlapping weights off the imagined towering spars.

"Hawks's shack's up there."

"Where?"

"In that tree. The big one." Lizzie was pointing a little farther along the palisade of forest at the pasture's edge. "You see how it's hollow? Boys started a fire in it once – cleared themselves a cave in it, but didn't kill the tree. A peculiar man. Didn't want to live in the shed; built himself a shack out of scrap lumber – way up in the branches! Drops down in the morning, climbs up at night, like a turkey roosting out of the reach of raccoons."

"Then that's where they are, isn't it? He's taken them! James? Laura!"

"Surely not, Kate," Annie cautioned.

"They would've answered by now, I'd think," Lizzie said. "All your hollerin' as we came across the field."

Kate hurried anyway towards the cedar with the deep black cleft wedged into its trunk. If there was a shack of some sort in its branches, it could not be seen.

"This way," Lizzie said. "They probably followed this cow trail back to the creek. That's an Oregon grape, Annie. A young hemlock there – you can tell by the drooped-over top."

Kate did not join the others on the cow trail. She moved in closer to the hollow tree. Her children were up there; Old Stonybrow had somehow got them up; he could have butchered them by now. She folded her umbrella and stepped in through the large inverted V of the opening to stand inside the hollowed tree trunk. A small, round room. Stones, moss, tufts of grass at her feet. Charred wall all around, curving up to a point – this might have been the interior of a teepee. A ladder of rough lumber had been spiked into the wall up one side as far as an opening where light entered. From there, presumably, you crawled out and climbed up through limbs. To where that man had made her children prisoners.

"Jack pine," Lizzie could be heard saying. "Fir cones. A patch of devil's club. Look how that young huckleberry bush is growin' right out of the rotten stump."

"Laura? James!"

"Here, what's this racket?"

Everything leapt within her at the sound of his voice. He stood with one hand on either side of the narrow slanting entrance, blocking her exit, and smiling. "You calling me?"

"I'm looking for the children."

"Well – you can see they ain't here."

Lizzie could still be heard, a hollow voice somewhere in the woods, cataloguing her possessions for Annie. "Cottonwood. That's a mock-orange. Holly." Not far away a barn owl commented: *Hoo-hoo! Hoo-hoo!*

"You have them up in your –"

Braided tower.

"Them brats? No thank you." He did not step aside, but seemed to let all his weight hang from his hands while he leaned in towards her.

"Then, do you know where they might –?"

No! We shan't fall. Uncle Paul, do take her away!

"You come to offer me a drink? It's about time we had a little talk."

The owl again: *Hoo-hoo! Hoo-hoo!*

"Mr. Hawks, we have already had all the conversation you and I were meant to have. Please, step aside and let me join the others." Her hands were wet, and cold. Rain had run up her wrist to dampen her sleeve. Would it be enough to raise the umbrella against him, if she should need to protect herself?

"We could go up." This was said with a crooked smile. "Them rungs'll hold a lady, easy enough." He added, with a grin, "I know that for a fact."

"I shall call them. Mrs. Sheepshank and my sister aren't far away. You can hear."

In fact you could barely hear. Lizzie's voice was still chanting out names, but now you could hear only the faded sounds without quite making out the words.

"It surprises me, how you act like there was never anythin' between us. No understandin', I mean. It surprises me how you like to pretend you never heard of me before. Now here's our chance to work a few things out between us."

"You *do* have my children somewhere!"

"It surprises me how quick you forget about them people you tossed over on yer way to the top, so to speak, the minute you gets yer hands on yer man and his money and his hotel. Only it ain't worked out the way you hoped for, has it? You shouldn't've been so quick to toss another man over on yer way to the prize."

"You ought to be confined to an asylum!" This was pure bravado. He must see that she was trembling. She clung with both hands to the wet umbrella. "If I had had any brains at all I would have arranged to have you thrown overboard before we were an hour out of Melbourne. There were those who would have been happy to do it."

"Come! Up you go! The ladder!"

"Step out of my way, sir! I shall scream!"

You cried out. I shall stay until I am content that you are safely asleep again.

"One rung at a time. You've been prancin' and side-steppin' and sashayin' your way towards my little shack for a year now or more. Anybody can see you made a bad choice. It's time you finished the journey. Up! Your skirts will be no hindrance once you've started. Let me help you place your foot on the bottom rung."

He would try to *talk* her up, as though the sounds and shapes of his words could serve as stairs to put your feet upon. One more man had built a universe out of words. His charred hollow tower was not wrapped in salvaged brand names like the Indian's barn, or inscribed with accounts of a fictitious career like Logan Sumner's tomb, or held upright like the Blue Heron by the sound of barroom tales, but the idea was much the same. When in her life had she bid farewell to the world of things and entered a world created out of nothing more than sounds and printed shapes? Was it something that happened, she wondered, to everyone?

One hand had reached as though to take an arm but she pulled back and began to protest. She would not go up! But she was, she found, no longer able to speak. Everything had tightened in her throat, there might have been hands around her neck, choking off the words at their source. Choking off her breathing as well. She would be strangled here without this fellow even touching her!

But there was a shout from somewhere – a man's voice. Then Lizzie's voice answering from a distance. The man again. The children? Someone had found them. She ducked, slipped quickly beneath his arm, and rushed out into the full rainy daylight, leaving the umbrella behind.

Horace Sheepshank was standing just inside the fence while Lizzie and Annie ran towards him. Kate hurried, into the gusts of cold rain that stung her eyes and dragged scraps of soggy hair across her forehead. "The race!" Lizzie said. Horace had started back towards the fairgrounds. "The children are safe, he tells me. He's seen them with their friends."

When they came around the stables an announcer's voice was naming the horses, naming the owners, naming the riders they could expect to see in completion, naming the two judges from the mainland who were down at the finish line, preparing to be wise and fair. Kate stood with Annie and the Sheepshanks behind the rail where they might get a good view of the starting-line, where riders were already mounted, and at the same time watch the royal party observing the race. Laura and Young James waved, out of the gathered mob. Like other children they were down on their knees in front, not caring about the mud.

She didn't care, she didn't care about any of this, she only wanted to go home. Her head felt as though someone were trying to peel off her scalp. She could not very well go fishing in her skirts for the bottle in full view of the city's entire population and the country's head of state and the Queen's own daughter. Let us get this over with as fast as possible.

Perhaps the Governor-General and Princess Louise were equally anxious to get this over with, though of course they didn't know that something more unpleasant than rain was waiting to happen. Huddling inside wraps and under parasols, they were close enough that Kate could see they were making a brave effort to pretend to be unaware of the disappointing weather. The ladies-in-waiting were not at all inclined to conceal their irritation, on the other hand. The rest of the crowd seemed determined not to let the rain spoil the occasion, which was, after all, the one event in the Fair that everyone could share at the same time. Their eyes could see precisely what Queen Victoria's daughter was seeing, and at precisely the same time she was seeing it.

Some youths had climbed up onto the roof of the stables, some sat in the branches of nearby trees, still others stood on the shoulders of their friends. Families passed food back and forth out of paper bags. What appeared to be the entire population of the town was here, with the inhabitants of up-island towns as well, and more than a few curious republicans from across in Washington Territory. Eating, talking, drinking, shaking the rain from their clothes, they waited for the starter to set things in motion.

Logan Sumner again! He detached himself from the crowd and started to walk this way; Annie moved to meet him. Kate would like to shake both of them. Fools!

Hastings and Portia's Knight were fastest away from the starting-line, inspiring immediate cheers from the crowd, but it was clear from the beginning that something was wrong with Norah; she ran as though no one had told her this was a genuine race. She behaved as though she had been propelled out into blinding light, unable to see, yet would give it a half-hearted try anyway, though her legs were not as reliable as they might have been. No more than fifty yards down the track she gave up the attempt; she came to a too-sudden stop, her front legs locked, and James Horncastle went flying over her head into the mud.

A great "Ohhhhhh!" went up from the crowd. Kate herself was part of it. An angry Horncastle stood up immediately, and made to climb back on. But the horse shied, as though to say she would have none of him. A few members of the crowd laughed. Horncastle cursed and tried again, and once again the horse stepped aside, whinnying nervously. More laughter. The horse dropped her head, as though ashamed, but would not let her owner come any closer. There could not be anyone unaware of the dangerous colour in James Horncastle's face. He tried to make light of it – bowed deeply to the royal party, scratched his head – but it was clear he was embarrassed, no, humiliated, by his own horse before a royal audience. He turned quickly, more quickly than the horse could leap away, and threw his leg up over the saddle.

But the horse would not be outwitted. This time, when James Horncastle flew through the air, he landed on his head and did not move.

There were many who got there before Kate. James was lifted carefully by a dozen hands and carried off the track and into the stables. She could only follow. Horace came behind, leading the horse. This awkwardness must be taken care of as fast as possible, away from the view of the visitors, so that they might quickly set about erasing it from official memory.

Inside their eyes had first to adjust to the shadowy dark, where sunbeams slanted down from cracks through stripes of floating dust. Nervous horses stomped and snorted. Logan Sumner went down on his knees in chaff, to hold James Horncastle's head off the floor. Someone else was there on his knees as well – Dr. Rae. Strangers were merely looking on, as though in hopes of entertainment. Kate supposed she had better drop to her knees, and take up her husband's hands.

The boy Jerome was suddenly there as well, on the other side of James, grabbing one of his father's hands for himself. "Will he be fine? Isn't it only a bump on the head?" His pleading eyes hoped for an answer first from the doctor, then from Logan Sumner, and finally from Kate, who looked away.

Behind her, Horace Sheepshank said, "There is something wrong with the horse. She's been tampered with."

Someone raised a voice. "You boys see any visitors come into the stables?"

Logan Sumner put his hand against Horncastle's throat. "He has a pulse, and his eyes are open, but he seems to be unaware of us."

"Will someone bring a wagon round?" said Dr. Rae. "We can't leave him here."

28

During the rush back to town, there was time for every emotion to have its turn with her. Though she spoke aloud to him, saying, "We shall be there soon," and "This is just something that will pass," and "You have given yourself a scare, you silly man, that is all," her thoughts were carrying on quite a separate monologue in silence. "Something terrible is about to happen to me, something *dreadful*, and I don't know if I shall be able to bear it." Sorrow followed, as if the something terrible had already happened. "I cannot bear to think that the whole world is changing this minute, and nothing will ever be the same." A glance at his frightened eyes brought pity. "Oh my poor dear James! What have you done to yourself?" And, yes, he *had* done it to himself – the foolish man. Had done it to her as well, though he would not care about that. When did he ever think that his moods and his actions might have an effect upon her? What had he ever cared about her feelings? Was he thinking about her now? If he was thinking anything at all behind the stricken face, he was thinking of himself. He thought of nothing else. "Go ahead and die," she eventually found herself thinking, to her own horror. "You'll have slipped away from me then, you'll have *escaped* me, and punished me as well. Isn't that what you've, isn't that what you've *wanted*? Isn't that what the whole world has wanted for me?"

But when they reached the Royal Hospital she would not allow them to stop. Dr. Rae could ride with them to the hotel, she insisted; he could examine the patient there. She knew that if James could speak he would demand that he be taken to the Blue Heron, which was only a few more blocks.

They had not been long at the hotel when she soon learned that her "punishment" was not to be his death. At least not yet. "First the blow on the head. Then perhaps a stroke at the same moment," the doctor announced. "But I have seen worse. I have

seen some live for ten or fifteen years afterwards, though I regret
to tell you they have been largely helpless. A few have gradually
regained much of their health. You will have your work cut out for
you, I'm afraid, if he pulls through this first part. I hope you are a
strong woman."

By the time an anxious Annie joined her, the doctor had
helped set up a bed in Horncastle's office, where they agreed he
would feel the most comfortable, surrounded by the familiar walls
of squared-off logs and his lithographs of famous racehorses – also
where he would be within convenient reach of those who would
help. Sumner and the Sheepshanks and the boy Jerome had been
sent away; she would allow no one else to come near. Guests had
been warned to be quiet from now on. Employees had been
already assigned additional tasks.

She had resorted several times to the bottle within the folds of
her skirt, and could see it all clearly now: her "punishment" – she
would think of it as punishment from now on, a punishment
meted out by a universe that could not bear to see a woman fight
for justice, let alone achieve it – her "punishment" was to be not
his death, but his continued existence. She would have to nurse
him, perhaps for the rest of her life. "I might as well be a slave. I'll
not have the time or the energy for there to be anything else in
my life but tending him. I'll be poor. The hotel will fail. I shall
work like a, I shall *labour* like a slave, shunned by everyone. While
he lies in this bed with his breath going in and out, staring ahead.
Drooling. Silent, silent, the entire hotel gone silent while he
barely breathes at its centre."

"Hush," Annie said. "We don't know how much he can hear."

They sat with only Horncastle's breathing between them
through the rest of the night. Occasionally one or the other dozed
off for a while, but never for long. Early in the morning, when
they had both been persuaded to take turns going to the kitchen
to eat and had come back to sit where they had sat before, on
either side of the bed, Dr. Rae returned and ordered them out into

the foyer while he conducted another examination. "Yes," was all he felt it was necessary to announce, when he had permitted them to return. "As I suggested last night."

Soon after he had gone, Wang Low entered the room, looking uncomfortable, and said that "the other Mrs. Horncastle" was outside. "We have turned others away, but she insists on seeing Mr. Horncastle. May I show her in?"

"Of course you may not show her in!" Furious, Kate stood up to shout this at her servant. "You may send that woman away. Tell her she isn't wanted here, she isn't *welcome*." When he had swung around and gone out, she breathed deeply for a moment, to calm herself, one hand over her heart. "Has she no feelings at all? I am sure her brats are just around the corner, waiting their turn."

But after only a few moments of silently studying her husband's face on the pillow, she found herself thinking: *I shall give him back. That's what I'll do. I shall hand him back to that fat, smiling peasant and see how she likes him now.* "Yes," she said to Annie, who sat with her head bowed, directly across the bed from her. "Let *her* slave for him. I shall let her have him, if that's what she wants. Let *her* wipe the spittle from his mouth and change his sheets and hold him upright on the chamberpot. Let her wipe his bottom and try to make sense of those gargling noises that come from his throat and try to keep the hotel from falling apart at the same time."

She stood up, smiling, and went to the glass doors that opened out into his garden. A greenish sunlight fell through the giant cedar and laid patterns along the gravel walks and across the rho-dodendrons and mock-oranges and currant bushes, all long-abandoned by their scented blooms. "Yes. That will give her reason to wonder, to be *amazed* that she wanted to keep him! She will beg me to take him back, but too late – I shall have sailed. To Manchester, Annie! I shall go back to where we began. Where we were girls. And never think of him again."

"Oh, Kate," was all Annie could think of to say.

But when Kate turned from the window, she had changed her mind. "No. She would move back into my home with that hideous loving expression on her face and almost enjoy making herself a slave for him. Ministering to him night and day. Wouldn't she just like that? All her patience, all of her *stupid kindness* would rise up. By God, Annie, I think she would make it her entire job just to serve him. And not just to serve him, but to heal him as well! And would quite likely succeed! No, I shan't give him back to her. They would both like that. To have me gone. They would both be happy if I did that."

"Kate! You mustn't think such things."

"He tries to say her name. During the night, while I sat here, I heard him try to say it. In that garble and spittle I recognize where he is trying to say it. 'Norah.' A hideous name! I shall forbid her to see him. She shall be forbidden even to set foot in this building. I shall make sure she does not even pass by the windows. Besides nursing him, we shall also have to stand guard over him. I have something at last which can injure her. She will never see him again."

Annie did not hide the tears that welled up in her eyes. "Oh, you mustn't speak so cruelly. You cannot possibly mean what you're saying. Please, think how she must be suffering too, to know that he is stricken, like this, and to be sent away."

She left, then, to offer some comfort to the other Mrs. Horncastle. "She must be so anxious for just a little news."

"There you go," Kate thought, "like everyone else. Deserting me for her." For some time she started at the immobile sleeping face of her husband, conscious of the slow, regular rhythm of his breathing, until she felt herself to be slipping into the sleep she had been denied in the night. She was not altogether surprised to hear, from inside her sleep, the sound of Annie returning to sit in the chair on the far side of the bed.

But it was not Annie who considered her from beyond the hump of her husband's breathing body; it was, she saw, the long, dark, expectant figure that had been following her everywhere. "Paul?" *You cried out. I shall stay until I am content that you are safely asleep again.*

"Not me, ma'am. I don't know any bloke named Paul."

"But Lilian. Where is –?"

Old Stonybrow again. Waiting. Smiling his insolent smile, as if he found everything about her amusing. He had removed his stockman's hat, the first time she had seen him without it since Australia, and held it with both hands on his lap, turning it constantly, feeding its brim through his fingers. How had he inserted himself into James Horncastle's private office?

He relaxed his broad, cruel smile when he saw that she had become aware of him. A satisfied chuckle came from deep in his throat. "A lovely performance! Very moving! The stricken wife confronts her future." He leaned forward and whispered hoarsely, "I'd applaud, but it might alarm the patient."

To avoid alarming the patient herself, and to avoid being overheard by others in the hotel, she hissed her response. "You must leave! Or I shall call for assistance, to have you thrown out."

At this, the chuckle rose up his throat to become outright laughter. "You think you can toss me off as easy as the fat woman?"

"My sister will be back. The doctor. You've no business, you've no *right* to be in this room."

Still smiling, he contemplated the motionless figure between them. Then he glanced about the room, as though searching for something whose value he might estimate. "Your fine indignation is wasted, lady. No audience for it." He even reached out and gently lifted a corner of the sheet up over Horncastle's exposed shoulder. "In the circumstance, I think you might be glad to see me."

"I have no business with you!"

Evidently he saw this as a great joke – he threw back his head and did not bother this time to restrain his laughter for the sake of the patient. "*All* of your business has been with me, like it or not. She's seen to that."

"What do you mean by 'she'?"

"You could've had me instead of this poor wretch. But you tossed me off like an old shoe. And look at you now. Naturally I wrote to yer sister in Ballarat when you turned me down, to keep her informed, and naturally she asked me to keep an eye on you in case you should be in danger of findin' happiness."

"You must go away!"

Kate closed her eyes, as though that were a sure way to dismiss him. And perhaps it was. He said no more. Perhaps she had only dreamed him, because even in his presence and in her agitated state she found herself slipping again into sleep, from which she fully awoke only when Annie had returned and taken her place in that same chair. It didn't matter to her whether he had been here or not, it didn't matter if he had said what she'd heard; she easily redirected the same antipathy towards the sister who had not supported her enough. "But you didn't want him. You certainly won't want him now, will you?" Both considered the pale face of the silent one, perhaps to avoid one another's. "I shall have him all to myself now, while you desert me altogether, like the rest of the world. The slave of a helpless cripple."

Annie's voice was barely above a whisper. "If I had decided to accept your offer, this should certainly have stopped things! But I would not desert you on that account. I would consider myself as much his nurse as you will be yourself. And I shall, I shall help when I can. But, dear Kate, I am guilty of keeping this from you just a little too long – you will think I am inventing it this minute. But the fact is, I have decided to set the course of my life in another direction. I have been invited to do some speaking – a tour in the United States. And when I come back, afterwards, I believe I shall marry Mr. Sumner."

Kate could only stare for a moment, half unbelieving. "Oh, Annie! Annie!" This was little more than a whisper. "You fool. What can you possibly see in that man?"

Annie seemed happy to admit uncertainty. "Impossible to know, or at least to explain. Only that we take such delight in one another's company, and that I think we will probably do so all of our lives."

But "fool" had already become "traitor." Kate made no attempt to keep her voice down for the sake of the patient, or for the sake of the silent hotel. "Did I invite you here to play this foul trick on me?" She felt she might explode with fury and grief. "You have become, you have *chosen* to become, my enemy, when you were my dearest sister! How did you join the others? They have been my enemies from the beginning. That stupid peasant woman! And her children. The wives! The sneering husbands! Even James!"

An embarrassed Wang Low stood hushing at her from the doorway. "You are upsetting some guests, who have heard." Wang Low, too, had decided to join the ranks of the enemy. "It all goes back to Susannah, of course. That's what that horrid man was suggesting. She *sent* him! Everything that has happened has happened because of her!"

"Now you are making me angry," Annie said. "You mustn't do this. It isn't fair. You have blamed everyone. Not even Susannah should take the blame for you. You have thought: *Because I have suffered, I must be rewarded for it, and it doesn't matter who else will suffer as a result.* In fact you have done everything out of spite, pretending to be a seeker after justice. From the beginning you acted only out of malice, and jealousy, and greed. And when you had got what you felt you deserved, you were filled with terror of losing it – am I right? You saw you *would* lose it, you were already losing it – and didn't see that you have chosen a life which could never be free of jealousy. Or fear."

But Kate would not hear. "It is Susannah, Susannah, Susannah, who is to blame for everything. It is Susannah who has ruined my life, ruined *everything*. Even from so much distance, she has controlled everything! For the rest of my life, for the rest of my horrid *life*, I shall devote myself to hating her." For a moment she blinked into the window light. A wagon could be heard rattling past. "I shall do nothing else but dedicate every act, every word, to this end, so that even across all this distance she shall feel it. If I am to be punished, you needn't think I shan't be strong enough."

SILENCE: WIDOWS OF THE GREAT BLUE HERON

29

J AMES Horncastle's funeral took place on a Tuesday afternoon in early December, a day in which sporadic rain showers and brisk gusts of winds off the strait alternated with brief intervals of sunshine. Sea-gulls wheeled in screaming circles overhead. By two o'clock, those who had arrived early enough to find seats for a service punctuated by periods of thundering rain on the iron roof of St. John's filed outside to join those who had been required to stand waiting around the door, where they formed a procession to move off down the street in the direction of the cemetery behind the hearse with its six black horses, each of them with black plumes standing upon its shoulders and black tasselled nets draped over its broad back. The veiled widow and her sisters rode in the first carriage, followed by the Sheepshanks, the families of other saloon-keepers and hoteliers, even a few carriages filled with minor city officials and naval officers. Window blinds were pulled down in all the houses they passed. Those on the street who were not part of the procession stopped and held their hats in their hands, and sometimes joined in with those who walked behind. By the time they turned in through the gates of the cemetery, the crowd had grown so large that it was Logan Sumner's impression the entire town must have closed down behind them to join the procession. "Few funerals could rival it for size – except, of course, for certain elected officials."

Years later, Sumner would still be momentarily surprised to recall that the crowd had been so large, even for the funeral of a popular man whose private life had been a matter of continuing public interest. But he would remember, then, that people had come not only to pay their respects to the departed but to avail themselves of the opportunity to view the controversial and provocative survivors.

"Perhaps this is always the way when rumours and suspicion surround the circumstances of a death," he would suggest to any visitor who expressed curiosity about the funeral. "Especially when it is known that an investigation is being carried out by the police. Perhaps all of us in the family felt it – eyes probing for tell-tale signs of a murderer's bad conscience. It gave them pleasure to think that all of us were capable."

At the graveside old rivalries were temporarily disregarded, if not forgotten. Norah Horncastle stood at the foot, a broad, solid figure anchoring the entire proceedings to her own sturdy calm, flanked by her children displaying faces filled with confusion and anger. Jerome would blame everyone, everything – even the Douglas firs – for this irrevocable loss of what had earlier been only filched. Beside him the eldest daughter, who had not spoken with either parent since their separation, gripped hard on his arm and directed accusatory eyes at one after another of the assembly as though she planned to record their faces for some future use.

Not exempt from her glare were Kate's two children, who looked back at Adelina from their position beside their mother at the head of the grave, their quivering bottom lips stuck out. A stranger might have thought two separate processions had converged from opposite directions at the same plot. For here, at the head of James Horncastle's grave and nearest to the Reverend Trodd, stood three of the McConnell sisters – the fourth would not receive news of the death in her Queensland home for several weeks, and even then would be so caught up in civic affairs that she had to assign responsibility for a sympathy note to one of her husband's secretaries. It had been a severe test of the sisters' imaginations to find black gowns and capes sufficiently different from one another to suggest their separate-but-equal griefs. Kate stood tallest, of course, in hers. And Annie's gown suggested only minimal respect for tradition. While Susannah McConnell, the oldest, the thinnest, the most haggard of face, managed somehow to suggest in every angle of her body that she, of all those gathered women, was the one true widow of the occasion.

It was an effect she would somehow manage to convey for years afterwards, even in the presence of those who had actually been married to James Horncastle by church or law, as she had not. As long afterwards as the time of the city's great nineties boom, she would still be a figure to be noticed – passing by the feverish activities of Klondike miners stocking up on sleighs, boots, mitts, hats, shovels, saddles, and stoves for their trip north – with the appearance of one who had gathered all of womankind's collective grief since the beginning of time to herself and nursed it, carried it in her dulled eyes, hid it in every fold of her perpetual widow's dress. Young men from Georgia, old-timers from California, if they later thought at all of the city where they had been persuaded by a foreign government to buy their miners' licences and to purchase their duty-free supplies before heading up to the Yukon, would think of it as the little seaside city cowering beneath spectacular snow-peaked foreign mountains where merchants did not even try to hide the glee with which they made the fortunes they had been waiting for, and where a tall, thin, elderly woman in black passed down the street with the air of eternal mourning in her face, and with whispered suggestions of dark deeds in her wake.

"By this time," Sumner would explain, "it seemed that all of the city's dreams were being fulfilled. As Horncastle himself might say if he were still alive: now the herons are being rewarded for their patience. We are thriving now, we all expect to be very rich soon. And we have every reason now to expect, once again, that this will soon be one of the great cities of the world. All that is necessary is that the supply of gold in the north last long enough for us to build, finally, the splendid city which has existed only in our dreams."

A short stroll up Government Street would be enough to convince the visitor of Sumner's claim. "Notice how the Driard has shot up to reach six storeys in height. Notice that construction is well along on a magnificent new post office on the harbour. And – across the bridge – you can see that the Bird Cages are being replaced with million-dollar buildings of a style even Londoners would be proud of! Here – evidence of the new sewer system, pumping everything into the sea! And if you have any doubts remaining about the bustling nature of life here, just climb aboard that streetcar and discover how crowded it is! If you wish, you may stay on for a ride which will take you all the way out to Willows Fairground, where the exhibition hall will make you think you have found a New World version of the Crystal Palace."

Drawn into Sumner's office on Wharf Street and invited up the staircase to his office, the visitor would find the view of the harbour an encouraging one. Boats of every description crowded several deep against the docks. Steamers waited to take on their cargo and passengers for the long trip north to Skagway. Dozens of those same passengers could be seen standing in a queue outside the Customs house, waiting to purchase the licences that would give them permission to become rich. But the much more important view was the vision of an imagined future to be found on Sumner's desk: great stacks of designs for elaborate mansions with turrets and cupolas and stained-glass windows, lodges reminiscent of Austrian *Schlösse*, giant warehouses modelled after Venetian palaces, stately hotels soaring ten, eleven, a dozen storeys towards the clouds, a dance pavilion to be erected on pilings over the water. "It is only the beginning, sir, madam. Reflecting more of the clients' taste than my own. But these will make the business sound, and strengthen our reputation, and make it possible for me to erect those splendid buildings of my imagination which will stand as monuments to this period when we have become mere history to future generations looking for something here they might admire."

Leaving Sumner Construction and passing deeper into town, the visitor who had manoeuvred his way through the stacks of tents, parkas, and sleds, and the mounds of canned salmon set out on shop verandahs would eventually be invited to regard The Great Blue Heron Hotel. Amongst all the obvious activity and apparent affluence on this street, it alone seemed to be enjoying little benefit from the city's boom. The verandah pillars required a fresh coat of paint. The faded sign needed to be repainted or replaced. There was no indication that any of the countless miners who were forced to spend a few days in town had made the Blue Heron their home – indeed, it seems they steered clear of the place after the few who tried it reported to others that they had not been made to feel welcome, claiming, "Them sisters got faces that'd chill your blood." Some travellers still stopped there, of course, but newer, larger, more elegant hotels had claimed the more affluent sightseers and visiting businessmen. The faces of those few who could be seen taking tea on the upstairs terrace, or strolling through Horncastle's garden, wore the haunted and rather tentative look of people who were not certain why they were where they were and could not remember where they were meant to go next. "I am here, I suppose, because I don't belong anywhere." A cousin of Mrs. Sheepshank had been here for several weeks, having discovered after a journey from Melbourne that she was unwelcome at the farm. At Christmas an actress from Toronto hanged herself in her room. The threadbare foyer carpet mourned the loss of heavy traffic which had pounded it bare.

"I believe I was more than half in love with that hotel at one time," Sumner would often say. "Or the *idea* of it. It was something of a dream place for me, a magic emblem of the very notion of family and home, a place I associated somehow with the future.

Of course, everyone didn't see it this way. To Mrs. Norah Horncastle it was, she said, a little home that grew too big to hold itself together. 'Somewhere along the way it lost its soul.' Not as harsh as her eldest daughter, who was heard to refer to it as a treacherous orphanage, and later as 'the house of succeeding whores.' Almost from the beginning, Kate Horncastle considered the building a mocking prison but did not realize, while Horncastle was alive, just how much of a prison she could eventually make of the simple family hotel which her husband had dreamed of turning into the grandest and most popular establishment in town.

"Two of the sisters run it now. My wife was invited to join them but of course she had other plans. She also has more sense than to enter into any business with her sisters. Though of course we visit, and try to help out occasionally when it is necessary. They have the assistance of a former cattleman who lives with them – an Australian, born in the States, a hired hand whose board is included in his pay but who conducts himself as though he were an equal partner with the others. He eats at the table with us when we are guests, but says little. The atmosphere is tense, but not so tense as it was while Horncastle was still alive."

Within a few months of Horncastle's accident, Susannah, the oldest sister, stepped off the boat and moved into the hotel – apparently for good. Sumner knew this from Annie, who had not yet moved out to become his wife; Kate was sent into a state almost as serious as her husband's when the tall, drawn woman put down her carpet-bag in the middle of the hotel foyer and, while hired boys hauled her trunks in off the street, studied every potted plant and framed etching around the room before looking hard at Kate, who stood pale and dumbfounded behind the reception desk. Then she stepped up to the blue heron at the foot of the stairs, placed a hand over its head, and turned it to face away.

"Have someone remove this, Katie. People do not wish to enter an hotel and find themselves looking into the glassy eyes of some stuffed ugly bird that belongs in the bush."

Kate was determined not to faint, yet felt the floor tilt beneath her feet. "I had no – You didn't write that . . ." In the confusion that resulted from the unwelcome surprise, it even occurred to her that Susannah might have been in town all along, in secret, and had only now decided to step into the light. "Where did you come from?" seemed an appropriate question.

"From Ballarat, of course. What else could you possibly think?"

"Then you are paying a visit. The boarding-house?"

"Has been sold. Do you think I would bring all these trunks with me if I were merely off on a holiday? I have come to help you with your burden."

Kate maintained her distance and her silence both. She had not written to anyone of James's illness. Yet, what other "burden" could be meant?

"Fortunately, you are not the only one capable of writing to inform me of your husband's condition."

Settled over a cup of coffee or a pot of tea at a window table in The Spindrift across the street, Sumner would lower his voice to confide in the curious visitor, telling what he knew about the several months that passed between Susannah's arrival and the day of Horncastle's death. "He failed, you see. They were forced to nurse him but were not rewarded with any signs of improvement. I sat for hours by his bed in his old saloon-office at the centre of his beloved building, now gone horribly silent around him. Guests were required to tiptoe about. Kate had can-celled the German gatherings, cancelled the Swedes, told the Scots to go somewhere else for their nostalgic meetings. When I talked to him, aware that what I was saying could very well be unheard or at least uncomprehended by my friend, I persisted in trying to see signs in him of the man I had known him to be; even in the absence of those signs I endeavoured to see the James Horncastle who was temporarily obscured by this cloud of his illness. But the two sisters seemed to make no such effort – they might have been tending some preposterously demanding plant which withered and failed before their eyes without comment or any sign of gratitude. Eyes and ears seemed to take account of all that went on about him, but nothing was ever known of how he felt or what he thought. Implored by Kate to give her some sort of response – a raised finger, a grunt, even a wink – he would mimic a state of unconsciousness. Except for the sound of his breathing, the rise and fall of his chest, he might already have been laid out by the undertaker and awaiting his coffin. While this perform-ance filled me with a powerful sadness, it infuriated Susannah – as though it were the act of a particularly stubborn and uncoopera-tive child who wished only to thwart her. And it drove Kate into states where she would lose control of herself in fits of shouted insults and sudden outbursts of weeping.

"It is a hard thought, I know, but I believe he knew what he was doing. This is a difficult thing to accept, when one recalls what a cheerful and generous man he was at one time, for all his obvious faults – prepared to help anyone who asked, hoping for everyone's happiness, surprised and upset to discover that he had been responsible for even the most insignificant distress. Yet I am certain I saw it in his eyes – he could not have been unaware of the contest which was enacted across his bed, a contest he inevitably controlled. There was a hotel in need of constant attention, indeed demanding considerable attention if it were not to turn away business and drive the Horncastles further into debt. Where once he had filled the building with his laughter and loud boasting and his even louder swapping of tales with the guests in his bar, he filled it now with a kind of deliberate silence which you could sense was already beginning to eat away at the foundations of everything he had built. And he remained, at its centre, a silent man in need of constant care, whether they liked it or not.

"When Susannah arrived she announced her intention to ease Kate's burden, but it soon became clear that while she was interested in easing the burden imposed by an invalid husband she was not very interested in easing the burden of a demanding hotel. Forced to devote long hours to keeping the business running, Kate was never unaware that while she supervised meals and checked beds and spent time behind the reception desk Susannah was free to spend as much time as she wished with her husband, a thought that drove her several times a day to abandon whatever task she ought to be doing in order to pay surprise visits to the invalid's room. At the end of a day she was so tired she dragged herself around on deadened limbs, yet insisted on spending long hours as Horncastle's only nurse. Resentful at being dismissed from the very task she incessantly complained about, Susannah was now set free to antagonize chambermaids, alter dining-room menus, order supplies from a different supplier, and supervise the children's homework with an iron will that soon had them both in tears. The hours Kate spent in the sick-room were hours spent frantically worrying about the damage Susannah was doing outside it, while the hours she spent outside the sick-room were filled with intolerable vexation about what Susannah was saying or doing inside.

"Occasionally Annie sailed in, drove both her sisters into their own bedrooms – where she insisted they stay – made certain the patient was comfortable, played games with the children, and smoothed ruffled feathers amongst the hotel help. When she had put everything into some sort of order she invited the sisters out of their rooms (where they had been only too glad to remain so long as each knew that the other was doing the same), lectured them briefly on the damage they were doing themselves and possibly even the patient with their silly competition, threatened

Susannah with removal by the force of law if she continued to make life so difficult for Kate, then left to take up her own life in another part of town."

Of course all of this was made more difficult by the presence of Hawks. He, too, insisted on "easing the burden" by taking his turn at nursing Horncastle. This was only further torture for Kate, who found that she now had two people whose activities out of her sight were a matter of anguished speculation. He moved in shortly after Susannah's arrival and became the man of the house in the sense that he took care of repairs, tended the garden, and disciplined staff. Eventually he also took over the books and established himself in possession of Horncastle's desk – now pushed to one corner of the office, behind a screen. This was not accomplished without a struggle, of course, but Kate was forced to acknowledge that she understood little of what she saw in the books and would soon have driven herself into bankruptcy. By the time Sumner learned of this new arrangement, and felt justified in protesting vigorously – as Horncastle's friend and Kate's brother-in-law – Kate herself defended the situation and demanded that he mind his own business. His lawyer assured him that neither Hawks nor Susannah could be forcibly removed from the premises without a request to that effect from Kate, and it was clear that she was unable or unwilling to take matters that far – whatever her reasons might be.

"I believe she had become dependent in some peculiar way on the internal agony their presence caused her, and could not imagine living without it. It was a most uncomfortable household to visit, let me assure you. Yet, as family, we felt we must not neglect them altogether. Mrs. Sumner still felt some fondness for the older sisters who had helped raise her, and a special responsibility towards the sister who had been instrumental in bringing her here. And I, of course, wished to make certain that Horncastle did not feel he had been totally deserted by friends. Believe me, very few were admitted. Horace Sheepshank. Captain

Trumble. And even these were made to feel so unwelcome that they soon began to postpone or forget their visits, all but abandoning the speechless hostage to the care of his grim keepers in that silent hotel.

"As I have said, I do not know the extent to which his silence was deliberate, though there was one day when it seemed that he would try to speak – in my presence only, of course. He was looking fully at me, and opened his mouth, and moved his lips – but he failed to make any sound and simply closed his eyes. It was as though he'd lost his language altogether, as though he'd tried to remember what words could do but found there was nothing there."

And indeed it seemed to Logan Sumner that something not unlike this had happened to all of them. It was as though some blow – Kate Horncastle's words during that first night's vigil, perhaps, as reported to the rest of them by Annie – had given them all a whack to the skull, just as the fall from his horse had affected Horncastle, leaving them unable to find, or use, or believe in a language that said what they wanted it to say, at least in one another's company.

Dinners were the worst instances of this, perhaps. The dining-room looked out from the back of the building, onto the gardens. The furniture was still the heavy oak that Horncastle had bought for Norah – its scorched portions only partly obscured by lace cloths. Norah's watercolour swans, the Queen, the family portraits still hung in their accustomed places on the fading wallpaper. Dinner was eaten off Kate's china but with Norah's heavy silver cutlery – though it may be that Kate and Sumner were the only ones who knew this. Susannah positioned herself where she might best hear, she said, any noises signalling a need for help in the sick-room – which put her against the long window wall. The children, Laura and Young James, sat on either side of her – obviously terrified of being within her reach, but more terrified of asking for any other arrangement. Sumner and Annie sat facing them, attempting to draw them into conversation but having little success – they would glance up at Aunt Susannah before answering even the simplest question, as though for permission, and would get it over with as fast as possible, to cut down on the risk of saying something in need of reprimand. More than once Annie would suggest when they had just escaped from a dinner at the hotel that it was the responsibility of herself and Sumner to remove the children from that poisonous household and make them part of their own. Eventually this was to happen, but not until circumstances made it imperative.

Hawks would come in to dinner at the last moment, ducking his head as he came through the doorway, and sit at the foot of the table beneath the portrait of Her Majesty, who looked down from above the plate rail upon these meals with silent, unblinking fortitude. He had come, everyone assumed, from Horncastle's desk, where he had been doing his best to keep the sisters out of the workhouse. One after the other around the table received a grunt from him, by way of greeting, as he snapped out his serviette and laid it across his lap, ready to eat. Both children cringed against the sound of the snapping linen, as though it had been his whip cracked under their noses. Now Kate would enter, with the final platters of food, and seat herself at the head of the table. It was always clear that she had taken time in the kitchen to talk herself into a determination to make this meal run smoothly – to be gracious, friendly, interested, even light-hearted. She had never for a moment lost her fondness for Annie, despite the disappointment of Annie's marriage. The sick-room was banished. So were the affairs of the hotel. Conversation must confine itself to cheerful gossip, news of the world, praise for the food, rumours of anticipated visits from amusing circuses and theatre people, and progress reports on plans for the home Sumner intended to build for his bride and their hoped-for family. Sometimes the conversation was quite animated, even pleasant, but a brief glance round the table was enough to make you realize that only the mouths were talking – behind the faces quite a separate sort of colloquy was going on. Occasionally just a fragment of these hidden monologues would find its way into some corner of the dialogue, making it possible for you to imagine the rest. I despise these people, thought Susannah, and shall eventually have James to myself, as I was intended to, and shall make them sorry for how they have treated me. I must, must, must, find a way of keeping these horrid people away from my husband, thought Kate, before I am driven mad. This contemptible lot will tear themselves to bloomin' pieces over a breathin' corpse, thought the stockman, but they'll soon discover who's in control around here.

Eventually, after several months of this, you became aware that the silent conversation had changed its nature. While it was clear that the thoughts of all three were still on the sick-room and the attention of all three was still focused on the other two, you now sensed that the jealousy had little to do with claiming control of either the hostage patient or the hostage hotel, both dying of silence. Rather, they watched each other as keenly as ever, but now with another purpose. Consider Hawks first: while he had been taking one of his turns at sitting with the patient, it had become necessary for him to retrieve a pillow from the floor and place it beneath Horncastle's head. While he was placing the pillow beneath the head, it occurred to him (how could it not?) that it would be an astonishingly simple matter to place the pillow on top of the head instead, and to hold it there until breathing had stopped, separating the patient from both his suffering and his property at the same time. The only question to be answered was how to make certain that it looked as though Kate had been the one to do it. This was the monologue going on now behind that face at one end of the table: how could one arrange to snuff out James Horncastle with a pillow and make certain that the same act that removed Horncastle from the scene would also remove Kate – to a prison, at least, if not to a gallows?

It was not a comfortable thing to sense this, however imperfectly. Especially when, at the same time, you were aware of

Susannah's thoughts across the table. She, too, did her best to contribute to the clatter of fake-cheerful noises exchanged over the meal, but just occasionally something else might slip in, in passing, a reference perhaps to the last time she had spooned food into James. And then you knew that behind those cold narrow eyes, behind the mask of that papery narrow face, she was remembering how in the midst of spooning Horncastle's mucked-up food into his mouth it had suddenly occurred to her how simple a matter it would be to spoon poison down this blackguard's treacherous lying throat. It seemed inevitable. Why else, after all these years, would she be holding the spoon that contained the food about to find its way into the stomach of the very man who had promised to marry her, who had kept her waiting for him even while he placed an engagement ring on the finger of her favourite sister and secretly married Kate? Anyone could see the justice in it. The only problem was coming up with a way of making certain that only Kate could be accused of the crime. It was not enough that Kate was usually the one to prepare the food – it was easily seen that the kitchen was never locked from the others. Perhaps she must arrange to leave town for a while, after stirring poison into food that would not be served to James Horncastle until she had become an innocent traveller seeing the sights of the mainland. It would be her duty then, she thought, to take over altogether the management and even the ownership of the Blue Heron Hotel, once the murdered and his murderer were both out of the way. Just as she would be taking over the hotel if she were the dead man's proper widow, as she ought to be.

And Kate. Even Kate. It could hardly be otherwise. Think of what she must endure every day! Consider that she almost certainly knew that Susannah would not be shaken off so long as Horncastle was alive. It was reasonable to think that afterwards she would have little reason to stay. Consider that so long as Horncastle lived – consuming her every thought, her every action, either directly or indirectly through her preoccupation with the behaviour of the others – she was hardly strong enough to stand up to the stockman and drive him off the property. If Horncastle was so determined not to recover his health and defend her against the enemy, she would be in a far stronger position with him gone altogether, and his property safely in her hands (as his will would ensure). She was expert at keeping the empty conversation alive – a letter from Lady Alice complaining of the cold rain in Weymouth, news of the new legislative buildings to be built in place of the Bird Cages. She laughed – or made noises that were intended to be heard as laughter. She proved to be skilful at bringing the children into the conversation, even though it was clear that they would prefer to be left alone. Yet her face was drawn, pale. There was little to be found of the strong, handsome countenance Sumner had first encountered in the cemetery. Married life had etched lines of disappointment and bitterness into her features, and drained the spirited energy from her eyes, and the nursing life with its attendant competitions had given to her flesh that grey papery appearance of the material found in wasp nests. Anger and shock had brought him to his present state, she was thinking even as she smiled into your eyes and asked after the health of your employees; perhaps still more anger and shock would finish him off. Tell him his horse had been shot dead by Samuel Hatch. Tell him the hotel had been lost – had fallen into the hands of the hated magistrate. Tell him the Americans had invaded, and set up their government in the hotel, and had handed all his possessions over to his cousin from San Francisco. There remained only to think of a way in which the results could be made to look as though Susannah and Hawks between them were responsible for the deed.

And so, on December third, after more than a year confined to that bed in his old saloon-turned-office in his quiet hotel, hostage to the care of the three competitors, James Horncastle ceased breathing and was declared by Dr. Rae to be dead, and was two days later recommended by the reluctant but dutiful

Reverend Mr. Trodd for a position in a heavenly afterlife, albeit in a voice that gave the Almighty permission to ignore the endorsement if He should prefer. Perhaps to aid the Almighty in His decision, the Reverend Mr. Trodd recalled the number of times that he himself had warned his little flock about the necessity for living a life of righteousness and the dangers in indulging in private versions of morality.

And who was responsible for the death? Did he stop his breathing behind a pillow? Did he wake up one night to discover poison sneaking through his system? Was he told false news of the death of his horse, the loss of his hotel, the collective suicide of his cricket team-mates – some shocking information powerful enough to finish him off? The Sumners and the Norah Horncastle family and Horncastle's closest friends were not the only ones to wonder. Everyone at the funeral had been aware of the tense rivalry that was going on in that household, the rivalry between sisters going back to the fifties, and all of them were relieved to learn that an official investigation had been launched into the affair. In a manner that would have met with the approval of Horncastle himself, several of his friends and old enemies put money on one or the other of the suspects, or upon the possibility of no guilt being found at all, with Samuel Hatch keeping book in his saloon and eventually taking responsibility for a sum of several thousands of dollars placed by more than two hundred citizens who eventually heard of the secret wager and did not want to be left out.

An investigation was carried out in a most discreet manner, though somehow everyone in town was aware of it, in the way they seemed to be aware of everything else that ever went on. No one was ever accused of anything, but it was accepted by each of the three that there was a possibility one of the others might have been guilty of wrongdoing, and so there was no trouble in securing their co-operation. No evidence of foul play was ever found, however. No trace was found of violence upon the deceased. No possible reason could be found for continuing to look with suspicion upon any of the survivors. The case, so far as the legal profession and the police were concerned, had to be dropped. It would make as much sense to say that Horncastle had died of his own recalcitrant silence.

Both widows might have agreed. The Reverend's graveside words had scarcely ceased their ambivalent reassurances when Norah Horncastle, whose thoughts had been as consistently directed towards that sick-room during the past year as the sisters' had been, detached herself from her children and approached the McConnell sisters at the distant end of the grave. She put out her arms and clasped Annie McConnell Sumner against her bosom first, then held out a hand to the narrow sister from Ballarat – who backed away from it as though from a tiger snake, and turned to find her way back to the funeral carriage. Though Norah Horncastle offered neither hand nor open arms to Kate, who offered nothing back but a dull defeated stare, Norah did eventually speak. "'Tis bitterness you're feeling, I'm sure. But we can feel united just a little in our loss."

"We are united in nothing," Kate said. "This is what you wanted, this is what you *prayed* for!"

Norah Horncastle gasped. "Oh, it is not! 'Twas only for harmony that I –"

"Have you no idea how much you are despised?" Kate said. "There is no reason for us ever to speak to one another again." She appealed to Hawks, who stepped forward and used his own body as a means of forcing Norah Horncastle to step away from the grave.

Adelina Horncastle stepped forward as though to protest this brutality, but almost immediately turned away again and disappeared into the crowd. She would leave town soon after that, to escape the persistent attentions of local males – including the young Customs official, Mr. Callow, who had recently become an alarmingly desperate suitor. She would sail for England, where she found a position as a governess in London. He would return to Ottawa. Miss Horncastle was not spoken of in town until several years later when she published a modest story in a London magazine, a romance in a style very similar to that of her mentor, Ouida. When a copy arrived at her mother's boarding-house, it was read and passed on to other households and eventually seen by perhaps half the population of the city. Few read it through to the end, however. Upon discovering that she wrote of imaginary people in imagined places, they soon lost interest and passed the magazine on to others. "If you want something to read, you can't beat a newspaper. It gives you all the information you need in a straightforward manner, nothing fancy."

One who relied on Logan Sumner to bring her up to date on matters concerning the death of James Horncastle was not a visitor at all in the ordinary sense, though her lifelong inability to decide where she preferred to live might allow her to be called one. This was Lady Riven-Blythe, now into her eighties, just back once again from her beloved England, which had once again disappointed her by refusing to align itself to her memories. "It was not so chilly in my childhood, I am certain of it, and we did not get so much rain. Weymouth still behaves as though George III were expected to pay a return call any day."

She had found England to be too *miniature* for her liking, she said, and much too resistant to change, just as she had found San Francisco, where she had imposed upon the hospitality of her childhood friend for most of a year, too indifferent to tradition, and Sydney, where she had taxed the patience of a younger half-sister living at Elizabeth Bay, too determined to shock you with its originality. Of course, she had discovered within moments of arriving here that the city had been transformed in a most unattractive fashion by the noisy chaos of the too many gold-miners who had flooded into the city and by the noise of too much construction going on, with businesses expanding and new shops going up, and larger homes being erected with the new fortunes being made by the merchants. Still, though she would not be able to return to her beloved house and gardens along the saltwater inlet, she would put every effort into overlooking the unpleasantness of a growing town and try to make it her home. The first step, of course, was to catch up on all she had missed.

Naturally she would soon be in a position to hear this story from the point of view of Norah Horncastle herself, and from the point of view of several other friends and acquaintances about town, eager to welcome her back. But she had only just arrived in town long enough to establish herself at the Driard when she encountered Logan Sumner on the street, and invited him to fill her in on all she had missed.

If she thought a visit to the cemetery to view the Horncastle grave would also provide the opportunity to visit Logan Sumner's tombstone – to bring herself up to date on what had happened to Logan Sumner himself in the intervening years, and to his wife and to his business and all his dreams, as it might have done in the past – she would soon discover this to be a waste of her time. Logan Sumner's troublesome gravestone was no longer part of the landscape of the cemetery, thanks to an order from the city council that he demolish his monstrous stone palace and replace it with a small plain marker, perfectly blank, in order to avoid competing with the stones of the city's leading families. This destruction of his romantic and exaggerated fictions was the result of a petition, signed by thousands of citizens, which demanded that city council do something about the offensive piece of architecture. One councillor, born in London, agreed that it was "more the sort of grotesque self-congratulating monument one might expect of a mad wealthy Yankee than something appropriate to a modest community on British soil." At the same time, a councillor who had been born in New York State found the stone equally inappropriate on the grounds that he wished the city to become the sort of place the citizens of the United States expected to discover when they crossed the line, a city that imitated Europe in its outer appearance, a city of dignity, good taste, modesty, and self-control – in short, as different from home as possible. When the question was raised of whether anyone on the council had been born, like Logan Sumner, on the island – or even in the country, or in the colony that preceded it – there was immediate general agreement that this was an irrelevant point, since the elected officials were unanimous in agreeing that such excess of the individual imagination was both unseemly and uncharacteristic of the nation to which they now belonged. Sumner was required to demolish his ridiculous palace of fantastical words immediately, and to replace it with a stone as small and insignificant as possible, and to promise to confine himself and his descendants, in his will, to the simplest historical facts, "which, being *actual*, will be far more interesting to the visitor passing through the cemetery at some future date than this fanciful nonsense about a person who, frankly, never really existed. Being smaller than the monstrosity it replaces, it will also suggest a modesty more in keeping with the circumstances of the man, the character of the city, and indeed the chosen attributes of the Dominion."

At first this directive incensed Sumner, who had just returned from his visit to Europe – the postponed search for a new home having become his honeymoon instead. He refused to obey, he wrote letters to the newspaper defying the order, he raised his voice to clerks in City Hall, and when it seemed that the city intended to do the task for him he set up a tent and camped beside his own tombstone for more than a week. But he awoke one morning to the sound of moisture dripping onto the canvas from the fir boughs and could not remember any more why the tombstone had been important; he certainly could not remember why it had been important enough to keep him like this from his work and to separate him from his new wife, already expecting a child, who had grown into the habit of bringing him groceries but insisted that he cook them himself if he would not come home.

Its eventual removal did not cause Logan Sumner any regret, he explained to Lady Riven-Blythe while they drove from the Driard towards his new home, where Annie (who had been warned by a small boy paid to run ahead with the news) was expecting them for dinner. "It had already become unnecessary. And since then, new wealth in the town has meant opportunities to build some of the buildings I have dreamed of, though none of them so splendid as I dreamt on the stone. And family life with Annie and the girls and the Jordan children has kept me too busy to be very conscious of the state of my inner thoughts."

I believe Mr. Sumner has proved himself to be worthy of my hopes, wrote Lady Riven-Blythe to her sister on Weymouth's Brunswick Terrace. *Though there were many times I doubted my own occasional glimpses of his possibilities. Perhaps it merely took an unconventional woman of his own age to see what I had seen as far back as when he took over his uncle's business, awkward and shy, and lost his bride in a boating accident and started hanging around the Horncastle family, sorrowful as an orphaned pup, looking for someone to love. Well, he has found his someone, and she is not at all someone he might have expected to find, though I was certain, after meeting her on board a ship, that she would be a perfect mate for him. I am delighted to discover that they have decided to agree with my opinion.*

Lady Riven-Blythe wrote this to her sister because it had become her habit while in Weymouth, evening after evening before the fire, to entertain her sister with accounts of her friends on Vancouver Island. While rain swept in across the esplanade to assault the windows and waves could be heard crashing upon the strand, the tiny woman spoke so much about the Horncastles and about the latest news of Norah Horncastle's expanding family – adored sons-in-law and a progression of enchanting grandchildren – about the Pearses and the O'Reillys and Mr. Logan Sumner's defeated romance with a young woman who wished to be a novelist that her sister occasionally said, "Honestly, dear

Alice, if you find these people to be so necessary, I don't understand why you have left them."

He has built the most peculiar house, not at all in the fashions favoured by other successful businessmen, reminiscent of homes in Oxford or Edinburgh or San Francisco or Rome. This has more in common with the houses built by the Indians in their villages, its great roof kept up by a structure of posts and beams carved from giant trees. He can be certain he will never discover another like it anywhere else but here, and I am equally certain that others will be slow to follow his lead.

It stands beyond the park, along the top of the cliffs which look south towards the strait and the Olympic mountains of Washington Territory. Also within view, he pointed out to me, is the location of the cabin where he was born, the former Pest House, long since burned down. Behind the house, half-obscured by trees, is an ancient barn once built by his late uncle, and a small shed once lived in by his Indian carpenter but long since abandoned – a funny little house scabbed over with bits of boards rescued off the shoreline from a shipwreck, each of them stamped with brand names and other words which have faded almost completely away in the weather. The gardens have not yet been completed, and of course I thought of my dear gardens left behind on the Gorge (whose new owners have discontinued my policy of allowing the public to enjoy them). "Oh, you must plant flowering bushes here," I said, and told him of the lovely bushes in your garden, and in the gardens of your friends. "You must allow me to send to England for a lovely mock-orange, and perhaps a rhododendron. All my sister's friends have so fallen in love with hers that they are imitating." He laughed at me! "Should I import from England what England has imported from us?" It seems that rhododendron and the mock-orange and that lovely red-flowering currant you have growing by the summer-house grow wild in all the forests that surround us. Here they are hardly more than weeds! "Now that England has declared our weeds to be garden flowers, are they more desirable than they were before?" He would wait a while, he said, before deciding whether to take a spade out into the woods to find *his garden, or to follow Annie's suggestion that he send to her sister in Brisbane for something more exotic.*

The children ran out into the front yard to join their father and the tiny lady beneath the giant hat – two small laughing girls with hair, alas, closer to their father's pale corn silk than their mother's wild red curls. The Jordan children, having become adults, no longer lived here, Sumner explained. The girl had married and moved to some northern part of the island, where she and her husband had built a small hotel. The boy, Young James, had gone north to join them, but would not necessarily stay.

The marriage is as unconventional as the house, by local standards, Lady Riven-Blythe would write, *but appears to be a satisfactory arrangement for them both. The children certainly do not seem to be suffering from their mother's frequent absences, though it is possible that even the most devoted mother could not compete with the maternal attentions of the Australian servant they have brought into the country. Of course there are many in town who disapprove of a mother who leaves her family for months at a time to cross the continent speaking in theatres on the subject of female shackles, but this seems to be of no importance to any of the Sumners. It is certain that his Uncle Charles, whose opinion always meant a great deal to Mr. Sumner, would not approve of this modern arrangement, but I remember his Uncle Charles as a fussy old creature who approved of very little in this world, a rather ridiculous relic from some imagined past with superb admirable ideals he did not know how to translate into the language of another place, perhaps because he had so little patience with the daily struggles of his fellow man.*

Since the visit occurred on the day before Annie was to depart on another of her speaking tours, dinner was declared to be a farewell party and a welcome-home party at one and the same time. Annie flew out of the house, laughing, and demanded that they all come in immediately, the meal was getting cold. "There has been something missing all these years," she said, "and now it has been made right."

They had not completed the meal, nor had they brought one another entirely up to date on the events of their lives, when they were interrupted by Zachary Jack, who came in through the front door without knocking or waiting to be invited, and pulled up a chair to the table, though he would not accept any food.

"Another visit from royalty?" he said, greeting Lady Riven-Blythe with a nod and at the same time hoisting the waist of his trousers up his enormous stomach. "We haven't recovered yet, from all the damage started by that last one."

Excited by the journey she would start on in the morning, Annie could barely sit still. "Sacramento, Salt Lake City, Denver, Kansas City, Chicago, Detroit, Toronto, Montreal. You *must* have more to eat than that, you'll starve. But it's getting harder every time to leave my darlings behind. It's almost time to think about taking them with me."

"You mean the girls, I hope," said Zak. "Or are you planning to put a skirt on the *tyee*-boss and parade him across the stages of all those hee-hee-houses you talk in? Maybe he can talk too. Maybe he can tell them how they don't have to put an axe in their husbands' skulls to get their freedom, they can just pack their suitcases and leave the poor buggers behind to find out how much they don't like living alone."

"Now Zak," Sumner said, "have you ever heard me complain?"

"I wouldn't know," Zak said. "You're always so busy making sure them girls are looked after right that I never get to hear you say anything, except maybe the odd 'No' whenever I try to tell you it might be safe by now to dig out the old plans for the flying machine again. Or to ask me what's the matter I haven't finished building John Powers's mansion all by myself while you were too busy building your own to remember you got a business."

"He doesn't forget he's got a business for a minute," Annie said. "Or that he's got the best carpenter on the coast working for him. If he doesn't make you a partner soon I'll divorce him. Then I'll marry you and we'll start a rival company together and put him out of business."

"Sure," Zak said. "But what would I do with a wife that's off in Kansas City? What would I do with the wife I've *got*, who's driving me crazy already with all her hollering that she wants me to build her a house like this one here instead of that tight little pointed *English* house we're living in. It keeps me busy slapping her around every time she opens her mouth."

"Zak, you do *not*!" cried Annie.

"Of course he doesn't," Sumner said. "And if he did, he knows better than to tell you. Besides, Big Berna would toss him right over the top of the house if he ever tried."

But the true purpose of his visit, Zak eventually said, was business. "Don't anybody move." He went outside and came back in with a croker sack under his arm, something inside it squealing and throwing itself around trying to get free. "Something I promised Annie." He squatted down and untied the neck of the sack, and released a small, pale piglet out onto the dining-room floor, where it set off screaming as if its throat were already cut, to race and skid across the floor beneath the table, manoeuvring its way between people's feet, and then across the room in another direction with two small girls squealing nearly as loud as itself close on its heels. Annie's mouth opened in an expression of surprise and delight, and stayed open while the pig could be heard going down a hallway and into the parlour, pausing for just a moment after something had crashed, then came squealing back down the hallway again and into the dining-room, where it raced around the perimeter of the room looking for some other way out. Lady Riven-Blythe closed her eyes, no doubt already writing a letter in her head to tell her sister about the crazy redskin and the even crazier pig.

"You said you wanted to put some livestock in that shed out back, I got you a start. This ain't no ordinary pig either. *Tyee*-boss will tell you, this one's great-great-grandma was a pig that flew!"

He scooped up the pig in his arms and handed it to Sumner, who in turn placed it in Annie's waiting arms. Then she and the girls went outside to settle it in its new home in the little shack whose coat of wooden words had long ago been faded by the weather while Zak and Sumner discussed some difficulty in the construction of Willet Goldfinch's new hotel. Should they or should they not stay with the original plans, or should they adapt to the unasked-for materials that had arrived from across the line? Naturally Lady Riven-Blythe did not take part in this conversation, doubtless making additions to her sister's letter: *The redskin was dressed like the poorer sort of white fellow in labourer's clothing, with holes here and there in his shirt, talking of roof pitch and floor joists like any white man.* But as soon as Zak had taken his leave and Annie had returned from the shed, she heaved in a great chestful of air – all that her tiny lungs could hold – and asked what she must have been wanting to ask since she had arrived.

"And is it true," said Lady Riven-Blythe, "but oh, I'm quite too frightened to ask this. But I must, before I see either of them again."

"About my sister?" Annie said.

"And dear Norah," said Lady Riven-Blythe. "Tell me, is it as her letters have suggested, that she and your sister have not spoken a word to one another in all these years?"

Annie nodded. "As Kate demanded at the graveside."

"Oh dear," said Lady Riven-Blythe, "I was so hoping to discover that it was no longer true."

It was true that Norah Horncastle and Kate Horncastle had not spoken to one another since the day of the funeral, Logan Sumner said, but if you wanted to discover just *how* it was true you would position yourself across from The Great Blue Heron some Tuesday afternoon, at two o'clock, or two-thirty, where you would not be observed by someone stepping out through the front door.

Eventually Kate Horncastle would step out onto the verandah in a travelling-dress and glance up at the sky. What she saw in the sky made little difference; she proceeded in any case out onto the street and turned left and walked along the shop fronts until she came to the doorway to the Red Geranium. The magnificent copper hair had faded to a pale grey that looked as though it had been stained here and there by tea, and the handsome face which had once confronted the world with interest and confidence, always prepared to laugh, was drawn tight and deeply cut as though with wires – yet she carried herself, when she walked, as erect and determined as ever. Inside the café she took her usual table by the window and ordered a cup of tea. As soon as the tea arrived she discreetly fished a bottle out of her skirts and splashed some of the liquid into the cup and then filled the cup with pale, thin, barely steeped tea from the pot. Only when she had removed her gloves, and loosened the bonnet ribbons at her throat, and taken her first sip from the steaming cup, did she allow her gaze to pass over the woman at the next window table, identical to her own, facing this way with a smile shyly prepared to manifest itself upon her broad, ruddy face. Six feet apart, no more, the two women barely nodded to one another, and silently sipped at their tea, and looked out upon the activity of the harbour, where ships prepared themselves for journeys – some to coastal towns of British Columbia, some to Alaska, some to San Francisco, and the occasional one to Melbourne or Shanghai, or Liverpool by way of the Horn. Or raised their eyes beyond the harbour to the great blue wall of snow-peaked mountains that hovered above the city.

For an hour, an hour and a half, the two women sat at their respective tables without speaking, apparently without needing to speak or not speak either, merely attending to their separate teapots and the view from the window and only occasionally allowing their glances to cross one another's, and for a moment lock, before returning to their private worlds.

The proprietor, Carrie Clover, swore that they had not spoken a word to one another in fifteen years and yet had sat in one another's company every Tuesday afternoon of that time, for at least an hour, and could not be imagined living now without the weekly ritual of silence in which, as Carrie would say, there was more spoken between them in their silence than was said in any of the excited, noisy conversations of the gregarious ladies who regularly met in small groups at the other tables to exchange gossip, recipes, news, opinions, predictions, and letters from family abroad, or in all the loud exchanges of men roaring their important sentences past on the street. In those split-second moments of coinciding glances from neighbouring tables, volumes were exchanged: despair and pleading, hope and reassurance, resentment and hatred, forgiveness and love, fear and calm, before the two ladies put on their gloves, tied up their bonnet ribbons, paid for their tea, and went out into the street to walk in opposite directions to their separate lives – one to re-enter the world of a hushed, deteriorating hotel saturated with the resentment of nearly half a century, the other to return to the noisy riot of a boarding-house overrun by her own unmanageable grandchildren determined to smother her with love.

"Not a word between them two in all this time," said Carrie, the former hurdy-gurdy girl. "I watched. Believe me, I kept an eye on them. I wondered if they would start passing notes but they never did. They didn't either of them ever speak. By now you can't imagine them speaking, any more than you can imagine them getting along without their meetings here. If anyone ever starts talking about selling the Red Geranium and putting some new sort of business on this site I will have to put a stop to it fast. I don't know exactly what's going on here, but I know that one of them is keeping the other one alive, and one of them is allowing the other to try it. Don't ask me how! And both of them are trying – while they sit there looking out on the ships that move out of the harbour under the eye of those mountains and disappear into the world or off to nowhere or into the future – they're trying to build some kind of new language between them, to build something out of silence that isn't death."

Acknowledgements

Although this is a fictional work about imagined people, some of the story's skeleton was suggested by the experiences of a family whose history was discovered by biographer/historian Terry Reksten. I am very grateful for her inspired lectures and for her subsequent co-operation.

I wish to express my gratitude to others as well: to librarian Peter Mansfield, who shared his time and his expertise with me while showing me the town of Ballarat, and who made his archives and his staff available; to Garry and Jo Kinnane in Buninyong, and to the generous staff of the Literature Board of the Australia Council; to the staff of the Provincial Archives of British Columbia; and to the writers of several books I consulted on the history of Vancouver Island and of the Australian colony of Victoria. Weston Bate's *Lucky City* (Melbourne University Press) was particularly helpful. "The Princess in Brobdingnag," originally published in the London *World*, was reprinted in the Victoria *Daily Colonist* on Oct. 12, 1882.

I am grateful to Kerry Slavens and Lorraine Calvert for their assistance in research, to Roger McDonald for his helpful advice, to Hart Hanson, and my daughter Shannon for their responses to the manuscript at various stages, and, as always, for support and understanding and patience and wisdom and love, to Dianne.

Jack Hodgins was born in 1938 in the Comox Valley, on Vancouver Island. After attending the University of British Columbia he taught high school English in Nanaimo, before teaching at a number of Canadian universities. He now teaches fiction writing courses at the University of Victoria.

His first book, a collection of stories entitled *Spit Delaney's Island*, was nominated for the 1976 Governor General's Award, and "did for the people of Vancouver Island what . . . William Faulkner [did] for the American south." (*The Gazette*, Montreal)

His first novel, *The Invention of the World*, published a year later, was hailed as "the major work of Canadian magic realism" (*Canadian Fiction Magazine*), and won the Gibson Literary Award. His second novel, *The Resurrection of Joseph Bourne* (1979), received still more critical praise and won the Governor General's Award. All three works are now in the New Canadian Library.

His later books include *Over Forty in Broken Hill* (about his travels in Australia) and *A Passion for Narrative: A Guide for Writing Fiction*, which has established itself as a perennial classic. His most recent novel, *Broken Ground* (1998), was a national bestseller and won the B.C. Ethel Wilson Prize for Fiction, the Drummer General's Award, and the TORGI Talking Book of the Year Award. He has been awarded the Canada–Australia Prize, among many others, and has received two honorary degrees. He was recently elected a Fellow of the Royal Society of Canada.